Short Stories from the World of Threadcaster

THE CURSES

Jennifer Stolzer

ISBN: 978-1-723-85539-9

Illustration: Jennifer Stolzer

Table of Contents

The Curses

Forgotten Tales

Resources

The Curses

This collection of four short stories was written throughout 2017 and 2018 as companion pieces to Threadcaster. Each of these stories contain at least one legacy character that also appears in the novel. Please enjoy them gathered here in one place.

Water Curse was originally published on May 1st, 2017 in volume 2 of the *Out of Darkness* anthology

The first of the Threadcaster short stories to be published, the story of Douglas being kidnapped by the farmer was an elaboration on a bit of Douglas's backstory that was cut from the final novel for relevance and space. Sometimes when you are writing, good ideas have to be dropped for the sake of the overall story. Threadcaster was Cat's story and her adventure and character development were more important than anyone else's. I decided late in the game to remove the character who delivered this bit of exposition. You can read the original context of this story in the "deleted scenes" section of this anthology, but for anyone keeping score, this is the canon way that adventure happened.

Water Curse

Douglas didn't know why he was sweating so much. It wasn't hot out, he didn't have a fever, and he wasn't nervous at all. Still, his hands were clammy and his clothes were damp and his shoes squished when he walked.

It felt like Douglas was always in doctors' offices. Everything from sports injuries to the recent weight he'd gained landed him at one specialist or another. No one else on his kickball team went to the doctor for sprains and stuff, but his mom was a huge worrier and his dad was a lawyer. The other boys' families couldn't afford doctors and medicine and stuff like this.

Douglas slapped his damp feet against the wooden exam table. Drops of water burst like fireworks from the impact of his swollen ankles. They didn't hurt or anything, but everything kind of flopped around in them, which felt weird.

Mom's muffled voice was barely audible through the closed office door. The doctor's tone lectured, while Dad's sounded more like a tantrum.

"But he's already ten!" Dad cried. "You said ten was too old!"

The doctor spoke again. Mom was crying.

"No, he's our son." Dad's voice cracked. "We'll do it."

Douglas stopped smacking his feet and sat at attention as the door opened. Dad always told him to handle himself professionally, because he was going to run the law firm someday. Douglas didn't know if he wanted to be a lawyer or not, but he understood why he needed to follow rules. How was he supposed to play kickball, or wrestling, or racket ball without rules?

Dad either didn't notice his effort or was not impressed. "Put your shoes on, Douglas, we're leaving."

He did as he was told. "Did the doctor figure out what was wrong with me?"

"We'll tell you at home, now get up."

Mom wiped her eyes with a well-used tissue as Dad took Douglas's hand and led them both through the clinic. Douglas knew all the doctors and nurses. They'd smiled at him when he came in, but now stared with sadness and disgust. A knot of shame formed in Douglas's stomach.

His socks squished as they swept into the cobblestone street. "Are you mad at me?"

His father didn't answer. Mom followed a few paces behind.

"Dad?" The knot swelled to a bundle in his ribs. "Did I do something wrong?"

"No son." Dad shot a pointed glare to Mom over Douglas's head. "No one did anything wrong."

They marched up the hill, past shops and offices, through the residential block to the heights where their mansion stood surrounded by a brick wall. Douglas's grandfather owned the mansion before they did. Dad grew up in it, now Douglas was growing up in it, too. It was built to look like the Prophets' old holy buildings. His grandpa really liked stuff from the old world. Dad said Grandpa was old enough to have lived it, but Douglas knew from school that the Prophets left hundreds of years ago. Grandpa just liked the look of it, even if he was really old.

Grandpa was sitting in the kitchen with a newspaper when the family arrived. "So what'd the doctor say?"

"Nothing," Dad said. "We're getting a second opinion."

Mom croaked through tears. "Ken..."

"It's not true!" Dad's roar echoed off the counter tops as he turned. "He's too old!"

"The doctor said it can take a while to present..."

"Five to seven!" Dad screamed. "Five to seven, that's what they tell you from the day they're born. He's ten goddamn years old! He is not a Cur –"

Dad cut short, but it was enough for Grandpa to understand. His wrinkled brow creased in horror. "Our God..."

Douglas's mouth was full of spit. He'd heard about Curses in school and when the monks came to visit. Curses were evil creatures hiding among normal people. Douglas's teammates called each other Curses when they made mistakes that lost a match. He'd told jokes and sung mean rhymes about them. Curses were the reason everything went wrong – why the rain stopped, and the animals died, and the crops all dried up. They were living sins in human bodies that destroyed the world for everyone just by existing.

Douglas didn't feel evil. He hadn't done anything to deserve being a Curse.

Grandpa opened and closed his mouth like a dying fish. "What do we do now?"

"We have to get rid of him," Mom said into her hands. "That's what the monks say. Send him to Water Town with his kind. There's even a service for it. The doctor gave us a pamphlet."

"We aren't hiring a stranger to get rid of our son," said Dad.

He met Douglas's eyes, his face full of pity but full of humanity, too. It was the first time since the doctors' that someone looked at him like a person.

"Doug..." Dad knelt and took the boy's shoulders. "I know this is bad news, but you are still yourself. No matter what people call you, you'll always be yourself. Do you understand?"

"Yes, sir." Tears welled. "Is the doctor right?"

Dad regarded Mom a moment and bowed his head. "He is."

"So I have to leave?"

"You have to live in Water Town with the other Water Curses." Dad tried to sound encouraging, but a shake in his voice spoiled it. "We don't know how to take care of Curses in Castleton, but Water Town will know what to do with your symptoms and all the changes – they see new Water Curses all the time! There's dozens of them living there. It'll be like a club."

"A club?"

"Like a family, you'll see." Dad sniffed with a painted-on smile. "You believe me right?"

Dad always talked about negotiation. Sometimes when you're a lawyer you have to tell people what they need to hear, so that your case can get settled and everyone can be at peace. Douglas wasn't going to be a lawyer anymore. He wasn't going to be anything except water. The thought sank in slowly, swelling in his chest, widening cracks and stretching sinew in his beating human heart. Did they play kickball in Water Town? Were there kids his age? Would Mom and Dad come visit him? He didn't want to leave his friends, and his house, and all the things he loved, but rules existed for a reason.

Drops fell from Douglas's eyes as he nodded. "Yes sir."

Dad rented a wagon from the stable near the south gate. Douglas waited in the street with a handful of possessions zipped up in a bag. Mom said he wouldn't need them in Water Town – that the church provided everything Curses needed through taxes – but he still kept his lucky ball, his favorite book, and a picture he drew of his folks. Mom wouldn't let him take his teddy bear, though. She said she wanted it to remember him by.

Mom said goodbye at the front door and stayed at home with Grandpa. Thinking about it made Douglas feel wriggly, like his belly was full of fish. He wanted her with him, but she wasn't treating him like she used to. It reminded him of when his grandma died. Mom refused to see the casket. She was always prepared and cautious, but she was grieving him before he even left – it wasn't fair.

At least Dad hadn't abandoned him yet... even if he'd left Douglas alone on the sidewalk while he talked to the stableman.

Farmers pulled carts of food past the stable from the irrigated fields outside the city wall. Castleton was lucky they had wells below the hill, because most of the Valley was drying up. Everyone talked about a water shortage, and now Douglas was filling up with it. Maybe he could give his water to the farmers instead of keeping it in his body. Curses probably didn't work like that.

The wagon Dad got was bigger and nicer than any Douglas had ever seen, pulled by a gorgeous white horse called Brutus. The stablemaster smiled wide. "So, where are you two going?"

"Chalsie-Veneer," Dad replied.

"Ah! A father son vacation? You should take the guy fishin', they've got the last lake in God's Valley down there, you know."

Dad sawed his teeth. "We know."

The stablemaster blanched. He spotted Douglas's damp hair and whispered an apology before hurrying back inside.

Douglas sat with Dad in the front seat as they drove through the city gate. He often left Castleton for sports and camping in the flat farm land beyond the wall. The un-tilled field where his team met for kickball was tucked between an orange grove and a cow pasture. It was the fifth field they'd used, since their old ones kept getting planted by new farmers. Misty fountains arched from irrigation pipes in rainbows. Despite everything that was happening to him, it was cool to see the rainbows – with the drought and all, he never saw them in the sky.

Dad kept his eyes on the road for hours as Brutus's hooves clomped past acres of colorful plants. The fields ended at a chain-link fence, making way for a barren wasteland that extended all the way to the distant mountains. Hot wind rushed through the parched desert and tossed dust into Douglas's already tearing eyes.

The temperature rose with the sun. Brutus pulled them southward toward the main highway where other wagons moved like ants in the distance. Douglas's sweat became a torrent running cold down his back until a puddle soaked into the upholstered seat.

"Hey Dad?" Douglas watched his father's face harden. He sucked water off his fingers and tugged his father's sleeve. "Dad?"

His father kept his full attention on the road ahead. "Yes, son?"

"How long to Water Town?"

Dad's brow furrowed, as if considering how to answer what Douglas thought was a pretty easy question. Every muscle tightened in Dad's neck. "Two days."

Douglas's stomach soured. It was already too hot; he didn't want to ride in the desert for two days. "Do we get to go camping?"

"Yes, we'll stop after we cross the Outer Bend. Then tomorrow, we're off to the forest and Chalsie-Veneer where Water Town is."

"It's in a forest?"

"Yes."

"Is that like the orange field?"

A tiny smile creased the wrinkles under Dad's eyes. "I guess you've never seen real woods, have you?"

"Only in drawings."

"This is going to be an education, then." Dad's voice turned instructional, like when he was talking about laws or taking responsibility. Douglas used to roll his eyes when Dad got like this, but now it was relieving. It was nice to hear Dad talk to him the way he used to. "The Gatekeeper's Forest is bigger than the orchards around Castleton. It's been around for hundreds of years, and the trees are so tall you can't see the tops. A lot of it has died off from the drought, but Lake Veneer is right in the middle, and its water keeps the trees alive."

"Water Town is in that lake, right?" Douglas asked. "So Water Curses saved the trees?"

Dad turned thoughtful. "Yeah, I guess they did."

The Outer Bend was a wide, unpaved loop that ran in a circle around Castleton like a giant belt. Lots of people moved on it in wagons and on foot. Dad waited for a wide break in the traffic and urged Brutus across the street to another road on the other side. A dark haze took shape at the foot of the distant mountains. The forest, Douglas guessed. He was both excited to see it and upset it was so close. At least there was still another day.

A cart came toward them from the south, pulled by an ancient-looking mule. The back of the cart was full of barrels and covered with a tarp. The driver sat hunched over his knees. At first Douglas thought he was old, close up he could see he was young, just hollow-faced and emaciated. The man's eyes were sunken with dark circles like a skeleton. He noticed Douglas staring and glared back. Douglas focused on his own swollen ankles, but could still feel those eyes boring into him as the wagons neared each other. Douglas chanced a look over his shoulder as the other wagon passed. The man's eyes were still locked on as his cart moved away.

The sun set over the mountain range to the west. Wind rolled down the slopes, waving fields of stiff, yellowed, prairie grass. Douglas shivered in the stretching shadow of the peaks. He pulled his damp legs to his chest. Dad noticed the change in position and tugged Brutus's reins. "How about we stop for the night?"

"Here on the road?"

"Sure, no one's here to bother us."

The thick wagon wheels crunched over dried grasses as he pulled over. Douglas hopped from his seat and snapped the stiff blades under his squelching shoes. He always loved camping, although he'd never done it on the road. Dad unbelted Brutus and tied his bridle to a hook on the back of the runner before helping Douglas erect their tent.

Night came in deep shades of blue and grayish lavender. Douglas shivered and hugged himself tight. "Can I start the fire?"

Dad's pursed lips were barely visible in the fading light. "The kindling has to be dry to start a fire."

"Sorry." Douglas hung his head, shedding drops from his bangs. "I was feeling so normal, I guess I forgot."

"You don't have to be sorry. It's not your fault."

Douglas sniffed as both shame and his illness filled his sinuses with water. Camping with Dad was fun before, but it felt different now. Everything was pretend.

"Hey, pal, don't cry." Dad lowed to one knee and squeezed Douglas's shoulder through the clingy fabric of his wet tee shirt. "Do you remember what I told you yesterday?"

A lot happened yesterday. Dad did a lot of yelling. Just thinking about standing in their kitchen felt awful, with Grandpa looking at him like he was a live bomb and Mom saying "we have to get rid of him." Douglas blinked tears from his eyes. "You said I was still me."

"That's right."

Breath shuddered in Douglas's lungs. "If I'm still me, then why are you getting rid of me?"

"We're not getting rid of you." Dad said with lecture-voice. "When a client comes to me in my office because he's being sued by the city, I have to defend him even though I know he broke the rules."

Douglas sucked spit through his teeth. "So I broke the rules?"

"No, no, son." He cleared his throat and searched the horizon, perhaps for clues to a proper answer. "When you play kickball and you accidentally trip someone while you're running, what happens?"

"You get time out."

"And when you're in time out you sit on the bench," Dad said. "Are you a worse kickball player when you're sitting on the bench?

Does it change how good you are at the game?"

"No."

"That's like Water Town. You didn't mean to trip the other player, I know it doesn't feel fair, but you still have to follow the rules." Dad looked him square in the eye. "You are still Douglas Miller. That's who you were born as, and *who* you are means so much more than *what* you are. As long as we share a name – as long as you're still you – no matter where you are or what happens, we'll always be connected. That's a rule."

Douglas sniffed. "And rules are for a reason."

"Rules keep us all safe."

Something snapped the dry grass nearby. Douglas broke eye contact as a shadow moved in the dark behind the wagon.

An axle wrench slammed hard into the side of Dad's head.

Douglas screamed as his father fell sideways into the wagon, revealing the driver from the other cart. The man straightened to six feet tall with wide, forward bowing shoulders and a stare as focused and intense as before. He lifted the wrench again. Douglas scuffled backward, but caught his foot on one of the tent poles and fell. His stomach sloshed as he hit the ground.

The man's unarmed hand thrust forward and caught Douglas by the ankle. Douglas was dragged forward, kicking and shouting. His swollen flesh squished through the stranger's fingers as he was yanked into the air and pinned under the stranger's arm like a bag of rice.

Dad groaned, blood seeping from his wounded head. "What are you doing? Give him back!" He grabbed for Douglas's reaching arm, but the stranger swung the wrench again and split the skin above his father's eye. The impact threw a ribbon of blood from Dad's face. He landed in a crumpled heap and didn't move again.

The stranger grabbed the lead rope and wrangled Brutus one-handed. The tired white steed reared and whinnied. The man flopped Douglas across the horse's back and climbed up behind him with a firm grip in the creature's mane. The stranger whacked the horse in the hindquarters and charged away from camp.

"Dad!" Douglas wriggled and punched the stranger's leg with both hands. "Let me go!"

"Shaddup." The man grunted and kneed him in the face.

Douglas's eye swelled and throbbed. A muffled whooshing filled his ears as the horse's hooves thundered beneath them. They diverted from the road and cut through grasses until they found the man's mule cart waiting with its load of barrels. The man carried Douglas with him as he leaped from Brutus's back and tossed the tarp back from his cargo. The half-dozen industrial-sized barrels were sealed with fitted wooden lids. The stranger pried one open with the bloody wrench and forced Douglas inside.

Douglas landed head first in a pool of standing water. He twisted, coughing and panting as the lid shut out the light.

The stranger thumped the side of the barrel. "You keep yer mouth shut."

Douglas clawed the lid and the walls, but the barrel was sealed. It didn't move when he thrashed or rock when he shook it. He was trapped, alone, and frightened in the cold, wet dark.

Fresh air flooded Douglas's starved lungs with as much shock as a slap to the face. He inhaled with pain and coughed mouthfuls of coppery liquid. The stranger grunted, but his voice sounded far away. "Still alive, huh?"

He grabbed Douglas by the collar and hoisted him from his prison. The boy tried to fight, but his arms and legs were like lead. They were on a farm, like those outside Castleon, with miles of wheat barely visible in the dim moonlight. The stranger hoisted Douglas onto one shoulder and started up a wooden ladder to the top of a water tower made of wood and metal, like the barrel.

Douglas didn't want to go back in the dark without space or air. He balled his fists in the man's traveling cloak, but his wet fingers lost their grip as the man levered him through an open hatch into the darkened tank. Douglas fell eight feet before landing flat on his back in a pool of shallow water. The stranger slammed the door shut. His work boots clomped down the rungs and vanished into the night.

Douglas sat in the pool with every inch of him hurting. Lost and alone, he buried his face in his arms and cried.

"Shhh, it's okay."

A hand touched his shoulder. Douglas flung his arms in fear and surprise. The mix of exhaustion and adrenaline sent him sprawling into the water.

The hand belonged to a girl, although she was little more than a shadow in the dim light. "Poor thing."

"Is it a boy or a girl?" Another child asked.

The sealed room filled with rippling echoes. Douglas's aching heart pounded faster. "Who are you? Who's there?"

"Don't be scared. We're like you." The girl's touch was cold, but warmer than the water he was in. She sat beside him. "I'm Imma."

"Imma?" Douglas stammered. "You're a Water Curse, too?"

"Yep. So is Noah, and Mira, and Wade over there. The farmer kidnapped us, too."

"Why?" Douglas trembled. "Why did he do this?"

"For our water," a young man gargled. "He keeps us in here for the crops."

"You water his crops?"

"His well's dry," Imma said. "I think everyone's well's dry."

"Where did he get you, kid?" The boy asked.

"We were camping by the road." Douglas's hands shook. "I was going to Water Town, and Dad was..." His cold tears surged and grew warm. "Dad was..."

"You don't have to say it," Imma assured. "But you can cry, if you want to."

Douglas drew a sharp breath and curled into a ball. "I want my dad!" He wept into his knees. "I want my dad. I want to go home!"

Imma put an arm around his shoulder. Another pair wrapped from behind. The rock of their small bodies in the pool added the soft lap of waves to his echoing sobs.

Douglas waited in the water tower for days, hoping someone would find him; his dad, the police, the stablemaster, anyone. He felt weak. Depression didn't make good sleeping – neither did shin-deep water – and the food the farmer threw to them was meager at best. Douglas prowled the slick walls of their dimly lit enclosure, searching for weaknesses.

He cupped his numb hands around his mouth and shouted at the ceiling. "Dad!"

"Ugh, stop," Noah groaned. He was the youngest – only seven

– with white-blonde hair so thin it was nearly transparent where it was stuck to his face. He was abducted off the same road Douglas was, a year ago. "Your yelling's annoying."

"I gotta let my dad know where I am. He's looking for me."

"No he's not."

Douglas kicked water at him and continued yelling. "Dad? Anybody? We're stuck in here!"

"Be quiet," Mira plead. "Shouting's against the rules."

Mira and Imma were abducted before Noah. The farmer got them both when a Curse transport service passed by. They were the same age, although Mira was significantly smaller. Rolls of swollen tissue gathered around the tiny girl's joins and under her jaw.

Imma was healthier at first glance, but her darker skin only masked the raised veins and magenta splotches covering her face and arms. Her eyes were swollen into a puffy squint, but her smile was still genuine the rare times she wore one. "We know you're trying to help, but we've tried everything already. No one else lives out here, and the farm is hours from the road."

"Someone has to come. The mail comes, doesn't it?"

"Yeah," she cleared her throat with a cautious glance to the wall, "but you already know about that..."

She turned her leaking eyes to Wade, slumped in a pile against the wall. He was the oldest – maybe twelve, although no one knew his actual age – and the first Water Curse the farmer grabbed. According to the others, his parents bribed a mail carrier to take him south, but instead of delivering him to Water Town, the courier sold him as a sustainable water supply. He was the farmer's first Water Curse, and his only one for a long time.

Wade hadn't spoken or moved since Douglas arrived, just sat by himself, gargling and wheezing with his flesh hanging off his bones like clothes dripping on a line.

Douglas felt bad for forgetting. He stopped pacing and hung his head. "Sorry, Wade."

"He can't hear you, he has water in his ears." Noah spat a mouthful into the pool. "Ears, eyes, nose, and everything else."

"Don't be mean to him," Mira peeped with a gargle. "Look, he's frowning."

Rivers of water drained from Wade's half-lidded eyes. His lip hung open to drain the spit. Every muscle was slack except Wade's brow pinched beneath his slick hair.

Heavy boots clomped up the outside ladder. Panic stirred the soup of Douglas's stomach as his companions scrambled. They pressed themselves flat to the wall opposite the hatch. The door squeaked as it swung inward.

In daylight, the farmer looked like any of the farmers tilling land outside Castleton. He had gray-streaked hair, worry lines on his brow, and an overall normal expression except for a hollowness behind his eyes, like a spark had died and left his soul dark. "You monsters back? Even the new one?"

Water squeezed from Douglas's tee shirt as he pressed against the wood. Mira told him the first day that the wall was the most important rule. If they didn't line up, they didn't get food. Noah got beaten bad when he first arrived. He still had a scar on his cheekbone.

The farmer was satisfied and emptied a bag of table scraps into the standing water. The group waited for him to close and lock the hatch before scrambling for the floating leftovers.

"I bet he heard you yelling." Noah shoved a piece of damp bread in his mouth. "He'da brought us more meat if not for you."

"You're dumb if you think he cares," Douglas said.

"You're dumb because you think your Dad is coming back."

"My dad IS coming back!" Douglas said.

"Stop lying to yourself." Noah scoffed. "No one's gonna rescue a Water Curse. Your dad is laying dead on the side of the road."

"Shut up!" Something in Douglas's heart snapped. His teeth bared and he charged Noah as hard as he could. It was like when he went out for wrestling. Douglas wedged his shoulder under Noah's ribs and threw him into the water.

Mira screamed. "Douglas, stop!"

Noah hooked his arms around Douglas's neck. His forearms were large, but the bones inside were tiny and malnourished. Douglas flattened him backward against the wall. "Don't say that to me! I could cream you!"

"O-o-okay," Noah's face paled like chalk dust. "Sorry. I didn't mean anything by it, I was just bein' tough."

"Yeah, I know." Douglas gargled. He dropped his hands from Noah's arms and let them hang limp. The sight of Dad bloody and reaching for him was burned forever into Douglas's memory. He wanted to believe he was still coming, but that's all it was – wanting. Even in a best case scenario, Dad was wounded with a wagon full of stuff and no horse to pull it.

Mira patted Douglas on the shoulder. "Come eat before the food touches the bottom."

Douglas doubted touching the bottom made much of a difference. They were standing in years of human filth. He was surprised it wasn't a lot grosser. Could crops grow if they were being watered with poison? Perhaps everything in a Water Curse turned to water over time.

Imma splashed to Wade with a handful of morsels as Douglas scrounged what he could from the remaining dregs. The only way to keep the wet trash down was to swallow before you tasted it. He balled a wet bread in his wrinkled fingers and took it like a pill.

"Ahh!"

Imma backed away from the wall, hands shaking over her open mouth. Mira swallowed hard. "What's wrong?"

Imma pointed her dripping finger at Wade. "He's dead!"

Noah choked. "What?"

"Dead! He's dead – he died in front of me!"

Wade sat slumped in his usual same position. The eyes below his half-closed lids were bloodless and white. Water poured from his mouth like emptying a bucket, causing the wad of food Douglas swallowed to shoot back up his throat.

Boots sounded on the ladder again. "What's all that racket?"

"Get to the wall!" Mira cried. Water filmed and overflowed Imma's vein-lined eyes. Mira grabbed her arm. "C'mon, hurry!"

The access hatch opened and the farmer leaned in. His bearded face scrunched into a deep scowl. "Why aren't you on your wall?"

"He died!" Noah said pointing. "It's not our fault!"

"Don't talk back to me!" the farmer seethed through his teeth. "You human sins got two jobs – keep quiet and get on the wall. You don't do that, you don't get fed, so I hope you liked your breakfast because you ain't getting dinner."

"But he *died*!" Rage edged Douglas's voice. "You killed him by keeping him stuck in here!"

The farmer grunted and reached to close the door.

"You can't just leave!" Douglas sloshed forward. "It's a dead body! You'll make the rest of us get sick and die, too!"

"You still turn to water after you're dead."

The hatch shut and locked. The farmer's boots clomped down the stairs. Imma sank into the water with a long, pitiful whine.

The body was already dissolving by the next morning. The muscles and tendons holding his thin bones stretched, creating a mound of flesh and clothing wearing Wade's tortured face. A sickening stink hung in the humid air. Douglas sat with his three companions on the far side of the tank, staring at the corpse in fascination and horror.

Imma clung to his right arm. "So is he just gonna leave him?"

"Looks like it."

"Can he really do that?" Mira asked from his other side.

Noah hugged her middle. "Who's gonna stop him?"

Boots clanged on the ladder outside. Mira tightened her grip on Douglas's arm. "We should get on the wall."

"We are on the wall." Douglas grunted.

"We're not on the wall the right way."

The farmer opened the door and leaned into the tank. His eyes moved to where he expected his captives to be, then drifted where they sat huddled. He scowled and slammed the door.

Mira sank further into the water. "No breakfast, either."

Noah grumbled. "I'm never eating again."

Hours dragged. Wade's body continued weeping into the standing water. No matter how tightly they pressed to the wall, there was no escaping the runoff, or hiding from the horrible vision of their own future deaths. Sounds of Imma's weeping and Noah's grumbles echoed around them. Douglas didn't move; he was too busy thinking.

Five days ago, he thought being a Curse was the worst thing that could possibly happen to him. The conversation in his parents' kitchen felt so long ago, it might as well have happened to another person. In a lot of ways it did, because *that* Douglas was a kid with a life and a future. He didn't feel like that person anymore.

Dad wasn't coming. The police weren't coming, either. No one cared what happened to Curses. But what he was was nothing compared to who he was, and he was a person. Not even 'Douglas Miller' – just a human being who deserved safety and respect. He was getting out of there, and his friends were leaving, too.

"Doug." Mira shook him. "Doug, it's the farmer."

The familiar 'clank clank' climbed the outer wall. Douglas rose from his seat. "Get on the wall."

Imma muttered. "Are you okay?"

"No. I'm angry." Douglas lined up beside her. "He has to pay for what he's done to us."

"You know he won't."

Water trickled from his furrowed brow. "Yes he will."

The farmer unlatched the exterior handle and swung the door inward. He leaned into the tank for a better look. "That's more like it."

Douglas fought the urge to scream. Injustice steamed under his skin. The farmer bent to get his bucket of slop.

"You're strong, Doug," Noah said. "Stronger than you look."

"I know." A dark thought took shape in Douglas's mind. He lowered his voice as the hatch creaked back open. "Give me a leg up."

The two rushed the hatch as the farmer reappeared with his bucket. The man paused when he spotted them below him. Noah boosted Douglas up the eight foot wall.

Douglas's ten year-old heart pounded as he grabbed for the man's wrist. His wet fingers slipped and grasped the lip of the metal bucket. Douglas brought his other hand around the farmer's filthy shirtsleeve. The bearded man squawked and dropped the pail. Douglas swung it into the farmer's face. The metal ran like a bell. Blood gushed from the man's nose, dropping spots of red up Douglas's arm and into the water.

The farmer covered his face with his left hand, but his right still supported Douglas's weight. The Water Curse walked his sneakers up the wall as he climbed the man's arm like a rope. His body weight dragged the farmer further through the hatch until he was folded over the door jamb with only his belt and the weight of his heavy boots anchoring him to the outside. Douglas avoided the farmer's waving fist hooked his knee on the open door frame. Cold air stung his moist skin.

"Run, Doug!" Imma shouted. "Get help!"

He could try to run. Douglas was lighter and younger than he was, but also sicker and hungrier. Maybe if he grabbed the farmer's legs, he could tip him into the water tower and escape, but that would leave him to take his anger out on the others. No judge was going to listen to the testimony of a Curse anyway, and no cop was going to stop the farmer from kidnapping more kids. There was only one answer if they all wanted out alive. Douglas climbed onto the farmer's back and put him in a headlock.

Mira coughed. "What are you doing?"

The farmer thrashed and swore through bloody spittle. He grabbed at Douglas's arms, but he couldn't fight back without falling head-first into the silo. His panicked fingers raked lines over Douglas's skin as the water beneath it rolled out of his grasp.

Doug's muscles ached, his grip about to fail. The farmer stole them, used them, disregarded their humanity, but more than that – more than anything else – this man killed his dad. Justice burned in Douglas's belly. He jumped back toward the water, twisting the farmer's head until the man's neck snapped with a sickening pop.

Douglas slipped and splashed down in the tank near Wade's body. His lungs were thick with fluid. His pulse whooshed through his ears like a squirt bottle, blocking out noise. Noah dragged him from the water. "Are you okay?"

Douglas could still feel the pop of the farmer's neck. It was like crushing a can. His hands shook and tingled with each slush of his heartbeat. Imma was crying. Mira stared in crippled horror at the farmer's dangling body. His eyes were white, like Wade's. Blood dribbled from his nose and lip. Dead.

"How..." Mira stammered. "Why...?"

"Because no one else was going to stop him." Douglas tried to sound tough, but his voice gurgled.

Imma put her arms around Douglas's neck. "I'm sorry."

They used the dead body to climb out of the hatch. The outside air was cold and sweet compared to the tank. Wind ruffled wheat fields fed by Curse water. Noah took off, running in circles and cheering. Mira fell to her knees. Imma just cried.

Douglas stood at the base of the water tower, his heart

was hardening by the moment. Nothing felt right or fair. Even his own actions were numb and separate from his thoughts. He killed somebody and he wasn't sorry. It made him sick, but it was real.

"Hey!" Noah shouted from an outbuilding where he stood beside a beautiful white horse.

Douglas smiled for the first time in days. "Brutus!"

"You know him?" Mira asked.

"My dad got him to take us to Water Town." Douglas patted the creature's nose. The farmer's wagon was parked near the house. The Curses hooked the horse into the harness and raided the building for food and supplies. They had to leave Wade behind. He was too heavy.

"The farmer's body will mix with Wade's water and poison his crops," Mira said as they rode away. "It'll be his revenge."

"Revenge doesn't do anything." Douglas said. "We're surviving. That's what matters."

"So what do we do now that we've survived?" Imma asked.

Douglas stared south toward the mountains. The weak glimmer of daylight illuminated the Gatekeeper's Forest, full of trees sustained by Water Curses hidden inside. "We go to Water Town."

Noah frowned. "After all that?"

"The rules say Water Curses belong in Water Town." Douglas suppressed another gargle. "Dad always said rules were made to keep everyone safe, but rules are only good when those making them are."

"You're good," Imma said. "You rescued us."

"Because of what my Dad taught me," Douglas said. "Who we are is more important than what we are. No one's going to take care of us because we're Water Curses, but that's why we belong together. As long as we've got the same name we're connected. Like a club."

Mira cocked her head. "A club?"

"A family." The tears in his running eyes turned warm. "And this time we'll keep each other safe."

The End

Elizabeth is named after Elizabeth Palmieri, winner of the Threadcaster Summer 2017 review drawing. Thank you Elizabeth, for your name, your review, and your support!

Originally published September 9, 2017

Wind Curse

Elizabeth couldn't remember much, but she knew a lot of things. She knew she had a life before coming to Wind Town, although she couldn't recall what it was like. The dress she was wearing belonged to someone who'd died, but Elizabeth couldn't remember her name. She probably should have been sadder about it, but that was one of the good parts about their terrible illness – it never took long for sad feelings to drift out of her head.

Realization of her condition made it all seem so dire. In addition to a weakening body and shortness of breath, Elizabeth could tell her mental condition was getting worse. She was still only a middle Curse – not young enough to be new, and not sick enough to be old – but had already lost track of date and time. She had no idea how old she was, or how long she'd lived in Wind town. Earlier, Ayer said she'd asked him the same question three times in a row. Elizabeth didn't remember the answer, or the asking, or even the question, she just knew it made her upset that he had laughed at her. It wasn't her fault she couldn't remember.

Elizabeth sat on the shoulder of the Goddess sculpture overlooking Wind Town. Piles of broken shingles and crumbled plaster heaped within the wooden frames of abandoned houses. Neighborhoods destroyed by wind and time. The Goddess stood in the middle of Wind Town with her arms extended toward the valley to welcome sunrise. Gale said the healthy people once lived here. He still had a memory for historical things. Elizabeth didn't know how he did it, but he had a way of getting her to remember things if he said them. It was probably his voice. Gale's voice and the Goddess both put her heart at ease.

A willowy, tan-skinned girl appeared over the Goddess's opposite shoulder. Camden appeared, her short black hair waving in her personal wind. "I should have known you'd be up here."

Elizabeth grunted. "What do you want?"

"Grouchy." Camden folded herself over the Goddess's arm like an old towel. "I came to say 'hi' and you're like 'rawr.'"

"Sorry." Elizabeth pulled her bony knees to her chest. "I was angry about something else."

"Is being angry why you come up here all the time?"

"I don't come up here all the time."

"Yes, you do."

"No, I – " She bit her tongue. It was just like with Ayer. Maybe she did come up here all the time? It was frustrating to not remember. "I like being up here."

"Why?"

"It feels safe to me," Elizabeth said. "Like being held."

"By the statue?"

"By a... mother." Elizabeth's voice caught in her throat.

Camden cocked her head to the side. "You remember?"

Elizabeth dredged her mind for scraps of her past. It wasn't a complete blank, she could still see her folks getting smaller as she rose to Wind Town, and hear the hum of her father's voice singing a lullaby about kittens. Her mother would carry her to the fields and back when she was a baby, but that was a long time ago. She couldn't remember their faces, but the feeling of being carried warmed a hollow place in her ever-constricted chest. "Not her face."

"What?"

"You asked if I remembered my mother."

"Do I remember my mother?" Camden gnawed her lip. "I assumed... I mean... aren't you my mother?"

The last of Elizabeth's anger eased with a thin-lipped smile. "I'm not your mother, but I love you."

"Oh good."

Late afternoon stretched the shadow of the Goddess over the dilapidated buildings below her. The sails of the windmill behind them extended like wings from the shadow's back. Elizabeth looked down on it with a growing sense of peace. It was like the Goddess was holding everyone: the new Curses lounging at her feet, those sheltered in the rest house, the ones working in the garden, and those making crafts. The buildings were crumbling but the Goddess never wavered. She was always watching over them.

At the edge of the plateau past rows of dilapidated houses, a shiny steel elevator platform was bolted to the naked rock. Elizabeth didn't remember the healthy people putting it there but she knew it didn't belong. It looked too different. A metal lever built into the platform swiveled in its crescent-moon housing as she watched. Elizabeth didn't believe it had happened until the gears started churning – as if a ghost had switched it on. "Did you see that?"

"What?"

"That! It turned on!"

"What turned on?"

"The lever! The – that!" She gestured to the distant platform, half expecting it to be back to normal, but the large metal gears kept turning. Elizabeth slipped down the Goddess, using the waves of the statue's long stone hair like steps. "Guys! Guys, the thing!"

Ayer's dark face appeared over the lounging Wind Curses, his hair braided tight into stripes over his scalp. Elizabeth always thought the tight braids looked painful. Maybe that was why he was always in a bad mood. "What about a thing?"

"The thing, you know the..." The word 'lever' didn't sound right any more. Trigger? Stick? Elizabeth pantomimed the shifting motion it made. "The thing."

"Calling a thing a thing doesn't help," Ayer said. "Can you think of another word?"

"The metal thing at the edge of town." Elizabeth wheezed. "It moved on its own. I saw it switch on and parts were moving!"

"You mean the elevator?"

"Elevator? No it's a – " She pantomimed harder, "THING."

"I want to see the thing." Camden chirped as she hopped from the Goddess.

"I do, too!" A new Curse asked. Elizabeth knew his name but it wasn't coming to mind. "Can you take us there?"

"I want to see the thing, too." Another new Curse said. So many little kids. Were there always this many?

Camden rallied several more into a chant of "show us, show us." Their over-sized clothes flapped as they dashed around.

"Okay, I'll show you!" Elizabeth said. "Follow me."

The rest of the Wind Curses flocked after her like chatty, hollow-boned birds. The wind rushed in Elizabeth's ears – both from the mountain breeze and from her own body. The air bolstered her as she pranced through the city on tip-toe, humming and weaving in and out of the skeletal house frames. It was like her own magic land collapsing from weather and time just like she was. She belonged to that place, and it belonged to her.

A shiny metal platform sat bolted on the edge of the plateau. Great gears turned, moving a heavy belt along the ground.

"Ah!" Elizabeth halted and jumped back from the unnatural sight. Ayer grabbed her shoulders. She huddled close. "What is that?"

"The thing!" Camden skipped to the structure and grabbed the stick's handle. "You said it moved! Why isn't it moving?"

"It's an elevator," Ayer said. "It'll stop moving when the car gets to the top."

"Car?" Elizabeth puzzled. The machine continued to clank until a slab of metal floor appeared over the cliff's edge. A residual memory emerged from Elizabeth's mind; the image of her mother and father getting smaller as she rose away from them on platform – an elevator platform.

Were her parents on the car? Her heart seized with the thrill of hope, but only for a moment. The elevator was occupied by six or seven adults surrounded by wooden crates and large camera boxes on tripods. The people on board gasped at the sight of them. They had no personal stake in Wind Town. Even with an affected brain, Elizabeth knew the disgust of healthy people seeing Curses for the first time.

A tall woman wearing a stiff, tight skirt, stood with her back to the town. Long red-blonde hair cascaded in waves down her back.

Elizabeth inched out from beneath Ayer's arm, astounded by the way stray hairs sparkled like a halo in the sunlight.

"Don't be afraid," the long-haired woman told the other passengers in a commanding tone. "These sad creatures won't harm you. Our sin has robbed them of everything from families and possessions to their very minds and bodies."

Ayer snorted behind Elizabeth. The people on the platform took frantic notes on the speech.

"This is why I, the mayor of New Torston, agree wholeheartedly with the Order of Holy Calligraphers. Their new law, effective immediately, declares the Curse Towns are the responsibility of their neighboring cities."

She gestured to the piles of boxes.

"Observe, food and clothing to last the Wind Curses through the winter. Also included is equipment to install one of Torston's state-of-the art electric generators. A gift from the inventor, my father, Howard Torston – " an old man near the back of the group bowed " – as a sign of our family's long history in this city and the valley."

Camden still stood at the lever, her tan skin pale. The mayor spotted her and smiled, revealing the soft lines of a gorgeous older woman. Elizabeth's heart fluttered. She knew those round cheeks. The wave of hair down her back only added to the familiarity. This woman was the mortal image of the Goddess.

"Come here, little girl." The woman beckoned Camden with upraised hands. "I have a new dress for you."

"A dress?"

The woman pulled a simple muslin smock from within the nearest crate. Camden reached out as a flashbulb popped. The tiny Wind Curse yelped and rushed to hide behind Elizabeth.

"No flash!" The mayor snapped to the photographer. "They're incredibly skittish!"

"Excuse me?" Elizabeth stepped forward.

Camden held tight to her over-sized shirt. "Liz, don't!"

"It's okay, I think she's nice." Elizabeth whispered. More cameras snapped as she ventured toward the crowd. "Miss?"

The mayor beamed down. "Yes, young lady?"

"I'm sorry. Are you...?" The breath caught in Elizabeth's throat.

"Are you a Goddess?"

"What?" The woman smiled and broke into a musical laugh. "How flattering, but no. I'm only a mayor. You can call me Henrietta. What's your name?"

Elizabeth was too stunned for words. She placed her bony hand in Henrietta's soft, warm palm. "Eliza-liza…"

"Lisa?" Henrietta reached back into the crate. More camera clicks went off as she handed Elizabeth the muslin dress. "This is for you, Lisa. It will keep you warmer than those rags."

"Th-thank you." The fabric felt thin, but it was new with real seams and real sleeves. Elizabeth clutched it to her heart.

Tension sufficiently broken, the others flocked to the elevator and received similar garments. Some started changing into the dresses right there, much to the anxious delight of the photographers particularly interested in their bony spines and prominent ribs.

The old man who bowed – Elizabeth couldn't remember his name – interrupted the frenzy. "You've got your story, now help unload these crates. When night falls, the wind picks up. We don't want to be stuck on this plateau after dark."

"Thank you, Father." Henrietta clasped Elizabeth's hands. "Can I trust to you to make sure this food gets shared? You shouldn't eat all of it. You should put some away for later."

Elizabeth's heart swelled. "You can trust me!"

"Thank you, pretty one." Henrietta smiled and returned to the elevator. "Alright, let's go."

Workers from the elevator car moved the boxes through town and put them in the windmill. Elizabeth didn't like it in there, it was old and it creaked. The propellers only moved when the wind blew, but it was enough to draw water up from somewhere deep under ground. The moist earth and stone walls chilled the air enough to make her shiver. It was spooky in there, but it protected their new boxes from the dust so it was a good choice. The healthy people unloaded lots of weird metal equipment and left the distribution of supplies to the Curses.

Elizabeth used her new dress as a satchel to transport an armful of dried meat and crackers to the rest home for the old Curses. It was a two-story building next door to the windmill where the very old

Curses stayed until their symptoms overtook them. Elizabeth loved the old people because they were the Curses who raised her, even if their appearances had changed. Their faces were like skulls with sunken cheeks and eyes receding into heads stretched tight with bloodless skin. She couldn't even remember these poor Curses' names except for Gale. Gale was different. He lived on the second floor of the rest house under one of the windows. Although he was too weak to move, he always smiled when he saw her. "Elizabeth."

"Hello, Gale," she sang. "I brought food. Open wide."

He did his best to wrench his mouth open, but the muscles in his face were as withered as the rest of him. Elizabeth broke one of the biscuits in small pieces and inserted it through his teeth.

"I have something I really wanted to tell you," she said. "I met the most wonderful person today."

Gale crunched slowly and listened.

"Her name was Henrietta. You know how much I love the Goddess? She looked just like her, and she brought us this food!"

"The Goddess came from the valley." Gale mumbled with his mouth full. "She walked up the hill on ropes."

"That's right! She rode up on the elevator." Elizabeth swooned with a breathy sigh. "She was amazing."

"She was a liar." Ayer coughed from across the room.

Elizabeth spun, short hair blustering. "Why did you say that?"

"She only brought us food because the Brushcasters said to." Ayer fed a bite of food to another elderly Curse. "Then she made a big show of it to impress her friends."

"Brushcasters?"

"The Calligraphers." Ayer groaned. "Don't tell me you've forgotten that, too. The Calligraphers hate Curses. They sent us here!"

Ayer was really angry, but Elizabeth had no idea what he was talking about. Her parents sent her up here, that's what happened on the elevator. There was a vague sense of it being the right thing to do, but nothing about whatever the Brushcasters were, and definitely nothing about Henrietta. "She was nice to me. I remember that part."

"I thought she was nice, too." Camden hopped over a sleeping Wind Curse to give out more food. Her new muslin dress billowed about her legs in soft waves. "Do you think she'll come back?"

Ayer scoffed. "I hope not."

Elizabeth's chest ached. "You're just being mean because she was nice to me."

Ayer flushed. "No I'm not."

"Yes you are. It's what you always do."

Gale closed his fingers around her clenched fist. "Elizabeth..."

"Yes?"

"The Goddess... is a symbol. You must remember."

"That's very nice." Elizabeth slid another cracker in his mouth. "You eat. I'm going walking."

Leaving her dress and the extra food on the floor, Elizabeth climbed downstairs to the street. The other Wind Curses were asleep. Wind whistled across the darkened plateau, stirring clouds of dust from the ruins. A full moon illuminated the square where the Goddess statue gleamed. Her empty hands reached up, as if to catch the moon in her arms. The thought warmed the hollow space in Elizabeth's chest. Perhaps if she climbed onto the sculpture's shoulder it would feel like she was being carried, too.

She mounted the base and scaled the skirt, using friction from her bare hands and feet to keep from falling. Using the hair as a staircase, she reached the sculpture's shoulder and sat, shivering in the cold night air. For some reason she thought it was going to be more comforting than it was.

A mysterious light bobbed somewhere within the ruined town. Elizabeth watched it from her perch, assuming at first it was imaginary until she noticed the elevator car had returned to its platform. The light circled the edge of town where the buildings met the mountainside and vanished from sight behind the windmill.

Elizabeth climbed back to street level and followed the light. Behind the windmill was a mountain passage where the Wind Curses grew food. Elizabeth pressed herself to the mill's cold stone wall. The winds from the valley barely turned the sails of the propellers, causing a steady "thump" to reverberate throughout the building. Elizabeth could feel it like a heartbeat with her bony hands against the wall. The tempo emphasized the pulse in her ears.

Light flashed between the trees at the edge of the embankment. Elizabeth followed up the hill and into the darkened passage between the mountains. Gnarled trees like a hundred clawing spiders stood between Elizabeth and the moving lantern ahead. Sharp rocks poked into her bare feet. Thoughts ran wild in the dark. How would she find her way back to Wind Town? What could be out there with her? How did she get there? Why was she out there at all?

There's no reason she would leave Wind Town. Something must have gone wrong. Elizabeth couldn't remember what happened but something forced her out – or abandoned her. It was all jumbled somewhere between air-choked breaths and her beating heart.

A light bobbed ahead; warm and yellow against the darkened trees. She was following it for some reason – that she could remember. In the darkness, remembering it was enough.

Elizabeth pursued the light through the dark shapes and scraping brambles until she stumbled into a clearing. Pale light tinted the sky above the mountains, illuminating a small cabin. The warm light shone still and welcoming in the windows.

The front door opened to a small front room. Two bags sat on the floor to the left; one with a jar of dried fruit visible inside. Elizabeth snatched the jar and started eating, suddenly aware of her aching stomach. Two voices murmured in a room further in. The man sounded vaguely familiar. He was in the middle of a speech:

"– we have relied all these years on the clout of our namesake. We descend from the original Torston back before surnames even existed. The place we now know as Wind Town used to be his mountain estate that grew into a city that overflowed to the valley hundreds of years ago. Our family is one of free thinkers: inventors, artists, musicians. We harnessed the power of wind, the power of steam, the power of lightning... but also the power of dishonesty."

"Father, I'm already a politician." The responding woman's voice was harsh, but musical. Somewhere in the back of Elizabeth's mind rose a vision of glistening rose-gold hair.

The Goddess.

The Wind Curse's full lungs constricted in an exhaled gasp as she peeked around the doorjamb and beheld the Goddess's blonde hair. The old man was the same one who joined her on the plateau when she arrived with the gifts. He lowered his lantern and twisted the lid off the top with a towel. "Our history is more than it seems. The part you know is true. Torston did found our city, his children did blanket the world in technological and cultural advancement, and you have inherited their wealth, power and intelligence, but you inherit something else tonight. Something darker and even more important." He removed the lid. Light swelled to reveal four walls lined floor to ceiling with books. Script Elizabeth didn't understand glistened on the spines.

The Goddess seized the nearest book in shock. "Is this – "

"It is."

"How long has this been out here?"

"For hundreds of years." The old man walked a slow circle around her. Elizabeth ducked back into the kitchen as he turned to face the door. "Torston was the ancestor that gave us our name, but his ancestor – his father – was more important than that. We descend from the man who stole magic from Our God."

"What do you mean 'stole'?"

He dropped to a conspiratorial whisper. "No one remembers he existed. He wiped his involvement from history for the sake of his four sons: Torston, Aston, Lonoto, and Chalsie. They kept his secret in the form of four libraries of scripture. This is Torston's library, and your inheritance. Along with the truth that the magic we stole killed the world and caused the Curses."

The flurry of names sifted through Elizabeth's head like a sieve but the last phrase hit her like an icy wind. Caused the Curses. She never considered that her condition had a cause before, but she certainly didn't believe it was the Goddess. She was a loving person who cared about Curses, Elizabeth could see it on her face.

The Goddess's voice trembled. "Do you have proof?"

"You had a cousin – a man named Penn Aston – who also had a library. He and his son lived in Castleton, I visited them a couple times. He had Uzzah's personal journals, letters, and writings. They confirmed everything I've said, although I cannot show you."

"Why?"

"They burned. Along with everything else." He took the book from the Goddess's hands and opened it to reveal an old scroll. He stretched the roll between his hands. "This is a scripture from the first Prophet at the beginning of recorded history. It is written in a language we no longer speak, but it still has things to tell us. Every scripture is dictated by the voice of Our God. The divine influence lives in the order of the words, existing out of space and time."

He rolled the page and cast it into the open lantern flame.

"No don't!" The Goddess shouted, but the sheet had already caught. As it burned, penetrating light glowed from within. The inked letters shone with a flame brighter than the rest.

Elizabeth was transfixed. She inched into the room, unable to look away. Sounds, sights, and smells washed over her: a warm breath of wind, the smell of baking bread, loud barking dogs, cold earth, wet mist on her face, and a chill that traced her spine. She saw a man standing in a field, spots of white light on his bare back. A woman stopped weeding to catch him as he fell. The image changed. Another flash and the Goddess stood at the edge of a basin of white light. She raised her arms and smoke and light consumed her. A flash more and Elizabeth was in the windmill surrounded by bodies. Cold, frightened, and lonely, she pitched forward and fell twenty feet to the ground.

The impact made Elizabeth scream. She jumped back and toppled to the floor of the woodland cabin, breath heaving in tiny puffs in the predawn light. Her chest was tight with air from her illness. The pressure filled her chest and gut, pressing down on all the organs until she thought she would be sick. When she looked up, the Goddess and her father were staring right at her.

"It's one of those Wind Curses," the Goddess said. "How long has she been here?"

"Long enough to see the vision!" The old man snarled. "We have to get rid of her!"

"No," the Goddess said. "They've got memory problems. It's fine. She'll forget everything."

Elizabeth's lip quivered in breathy sobs. She couldn't imagine forgetting the way the vision felt, even trying caused a headache.

"There's no time." The old man huffed. "Henrietta. Each scripture contains the past, the present, and the future. Upon the death of my friend Penn, I traveled to Castleton to pay respects, but his home was under siege by the Calligraphers. I tried to save his scriptures, but the house was already on fire. I saw... so many things."

He staggered. The Goddess turned and caught him before he collapsed, but his strength was entirely spent. She laid him against the bookshelves. "Father? What's wrong? Are you sick?"

"The world is ending, Henrietta..." the old man's voice cracked, his face ghastly white. "I had to tell you about this library... before the same happened to us. Penn's son died in that fire. We are the only ones left to carry this burden."

She clung to his arms. "What is this? You're burning up!"

"I am sorry, my dear." His hand fell to his side. An empty glass bottle tumbled across the wood floor. "I saw this moment in that fire. It had to be done."

"Father!" The Goddess shook him with no effect. White film glazed his eyes. "Father!"

Elizabeth knew what death looked like, she'd seen it many times in Wind Town when Curses got too sick to continue, but she'd never seen a healthy person die before – and so suddenly. It felt wrong. Pressure rose in her chest again, sending pain through her body. The Goddess wept, and that was wrong as well. She was never supposed to weep. She carried the sun and moon. And Elizabeth. The Goddess protected her from sadness, and loneliness, and harm.

Elizabeth's tattered dress fluttered as she crossed the room and placed a bony hand in the mane of flowing hair. "Please don't cry."

The woman's brow furrowed. "W-what?"

"Gale says when we die our bodies join the air," Elizabeth said. "You show me, when I sit on your shoulder. The bodies fly up like a veil and go back to nature. It's why we die at all."

"You're the Wind Curse from earlier. You called me Goddess." The Goddess stood, face wet but eyes stern. "Do the other Wind Curses believe like you?"

Elizabeth remembered Ayer, so skeptical of everything, and Gale. Gale could remember so far back, he always told her about things that happened long ago, even if he wasn't there to see them. He would probably know the answer, but she couldn't recall. "I guess so."

"Then you tell them this for me," the Goddess said. "Their Goddess is watching over them and everyone else who's suffered because of these awful scriptures. No one else is going to die from this, do you understand me? I will find a way to stop it."

Elizabeth's lungs ached. "You can stop us from dying?"

The Goddess faced the shelves. "It all ends with me."

"Ayer! The Goddess is real!"

"Of course she's real," Ayer scoffed as he lounged in his new muslin gown. "She's super tall and made of stone."

"No, I mean she's alive!" Elizabeth insisted. "The Goddess spoke to me. She said she was going to save us from dying!"

"Oh, so you had the dream again."

Elizabeth paused, taken aback. Anger kindled like fire in her chest. "It wasn't a dream."

"You always say that."

"Stop it!" She stomped a foot, but doubt had taken hold. Had she told him about this before? "It wasn't a dream! You didn't see it! She gave me visions. I saw food and magic and..." A blink and the image of the bodies in the windmill extinguished her fire. Elizabeth gripped the knobs of her elbows. Her red hair rose off her neck as fear intensified the wind from her scalp.

Ayer sat up. "Wow. Your hair... was it always that long?"

Elizabeth blinked her dry eyes and the world focused again. "What? Oh..." She tugged a strand. "No, I'm growing it out."

"Why?"

"Because I wanted to look more like the Goddess."

"I want to look more like the Goddess, too! Can I grow my hair long?" Camden came twirling around the base of the statue. "Elizabeth! Look how my dress moves!"

She smiled. "It's very pretty."

Ayer rolled his eyes and pried up from the ground. "We should hand out lunch food."

Camden stumbled to a stop. "Do we have to?"

"You don't like taking care of the old Curses?" Elizabeth asked. "They are so sweet."

"No, they're skinny and creepy." Camden shivered.

Elizabeth drew back in shock. "You said you wanted to be more like the Goddess. The Goddess would never say something like that! She loves all the Curses. She came here to save us!"

"I do want to be more like the Goddess," Camden sighed. "I'm sorry, Liz. I'll help feed the old Curses."

Elizabeth ruffled her dark hair. "I'm proud of you."

Ayer led them to the windmill. Several huge machines hummed just inside the front door. Elizabeth didn't remember them being there before. The machines gathered dew like glass in winter. She reached but Ayer caught her hand. "Do you forget everything?"

"What is this?"

"They called it a generator."

Another machine was in the windmill with the supply boxes. It was wired into the crank that usually brought up their well water with a lot of strange cables that didn't make sense. Ayer and Camden sorted through the boxes. Elizabeth bit her knuckle. "Was this always here?"

"Um, yeah," Ayer scoffed. "It's the windmill."

"Not the whole mill, just this metal thing."

"Things again? It's always 'things' with you."

Camden tugged an open crate. "Lizzy help me with this box!"

"You don't have to take all of it with us." Elizabeth piled the packets of dry biscuits in Camden's arms, loaded the front of her skirt like a bag, and headed next door.

The rest house was less full than it had been. Good food and warm clothes kept some of the middle Curses "middle" longer. Some were even able to get up and walk back outside. Most couldn't though, even with better care they were too sick.

Gale was one of the sick ones. He was still on the second floor under the courtyard window. Elizabeth took her load of food up to him first. She had to tell him about the Goddess, and the weird machinery, and her visions. Maybe he'd be able to tell her what they meant.

He was sleeping when she arrived, his thin-lipped mouth slightly agape as his head lolled against the wall. Elizabeth settled next to him. "Hello, Gale! I brought lunch for you." He didn't move. Elizabeth shook him gently by the shoulder. "Gale?"

The air wafting out of his body was colder than she was used to. It took a moment to realize no air was going in. His pale face was almost waxen, with no movement of blood. Elizabeth dropped the load of crackers and took him by the arms.

"Gale! Gale!" She shook hard enough for his head to thunk against the windowsill. The skin broke across his forehead, but no blood flowed out. Regret and sadness swelled through her insides until she thought all her organs would pop under the strain. Elizabeth pressed her hand to the cut and cradled him. "I'm sorry. I didn't mean to. I'm so sorry, Gale."

"Lizzy, what's wrong?" Camden asked, but Elizabeth barely heard the words. The wind howling in her own head muffled everything else. Camden hugged Elizabeth's chest, as if the wind of her emotion might blow them both away.

"He was an old Curse." Ayer's hand pressed the back of her head. "You knew this was going to happen."

A hundred angry responses shifted through Elizabeth's head but her body was too stormy to properly think or speak.

The hand on her head slid down to her shoulder. "I'll help take him to the graveyard."

Elizabeth was too weak and short of breath to stand. Camden pulled her up as Ayer gathered Gale in his arms. The body was so thin and limp, like the piles of rubble heaped about the streets of the plateau. Elizabeth passed them in a blur, unsure of where they were going. All she knew was she was sad. She was horribly, terribly sad.

The graveyard was only called that because healthy people had them. Really it was a yard where Wind Curses slowly disappeared in a huge column of displaced air. The dead lay in unidentifiable heaps. Ayer added Gale to the collection of stiff, withered husks as Camden bounced and danced in the swirling wind. It made Elizabeth sick.

"You don't look good." Ayer put an arm around her back. "It'll be okay, you know. You'll forget soon enough."

"I don't want to forget," Elizabeth muttered, throat tight.

"You're not going to have a choice."

"Yes I do," she said. "I'll make myself remember."

His hand tightened on her shoulder. "I try to make myself remember things all the time."

"You do?"

"I repeat stuff to myself, like what day it is, how old I am, and everybody's names."

"Does it work?"

"For a little while." He hung his head. "It leaves when I least expect it, then it's hard to get it back, but if I practice I can keep it."

"I can keep him if I practice." Elizabeth leaned into Ayer's bony shoulder. "Thank you for telling me. I needed to hear that."

Elizabeth repeated Gale's name over and over. Every time she said it, she was afraid it wouldn't sound right. Thoughts felt so slippery in the back of her head.

She didn't want to feed the old Curses anymore. She wandered the edge of Wind Town, muttering to herself. Gale was fading away; she was already losing his face; she loved his voice but could only remember the fact that she loved it; and every piece of wisdom – every story he ever told her she had to remember was gone.

The breeze was cold and tangled Elizabeth's long hair. She wandered behind the windmill for protection from the gusts that buffeted the canvas sails high above. Even in cover, her own wind persisted. Her hair always blew in her eyes.

"Gale. Gale. Gale. Gale." She concentrated as hard as she could, trying to fill her head with him, but it was too full of her own air. In the struggle she saw a flash – a man with white lights falling to his knees. The image sliced through her like a knife and stilled her breath.

"What was that?" Elizabeth pressed her back to the windmill. A thick cable snaked out of the ground at her feet. Was that an animal? No it wasn't living. Was there always a cord like this back here?

Maybe Gale had a saying about cords? Did he ever mention cords? Something about the Goddess coming up the mountain?

Hair stabbed her eye. She blinked and saw the Goddess standing at the misty basin with light all around. She said she'd save people from dying.

Hope lit Elizabeth's heart for what felt like the first time. Perhaps the Goddess could help her bring Gale back to life. She said she could save them, Elizabeth remembered it clearly as long as she focused on the vision in the flame.

She followed the cord along the ground and up the hill. It twisted away through the trees into crevasses between the mountains, all the way to a cabin tucked deep in the heart of the woods. The sun was setting – it took all day to get there – and her stomach growled. Everything felt oddly familiar.

Elizabeth slipped in the front door to find a well-stocked kitchenette. Baskets of fruit and vegetables waited on the counters with salted meat hanging from hooks on the wall. Glowing orbs like tiny suns hung along the ceiling. They flickered as she stood amazed before going suddenly dark.

A woman's harsh voice burst from the next room. "Damnit!"

Elizabeth jumped. Lantern light swelled through the interior door. The warmth kindled hidden memories and drew Elizabeth into the room with the bookshelves where the Goddess sat on a straw mat surrounded by scrolls and empty boxes.

"This accursed world," the Goddess grumbled and stretched another scroll. "Grandfather killed God, now the wind is dead too."

"E-excuse me?" Elizabeth stammered.

The Goddess spun in her seat, firelight tracing deep wrinkles and valleys in her once youthful face. "Who's there?"

"It's me, Goddess. Elizabeth."

"Who?" The Goddess stood, shedding leafs of parchment from her lap. "Oh that Curse girl. How'd you get back here?"

"I-I, uh," Elizabeth's voice shook. She moved her waving hair from her face. "I wanted..."

"I thought you people had memory problems. You aren't supposed to be here."

"I... I'm sorry. M-my friend died."

"Who?"

"My friend G – " She stopped. It didn't sound right. The name was so close, she'd recited it so many times, but in the face of the Goddess with the swirl of emotions the name slipped away, replaced by horror. "It was... It was... Our God, I couldn't have..."

The Goddess grabbed her. "Hey, calm down."

"He's gone!" Elizabeth collapsed against the woman's shoulder, wailing with all the air in her lungs. "I tried so hard!"

"Hush, now, I know," the Goddess bade. "Your friend is turning back to nature, that's what you said. Like the wind... that turns the mill."

Fresh tears evaporated off Elizabeth's cheeks. "When you burned the scroll you said you'd stop us from dying."

"You remembered that, too?"

"I see it in my dreams."

"Hmm." The Goddess glanced at the mess on the floor where the flame in the lantern flickered on the shiny script. "Maybe I could if I had more time... or more power."

"Power?"

The Goddess softened and maneuvered Elizabeth back to the door. "How about you sleep here tonight? When you wake up we'll go back to Wind Town together. Then I'll take care of your friend, okay?"

The pressure in Elizabeth's chest vanished. "Really?"

"Of course." She brushed Elizabeth's hair from her eyes. "I'm the Goddess, aren't I?"

She mixed Elizabeth a mug of very bitter tea, built a bed of blankets under the table in the kitchen and eased the door to the library closed between them. Elizabeth sipped, warm and relaxed. The calm brought relief to her swollen body and clarity to her mind.

"Gale." She smiled and fell swiftly to sleep

Night passed with a series of terrible dreams. Elizabeth saw dark-skinned faces she didn't recognize, the Goddess at the basin of white light, and monsters made of fire and water fighting in the field. She saw the Curses back in Wind Town with long tangled hair. The Goddess was with them, only as an old woman. Elizabeth wasn't sure if she was seeing the future or imagining it. Every dream ended in the windmill, surrounded by piles of bodies. She saw herself fall and woke on the floor of the Goddess's cabin, head pounding.

Dust covered the surfaces. Fruit rotted on the table. Elizabeth crawled, dizzy and disoriented, from the kitchen to the library. Empty boxes lay about a cold, unlit lantern with only a couple of scrolls left unsheathed on the floor. The Goddess was missing. Only her straw mat and a mound of packed dirt remained.

Elizabeth's chest inflated like a balloon. She had to get back to Wind Town. Stumbling outside, she followed a line of cables through the gnarled forest. The sun rose behind one line of mountains and descended beyond the other as time and distance blurred. Elizabeth's feet ached, her muscles were tight and stiff, her fingers refused to straighten as she steadied herself on the trees. She could see the windmill at the edge of Wind Town. The propellers moved, although no wind stirred the trees in the passage. Had it ever turned so fast before? She couldn't remember.

It was dark when she reached the town square. The Curses were lounging below the Goddess statue as usual. Strings of odd lights like descended stars dangled above them. Elizabeth staggered into the courtyard, starving and in pain. She clenched her sore stomach to force air up her throat. "Help..."

"Ahh!" One of the new Curses jumped up, long hair swirling like a cape from their head. "What's that!?"

"It's a person!" another Curse with long hair cried. Others circled. They all looked the same. "She's wearing one of our dresses."

"Out of the way." Ayer's tight braids still looked painful, but in that moment Elizabeth found them gorgeous. His brow furrowed in the hanging starlight. "Our God – It's Elizabeth!"

He scooped her up in both arms. She didn't remember him being so strong, or his neck being so warm as she fell limp against it. A woman's voice boomed across the yard. "What's all this?"

The Goddess exited the rest house, her rose-gold hair shining in the hanging light. Camden bounced out from behind her, wearing ribbons in her mop of twisted dark hair. "She looks like an old Curse! Goddess, can you help her like the others?"

Others? Elizabeth studied the darkened windows of the rest house, but no silhouettes were visible. The dust cloud over the graveyard was also missing. Something felt wrong.

The Goddess's eyes bored into Elizabeth like a pair of hot pokers. The Wind Curse's heart clenched into a quivering knot under the woman's gaze, her mind surging with images of monsters, fire, light, and bodies.

The Goddess's menace vanished behind a smile as she took Camden's hand with a motherly tone. "Yes, I can help your friend."

Ayer handed Elizabeth to golden-haired woman, who led the flocking crowd toward the windmill. Elizabeth struggled, pleas and protests spinning a whirlwind through her head. She opened her mouth but the wind inside poured out of her throat so fast she couldn't get more air in to scream.

"It's okay, Lizzy, you were right!" Camden said. "The Goddess says we're holy, that we will turn into light and never be sick again!"

The windmill turned. The Curses cheered. Ayer was the only one not smiling. Elizabeth reached for him as the Goddess carried her over the threshold, but he stopped at the open door.

"Don't be scared." His eyes were moist. "I'll repeat your name every day. So when I ascend I can find you."

"No..." Elizabeth choked. "Wait..."

The Goddess shut the door behind her, sealing out the heat and light. A whirlwind raged within the building. Its roar overwhelmed Elizabeth's senses. The Goddess dropped her to the earth beside a pile of other bodies. People from the rest house, all dead. It was just like the vision she saw in the burning scroll.

"Wait!" Elizabeth reclaimed her voice in the prophetic moment. "I thought you were going to stop us from dying!"

"And as far as they are concerned, I have." She sneered. "Enjoy your ascent."

"Don't leave me!"

The door opened and shut and the Goddess was gone. Elizabeth tugged the handle, but the adrenaline that fueled her outrage was officially spent. The Wind Curse sank to the floor and hugged her knees to her chest, cold, alone, and trapped in the old mill.

Piles of stone littered the floor from a hole high above. Someone had ripped the forward window out, revealing the sky and turning propellers. Elizabeth followed the center joist with her eyes, tracing it across the ceiling to a high platform where the propeller turned the gears. The gears moved a piston that cranked a pump on the floor where the thing Ayer once called a generator hummed. A withered hand stretched from behind the machine. It was Gale.

Elizabeth crawled alongside the body. She remembered laying him in the graveyard mere days before, but the corpse lying in the windmill was shriveled and twisted with weeks worth of steady decay. The Goddess must have moved him, but that didn't account for the deterioration. How much had she forgotten? So much missing time.

This was the new rest house, and Elizabeth belonged in it. She was weak and confused and completely defeated. The stairs to the upper platform yawned before her. Elizabeth didn't know much, but she remembered the vision. And she remembered the drop. And as she struggled to climb the wooden staircase, she was more certain than ever about how it would end.

The End

Fire Curse

Originally published on October 29, 2017

Fire Curse was a chance for me to breathe new life into two deleted characters who were a thorn in my side for many years; Ildri's mom Sharon and her younger sister Kindle. Sharon and Kindle were in the novel from the very beginning. They joined the party when Ildri did and followed all the way through to Water Town. I wrote several drafts trying to get them to work (evidence of that can be found in this anthology) and ultimately cut them and the change was like night and day.

Threadcaster without Sharon and Kindle was a simpler, more focused ordeal with the attention squarely on Cat, her mission, and her relationships to her friends. Even in a third-person story like this one, the main character is the heart and soul of the tale, and should therefore be the driving force. Sharon, specifically, was a strong personality who dominated any scene she was in. When I realized these characters were stealing control of the story from Cat, I knew they needed to be in their own story; somewhere they could shine.

Even thought these characters will appear many times in this volume, this short story is the canon incarnations of these two people. It's so good to be able to give them new life.

Fire Curse

Ildri thought she'd never get to Fire Town. Back home in New Torston everything was shiny copper and old paint and carvings, but out in the desert everything was bare and brown. It was a really long trip by wagon, with a lot of stops to towns and farms to pick up or drop off shipments of things. Ildri and her family were one of those shipments.

Mom sat next to Ildri with with one arm cushioning her back as the wagon bounced and rocked over the dirt road. The wooden seat rubbed Ildri's legs like sandpaper. Jude sat across from them, pouting. She didn't want to get close, not since Ildri was discovered to be a Fire Curse. When Ildri was a baby, Jude carried her around on her hip like a doll, but Jude stopped playing with dolls a long time ago. Since then the teenager kept her distance, even on this trip when there wasn't a lot of room and the night air got so cold it stung Ildri's tight skin.

Ildri was so tired by the time they reached Dire Lonato she felt sick. Days of not sleeping, barely eating, and doing nothing but sit quiet put them all in a sad mood. Mom paid the wagon man and he turned his wagon back to the desert for more drop-offs and pick-ups deeper into the Valley. Ildri wondered what his life was like, if he saw a lot of interesting things. Maybe he felt lonely like she did, dozing on her mother's shoulder.

Dire Lonoto was dirt and smoke and that was about it. The wall around the outside was made of sand. The buildings inside looked like sand. Everything was square like the castles she used to build on the playground at school. That was when her hands started hurting. She was playing in the sand and her skin got red and swollen. The doctor called her a Curse. Somehow being sent to a giant sandbox after that seemed mean, or maybe the sandbox back home was trying to tell her what was coming next for her.

Jude groaned. "I hate this place!"

Mom rolled her eyes. "Don't make a fuss."

"It's too hot here. And it stinks."

"Don't insult a place you just met."

"It's not an insult if it actually stinks! The whole place smells like vomit." Dust powdered Jude's curly black hair. She looked like an old woman. "Why did I have to come on this dumb trip?"

"To support your sister."

"She's not my sister anymore, she's sin incarnate."

Ildri hated that saying. The priests and monks always said it to convince people that Curses were bad. She wasn't even sure what it meant except that it made her not sound human anymore, and the words coming out of Jude's mouth felt even worse. Mom's arm tightened under Ildri's legs as she whirled and slapped Jude straight across the face.

The sound rattled in Ildri's head and echoed off the buildings. Jude's bag hit the ground and a stack of crumpled photos scattered at her feet. She squatted and snatched them back up. Her cheek was as red as Ildri's hands were.

"How dare you!" Mom hissed. Her free arm trembled at her side. "Don't say things like that about your own flesh and blood."

"She's only half my flesh," Jude shot her mother the angriest look Ildri had ever seen. "And definitely not my blood."

"It could have been," Mom said ominously. "Don't forget."

Jude returned the bag to her shoulder and they continued into Dire Lonato, down lots of narrow streets with shuttered windows and closed doors. Shops selling all kinds of things kept curtains on their entrances to keep out the columns of thick smoke flowing up from the center of town. The cloud dropped soot and ash in flakes over the dust-coated people. Everyone wore colored scarves over their noses and mouths to keep from breathing it in. They watched Ildri as they passed. They were also taught to hate her because she was a Curse, just like Jude was when she was in school. Ildri tightened her chapped fingers in Mom's shawl. At least someone still loved her.

There were fewer people the closer they got to the smoke columns. The sickness in her stomach worsened. Fewer people meant they were getting closer to Fire Town, and Mom and Jude would have to leave her. The last few days traveling weren't any fun, but at least she was with her family. The smoke was getting thicker. It hid the words on the shop signs. A sweet, burning smell filled Ildri's head and put a knot in her throat that tightened with each of Mom's steps.

A sculpture peeked through the smoke above them. It looked like a woman – the Fire Goddess. That meant they were there. Shapes moved in the haze, hidden in shadows cast by the surrounding buildings. Ildri tightened her grip on her mom as they stopped at the foot of the sculpture.

Mom cleared her throat. "Are you Fire Curses?"

"Yes," a timid voice said from the smoke. "Who's there?"

"My name's Sharon Fiammetta," Mom said. "This is my daughter, Ildri Fiammetta."

"We don't keep family names. Is she like us?"

Mom's hand pressed to Ildri's back. "Yes."

A boy stepped out from behind the base of the statue. He was covered in soot and gross open sores with points of light glowing in the oozy parts. He reached for them, but Ildri shrank away, her heart beating fast.

Mom turned to put herself between the two. "Hold on."

"She's a Fire Curse. You brought her to Fire Town. Don't you want us to take her?"

"The Calligraphers tell us to give up our sins, that doesn't mean I give up my child," Mom said. "I brought my daughter where I was supposed to so Our God should be satisfied."

The fire in the Curse's eyes glowed brighter. "What exactly do you mean by that?"

"We live here now," Mom said. "The three of us."

Jude's bag hit the road a second time. "We *what*?"

Mom bought a house for herself and Jude on a side-street near the Goddess. Most of the houses there were empty because of the smoke and the smell. It came with furniture in it already, which was good since all their stuff was still in New Torston. It was square inside with low ceilings and more wood than the other houses they'd passed on the way in. Mom said that was because it was older. Ildri liked the new house because it was bigger than the one they used to live in. Jude even had a bedroom to herself, but she didn't seem happy about it. The minute Mom pointed it out, Jude stomped in and slammed the door. She didn't speak to them again, not even to say goodnight.

Unfortunately, although there was a room for her in Mom's house, Ildri still had to live in Fire Town to keep the monks' rules. Mom kissed her hair when she dropped her off with a blanket and her rag doll and waited for her to lay down with the others before walking back up the street. Ildri curled up on a stained burlap mat, surrounded by bodies that glowed in the dark. She whimpered into her blanket, but she couldn't cry. The tears hurt her cheeks. The Curse sleeping next to her rolled toward her.

"Hey, you're the new girl."

Ildri sniffled and nodded.

"I'm glad you're a girl. The boys were outnumbering us," the other Curse smirked. A dull orange light shone in the corners of her mouth. Ildri clutched her doll tighter. The girl squinted her glowing eyes. "Don't you talk?"

Ildri shook her head again.

The girl sighed. "I'm Kindle. You're my friend now, alright?"

Ildri's heart skipped. She nodded. Kindle went back to sleep and Ildri relaxed her grip. It was still strange and scary, but now she had a friend, and with so many other Fire Curses around Ildri was finally warm. Sleep didn't come without nightmares, though. All night she was chased by boys with glowing orange eyes, oozing slime from their skin as they reached toward her in the dark.

Ildri woke up to the sound of her mother's voice.

"Where is your blanket!?"

Ildri rubbed her sore eyes. The skin on her face was more raw and swollen than ever. Maybe she was crying in her sleep again. Maybe it just got worse on its own. Jude sulked up behind their mother,

her eyes as red and puffy as Ildri's probably were. The spot on her cheek where Mom slapped her was starting to bruise. "What are you panicking about now?"

"Ildri's blanket!" Mom snapped. "One of them stole it. Help me look for it!"

"You mean this?" Kindle held the knitted wrap up. She wasn't scary in daylight; only a year or so older with spurts of shoulder-length curly hair and a leathery blush across her nose. "She kicked it off in the middle of the night so I put it aside – "

"Give me that!" Mom snatched it fast enough to make Kindle flinch and cradle her hand.

"Ow!"

Ildri grabbed Mom's dress and tugged with a pleading look. Mom snorted, her eyes still angry. She handed the blanket to Jude. "Come on, Ildri, it's time for breakfast."

"Yeah, that's right! It's your first breakfast!" Kindle grabbed Ildri's wrist. "Come on! Before all the good stuff is gone!"

They rushed past the Goddess statue to where the other Curses were gathering. There were maybe fifteen Curses all looking very sick. They wore tan shirts and pants like prisoners in a jail. Kindle let go of Ildri's hand to join the food line in front of a man in a stiff suit and powdered wig.

"Okay, you lot! Your rations for the day." The man snapped his fingers and a couple of assistants set several brown boxes at the edge of the square. "Now say your 'thank you's."

"Thanks to the Calligraphers and Our God," said the Curses.

"Very good. Now eat up."

The workers cleared out so that the Curses could get at the packages. Inside were crackers, dried meat, and jars of water with straws stuck in them. Kindle gathered as many meat sticks as she could carry in her blistering arms and ran back to Ildri with a piece held out in front of her. "Here! You want to aim for these. They taste the best!"

"She doesn't eat garbage." Mom took Ildri's hand. "She eats her meals at home with us."

"Excuse me?" The man in the wig avoided the Fire Curses and headed straight to Mom and Jude. "What are you two doing here?"

Jude glowered. "My question, too."

"Hush." Mom stood extra straight with her face held tight in an emotionless expression. "Nothing, Mr. Mayor. This is my Fire Curse daughter. I'm... dropping her off."

"It is good of you to be obedient, Ms..."

"Fiammetta."

"Ms. Fiammetta." The mayor pursed his lips. "Not everyone is so willing to come on their own. Unfortunately that means you should say your goodbyes. No healthy people are allowed In Fire Town."

Jude's eyebrow raised. "Then why are you here?"

"I'm here by Calligraphers' orders," the mayor said. "You know that the founder of the Calligraphers came from our town, yes? We still have a priesthood at his old church. We provide food, clothing, and shelter for these young sins. All their needs are taken care of, your daughter will be perfectly safe here."

"Good," Mom said, stiffly. She dropped Ildri's hand and grabbed Jude by the arm. "Let's go."

Jude scowled. "I thought we were fetching the spawn for breakfast – "

"Shut your mouth." Mom faced away from the mayor and whispered to Ildri. "See you later."

The mayor lingered as the two women hurried away. His cold, judgmental eyes settled on six year-old Ildri with a sneer. "Join your kind, Curse. You only get fed once a day."

Kindle hooked a hand on Ildri's elbow and steered them back to the group. A chill tingled down Ildri's neck. The mayor reminded her of the priests that sent her to Fire Town in the first place. The ones that didn't treat her like a human anymore. The mayor stared after Mom and Jude until they vanished around the corner, then rounded up his helpers and left without another word.

"Don't talk to the healthy people. They're really rude." Kindle thrust the bit of dry meat back into Ildri's face. "Eat it. It's good."

It was not good, but she didn't want to upset her new friend, so she tried to eat it anyway. Kindle ground the stiff meat between her teeth and led Ildri on a tour.

The place was a lot less scary in daylight. The wind had changed in the night, blowing the smoke into the desert instead of the street. Ildri could see that a lot of it was coming from a line of old-looking houses circling the square. They reminded her of home – her old home back in New Torston. There was even some detail on the frames, although most was hidden by soot and black charring. Most of the smoke came from within these tall houses, drifting out of the windows and through a huge open gate behind the Fire Goddess. The Fire Curses gathered in this open space, with the Goddess as their guard. Kindle shared each of their names.

"That there is Firenze. His parents found out he was fire cursed when he dropped a glass of cold water on his arm and burned all the skin off. It never really grew back. How's it going, Frenzy?"

Firenze waved a bandaged stump at them. "Going okay!"

"That over there is Blaise. He came from Castleton. He found out he was a Fire Curse when he burned himself on a cold pipe. And the guy he's with is called Bunsen, he's like Blaise's twin. The two showed up together which I hear is really rare. Usually we get a new person every year or so."

A pair of kids a little older than they were ran past playing tag. Kindle pointed as they passed her. "They're Tyson and Ashlyn. We should go play with them!"

"Don't run!" Another Fire Curse called. "You'll overheat!"

"That's Dawn." Kindle said about the speaker. "She took care of me when I came here."

Dawn's feet were wrapped in scraps of paper. The bottoms were soaked through from hidden sores. Beside her was a horrible looking boy, covered head to toe in rippling burns. Ildri stopped, scared and repulsed. It was the gross boy from her dreams. Popped blisters covered every inch of his skin, and stained yellow bandages were wrapped around bloody sores. There was no hair left on his head, and his eyes were slightly cloudy. When he smiled the inside of his mouth glowed even in daylight. "Hello there."

"That's Branton." Kindle tugged, but Ildri was rooted firmly in place. "What's wrong?"

"Don't be rude," Dawn said. "You're looking at your future."

Ildri's face flushed with a rush of wooziness. The salty taste of the dry meat in her mouth was suddenly disgusting and she hugged herself, afraid she might be sick all over.

Branton got up. "Whoa, kid. Take a deep breath." He reached

forward and a rush of heat swirled into her head. The world dropped out from underneath and Ildri fell backward. Kindle caught her before her head struck the cobblestone street. "Whoa! Ildri!"

"Get her in the shade," Dawn directed.

Kindle propped her next to one of the buildings. The smell was particularly bad, and it made Ildri feel even more sick to her stomach. Her head hurt, as well. Kindle tried to give her water from one of the jars but the wet made her throat hurt. "This has been hard for you, hasn't it?"

Ildri sulked and nodded.

"I guess I forgot what it was like to be new. My mom asked my uncle to drop me off." Kindle hugged her knees to her chest. "The first day was bad, but then Dawn took me in and I felt a lot better."

One of the other Curses brought Ildri's rag doll from the sleeping mat where she left it. She took it almost desperately and hugged the doll tight.

Kindle thanked the Curse as he left and scooted closer to Ildri. "Have you always not talked?"

Ildri shook her head 'no.'

"Did you hurt your voice?"

'No' again. It wasn't that she couldn't, just that for the last couple of months she didn't really want to. Mom usually took care of anything she needed and no one wanted to talk to a Curse anyway.

"I hope you get your voice back," Kindle sighed. "I've wanted a friend I can sit down and talk to."

They sat together, quietly through the afternoon. The wind changed again, blowing the smoke cloud back to the street like when she arrived. Ildri wondered if that was a normal thing – the smoke being gone in the morning and settling in the afternoon. The fog back home used to do that. It felt very peaceful. Ildri was just starting to doze off when Mom's voice entered the square.

"Hello!"

She stood near the Goddess. Jude was with her, carrying a heavy wooden box.

"Fire Curses!" Mom called. "Come here, I brought food."

"She brought food?" Dawn waited for Ildri to explain, but she could only shrug.

Jude put down the box and stepped back as the Fire Curses searched through it. Mom crossed her arms, importantly. "I couldn't stand by and let that good-for-nothing mayor feed you chaff. Here you've got bread and real fruit and actual vegetables shipped in from Castleton. It's the same everyone else in town eats and it's all for you."

"Thank you, Ma'am!" Firenze, the one with one arm, cried.

She nodded 'you're welcome' and scanned the crowd. "Where's my daughter?"

Kindle waved. "Over here, ma'am!"

"Ildri!" Mom ran across the clearing. "What happened? What did that awful man do to you?"

"He didn't do anything," Kindle answered. "She fell over because of the heat."

"The heat..." Mom petted her daughter's hair. Ildri shut her eyes as Mom pulled her close. "I don't know how all of you haven't collapsed. Why don't you stay in the buildings?"

Kindle pressed her chapped lips. "Only the dead people go in the buildings."

"The dead people?"

"Because of the smoke."

Mom took in the hazy surroundings and scowled. "Of course."

The nightmares weren't as bad the second night. Knowing Branton's name didn't make him any less scary. She could see herself turning into him with lots of dripping wounds, but Kindle was there, and that helped a little. Every time Branton reached for her, Kindle tugged her away. And when Ildri woke up Kindle was sleeping right next to her like before.

The mayor came back with more food. The Curses lined up and thanked him, but the minute he was gone, Mom and Jude arrived with five other townspeople. All seven of them dressed in the traditional Dire Lonato coats and scarves and each of the new people carried crates that they set at the foot of the Goddess. Ildri joined the other Fire Curses as they picked through the new foods. There were the same breads, fruit, and vegetables but also candies and a package of cooked meat that tasted way better than the dried sticks the mayor had brought.

Mom made sure none of the mayor's men were still around before pulling the muffler away from her face. Ildri ran out to meet her and was lifted onto her hip. Mom sighed into her hair. Even with Ildri's higher temperature, Mom's breath still felt warm.

"Is this the one you mentioned, Sharon?" An older man in a green turban asked. "Ildri, was it?"

"Yes, my daughter."

"Are you comfortable calling her that?"

"Of course I am," Mom retorted. "I bore her and raised her, what else can she be?"

"The priests say they have no souls."

"The priests say what the Calligraphers tell them to say."

"I think it's lovely. My nephew was a Curse, you know," said a woman in a pink scarf. "A Water Curse. Losing him broke my sister's heart. She was never the same."

"All the more reason why we should take care of the ones in front of us," Mom said. "Can all of you keep donating goods?"

"I can't," a red-scarfed man said. "Goods from Castleton get more expensive every day."

"Then we'll have to get more people to help us." Mom lowered Ildri and knelt beside her. "Here you are, dear." She pulled the scarf off her head and tied it over Ildri's greasy hair. "To protect from the sun."

Ildri's raw fingers tugged the tails of the knot as her face and neck warmed in her first smile since leaving home. Kindle hurried up, eyes wide. "Wow, is that yours?"

"Oh look at that!" The woman in pink removed her own scarf. "Here you go, dear, you can have one, too."

"Really?"

"Yes. My husband dyes them. I can bring enough for the rest of you tomorrow, if you'd like."

"Yes!" Kindle hopped up and down. "Thank you so much!"

Jude stepped to the forefront as the others wandered off. She scowled. "Mom are you crazy?"

"Don't take that tone with me."

"This is breaking the Calligraphers' law. You're going to get yourself arrested."

"Not if we're careful," Mom said. "I know you're reciting what has been told to you. I believed it, too, before it happened to our family, but Curses aren't creatures, they're helpless starving children. If more people saw it they'd agree, too. We have a chance to enact real and important change."

"I didn't come here to be in your social revolution," Jude said. "I wish you'd left me at home."

"You are home, Jude."

"No I'm not." She kicked over a box of vegetables and stormed away from them up the street.

The swell in Ildri's chest became a low, shameful burn that cooked the contents of her stomach into a stone. Mom pulled her close. "It's okay. She's still adjusting."

Jude had been "adjusting" for as long as Ildri could remember. The two of them were never really close. Ildri wondered if having a little sister was something Jude never really wanted. And after they found out she was a Curse, Jude turned downright mean. It made Ildri feel like the worst thing in the world.

Kindle shifted weight from foot to foot. "Come on, Il, let's show Dawn our new hats."

Ildri looked to Mom for approval. Mom's eyes softened with more than a little sadness. "Go ahead. Make some friends."

Ildri followed Kindle past Tyson and Ashlyn this time playing stick ball with a heap of old rags. Tyson stopped mid-swing and furrowed his wrinkling brow. "Where'd you get those?"

"It was a present," Kindle modeled her scarf. "Do you like it?"

"No," he snapped, but his face flushed to red.

She winked. "Do you want one, too?"

"Yes."

"Ildri's mom's going to bring more tomorrow. Right, Ildri?"

Ildri nodded and beamed back at Mom, but she was gone, probably after Jude. Ildri's heart sank.

Ashlyn snuck behind and stole the purple scarf off her head. "Come catch me, new girl!"

Kindle gaped. "Ashlyn! That's mean!"

Tyson took off after her. "If I get it first, it's mine!"

Ildri and Kindle joined the chase. Exercise warmed Ildri's chest until it felt weird, but Ashlyn didn't seem to mind. She rounded the Fire

Goddess and passed Dawn and Branton.

Dawn waved her hands. "Don't run!"

"Stop worrying!" Ashlyn climbed through the window of one of the buildings with Tyson close behind.

Dawn raised her voice again. "Hey! Don't disturb the dead!"

"I'll get them!" Kindle climbed in after. A steady stream of smoke filtered out of the darkened building. Ildri hefted herself over the wooden windowsill and onto the floor on the other side. The air was extremely hot and the smoke made Ildri cough. Her shoes trudged through mounds of ash, following the prints of Kindle's bare feet along the damaged carpet toward a back room. The house was really pretty once. Smoke had blackened the decorated wallpaper and fancy ceilings with blackness where weak fires had worked their way up the walls. Stone crumbled from behind the peeling wallpaper – that must have been why the walls hadn't burned. Big weather-proof blankets covered smoking mounds in the corners and across the floor. Her heart seized. She'd never seen a dead person before, and here there were probably hundreds of them in piles. Light glowed up through the blankets where fires still blazed. She felt dizzy again, but didn't want to pass out. Everything around her got really dark.

"Hey, Ildri?" Kindle asked. She sounded far away. Ildri felt her knees wobbling. "Hey Ty! Ash! Something's wrong!"

A light moved in the settling smoke. The shape of a man covered in burns with his eyes and mouth glowing. He reached a skinless hand toward her, but Kindle jumped in the way.

"Wait, Branton, I'll get her. I think she's just scared."

"You know Dawn told you kids not to play in here." Branton spoke with the same timid tone as the night Ildri arrived. "It's disrespectful and the floor is broken upstairs."

"I know that! It was Ashlyn's idea." Kindle took Ildri's hands. "It's okay, nothing's gonna hurt you. We're here together now, see?"

Tyson and Ashlyn hurried over, their eyes pleading and sorry. Branton squatted down. His face was blotched and peeling with ridges and scars, but up close she could see his eyes were still an emerald green. "She's right. We're all a big family. That includes the people in these houses. They died, but we're all fire. We've got the same flame, and that flame won't go out, so we're still part of the family. It's not as scary when you think of it like that, is it?"

Ildri's heart was still pounding, but Branton's voice was nice. Even if his body was gross, the person inside was very gentle. The heat she felt inside her was the fire he mentioned, the fire that made his wounds but also the fire that let her know she belonged. She wanted so badly to belong somewhere.

Ildri met his eyes, feeling calmer as she breathed. "Yeah..."

Kindle gasped. Branton's smile glowed. "Good. Now, let's get out of this smoke."

Kindle took Ildri's hand and the group returned to the street. Dawn was practically shaking in her seat with her bandaged feet still splayed in front. "What were you guys thinking? I've told you a hundred times not to play in there."

"Sorry, Dawn." Tyson sulked.

"Don't apologize to me! Apologize to the new girl!"

Ashlyn put the purple cloth back on Ildri's head. "Sorry Ildri."

"It's...okay." Ildri adjusted the knot so it was under her chin. "I wanted to play with you."

"Then how about we play stick ball instead?" Tyson asked and smirked at Dawn. "I promise we'll play outside."

"Well, Il?" Kindle glowed with pride. "What do you say?"

Ildri managed a smile. "Can I throw the ball?"

"Sure you can!" Ashlyn said and led them to the square.

The scarf lady kept her word and returned with Mom the next morning to give everyone colored scarves. Tyson and Ashlyn each picked blue ones. Dawn's was a happy orange color. Ildri picked a pretty green one to match Branton's green eyes. When she gave it to him, the light behind the emerald glowed in thanks.

Along with the scarves came more people carrying boxes of food. There were also bandages and ointment for everyone's burns. Mom introduced Ildri to the volunteers, making a point to say "her daughter." Ildri's fire made her a Curse, but love and pride was what kept her close to her Mom.

The visitors made sure to leave before the mayor showed up, and the Curses hid their new headscarves to keep their secret safe. The next day was similar with even more helpers. Ildri smiled and actually laughed, although Kindle did all the talking and thanked the locals over and over for everything they'd done. Mom brought breakfast and dinner the day after that, but the fifth morning Fire Town woke to a different kind of sound.

The mayor's voice boomed in the square. "Fellow citizens!"

Ildri sat up on the sleeping mat and pulled her purple scarf from her eyes. Fire Town was filled with hundreds of people. The mayor stood in the back of a cart lashed to a horse, flanked by guys carrying buckets and priests dressed in black robes. The townsfolk before him carried torches to light up the dark shadows of the early morning. Kindle sat up next to her. "Is that your mom?"

"No." These people were angry. Mom wouldn't trust them.

"You are all aware of the movement taking place in our city!" the mayor cried. "The priests warn us every day about the danger of sin. The Calligraphers' scriptures tell us Our God disapproves. That he wants us to reject these Curses. Their smoke fills our lungs and our streets, their smell permeates our homes, the ash from their evil bodies makes our young and old sick. This is why, as elected mayor of this town, I've decided to dedicate my administration to taking back this quarter of our city!"

The townsfolk gave a cheer. Ildri noticed Mom and her group shove to the front of the pack. Mom gaped. "What is going on here?"

"Ms. Fiammetta," the mayor said. "I've heard about your little charity. We're here to help."

"Help?" She set down her supply box. "How?"

"By removing your temptation." He waved his hand to the people. "For the beautification of Dire Lonato! Get these corpses out of our town."

At that signal, the group stormed the square below the Goddess. Wagons came to the doors of the smoking houses and people with shovels piled the dead bodies from inside into them. More people descended on the Curses. One grabbed Ashlyn around the waist and tossed her into a wagon that looked a lot more like a cage. "Ty! Help!"

"Leave her alone!" Tyson punched at her captor, but the man seized him and tossed him into the wagon as well. More grabbed Bunsen with ropes. A woman took Blaize and shoved him in with a hook on the end of a stick.

Fear rolled to a boil in the pit of Ildri's stomach, making her sick and feverish beneath all the fear. She searched the crowd for her mother and saw Firenze get captured. Kindle grabbed hold of Ildri's hand. "Run for your life!"

They dodged the chaos and headed for the open back gate. Smoke and fire spilled into the street from the disturbed piles of bodies. Pink dawn became hot and red in the flames. The wood in the houses caught fire. The wagon beds were like torches. Townsfolk doused the buildings in water to save them, while the bodies of dead Curses lay in pieces nearby.

"Help!" Dawn shouted. Kindle pulled Ildri to a stop and steered them toward the other Fire Curse, struggling to stand.

Branton grabbed her arms, but was kicked down by an attacker who emptied a whole bucket of water on Dawn. She screamed, steam rising as her skin blackened and cracked. Kindle shrieked and fainted. The men with the water turned on Branton. He backed toward the gate. Ildri covered her steaming face and let out a loud scream.

"Ildri!" Mom swooped in and grabbed her up. The girl's face pulsed with heat as she fought to stay conscious. She couldn't leave Kindle, but Mom was already running. The wagons full of bodies headed through the gate toward the desert. Mom pressed Ildri's face to her shoulder and dashed back toward town.

Ildri woke up in a bedroom she didn't recognize. Her blanket was over her shoulders. Her rag doll was propped on the pillow by her head. It was very cold.

Dishes clinked in the hall outside the room. Ildri slipped from the bed and out into the main living space where Mom stood frying something in the kitchen. It wasn't New Torston. Something felt very wrong. Mom smiled. "There you are, dear. Come eat your dinner."

Jude sulked at the table, stirring soggy vegetables with a fork. Ildri sat across from her, feeling sick and raw like the skin inside her throat was sunburned all the way up and down.

"Did you sleep well?" Mom asked.

"Was I dreaming?"

Mom's face brightened. "Yes, dear! You were dreaming!"

"Is Fire Town... okay?"

"Don't worry about Fire Town, you won't live there anymore. You'll live here with your family, where you belong."

"I saw... lots of fire." Ildri hugged her arms. "And attacks. And people dying."

"Don't. You'll upset yourself," Mom said. "Eat your food."

"But Mom..."

"It was a very bad dream, but you're safe with us now. Nothing is going to happen to you when your mother is here."

"Stop lying," Jude growled. "She's not supposed to be here."

Mom steeled. "You're upsetting your sister."

"Mom, she's a Curse!" Jude cried. "You came here to sacrifice but you haven't sacrificed anything. You only care about yourself when the whole world is going to die if you don't give up your sin. What about my life, Mom? What about me? "

"Jude, go to your room!" Mom shouted. "The neighbors will hear you!"

"Good. Let them." Tears filled her eyes. "Someone has to remove your temptation!"

Ildri's body twinged – it was the phrase that the mayor used to start his attack. The attack was real and her friends were real and Jude must have been there to see it. Fever and chill rushed through her, but she breathed deep to tamp it down. Ildri looked across the table. "You're mean."

Jude staggered. "What?"

"You've been really mean to me." Ildri stood in her seat. "Just because I'm sick doesn't mean I'm not here, even if you treat me like I'm not. You're the one who's selfish."

"Don't talk to me like that, you little worm," Jude snapped. "I'd be home if it wasn't for you."

"And so would I." Ildri's voice shook. "You told them about Mom helping us. It's your fault Fire Town was burned...because you were jealous."

Jude's anger flashed to horror. She backed out of her seat. "I didn't mean for it to go like that."

"You did that?" Mom asked. "You told him."

"You were breaking all the rules," Jude said. "You didn't listen when I warned you. I had to force you so we could go home."

"You stupid, foolish child," Mom hissed. "I brought you along because I love you and wanted us to be together. Now those Fire Curses are homeless or dead because of you. You could have killed your sister. Was that part of your goal?"

"It wasn't about that," Jude said. "I thought being a Curse meant she already was."

"Ms. Fiammetta!" A voice shouted. Fists pounded on the door.

Mom covered Jude's mouth. "Do not speak a word."

"Ms. Fiammetta," the knocker called again. "It's the police. We know you have a Curse in there!"

Mom snapped. "You told them, too?"

Jude shook her head 'no.'

Mom released her and whispered. "Take your sister out the window. Escape into the alley."

"But Mom – "

"Obey me for once in your life," Mom said. "If you aren't soulless, yourself."

Jude glanced between Mom and Ildri, face pale and eyes wide. The knock became a slam. The door rattled on its hinges and burst open, releasing what felt like an army of policemen into the room. Jude grabbed Ildri and ran back to her bedroom. Mom was flattened onto the kitchen table and her hands and arms tied with ropes.

Ildri reached out. "Mommy!"

Mom met her eyes before Jude barred the door with a chair. She opened the window. "Go on. Run for it."

Ildri's face pulsed. "But Mom – "

"I'm the reason they arrested her, I'll try and get her out," Jude said. "Hide back in Fire Town and I'll find you there."

"You want to help me?"

"I..." Jude bit her lip. "I'm sorry it came to all this."

The bedroom door slammed against the chair. Jude shoved her into the street. "Go!"

Ildri didn't wait to see what happened. She hurried out into the dark, tears and dizziness blurring her eyes. The veins in her hands glowed through her skin, so she stayed behind the houses and followed the smoke through the city to where the Fire Goddess stood.

Wisps of steam trailed from the dark houses. Water dripped

from the frames. There was no glow anywhere in the whole square. No fire left burning. Ildri sniffed back tears burning in the corners of her eyes. When her family came to Dire Lonato, she thought it was the worst it could ever get, but then this happened. It felt like her fault.

"Ildri?"

A man stepped from the desert beyond the open gate. His eyes and mouth glowed orange, with branching veins and cracks illuminated on his arms and legs. Ildri gasped. "Branton!"

He wrapped her in his green scarf to protect her from the sores on his arms.

"Is it her?" Kindle joined them, her face spotted with new sores around her eyes. "Is she okay?"

"I'm okay," Ildri muttered. "The guards took my mom away. I thought everyone was gone."

"They're all in the desert," a third voice said. It was the scarf-dyer's wife. The one that gave everyone their head wraps. "You're the only one they couldn't account for, so they asked me to bring them back here to look for you."

"It's dangerous here, but Fire Town is a family," Branton said.

Kindle nodded. "We have to stick together."

The four of them climbed into a wagon parked outside the gate. The column of smoke lingered in the desert, somewhere among the rolling dunes. The scarf lady talked about a new Fire Town, and that the volunteers Mom had gathered still wanted to help. They were going to dig new houses for them and bring better food. Kindle sat hugging Ildri as the wagon rolled into the desert, leaving Dire Lonato and all of its people behind. As she looked back, a girl ran through the open gate.

Jude. She kept her promise. Hopefully it meant Mom was safe, now too. If she shouted, Jude would hear her, but Ildri kept still and quiet. There was nothing gained by going back to her old life, and she had a new family now. It was going to be different, and it was going to be hard, but she was a Fire Curse and she finally knew where she belonged.

The End

Earth Curse took the longest to write of all the short stories because although I had spare characters I could include, I did not have a story starter left over from Threadcaster like I did with the other short stories. I took this opportunity to write a more political story. I also used it as an experiment in writing the non-gendered pronoun.

The singular use of "they" in spoken English is a very old practice. it is documented in Shakespeare, the writings of Jane Austin (1814), and Lord Byron (1823). In official language studies at the time, the preferred choice for situations when the gender of a person is not certain was a common "he," which we can see affects of as modern readers in everything from male-character-as-default scenarios to female participation being erased in stories about groups or events. Nowadays the nonbinary pronoun is often a very personal one and can be anything from ze, sie, hir, co, and ey to a complete lack of pronouns altogether. According to Wikipedia, the most commonly used gender-neutral pronoun in the 2010s is the singular "they," and so I wanted to give the usage a try.

The singular use of a plural pronoun can be a challenge to readers, especially when the character in question is participating in a group. I won't pretend I pulled the usage off perfectly, but it's important to stay current with language and with more and more people coming out as nonbinary, respectful usage of their preferred pronoun is important for everyone.

Earth Curse

Clayton dragged his heavy legs across the courtyard, the handle of a metal bucket grasped in the stiff fingers of his left hand. Breath raked in and out of his lungs as he hefted one stone leg in front of the other. Not long ago, the walk from his house to the well was no big deal. He'd make the hike three or four times a day, especially when Jade was at her sickest. But Jade was gone now, long past needing a Helper, and he was crossing into old age himself, at least old for an Earth Curse. Jade only made it to fourteen and that was only a year and a half away. Clayton knew he really should be resting, but his new Helper was missing. Plus, chores made him feel younger, and that was harder to give up.

The town well was a hole in the ground dug by generations of previous Earth Curses. A crossbeam with hand-made pulleys hung over the open mouth. Dangling ropes coiled around the beam, ready to descend. A small child sat on the edge of the well, staring into the dark. Mica, Clayton's new Helper. They were five years-old at most with close-cropped dark hair and no discernible gender. And when Clayton asked they avoided the question, so genderless they stayed. Mica scowled into the well and kicked their swollen feet against the wall.

"Hey, Meeks," Clayton said. "Whatcha doin'?"

Mica's squeaky child-voice had a grown-up amount of anger in it. "Nothing."

"Bouncing your heels like that is only gonna make them swell."

"Leave me alone."

"Okay, if that's what you want." Clayton lowered the bucket to the ground before releasing his grip. "Could you tie one of those ropes to the handle so we can lower it? I can do it but it'll go a lot faster with two hands."

Mica growled.

"You're my Helper. It's not a big request."

Mica rolled their eyes and pulled their legs in. "Fine."

The handle for the rotating crossbeam was installed near the ground. Clayton stooped to grasp it, but a growing lump on his left hipbone jabbed his ribs as he bent so he decided to nudge it with his shin instead. The rope descended on the far side of the well. Mica grabbed it easily and plopped down on the ground to string it around the handle.

"Make a loop first and use it to make the knot," Clayton said. "It'll be easier to untie."

"I can do it."

Another pair of Earth Curses – an older girl, Emery, and her helper Jared – swayed up to the well. Emery was only a year older than Clayton, but was given a Helper early because of how quickly her symptoms affected her hands and elbows. Her face was deep-set, but not enough to hide her eyes which were a beautiful green color. Clayton loved her eyes. He tried to play it cool as she approached. "Mornin' Em."

"Morning," she said. "What are you two doing?"

"Nothing special. Getting water."

"Yeah, us too." Emery shuffled her overlarge feet. "How's your new Helper?"

"Ah, well, you know..." Clayton paused as Mica looped the rope around the handle ten more times.

Jared, a ruddy-skinned kid with a large tumor over his right eye, inched closer to Mica. He was a couple years older than Mica and more than twice as big. He'd been with Emery for years already and it was showing on his knees and elbows. Helpers did a lot of lifting and bending. "You okay, Mica? Can I help you with that knot?"

" No."

"It's gonna fall in if you don't tie it tight."

"No."

Clayton shook his head with a sigh. Emery nudged the back of his leg. "Don't feel bad, it's not Mica's fault. I mean, they only got here two days ago."

"I know." He lowered his voice and leaned toward her. The ridge in his hip pinched again. "It was nothing like this when I helped Jade. I don't understand what Mica's problem is."

"They're still adjusting. Plus there's no telling how long they sat outside until Georgia found them."

"And we both know how comforting she can be," Clayton scoffed, but the humor faded quickly. "I wish Jade was here."

"Here, Mica, just let me do it." Jared fixed his two strongest fingers around the pail handle and pulled it free of Mica's rope. The younger Helper snarled and pouted as Jared tied one of the other descending ropes easily and kicked the bucket into the well. It clanked off the walls and hit the damp bottom with a squelch.

Clayton grimaced. "Dude, you'll get mud in it."

"It's great, don't worry!" Jared tugged the rope with his more useful right hand, transferring the slack to his stiff, heavy left hand one arm-length at a time. He was an odd kid. Clayton had never seen someone whose symptoms were so lopsided. When he first arrived it was just his left wrist, but time and all the chores he had to do spread the swelling to his shoulder. The added weight was causing his left knee to swell, too. There was no telling how anyone's illness would progress, but Clayton couldn't help wondering how much the constant errands and chores affected the way their symptoms advanced. Perhaps if they had a chance to rest, they'd be able to do more when they were older. The grip on Clayton's left hand was his most prized possession and he only had that because he took care of it.

Jared was losing steam with each tug, but continued diligently onward. The bucket rose, mud-caked and swaying, with each tug. It clunked off the wall and Jared's improvised knot gave way, dropping the pail back to the wet bottom.

Jared balled up. "Oops."

Mica snorted.

"Jared!" A girl's voice barked from across the yard.

Emery and Clayton jumped. Georgia stood with her two lackeys in front of her stone hut. She was still young – maybe nine or ten – younger than Clayton, but she was already a brute of an Earth Curse with thick, overgrown legs that made her tower above other Curses her age. They also made it hard for her to walk quickly. That's what her lackeys, Evan and Steiner, were for. Neither boys had much personality, but both had use of their elbows and that made them a powerful intimidation force.

Georgia shifted her immense weight onto her back foot. She propped her swollen elbow propped on one of her hips. "You lost a bucket down the well. I saw it."

Jared went pale.

Clayton stepped between them. "It was an accident."

"We don't have extras. You need to get it back."

"And how should we do that?"

"I don't care." Georgia's voice was flat, almost disinterested. "Every house has exactly one of those. You lose it, you get no water."

"That's not fair!" Jared cried. "It was Mica's bucket."

"The four of us can share a bucket," Emery's voice was small and shaky. "It's okay with me. It wouldn't be much trouble... "

"No," Georgia said. "This is not your problem."

"We can share for now, then," Clayton said. "When it rains again, the water will rise and the lost bucket will float to the top where we can reach it."

"It hasn't rained in six weeks," Georgia snapped. "Before that, it was two months. The well is all the water we're getting and who knows how long that's gonna last. You need to get that bucket back. There's no other solution. That's the way it is."

"Fine." Mica stood at the edge of the well, the rope from their pail tied in a knot under their arms. "I'll go."

Clayton's stomach dropped. "That's not a good idea."

"It'll shut everyone up. Lower me down."

"Don't be a brat," Clayton said. "It's dangerous. I won't let you."

Emery tried to be a little kinder. "I know it seems easy, but you'll hurt your ribs."

"Let them," Georgia said. "It's what Helpers are for."

Clayton bristled. "Helpers are still little kids. We're older, we should take care of them."

"No, they take care of US. That's their job. You used to be a Helper, now you're Helped. Soon you'll be a wall. There's an order to everything."

Clayton narrowed his eyes. "I'm going to be a house."

"My mistake." Georgia cut. "Evan, lower the kid into the hole."

The thug on her left grabbed the loose end of Mica's rope and tugged. The child was small, but still heavy for an Earth Curse of any age to lift. The knot at their chest held as they were lifted into the air. Clayton's ribs tightened. A tumor deep in his neck poked up into his windpipe as Mica twisted in air and was lowered into the well.

"This is bad," Clayton stammered.

Emery pressed tight to Clayton's arm, her whole body shaking. "Be strong for Mica. It was their idea. Show them you're confident."

He gulped. "I'll try."

Jared leaned forward over the well, hands supported on his knees. "Be careful!Watch the walls!"

There was a splash and a clatter. The descending rope went slack. Steiner added his strength to Evan's and the two started to pull. Seconds passed without a sound from any of the onlookers until Mica emerged with the handle of the lost bucket held tight in both hands.

Jared pulled them back to solid ground. "Good job, Kid!"

"Thank God," Clayton's slouched his massive shoulders. "Meeks? You okay?"

Mica focused on undoing the knot and did not reply.

Clayton turned, instead, to Georgia. "That wasn't cool. Laird is going to be mad."

"Why? Are you going to tattle?"

"Maybe I will."

"Good, go ahead," Georgia dismissed. "Laird hasn't gotten rid of the Helper system yet."

Clayton hefted himself on stiff legs, shuffling as defiantly as he could past Georgia and toward Laird's hut near the outer wall. Earth Town was surrounded in a ring of stone accumulated from generations of Curses. It sloped on either side – a healthy person could probably climb it if they really wanted to – but it kept the wind out. The farms beyond were all closed down, choked to death by lack of rain. A brown haze drifted in the world beyond the wall, reminding Clayton that as bad as the Earth Curses had it, at least they were safe from the dust.

The Earth Curse leader's dirt hut was small and uneven like everyone else's. When Clayton was found outside the wall, Laird was the one who told him who to serve and where the stone inside him was going to go when he died. It was a tough job, but Laird insisted he be treated the same as everyone else. It was something Clayton appreciated about him. Clayton ducked in through the low doorway but Laird wasn't home.

"Is he walking?" Emery asked.

Jared bit his lip. "I thought his legs were too stiff."

He was right, Laird hadn't moved in days. This felt wrong. Clayton exchanged a glance with Emery. "We should try to find Ila."

Emery sent Jared around the house calling Laird's Helper's name. Ila was a quiet girl, but wholly devoted to Laird and never left his side. Other Curses heard the shouting and poked their heads from their huts. Clayton called to them. "You seen Laird?"

"Not since yesterday."

"What about Ila?"

"She's not there?"

Mica joined him outside Laird's hut, their sour face not even a little concerned about the missing leader. Clayton did his best to show disapproval without saying any words. There were more important problems than his Helper's bad attitude. At least they didn't seem hurt by the rope incident unless they didn't care about that either. In the short time they'd known each other, Clayton had yet to see Mica care about anything.

Jared galloped back up, panting heavier than the short walk usually required. The seven year-old's eyes were wide and hollowed in fear. "I – I found them."

"What happened."

"She... They..."

The sound of weeping echoed faintly in the quiet, and Clayton's heart dumped like a stone to his stomach. "Take us there."

He gulped and followed. Ila stood sobbing at the base of the wall. Laird lay face-down against the uneven stone. Spears of rock like spines split the skin of his back, arching upward from cakes of dry mud that used to pump through the Curse's veins.

Laird was dead.

"He asked me to help him up," Ila blubbered into her gnarled hands. "Then sent me out for food."

Clayton laid his heavy arm as softly as he could across her back. "It's not your fault. You're supposed to help when he asks. You did the right thing."

Emery's lip quivered. "He used the last of his strength to get in this position. He didn't want Ila to watch."

"So he's dead?" Georgia limped into their midst, her face as pitiless as her voice. "I guess the Helper system stays, then."

Ila's sobs increased in strength and volume. Clayton tucked her to his side. "Show some respect."

"Respect for what?"

"He's dead!"

"No, he's a wall."

Emery gawked. "He was our leader!"

"Yeah, 'was." Georgia said. "This is a natural progression. I'll be a wall, too, at some point. And you, and Jared and Mica and everyone else. We all know the purpose we're going to serve. Laird was a leader, now he's doing the job he was meant to do, and someone else gets to be leader. I propose it be me."

"You?" Clayton turned so quickly he lost his balance. Emery was at his side in an instant, but no amount of steadying would ease the sense of "stagger" he got from such a thought. "You're joking."

"No. I'm the only one with my head on straight around here."

Jared snorted. "Only 'cause you can't move your neck anymore." Emery shushed him in a panic.

"Laird thought the same," Georgia continued. "I'm the only one for the job."

"I could do it." Clayton said.

"But you won't."

"Who says?"

"Please." A sardonic smile split Georgia's craggy face. "Like you'd stand up to the Brushcasters. Or tell the new arrivals where their stone is needed. Or keep track of how everything works. You're shaking to dust just thinking about it. Earth Town won't last a week with you leading."

"Earth Town would do more than last, it would sustain itself better than ever because we'd work together to make it happen." Saying it made Clayton's heart swell. He met Mica's eye around Emery's leg. They were still upset but obviously listening. Did he see a hint of hope? Clayton straightened taller. "I don't think we even need a Helper system anymore! The thing at the well just now is proof that I'm right. It's time for us to change things around here!"

"I guess we're officially rivals, then." Georgia gestured to her two lackeys. "Round up the rest of town. It's time for a fight."

Jared gulped. "Fight?"

"Not with violence," Emery assured. "Only words and ideas."

"Those can be violent." The spark of sadistic humor on Georgia's face fanned to flame. "Hope you're ready."

Clayton flexed his left hand into the tightest fist he could manage. "More than you know."

Rounding the townsfolk up was not an easy thing. Earth Town wasn't very big, but its residents were very, very slow. The oldest Earth Curse, now that Laird was gone, was an immobile girl named Amber who just turned fifteen years old. Her hips were fused solid, so they agreed to hold the vote outside her house so she could still participate. The other twenty-two Earth Curses were split between Helpers and Helped with a couple of solo acts in the middle. Clayton didn't know why he was nervous to talk in front of them. These people were his family, and he was never this nervous before.

Besides, he was pretty sure he was going to win. Georgia was a lot younger than he was, but her body was worse in a lot of ways. He could still walk easily, not to mention grip and carry things. She relied on not one but TWO Helpers, if you counted Evan and Steiner as Helpers (which technically they weren't). Plus, no one liked Georgia that much. Ever since the two of them were Helpers, she was like a robot who did what she was told and no more.

The girl she was helping back then, Ruby, wasn't "all there" so to speak. Emery said she probably had a bone growing in her brain. Clayton shuddered at the thought. What a gross way to go. It left Ruby in a kind of waking sleep state. Georgia did everything for her until she

72

died. That was almost a year ago, a little before Jade died.

Boy, he wished Jade was still with him.

"Okay everyone!" Jared waved his better arm. "Attention here, please! Emery wants to say something!"

"Yes," Emery croaked and cleared her throat. "I have some sad news to share with you. I know it will come as a bit of a shock. It shocked us for sure, so I want you all to prepare... "

Georgia cut her off. "Laird's dead."

The other Earth Curses paled with shock. Helpers, most of which were probably found by Laird outside the gate, started crying on their older counterparts' swollen legs and arms. Ila's face twitched as fresh tears wet the mud drying on her cheeks. Even the human shapes that made up the buildings seemed sad.

Clayton's pounding heart doubled its beat. He couldn't stand seeing his family so upset, and Georgia wasn't saying anything to help them. That was why Georgia wasn't going to be a good leader. That was why she wouldn't win.

"I know you all feel bad," Clayton called over the sounds of mourning. "It's okay to be sad when someone dies, especially someone as important to all of us as Laird was. He took care of us. And looked after us. And he's still looking after us now, because he donated the stone of his body to reinforce our wall."

One of the Helpers looked up, eyes clouded with mud. "He's still looking after us?"

"Yeah, he's helping keep out the wind and cold," Clayton replied. "It's the job he's always prepared for, and he's happy to protect us, just like he was before. Right?"

The child nodded, more hopeful. "Right!"

Georgia rolled her eyes. "The important part of all this is that he's dead now and we need a new leader. I think it should be me."

"And I think it should be me." Clayton frowned. "That's why we got everyone together for a meeting."

Ila's eyes swam with tears. "How do we pick?"

"We have a vote," Emery said.

"Vote?" One of the Helped asked. "But, I can't raise my hand any more."

"That's okay," Clayton said. "We'll let Amber vote first, and then whoever agrees with her can stand next to her on that side of her house and whoever votes for the other person will stand on the other side of her house."

"You're making it too difficult," Georgia said. "We'll do it by 'aye's. Everyone who votes for me say 'aye.'"

"Don't just flat out ask," Clayton cringed. "We have to debate!"

"Why? The correct answer is obvious. I do all the work around here anyway."

"She's not wrong," Flint, one of the Helped said.

Emery scowled. "Clayton would do the work, too!"

"Yeah, but Georgia already knows how."

Amber's strangled voice spoke from the ground. "I want to vote for Georgia."

"No, wait – " Clayton bade, but the Earth Curses were already shuffling back and forth across the lawn. The Helpers clung together or followed their assigned Helped Curses to their different voting locations. Emery took Clayton's side, but most of the older Curses were picking Georgia. Mica remained firmly and stubbornly neutral.

Georgia's chest puffed with pride. "See? I win."

"But Clay barely got to talk!" Jared cried.

"He didn't have to."

"No you didn't let me, because you are a bully," Clayton said. Those still wandering stopped to gape. Clayton cleared his throat around the stone barb in his neck as an equally large knot tightened in his stomach. "I mean, you probably don't know it, but you're really mean sometimes. You don't care about how people feel as long as you get what you want."

"Feelings are stupid," Georgia said. "We've got what? Ten years of mobility? Am I supposed to waste time making people feel good, or am I supposed to keep this town running?"

"Taking care of people is part of that, though. Our feelings make a difference with our illnesses, too."

"Yeah, more reason not to waste time on them," Georgia huffed. "It's dumb to even bring it up. Everyone's already chosen my side."

"Clayton?" Ila's strained voice spoke through sniffs. "If uh... If you were in charge, who would I be helping? Now that Laird is gone I don't have anybody. Do I have to live by myself? I don't want to live by myself."

The pulse pounding in Clayton's ears eased. He bent forward as far as the pinch in his hip allowed. "No, Illy, you don't have to live alone. We'll all help each other when we need it. You don't need to be assigned to someone."

"You mean no more Helpers?"

"Yeah. No more helpers." He set his jaw and stood tall. "Picking me is more than just running Earth Town as it has been. From now on people who can move easily will help those who can't move easily, regardless of age or assignment, and those who are sick get cared for and taken care of until they die."

Amber coughed. "And what happens then?"

"Then... uh..." Clayton hadn't put a lot of thought into what happened when he died. He was going to be a house, and was told so the day he arrived. Heck, Amber was sitting in front of her house for the very same reason. Laird worried so much about everyone, then sent his Helper away so he could sneak off alone to die. Laird needed to be honored the same way Ila needed to be protected.

Amber blinked uneven, partially blinded eyes. Clayton returned to his present mind and held her gaze. "After you die, you'll get a funeral. And you'll be respected. And your stones will go to wherever the town needs them the most."

"Sentimentality," Georgia scoffed.

"But kind!" Emery said.

"Kindness doesn't assure anything," Georgia said. "If you like having buildings and getting food, you need rules and jobs like we had."

Amber grunted and shifted in the spot near her house. "I'm changing my vote to Clayton!"

Georgia grunted. "You already voted."

"Clayton said I could go first."

"He's not in charge."

"Neither are you."

Jared laughed out loud and slapped his hand over his mouth. Giggles rippled behind him. Georgia's face flushed umber. "It doesn't matter who is in charge. Facts are facts."

"Then it wouldn't hurt to vote again," Clayton said. "We'll each say one closing thing before Amber starts."

"Don't be fake generous," Georgia snapped. "Your feel-good stuff is all fluff. A vote for me is a vote to make sure everything keeps going as it has. Everyone's going to have food. Everyone's going to have shelter. Everyone's going to have a purpose."

"And voting for me is a vote to change for the better," Clayton said. "So Amber? What do you say?"

Amber coughed again. "Clayton!"

"Clayton!" Emery and Jared agreed. They joined the other Curses as everyone changed positions. A lot of the voters stayed where they were, but even more changed their minds until the group was sorted into two camps. Nine people for Clayton; nine people for Georgia. Mica still stood defiantly in the middle.

"Mica!" Emery fretted. "What are you doing?"

"Nothing."

"But Clayton's your Helped Curse." She looked worried.

Clayton reassured her with a nod. "Mica's their own person. They can pick whoever they want to."

"But they still have to pick *someone*."

Mica's tiny brow was creased deeply over the bridge of their nose. They pouted with such determination it was obvious to all they would not be moved. Clayton regarded Georgia. "Seems we have a tie."

"This is stupid," Georgia said. "Vote again."

"We'll wait until tomorrow morning, so people can think about it," Clayton said. "In the meantime, everyone can ask us questions. It'll be a real election, like the healthy people do in Astonage."

"I don't care about what healthy people do," Georgia said. "We're Curses. We're not people. The important part of all this is that we survive."

The tie was a good enough reason to throw a party as far as Emery was concerned. By nightfall, she had all the food they could spare out in baskets for guests. The huts around Clayton's and Mica's house were strung with banners of string and knotted fabric. Helpers played drums and rattles around the central bonfire and pulled buckets full of water up from the well in teams. Mica wandered around the outside ringing a bell left by some long-dead Curse. Clayton watched from the door of their house, amused his Helper could be so captivated as they played their tiny instrument and barely – almost – smiled.

"They're coming around." Emery's voice made Clayton jump. She nudged him with her thick elbow. "Do you think they'll open up when they aren't a Helper?"

"I don't know. They don't complain about being a Helper, but they do seem happier when left to themselves." Clayton leaned back into her. "Maybe they'll be our first lone wolf?"

"That or they'll have a change of heart."

"I hope so." Clayton thought of Jade. "It's hard to live alone."

Emery and Clayton moved throughout the crowd, smiling and nodding as people toasted with heavy-handed gestures. A Helper raised a cup of water for her Helped Curse to drink from. The seated Curse looked up. "Congrats, Clayton!"

"Heh, I'm not leader yet."

"But you will be!" The Helper called out. "You beat Georgia, that's almost impossible."

"No, it's not. You just gotta care about more than a schedule."

"Clayton," Amber's rough voice whispered. She was no longer in front of her house, but set a few feet away, near the fire. The space between was marked by foot steps and deep drag marks. It was hard work to move her, but Clayton could tell in Amber's smile that those few feet meant a lot. "Do I really get to have a funeral?"

"Absolutely!"

"Will there be flowers and music and everything?"

"We probably can't get flowers, but music – you bet."

"Wow," Amber sighed. "Just like real people."

Clayton's throat tightened around the knob. "Don't think like that. We are real people."

"We're Curses."

"That's what we're sick with, it's not who we are," Clayton said. "The rest of the Valley can shovel us into a pile out here if they want, but that doesn't mean we should treat each other the same way."

Ila played with the hem of her skirt in the firelight. "Is that why you want to get rid of the Helpers?"

"Helpers as a concept is not the same as Helpers as a job," Clayton said. "I want to make us all in to Helpers and at the same time make all of us in to Helped. A big community. Like a family."

Flint shifted his weight onto his stronger leg. He was one of Georgia's supporters and voted her way both times. "That's a nice thought. I don't know if it's going to work."

"It'll work because it's the right thing to do."

"Yeah, okay."

"No, we can do it!" Jared chirped. "I don't mind helping more than one person."

"Yeah, but that's because you're you. I wouldn't have done that when I was a Helper."

"Was that because you didn't like helping, or was it because you were being treated like a servant?" Clayton asked. "We all remember Jade. She was my Helped Curse. She was nice to me, and I was happy to help her because I knew she couldn't do a lot of the things I could do. It feels good to make others' lives better – to be a part of a community."

Flint blew a dusty snort. "It's real easy to tell others to step up when you've still got a working hand."

Clayton closed the fingers of his working limb. "I'm getting sicker just like you are, but it'll work out because I know everyone will be there for me."

"Says the guy whose own Helper doesn't even step up," Flint scoffed. "Mica hates your guts. You really think a kid like that's gonna magically start helping you out of the goodness of their heart? I mean, have you met them?"

Across the fire, Mica's scowl returned. Their eyes flashed to meet Clayton's before stomping away into the darkness. The bell dropped near the fire with a muted thunk.

Clayton glared at Flint. "Why'd you have to take it there, man? This isn't about them."

"They're the only undecided." Flint shifted his weight again. "Maybe you better reconsider."

Clayton gritted his teeth and hobbled after Mica. Only Georgia's most steadfast supporters weren't attending the party. Most slept in their houses, but some sat hunched outside their doors or against the outer wall. Clayton knew all of them inside and out, yet they glared at him as he passed. Nothing like an election to learn who was a fair-weather friend. He wondered if things would go back to normal after he won. Assuming he won. Even if he didn't, would these people be friendly? Everyone's lives were so short, it'd be a waste not to be friendly. Still, it seemed like some people couldn't help but hold grudges. Like Mica. Clayton found them crouched behind a box.

"Hey Meeks," Clayton said. "It's me. Come on out."

"No."

"I know what Flint said upset you, but that's no reason to hide."

"Flint's stupid."

"Sometimes he can be." Clayton's ribs ached. The air was cold away from the fire. Dust escaped with steam from his lips. "Do you want to talk about it?"

"No."

"Are you sure? It seems like it really bothered you." Clayton dragged his feet to the edge of the box pile. "If it helps, I don't agree with what he said. You aren't angry because you want to be angry."

"Who asked you?"

"If it's about being an Earth Curse, I understand," Clayton continued. "It's tough being dumped by your folks. Then, in the same moment, made into a servant for some gross-looking person you don't know, and realizing that deformed person is what you're going to look like when you get old and die. It's cosmically unfair."

Mica grunted. "It's dumb."

"Yeah, it's real dumb."

"Everything's dumb." Mica sniffed, their shoulders shaking despite how tightly they were gripping their arms. "We're all doomed, so nothing matters."

Clayton leaned against the boxes, the knob on his hip poking up into his guts. "That's not true. You matter."

"No, I don't." Mica glared over their shoulder. Their eyes were bloodshot brown from crying. "You don't care about me. This is about getting votes for your dumb election. What difference is it gonna make who wins or who doesn't? I'll still be fetching stuff and getting ugly and dying just like you're doing. Who's leader won't change that."

The neck tumor pressed Clayton's windpipe again. "Yeah, okay," he croaked. "Maybe you're right. If I lose and Georgia wins, it's not going to stop anyone from dying. If I win I might die tomorrow and she can take over again anyway, but that doesn't mean I can't try my best to make living better."

"For what? Like a year?"

"A year is a long time."

"Yeah and healthy people live a hundred years."

"And if you talked to one who was ninety-nine would they say the last year didn't matter?" Clayton opened and closed his left hand. "None of us have as much time as we'd like, but we're all alive for now. And you're gonna live on after me. That's true right? There is a future, even if I don't see it. It's how I can still help. What I'm trying to do isn't pointless if it makes life better for other people."

"They're just gonna die, too."

"Yeah, but they might not dread it so much." Clayton extended his hand. "I know you're scared, Mica. I bet you never thought about dying before all this happened to you, and it's okay to be upset about it. I am. But that's why I'm trying to change things."

Mica's tense shoulders slacked. They regarded Clayton's hand.

"I don't care if you vote for me or not. I don't care if you serve me. Really, I just want you to be happy. You believe me about that, right?" Clayton flexed his fingers. "Come on back to the party. Put all that energy toward living instead of dying."

The scowl returned. "You don't know me!"

"Mica?"

"Quit lying! Leave me alone!" Mica ducked the extended arm and dashed into the shadows beyond the supplies. Clayton shuffled after, but was blocked by two taller figures.

"Shouldn't you be sucking up somewhere, Clay?"

It was Evan and Steiner. Clayton steeled. "And shouldn't you two be flanking Georgia like furniture?"

Evan snorted. "You talk brave now, but Georgia sent us with a little message."

"She doesn't like the changes you plan to make to town," Steiner agreed. "Sent us with a little message."

"Anything she wants to say, she can say in front of everyone."

"It's not that kind of message."

The two hemmed him in, their bodies forming a wall that bent around Clayton and pressed him into the stack of boxes. His throat constricted around the lump as he teetered off-balance. Evan used the gripping claws of his two hands to grab Clayton by the wrist, pulling his arm straight.

"This is the one you can close still, isn't it?"

Clayton gulped.

"Steiner's got one of those too. See, he'll show ya – "

Steiner raised a length of metal pipe and slammed it down on Clayton's forearm with the momentum and weight of a wrecking ball. The stone replacing his skeleton fractured to pieces. Chunks shifted under his skin. His arm skewed from the weight. A sharp ridge sliced through with a swell of mud-stained blood.

It took a moment of horrified staring before the pain kicked in. It throbbed with fire up his arm, across his chest, and down every vein. The spaces in his ribs hardened and the muscles tightened. His throat collapsed around the tumor. His next breath was a strangled gasp.

Evan dropped Clayton's hand. The weight of the broken stone stretched his screaming flesh toward the ground. Clayton pitched forward to touch dirt and stop the drag, but it only made him stumble and fall against the supply boxes.

"Gross," Steiner snorted a laugh and levered Clayton off into the wall. "There. Just like Laird."

Evan grinned. "Thought he said he was supposed to be a house."

"I thought he said he didn't care about that anymore."

"Good point." Evan loomed over the prone Curse with a toothy grin. "Well, Clay, that's all Georgia wanted us to say to you. We'll miss ya at the vote tomorrow."

"Maybe if you're still alive we'll tell you the results!"

The two laughed and shambled off, dragging the murder weapon behind them. Clayton wheezed. His mind and heart raced as pain and dread twisted to nausea in his stomach. He was going to die here, like Laird. Like Jade. Like so many Curses before him. Boulders that used to be heads and legs and arms packed in around him, blotting out the moonlight. Through fading consciousness, Clayton saw another shadow, tiny compared to his attackers. Mica. They stood in the lighted gap between two huts. Clayton tried to call but hadn't the breath or strength. Another gasp and he slipped into spinning darkness.

Clayton didn't have any siblings as a kid, although his mom was pregnant last he saw her. Six year-old Clayton was so excited to help look after the baby, but never got the chance. A bruise on his knee no bigger than a fingerprint calcified under his skin just a month before the baby was due. Curses were bad omens and invitations to misfortune. If it meant protecting his wife and future child, Clayton's dad was willing to get rid of his son. It hurt, but leaving meant he was still looking out for his kid sibling. It wasn't so bad if it was to protect someone. That's what he was told.

When Clayton was dumped at Earth Town he was assigned to Jade. She was sweet. She told Clayton he reminded her of the baby brother she had when she lived with her parents. She also told him he'd grow up to be a house, which didn't make a lot of sense at first. Not until he woke up one night and saw two eye sockets staring at him from near the ceiling of his hut. That's the first time it really clicked that he was going to die, and how, and why. At least he knew what to expect, she told him. It didn't help.

Emery's voice pierced the painful darkness. She bent over him, sunken eyes wide. "Clayton! Can you hear me? Say something, please."

Clayton opened his mouth but it hurt to move that much. The effort was enough. Tears flooded Emery's eyes.

"You're still alive. Thank goodness."

Jared appeared at her side. "What happened?"

"Georgia..." Clayton rasped.

"She did this?"

"Her goons." Mica hugged themself. "I saw it happen."

Emery gaped. "Because she didn't want to lose?"

"Not killed," Jared said. "It's just the arm, see?"

Clayton risked a glance at his arm. The limb was bent unnaturally over the broken box beside him. His forearm had already tripled in size. Great crags of stone jutted from the raw ends of broken bone like fireworks frozen beneath his stretched skin.

Emery sniffed. "Sometimes it doesn't matter what's broken. If it's bad enough, the rest of you can't recover."

"I'm...." Clayton's ribs creaked with every labored breath. "I'm not dead yet."

"Clay," Emery whimpered. "Stay calm."

"You're going to be okay, man," Jared assured. "We'll get you back home and you can rest there until the arm knits back up. You're gonna have a monster arm, but we'll help you with it."

Clayton hissed past the lump. "Thanks, Jared."

"What about tomorrow morning?" Mica asked. "Will it grow together over night."

Jared's hopeful face fell. "It's fast, but not that fast."

"If he moves, he'll just rebreak it and it'll grow in bigger than ever," Emery said. "We'll align it right and put a splint on it, but he'll have to sit here for days before we get him up."

"If I can get up at all," Clayton sighed. "Everything's so stiff."

"But you have to." Emotion squeaked in Mica's high voice. They hardly looked like themselves without the anger on their face. Mica hugged their arms so tight their hands shook. "Georgia did this because she wanted to make sure things stay the same."

Clayton glanced sidelong. "I thought you didn't care about that."

"I – I don't." They bit their lip. "But, like... those guys did this on purpose. They picked the arm you could still use to make it hurt as much as possible. She's awful. I don't want her to win."

The tightness in Clayton's chest subsided. He smiled. "Does that mean I got your vote after all?"

Mica pursed their brow. "Not that it matters."

"It matters," Clayton said. "This isn't going to end with me. Georgia did this as an example. She wants people to be scared to oppose her, and she's going to make everyone's lives miserable. I won't let this happen as long as there's still a way I can get to the election tomorrow."

"How?" Emery asked. "We can't bring it here. No one will vote for a leader who can't move. Especially after seeing Laird laid on the wall in the same way."

"That's not what I mean." Clayton drew a shaky breath. "You have to take the arm off."

"Wh-what?"

A cold sweat broke over his neck, but Clayton steeled his resolve. "It's mostly off already anyway. You just gotta cut the rest."

"That's awful!" Emery cried. "You can't do that! It'll kill you."

"Aren't I dying anyway?"

"You can't risk it."

"I have to." Tears overflowed his eyes. "For everyone's sake."

Emery shuddered and stretched her hands, neither of them able to grip or extend. She let them rest at her sides. "Jared, it's up to you."

Jared blanched. "You mean for real?"

"Once it's free you have to bandage it or he'll bleed too much."

"No way! I don't want to do it!" Jared cried. "I'm not gonna cut up one of my friends, no way! I'll do anything else, I can't do that."

"It's what he wants."

Mica blinked mud away from their eyes. They studied Clayton with the same look of silent terror he was feeling himself. He didn't want to lose an arm, but that decision was made for him already. Mica saw it, too. The two shared an understanding as a frown returned to the younger Curse's face. "I'll do it."

Jared rounded on them. "Dude, this isn't like the bucket in the well. This is a big deal."

"I know it is," Mica nearly shouted. "But, I'm his Helper. He needs me to be his hands for him because I can do it and he can't. That's what my job is."

Emery's massive shoulders sagged. "Mica, Clayton doesn't care about Helpers."

"But he cares about living." Mica gave Clayton a nod. "And he cares about me."

The next morning the Earth Curses gathered close to Amber's hut. A mull of human voices hummed over the stone buildings. Clayton's name bounced between structures amid calls of "Where is he?" "Have you seen him?" "Have you seen his Helper?"

"I checked his house. Both he and Jared are missing," Ila said. "Emery and Jared aren't home either."

"Did you check the wall?"

"N-no," Ilya whimpered. "I couldn't..."

"Baby," Flint spat. "Mica's gone, too. Maybe both ran for it."

"Shut up, Flint, you know he can't run."

Georgia cleared her throat boomed out over the crowd. "I think we've waited long enough. If Clayton can't be bothered to show up to this election, then I think I should win by default. You can't trust a leader that bails."

There was a medley of agreement.

She bellowed again. "All who pick me to lead them say 'Aye'!"

"Wait."

Clayton's voice was weak. He drew a constricted breath. It had been the longest night of his life. He was still hurt and woozy, but he was up on his feet. With Emery's help and Mica's bravery, he'd made it to the vote – missing his left arm below the elbow.

The crowd gaped at him, horrified and curious about his new body. A flash of anger twisted Georgia's face for a moment before her emotionless veneer returned. "Took your time."

"I came as fast as I could. I promise." Clayton rasped.

Without the weight of his left limb, his body shifted heavily to the right. He dragged the remaining arm behind him, supported by Mica who hugged it tight to their chest, their hands stained with Clayton's blood. Emery stood on Clayton's other side, supporting the shoulder above his amputation with her own from behind.

Flint's face paled. "What happened to you?"

Emery's brow leveled. "Why don't you ask Georgia?"

She blinked. "I have no idea what you're talking about."

"Don't lie!" Jared shouted.

Clayton shushed him with a glance and straightened to full height. "This isn't about who did what to who, although anyone with half a brain can probably figure it out. Everything I said yesterday still stands. You're a rotten person and you'd be a rotten leader."

"I'm an efficient person and I'd be an effective leader," she corrected. "Anything you're implying is unproven at best."

"You're really going to stand by that?"

"Just saying, you could have fallen."

"He didn't." Mica said. "I saw."

"You're his Helper," Flint said. "You'll say anything he wants."

Clayton couldn't help but smirk. "I thought you said they wouldn't obey anyone."

Georgia groaned. "Whatever. Let's vote."

"Sure," Clayton said. "Amber?"

Amber gaped at Clayton's bandaged stub. "Clay."

"Everyone else?"

The group sifted to either side, just as they had the day before. One by one, those who chose Georgia in the first vote moved toward

Clayton, eyeing her with suspicion and some of them fear. There was no denying the winner – except for Evan and Steiner – all of Earth Town was on Clayton's side.

Mica kept their hold on Clayton's right arm. They hadn't spoken since the night before, as if they'd left a bit of themselves on the wall along with Clayton's severed limb. Clayton felt stronger looking down at Mica, knowing how much they'd stepped up and how much they'd changed. Clayton shook the stony arm in Mica's hands. "We won."

Mica hugged tighter. "You won."

"I couldn't have done it without you."

"I guess."

"You okay?"

Their eyes lifted, not angry or frightened just... tired. "Maybe."

"Maybe?"

Mica sighed and rubbed their cheek into Clayton's uneven forearm. "Living is stronger."

"Living IS stronger," Clayton nudged them. "Thank you for helping me."

"I guess this vote is official then," Emery announced. "Clayton's the new leader. Right Georgia?"

An angry twitch flickered behind Georgia's frigid exterior. "For now. But I can wait."

"Good," he said. "You're gonna have to."

The stump at the end of Clayton's arm hardened into a stone cap in a matter of weeks, followed by his upper arm and part of his shoulder. He could tell he was still deteriorating – the damage done that night put his death on a swifter course, but just like what remained of his arm, he was determined to do the best he could with what he still had. Plus the extra weight of so much solid stone actually made walking easier. Mica helped. Emery too. Everyone helped everyone.

Amber got her funeral. Afterward, she was laid with honor outside her hut, buried under more rock and dirt so she would not waste away in open sight like her forerunners. In time the stone both inside her body and outside her body mingled together underground, and that remaining stone was used to reinforce the house, like it was always intended, but anonymously. She would be remembered as a person, not as an object.

Mica took charge of all the Helpers, making sure they were well distributed with tasks to help the whole community. Clayton took care of talking with outsiders, portioning resources, and most importantly, making introductions. When new Curses arrived, they came to him. He learned their names, what they were like, and where they came from. He showed them his arm and how it was progressing and explained as gently as possible what it meant for all of them. He held them while they cried. And when Clayton died, these children came together as one community and put him in a place of honor. Eventually he turned to stone, and was used to build so many houses. It was like he sheltered everyone for as long as Earth Town stood.

The End

Fogotten Tales

When you buy a movie, it often comes with a disk full of special behind the scenes featurettes and deleted scenes. That's what you will find in the next collection of pages. These elements are not all canon to the story, but are still fun moments of world buildings and storytelling that helped me grow as an author and make Threadcaster the book it is today. It is my hope that these elements will speak specifically to my fellow writers, to give a peek into the mind of another creator trying her best to craft a compelling and emotionally effective story.

When I first started writing Threadcaster, I planned a world with not four elements, but five; fire, water, earth, wind, and lightning. Of course in this book an extra element is more than an extra spell. Lightning meant lightning symbols marked on Runians bodies, lightning golems cast by Calligraphers, a Lightning Goddess statue, and perhaps the most essential addition; Lightning Curses, which come with their own symptoms, a town to live in, and a healthy town to be located near. I had everything planned out in outline, but after my initial zero draft I realized that the book was already getting long and kind of repetitive, so I scrapped the lightning element before I even got to the portion of the novel where it was supposed to go.

Fast forward almost a decade later, I start to brainstorm this anthology of additional content. I wanted to include the four short stories and some samples of my early drafts, but I also wanted to include a special additional story unique to this anthology, that was when Nell came to mind.

The only major regret I had removing the lightning element was removing the lightning volunteer. I had drawings over her everywhere, and she was never given a chance. So in an anthology called "The Curses" in which scraps of the past are preserved, I decided to give Nell a second chance.

This novella is a "what if" scenario. It is not an excerpt from the book, it is an entirely new piece written specifically for this anthology as a glimpse into what could have been. It is not canon, although some things that happen in the background (Vivian and Quill, the limestone mines, Castleton politics) are hints of what was going on at this point beyond Cat's perception.

So please enjoy this little "what if" and for all those creatives out there, don't be afraid to think outside the box of your outline, or your finished novel. And hold on to those old writings either in a folder in your office or a file on you computer. You never know when they'll come in handy.

Lightning Curse

Twilight broke pale blue against the mountains, casting weak light into a wider canyon further up the path. A dense forest covered the steep slopes. Cat exhaled a cloud of steam. Her head hurt and her body ached. Nothing about her felt rested. The Curses slept in the wagon behind her; Aiden and Lynn on the benches and Peter propped in the middle with the Wind Curse curled against his chest like a child. Cat watched her short hair wave in the wind from her scalp.

Peter noticed her over his shoulder. "Hey."

"Hey," Cat whispered. "You okay?"

"I'm okay. How's your side?"

"Hurts." She touched her knotted scarf. "The blood's dry. That's good at least."

"You're lucky to be alive."

"It wasn't that bad." She pulled the comb from her sagging bun and scrubbed dust out of her hair. A bit of porcelain fell into her hand. The two middle teeth had broken off her grandmother's comb. Cat sighed and slipped the comb with the rest of her things. Another precious thing lost in a reckless escape.

The Wind Curse rubbed her face into Peter's mud-stained shirt. She opened her eyes and drew back with an airy scream. "Ah!"

"Shh, it's okay. My name's Cat. I'm a friend. We met yesterday."

"We did?" The girl looked from her to the Curses. "What are these creatures?"

"This one's Peter—" Cat patted his head, "—and the other two are Aiden and Lynn."

Lynn rolled over and rubbed her eyes. "Did we make it?"

"So far," Peter said.

"It's freezing out here." Aiden yawned. "Where are we?"

"We're still in the mountains."

"Better that than caught, I guess." He wrapped his arms around his chest. "How's our new addition?"

"A little disoriented."

Lynn noticed the girl looking around and leaned forward. "What's your name, little one?"

"Zephyr." She blinked her wide eyes. "Are we in Wind Town?"

"No, thank God," Aiden grumbled.

"She's lost," Cat said. "Zephyr, is it? That's a very nice name."

Her tight brow furrowed. "Am I dead?"

"No, you're not."

"Then I must go back. The Goddess needs me."

"Your Goddess is a fraud," Aiden said.

Lynn coughed. "What he meant was, you've got an even more important boss, now. Your Goddess wanted you to save Wind Town, but our God wants you to save the world."

"The world?" Zephyr's lip trembled. "I don't understand."

"The whole world," Peter said. "Wind Town, too."

"Save Wind Town?" She touched the braided noose around her neck. "I guess that's okay."

They plodded down an embankment into a grove of thin, bowing trees. Strawberry was exhausted from a long night of walking. Lynn gave her food and water as the others searched Peter's atlas to find their bearings.

"The eastern range is largely un-mapped," Peter said. "My great-grandfather drew this himself, so it was probably too harsh to travel in his day. The path we took isn't even marked."

Zephyr petted the pages. "Pretty drawings."

"My ancestors thank you," Peter said. "If only they gave some indication where we were."

"Well, here's Wind Town." Cat pointed to Torston. "If we've been heading north this whole time, we could be in this spot he called "The Spires," but it was so dark last night, there's no telling where we've ended up."

"This mountain used to have a coal mine somewhere." Peter spotted it further north. "Here. It's closed down now, but the mining road will get us to the valley floor and down to Ebensmith, which is where Lightning Town is."

"Our last Curse." Lynn paused. "It's a bit hard to believe."

The glade extended further into the forest. Daylight dissolved the residual morning fog, exposing the path as an old mining road overgrown with tree roots. The road dipped gradually deeper, sloping north and west toward the valley until it emerged at the mouth of the mine Peter mentioned. Cat had assumptions about what mines looked like based on those she knew from the Western Mountains where metal and coal came out of hand-carved shafts. This mine was grander and more uniform. Huge openings like honeycomb lined the fissured mountainside. Snaking roots, dark brambles, and the curled branches of crusted trees clung to the shaft entrances, many of which had collapsed in the passing years. High above, the silhouette of sharply slanting roofs stood like a line of upright spears against the gray stone.

Zephyr raised a bony hand, her fingers shaking. "Teeth."

"More like turrets," Aiden said.

Lynn gulped. "Do you think they can see us?"

"I don't know," Peter said. "I mean, it's just the rooftops, but if we can see them..."

A chill prickled Cat's sore back. It was upsetting enough to know the Elder and his two lackeys were camped in New Torston, but a monastery full of other Calligraphers was more than she was ready to take. Past the mine, the main road widened as it descended toward the valley where Ebensmith waited at the foot of the hill. Multi-story buildings—larger than any in Castleton—clustered around a huge government building in the town square. The rest of town sprawled in neatly organized blocks before abruptly turning to desert.

Aiden peered over Cat's shoulder. "Where's the Curse town at?"

"It's usually by the Goddess statue."

"Unless they moved it for 'beautification.'" Aiden puffed a cloud of steam through his nose. "Where's the Goddess statue, then?"

"According to the map, Ebensmith should have the Lightning Goddess at its center," Peter reported. "I don't know where Lightning Town is, the maps predate them."

Lynn swallowed a mouthful of water. "Does that mean we have to go in?"

"No way," Aiden said. "We barely made it through New Torston, there's no way we're making it through a city as big as this. Not with all the Brushcasters after us."

"You're both right," Peter said. "We need to find Lightning Town, but it's too dangerous to go in ourselves."

Dread splashed cold in Cat's gut. "What are you suggesting?"

"We should stay here, you should go in."

"Leave you all in the woods?" Cat asked. "But the Brushcasters—"

"Are less likely to find us in this mine than they are in the city," Peter said. "I'm sorry, Cat, I know you don't like it."

"I don't." Her tone steeled. "Not after Chalsie-Veneer."

"Chalsie-Veneer is exactly why hiding's the best option." Peter nodded ever so slightly toward Aiden. Cat's stomach dropped.

It was less than a week ago, yet somehow in the chaos of sneaking through New Torston and the destruction of Wind Town, the pain and horror of Ildri's death had numbed. She hadn't forgotten it happened, but had let it go distant. Fresh guilt rose behind her breastbone to her throat. She swallowed hard to tamp it down and whispered, "If I was there it wouldn't have happened."

"No, if we'd been more careful that wouldn't have happened." He raised his voice to include the others. "Cat can lie about her name and where she comes from but the four of us are too obvious if we're found."

Aiden crossed his arms. "True."

"But what if something happens?" Cat protested. "This is too big and dangerous for one person."

"Sometimes one person is all it takes," Lynn urged. "You can do a lot, but not if you're worried about us. We can hide up here and be safe while you scout ahead."

Cat swallowed a knot and pressed a hand to her wounded side. "Okay, but you guys keep the horse and wagon. If something bad happens, I want you to run for it."

Peter's brow pinched. "You're going on foot?"

"Unless you have a spare horse."

"But you're hurt."

"I'm fine." She set her jaw and straightened as best she could. "No worrying, remember?"

Peter regarded her with a skeptical smirk and a hint of regret. Cat patted his shoulder and parked the wagon deep in one of the mine shafts. She made sure the Curses had everything they needed, and they in turn helped her pack a bag for the journey. Cat changed out of her soot-covered clothes into a fresh white shirt. She folded her ruined yellow one into a compress and bound it to her side with her checkered scarf—it was already ruined from use as a bandage, even if the checks might give her away. If anyone asked, she found it somewhere. She doubted anyone would. It wasn't in her plan to actually talk to anyone in town.

"You sure you're okay?" Peter walked her to the door of the cave. "You can take Strawberry with you. We'll be fine hiding here."

"I can move better than you can," she said. "I'll be back as soon."

"Promise you'll be careful."

"Pete, please," she lilted. "If I get in trouble, I'll use magic."

He shook his head. "I can't imagine how you'll blow your cover with that strategy."

"Keep everyone else safe." She hugged his heavy arm. "I'll be back as soon as I get a Lightning Curse."

The stony path crunched under her boot heels on her way down the mountain. The road from the mine was better defined than the mountain paths, with mile markers and weak sprouts of wild grass poking through the gravel pavement. Deep slats left by centuries of wagon traffic braided down the hillside toward Ebensmith, which didn't seem to be getting any closer as she went. She drank most of the water she brought to stave off the headache forming from exhaustion and heat.

The road vanished as it emerged from the forest, overtaken by dry grass and thick, thorny brambles. Arching vines snapped and twisted under foot, flicking up to bite at her knees like a swarm of insects. Cat tried to walk gingerly, but the flinches and twists made her side hurt even more. She ran out of water around sundown, still half a mile from the city. Behind her, the road to the mountain was hidden beneath the carpet of dark forest. She could also see the entrance to the Monastery, marked by a steepled gatehouse at the base of a narrow canyon. Flecks of black moved along the white outer wall, but no other Calligraphers were visible on the path. Lights from the hidden buildings winked deep within the shadows. They blurred and doubled with each throb of Cat's pounding head. She pressed a hand to her temple and checked her empty canteen for drops of water before taking her next step. Blood from her bandage spread through her sweat-soaked clothes. Dizziness rocked the landscape ahead. She missed her footing and fell to her hands and knees in the brambles. The impact rattled her head, her side, and her stomach. She locked her elbows, stealing a moment to process the pain before losing all strength and collapsing face-down on the parched earth.

Noise reached her first. Metal instruments clinked against a tray. A door opened and closed across the room, just far enough to echo. Her head hurt a lot less, and her side not at all. Blinding light forced its way through the skin of her eyelids.

"She's coming around," a man's voice said. "Another dose."

"No need, we're done here," a woman answered. "Clean up the space, keep the fluids coming. We'll talk to her when she's up."

The words took time to make sense. Was she captured? The voices muttered a bit more as she was turned onto her back. The bed started moving. Carried? Rolling on wheels? Electric lights slid overhead like moonlight on a river.

Cat woke next in a small room. Her right hand was strapped to an armrest with a length of clear tubing taped to the back of her hand. The tube extended to a glass jar hanging from a leather sling above her. A young man stepped into view. "Good evening, stranger."

"Whaaa?" Cat flapped her lips but they felt slow. "Wheeeh?"

"It's okay, I'm a nurse. You're in the hospital. The police found you lying in the desert."

"Police?"

"That's a nasty wound, too. Can you tell me what happened?"

Cat plumbed her brain for excuses. She couldn't admit she was near New Torston. What other reasons would she be traveling west from the mountains? Something with the Monastery? She got lost?

The nurse paused. "Were you mugged?"

"Yes!" Cat sat forward. A flash of muted pain radiated from her wound and she dropped her back against the bed.

"Ah, ah, careful now." The nurse tucked her in. "The numbing is wearing off."

"Numbing?"

"Dr. Tyrus performed surgery on your wound. It's clean and will heal much better now."

"How? But..." Cat tried to check the wound but her arm was still tied to the bed. "I can't pay for all this. I have literally nothing."

"Because of the mugging? Don't worry. The doctor does a lot of charity work."

"Does that mean free? How can you do that?"

"This hospital gets lots of donations," the nurse said. "Ebensmith is a good community full of generous people, and Dr. Tyrus turns all their donations into help for the unfortunate—even the Curses. The doctor is comptroller for tax money to Lightning Town."

"He has contact with the Curses?" Cat sat up again, more slowly this time. "Can I talk to him?"

"Of course you can." The female voice from before preceded the doctor into the room. She was a tall blonde dressed an immaculate suit jacket and pressed pants. She took Cat's medical chart off the door and flipped the pages. "I'm Dr. Tyrus. You're quite a mystery, miss..."

The turn in her voice prompted Cat for a name. She swallowed to wet her dry tongue. "Er... Ildri." She gulped. "Ildri... Traveler."

Cat cringed, but the doctor took her alias in stride. "Miss Traveler. It's not easy for a lone person to walk this desert on foot, especially a young woman. Do you recall what happened to you?"

"I- I was on my way here," Cat stammered. "My home was a small farm town, but our farms failed so I came out here."

"A town nearby?"

"Not... really?" She felt the lie collapsing like a tent atop her. "It's gone now. I'd rather not talk about it."

"Of course. It must be hard to lose one's home." Dr. Tyrus pulled a telescoping magnifier out of her jacket pocket and took Cat's chin for a better look in her left eye. "And how were you hurt?"

"She was mugged," the nurse answered. "They took everything but what was on her."

"Do you remember who they were?"

Cat winced. "It's hazy."

"That's probably to be expected considering the trauma and exposure. Draw up a report, Damini. See if we can track those villains down. Can't let such flagrant crime go unpunished." The doctor flashed Cat a smile. "In the meantime, don't worry about a thing. This is the foremost medical facility in God's Valley. As long as you're with us, you'll be well cared for. Open wide for me?"

Cat obeyed. The doctor clicked her tongue as she tilted Cat's head toward the light.

"You're a bit dehydrated still, but recovering well as far as I can see." She let go and made a note on the pad. "That wound in your side still concerns me, so I'd like you to stay another day for observation. Otherwise you seem alert, mentally clear, and physically restored once you're done with that saline bottle. You're a lucky one, Miss Traveler. I'll be back to see you later."

"Wait!" Cat's cry halted Dr. Tyrus on her way out the door. "I was hoping to ask you about the Lightning Curses. The nurse said you were in charge of them."

Dr. Tyrus snapped a pointed glance at her coworker. Nurse Damini blanched. The doctor smiled back at Cat. "He exaggerated. I manage the use of the Calligrapher-required supply taxes, but I'd hardly say I was 'in charge'. What would you like to know?"

"I have an interest in Curses." Cat attempted a conspiratorial tone. "It's why I'm here, to maybe do charity work with them? I know the Brush—the Holy Calligraphers are responsible for making sure the Curse towns get supplies, but you're one of the people on the ground who actually gets close to them. Takes care of them."

Her eyes narrowed. "Be careful how excited you are about the Curses, especially around the monks. It's a sin to be too accepting."

"O-oh of course." Cat waved her free hand nervously. "I don't approve of them or anything. It's just fascinating to think of humans changing from flesh to something else. Like watching a house collapse. Plus, I mean, the Curses are the reason my farm went into ruin. I'd like to figure out how they affect the world around them. Maybe I can help your efforts? Figure out how to protect the normal people from their gross evil influence. Or something."

The words tasted dirty as they crowded her mouth. Nurse Damini studied her closely as the doctor tapped the butt of her pen on the paper. "Interesting proposal." She slipped the pen and magnifier back in her coat pocket. "I hate to discourage a scientific mind, but Curses—especially the Lightning Curses—are very dangerous to be in close quarters with. Their bodies generate a constant electrical force both before and after death. I would recommend traveling to Chalsie-Veneer and observing Water Curses instead. I know it's far, but they are a much less volatile type of creature. I can get you some travel information if you're interested."

Cat mustered the most pathetic look she could manage.

The doctor sighed and dropped her formal tone. "I can bring some notes by when I check on you later. Perhaps we can work something out."

"I can still meet a Lightning Curse?"

"Don't push yourself too quick, you need to rest."

"I'm fine," she said. "I mean, with your help of course."

The doctor snorted. "Good. A positive attitude is important for healing. Almost as important as rest. I'll see you in the morning, Miss Traveler."

"Wait! I have more questions," Cat called, but Dr. Tyrus ignored her and left.

Nurse Damini leveled his brow. "I wish you hadn't brought the Curses up with her."

"Why?"

"Because it's dangerous, Miss Traveler," the nurse said. "Being kind to Curses is illegal and the electricity is a risk."

"That doesn't scare me."

"Maybe it should."

"You're the one who brought it up to start with." Cat said. "Are you protecting me or her?"

The nurse blanched nearly as white as his uniform. "This is a house of healing, Miss Traveler. I'm telling you this for your health."

"With all due respect, Mr. Damini," Cat said, mimicking his

tone. "I'll let my doctor make that decision."

The nurse fumed a moment. He drew a deep breath and swept in a huff into the hall.

The Holy Elder's scroll arrived by golem early in the morning, stirring Senior Vivian Arch from her dawn hour of prayer. There was a crisis. Chalsie-Veneer was in ruins, Wind Town was destroyed, and probably the most telling of all… the Elder needed help to deal with it. In the decades Vivian had known Artemis Tarlov, she never once heard him admit weakness. A call for personal assistance betrayed more about the crisis than any of the words he'd painted on the page.

She spent the morning preparing and within hours she was ready to go. Despite the anxiety of dealing with a destructive False Prophet, the monks of the Calligraphers' Monastery kept a sense of normalcy, studying, practicing magic, and tending the grounds. Vivian planned to continue cataloging holy references in the library, searching as always for better verses and prayers to use in golems. No matter how many lifetimes the Calligraphers spent transcribing and memorizing, there was always more to discover in the texts of the Prophets. Her current task involved reading the whole of the lower library, marking contextual references to changing direction. Nuance was important, and a word here or there vital to drawing the most compact and efficient casting circles. She hated leaving the works of Deborah half-read, but the reliable thing about scripture was that it was always there waiting no matter how long or short a task might take.

There was no time for horseback, the Elder was explicit. Travel by golem, arrive by sundown. Vivian followed the path to a protected courtyard dedicated to painting golems. A dark-skinned young man waited, weighed down with four bags of supplies.

Calligrapher Quill Gravadain tapped his foot impatiently. The blue tassel on the monk's polished brush swayed back and forth with the vibration. Despite years of Vivian's repeated warnings about modesty and uniformity, Quill insisted on decorating the bristles of his brushes. No harm intended, of course, he was an artist long before he became a monk. And deep inside she admitted she was glad that in this one area her old apprentice remained stubborn. "You needn't pack so much."

Quill jumped. "But Master, you said the—" he checked for possible witnesses and whispered, "—the Holy Elder sent for us?"

"He did, but you've packed for a week's journey. He's sending us to Ebensmith. Bring enough for a day."

"I see. I wish I'd known." Quill arched an eyebrow. "Although I assume you couldn't tell me."

She warmed. He had always been perceptive. "I invited you because I trust you, but yes, some protections are still required."

"Forgive me, Master, I didn't mean to sound ungrateful."

"I would never accuse you of that."

"Now that we are being honest, may I ask what exactly the Elder's mission entails?"

Vivian slid her well-worn brush out of the holster on her back. "We are hunting the False Prophet."

His brows arched. "Just us?"

"Staying discrete is important." She poured white paint from her goatskin into the concave stone palette built into the field. "Her name is Catrina Aston. Brown hair, sixteen, last seen wearing blue with a pink and yellow scarf. She slipped the Elder's grasp outside of New Torston. She is either hiding in the forest above the city, or headed for Ebensmith."

"Divide and conquer."

"That's right."

"So we're hunting for a False Prophet—but in secret so as not to scare her into destroying another town." Quill gnawed his lip. "With permission, may I keep my things packed as they are? Just in case."

Vivian sighed. "As long as you can paint a golem with them."

Quill pulled his tasseled brush free and took a portion of the paint into the bristles. Vivian did the same with hers and stood ten paces apart from him. The clay ground was perfect for painting, there was nothing like the feel of paint coating smooth earth. The two began together, like a dance, laying first an outer circle, then painting the verse designed for travel. Vivian mouthed it as she painted. For many the verses were tools, but to her, the poetry was art unto itself.

Lo, our God sent me southwest//A city of white near the mountains//Our God carried me upon his shoulder//Swift is the stride of nature's passing//Wind

The holy symbol brought the spell to dancing life. The air above the rune twisted together, solidifying into a massive feline creature with a long, rope-like tail and narrow starlit eyes. Quill's activated as well, braiding like hair into a serpentine shape supported by two legs on each side of its long body. The Calligraphers nodded to each other and climbed aboard their mounts. The wind golems dashed from the painting field down the mountain pass to the monastery gates. Vivian held on with her heart more than her hands. The exhilaration and speed; riding air was just like flying.

Vivian nodded to the lookouts flanking the monastery entrance but the golems were gone before the acolytes could finish their bows.

It was impossible to map the passage of time in the small, windowless room. Cat dozed for what felt like a minute and woke to Nurse Damini unbinding her arm from the bedside. The saline bottle was empty and her arm was free of tape or needles.

"Your things have come back from the cleaners." Nurse Damini was more subdued than previously. "I'm afraid your shirt was ruined so I've supplied you with a similar one. There are still stains in this scarf of yours as well, but I had a feeling you'd want it back."

"Yeah, thanks." Cat flexed her stiff elbow. "Is it morning now?"

"Yes."

"Has the doctor been by?"

"No. She said you were improved enough to go."

Cat frowned. "She told me she was going to show me her notes."

"She said that to placate you."

"I don't think she did," Cat said. "Ask her. She promised."

The nurse dropped Cat's knapsack and the bundle of clothing in his patient's lap. "Get changed and meet me at the desk."

Cat waited for him to close the door and kicked her way out of the covers. Her limbs were weak and the ache in her side was back with a vengeance. She planted her bare feet on the wood and used the bed frame to stand. Nothing was missing from her belongings except her ruined shirt. For the first time she felt lucky to have lost the scripture case back in Chalsie-Veneer, even if remembering it made her guilty. Cat wound her string back to her wrist and sighed with relief. Hurt as she was, at least with string she wasn't helpless.

Dressing required a lot of time and care but allowed her a chance to see what had been done to her. A thick white bandage wrapped around her ribs and midriff with layers of tape to hold the whole thing together. She took care putting on her new white shirt and the clothes she was wearing when she arrived there—all cleaned and mended by the hospital staff. Someone had even repaired the hole in her leather vest. The brown skin pressed on her bandaged wound just enough to remind her not to twist or bend.

Her room was at the end of a cream-colored hallway lined with similar doors. Nurses and patients paced the hardwood floors. Machines waited on wheeled carts outside different rooms. There was no telling which one the doctor was in and Cat hadn't the strength to check each one. She heaved a sigh and made her way slowly to the desk at the end of the hallway.

Nurse Damini's brow knit when he saw her inch forward. "Are you still in a lot of pain?"

"Yeah, I had surgery yesterday."

"I assumed you'd be feeling better than this..." He gnawed his lip. "Maybe you should go back to bed."

"You're the one who got me out of it!" Cat shouted. "Stop yanking me around."

"I wasn't..." He ran hands through his tangled hair. "I was trying to get you out early."

"So I wouldn't get to talk to the doctor."

"That's correct."

"I don't know what your damage is with Dr. Tyrus, but this has got to be violating some kind of rights or something," Cat said. "I have literally nothing – nowhere to go, no money or anything. You said you'd take care of me but I could die in the street this afternoon and who's to blame for that?"

"I- I'm sorry." The nurse flipped through pages in a folder in front of him. "Let me move you to a convalescence room."

"Are you suggesting I trust you?"

"Please," he said. "I wish I could explain—"

"Miss Traveler!" Dr. Tyrus's voice echoed toward them up the hall. Nurse Damini ducked his head. The doctor wrapped an arm around Cat's back. "What are you doing up? You should be resting."

"I should." Cat flashed a look at the nurse, but Damini was buried, red-faced and sweating, in his paperwork. Cat shook her head and stepped out of Dr. Tyrus's support. "I was anxious to see your research, though. Do you have time to do that now? If not, the nurse was setting me up with a convalescence room."

"You've got an indomitable spirit." Dr. Tyrus grinned. "If you're really feeling up to it, I'll take you to my office, but it's up a couple stories so I insist you use a wheeled chair."

"I'll get one!" Nurse Damini burst up and hurried away before either she or Cat could protest.

The chair was like a normal wooden chair with four wheels to help it move on an even keel. Cat knew older people in Mason Forge who needed a chair like this to move, although those were much less fancy than this one. Cat sat on the cushioned seat and let the nurse wheel her after Dr. Tyrus up the long hallway onto a shallow ramp that wrapped around the inner wall behind the patient rooms. The incline wound a circle around the structure for two floors. Windows lined the ramp at an angle, following it up the slope six feet at a time. Cat could see little more than the blue sky from her seat in the chair, with a glimpse of other buildings and the very tops of the distant mountains as they climbed higher and higher.

Her friends had been on their own for almost a full day. Hopefully the Calligraphers weren't flooding the mountains in that moment, hunting through every nook and cranny. Perhaps the whole monastery full of them rested the night in New Torston. Or made it back to the Monastery to rest. If the Elder was waiting for reinforcements he'd have to wait for messages to be sent too, although with all the golems he could paint at once she couldn't believe that took a lot of time.

Cat cleared her throat. "Um, weird question."

The doctor replied without looking. "Yes?"

"You have contact with the Calligraphers, right? Has anything... weird been happening with them?"

"Weird?"

"I uh..." She sucked her teeth. "Just noticed a lot on the road before. Didn't know what was up."

"A False Prophet was spotted out west a couple days ago." The doctor smiled back at her. "Don't worry, that's the other side of the world from here. It has nothing to do with us."

"Heh, yeah." Cat shifted in the wheeled chair. "What a relief."

They made it to the top floor and turned right down another long hall. Dr, Tyrus's offices were along the left-hand wall. She took Cat's chair from the nurse. "Thank you, Damini, that'll be all."

"But—"

"Wait downstairs until I ring," she said. She moved Cat from the hallway and closed the door.

The lab beyond was full of chemistry equipment. Machines Cat had never seen hummed on half a dozen tables with charts and notes scribbled on paper canvases along the walls. There were a lot of figures and equations she didn't understand, but she could see it was about the Curses. Wall after wall after wall. Curses, Curses, Curses.

"You see we both share a curiosity." She took a seat behind her cluttered desk. "Being comptroller has given me a lot of opportunity to study them in a controlled environment."

Cat moved from the wheeled chair to the plush one nearby. The doctor pulled a thick binder from one of the drawers and flopped it open between them.

"The Lightning Curses are a fascinating species. In addition to generating a charge, they actually make and maintain their own magnetic fields. That makes it a little dangerous to interact with them, but with protective clothing I'm able to get very close and examine them." She opened her book to a page featuring the outline of a human with over a dozen notes attached. "The electricity affects the organs and tissues a lot like burns, but it affects the mind more like a stroke or a seizure. I have tried the typical medications for those conditions with little success but there are other more obscure treatments for nervous system disorders I suspect will offer possibilities."

"Wait." Cat flipped through the pages of the binder. "You're trying to cure them?"

"Before I became comptroller, brain disorders were my specialty." Dr. Tyrus could hardly contain herself. "There's a lot of overlap between the fields, ignoring the supernatural element. Cure is asking too much at this point, but I've seen improvement already in the ten years I've been experimenting so anything's possible!"

Cat gripped the arms of the plush chair, heart pounding in her throat. A medical cure for Curses. No one in God's Valley would dare, but here was Dr. Tyrus experimenting with medicines. Could this make her mission unnecessary? Could it make Peter well? Emotion swelled from her core until it filled her to the brim.

The doctor's brow knit. "Are you alright?"

"I'm fine." Cat suppressed her welling tears and leaned forward through the pain in her side. "How can I help?"

"I'm glad you asked." Dr. Tyrus folded the binder closed and lowered her voice. "As you know, I'm comptroller for Ebensmith's Curse Town, which funds my ventures but limits my subjects to Lightning Curses. I've worked for the last year to increase my revenue stream but I need a collaborator to expand my territory. Interested?"

Breath rustled the flurry of hope in her tight chest. "Very."

"Good." Dr. Tyrus opened her desk and handed Cat a pack of papers. "I'm sending you to Chalsie-Veneer. Water Town is right in the midst of things. There should be enough for you to get one of the waterfront properties."

"Enough?" Cat unfolded the package to find a map and more money than she had ever seen in one place before. "Are you serious?"

"Of course!" The doctor was grinning. "Send me a letter when you set up shop. We're going to have to be discrete but I've already set up a shell address for me. When you're better, I can teach you basic chemistry for the simpler recipes and send my more complicated medicines by courier to try on the local Curse population. If we pool notes we can make real progress, but it's got to stay hush-hush. The Calligraphers are all for keeping them alive but curing them is a different story..."

Cat gulped. "I don't know about experiments... "

"Don't worry, I'll direct you every step." Dr. Tyrus extended her hand. "What do you say, Ildri? Partners?"

Cat gut twisted. A surge of adrenaline reinvigorated her tears. She took the doctor's hand with a shake. "Partners."

"Excellent!" The doctor hid her books back in the desk. "I know we're both anxious to get started but priorities are on your wound. I want you to stay in bed for a few days."

"Yes, of course."

"We can talk more once you're settled. I'll ring for the nurse." Dr. Tyrus opened the door. Nurse Damini was waiting just outside. They both jumped. "Oh. I was just about to—"

"I'm, uh," the nurse stammered. "There's a patient waiting."

"Thank you. We're done here, please take Ildri to her room."

"Yes doctor."

Cat hid the papers in her bag as she moved back to the wheeled chair. The nurse steered her out of the doctor's office and back to the ramp. Cat's hands shook. The idea of experimenting on people upset her, but if this medicine worked... no Prophet mission. No sacrifice. Her friends could help her, or go home to their loved ones. Peter would live. Her chest seized in a sob, forking pain up her side. They'd live— the two of them together for as long as he had. Another year, or if the medicines worked, maybe much longer.

Nurse Damini exited the ramp on the second floor and into another windowless bedroom. He paused the chair several paces from the bedside, put a brake on the rear wheel, and latched the door lock before returning to view. "I know what she told you."

Cat gulped in attempt to sound calm. "You were listening?"

"Can you blame me?" He squatted in front of her. "I could tell it was coming. I've been helping her keep this secret since I graduated school, and I know that spark in her eye. Why did she trust you? It's nothing about your demeanor, you're obviously a huge wreck. And you've been lying to us from the beginning."

"I don't know what you mean."

"What's your name?" the nurse prompted. "Your real name."

This was the worst time for confrontation. Cat ran a finger under her string in attempt to still her conflicted emotions. The last time she was interrogated like this was Lord Creven's table in Castleton when Lady Creven's piercing eyes cut through her charade. The lady wasn't fooled by a story, she needed a little truth mixed in. Hopefully Cat could keep herself together enough play the trick a second time. "Traveler is right. My first name was a lie."

"Your first name?"

"It's Cat," she replied. "Cat Traveler."

"Why did you lie about your name?"

"I was scared." Her voice trembled. "I'm on the run."

"Are you in trouble?"

"Yes." This was too much truth. Tremors rocked through her body. "From Brushcasters."

"Why?"

"Because."

"I need more than that."

"Because..." She was weak, and tired, and bursting with anxiety. "Ildri was the name of my friend. The Brushcasters attacked us and... killed her. So I ran."

"That's not like them. Why would they—" His eyes flashed with realization. "Your friend was a Curse, wasn't she? Ildri was a Curse and they killed her because she wasn't in a Town."

Cat sniffed.

"Of course! That's why the doctor trusted you. Why you cared about her research." He ran his hands through his hair. "I've heard of that happening but didn't assume... I mean it's a crime they'd lock you up for. No wonder you escaped."

Cat covered her face in her hands. It was too much truth. Ildri's death, Peter's eviction, her wanted status in the Valley. She couldn't say another word, not if she wanted to stay hidden. Not with her friends hiding in the hills. How could she think about working for Dr. Tyrus without first saving them? She wanted Peter.

The nurse took her hands in his, moving them gently from her face. His eyes were moist. "They won't find you. I promise. This hospital hides a lot of secrets, I'll make sure it hides yours. And I'll keep calling you Ildri, to keep your new identity intact." He waited for her to look up and smiled. "You can call me Dustin."

"Dustin." She nodded. "Thank you."

"Of course," he said. "Get some rest. Your secret is safe with me."

Vivian and Quill arrived at Ebensmith just before sundown and immediately sought an audience with the mayor. He was standard Castleton stock wearing a green waistcoat and white wig. He shook both Calligraphers' hands as they entered. "Welcome, welcome! It's a pleasure to see members of your glorious Order as always, although I hope it is not for the reasons I assume..."

"You mean the situation in Dire Lonato?" Vivian asked.

The mayor nodded. "And Chalsie-Veneer and New Torston. This False Prophet is making her way around the entire valley. I was hoping they'd stop her by now, but I'm guessing since you're here, that's not the case. Did you bring reinforcements?"

"No, it is only us two."

"Do we need more?"

Vivian stiffened. "What news has reached you? I'm surprised you are so well informed this far from the events."

"City governments are closely tied nowadays. I get my news from Castleton." He sat behind his orderly desk and readied a pen and paper. "So, what do we do to prepare town for invasion? Rations? Guards?"

"No need to cause a panic," Vivian replied. "The Holy Elder wants Ebensmith to be prepared, not frightened. Have you received any reports of strange activity lately? Any sign that False Prophet has already arrived?"

"Nothing out of the ordinary has been brought to my attention," the mayor said. "Of course, remember, your honors, that this is more than a small town. We're the third largest after Astonage and growing every day. People come and go constantly for any number of reasons. Is there anything more specific I can ask the people to be mindful of?"

Vivian pulled the letter she'd received from inside her black tunic. "The Holy Elder has provided me with a name and full physical description of the False Prophet."

"Excellent!" The mayor reached forward. "May I?"

Vivian drew back. "This is confidential monastery correspondence. My associate and I will transcribe the relevant parts."

"Very well, please turn that around for me right away. My people will draw up a poster. We'll paper God's Valley until she is stopped."

"Thank you for your cooperation," Vivian said. "May we have quarters in which to work?"

"Of course, the VIP chambers are in the next wing. My secretary can show you."

"Thank you, again." She placed a hand over her heart with a slight bow and gestured for Quill to follow her out of the room. The secretary ushered them along carpeted halls to the residential portion of City Hall, where several grand suites waited for dignitaries and personal guests. Vivian had stayed here often under different administrations. The current mayor had installed a large painting of Lord Creven at the entrance to the guest hallway. It was more than a little suspicious.

Quill placed their bags on the dresser. "You seem tense."

"I was taken off guard," Vivian admitted. "The world has changed since I was out in it."

"How long has it been?"

"Years, certainly." She retrieved the letter and scanned it again. "Too many, it seems."

"Shall I start to work on the transcription?"

"Yes." She handed him the page. "The portion you'll need is at the bottom. Please do not read the rest, it was sent to me exclusively from the Holy Elder."

He smiled. "I understand, you can trust me."

"I know I can." Vivian sighed, taken by sudden and consuming exhaustion. "I am going to meditate in prayer for a while, will you be all right on your own?"

"I will, Master." Quill nodded encouragement. "Afterward we can go into town ourselves and conduct our own preparation. The Elder will have nothing to fear."

She patted his shoulder. "A wise course. You will make Senior before we know it."

"With Our God's blessing and your glowing recommendation." Quill winked and the two moved to different rooms of their quarters to begin their occupations.

Vivian sat cross-legged on one of the beds with her paintbrush across her lap. There was something comforting in praying to a god who wasn't listening. To think that she, a small, insignificant thing, would dare speak with the creator of the world... an undying divine personage with the power to give and take life at a thought. It shook her to her bones. But knowing that he was far away, listening through distance, or time, or not at all, created a buffer of doubt that curbed the panic. Vivian often started her prayers not with the plea for his return, as she was taught to, but with a private admission of relief that his divine and all-knowing presence wasn't forced to listen to her petty complaints. Unless he was. That possibility kept her faithful, because if he *was* listening, he would know that she could relate to his isolation and disappointment in mankind.

No one knew the contents of the lower library better than she did. The scrolls were full of promises made and kept, miracles performed, evidences of his attention and affection for his people, but his Prophets often spoke of deep and permeating loneliness. She related to that. Mankind could not understand what it was like to be closer to the true and eternal than the mortal and immediate. She understood the attitudes and inflections of every Prophet, and those of the divine as well. Every prophet regardless of writing style or personality had the same curl of humor to them. A word with double meaning or a pun. Even the words he chose to leave out betrayed his clever mind. She understood him more than everyone except the Elder, and this is why she was so good at spell-crafting. The monks took the words she shared with them and forged miracles. The greatest miracle, she thought, was that the scriptures survived at all. The common man was so careless. Selfish. Like the Mayor. Like Catrina Aston.

The False Prophet was evidence for why the monastery needed to protect the words of the Prophets and the art of drawing golems. She was a bastardization of nature that undermined everything the monastery stood for. Artemis wrote to her about the False Prophet with bitterness. How she attacked the citizens relentlessly and protected the Curses with her life. This was a troubled girl driven mad somehow by her approximation to sin. Someone must have put her up to it. How else would she learn the symbols? And with string no less? Confounding. Which brought her to the behavior of Ebensmith's mayor. Got his information out of Castleton, he said. How would Castleton know? Unless there was foreknowledge of the False Prophet's campaign, the timelines could not add up to the mayor's cool, informed demeanor. Or perhaps if the stars aligned they could. She was a librarian, not a mathematician, and it had been a while since she took the roads. Perhaps this was overthinking.

"Master?" Quill interrupted. Vivian turned on the bed. "I'm sorry if I'm interrupting."

"Is something wrong?"

"No, I was checking on you. It's been an hour."

"An hour?" It felt like she'd just sat down. Did she fall asleep? Or had she honestly fretted for a full turn of the clock?

"Shall I let you continue?"

"No." Vivian unfolded herself, confirming through aches that her legs had definitely been crossed for an hour. "Have you completed the transcription?"

"That and more. Would you like to review it?"

"Of course."

Quill presented a sheet of paper with the transcription of the Elder's letter along the top. Below, in pen and ink, was a portrait of the girl described. Vivian could recognize Quill's work anywhere, but looking into the face of the False Prophet struck her cold. She didn't expect an agent of evil to appear so young and harmless.

Quill's brow pursed. "Did I overstep?"

"No, no." Vivian took the page. "Your skill is top-notch as always. Good use of time, Quill."

"Thank you, ma'am."

"Let's get this to the mayor and his printers. Then you and I will spread the warning on foot." Vivian eyed the portrait of Creven as they left their quarters. "This city may need more help than we thought."

Cat knew she'd fallen asleep when she woke in the dark. What time it was or who turned the light off or when was a mystery, but the wheeled chair was missing and a plate of food was set on her end-table. Cat hadn't eaten in a full day. She devoured the whole plate and tucked the glass water bottle in her bag before wedging her feet in her boots without bending over and creeping to the hallway door. The second floor was less active than the first with nurses, doctors, and orderlies moving between the many convalescent rooms. A single window stood on the far wall, revealing stars and a bath of moonlight on the eastern mountains. Dustin was nowhere to be seen.

She needed to tell Peter and the others what she'd learned. Medical treatment. For Curses. This could save everyone—not just the four hiding in the mountains, but all Curses in God's Valley. She had to involve them in this decision, she had to talk about next steps. Peter always had a level head about this stuff, and she was still so tired from the previous day. It might take her all night to get there, but at least night meant no beating sun. She knew she could make it back to the mines by morning and the hope of sparing her friends' lives gave her the courage to try.

Cat grit her teeth and limped as quickly and inconspicuously as she could toward the ramps. Moving still hurt, but she could muscle through it for the sake of Peter and the others. She hadn't realized before descending the ramp how many muscles in her core worked on maintaining her balance. It took extra effort to act casual as she passed the night workers on the slope.

She quickened her pace down the final slant to ground level. Hospital staff bustled between doors and desks. The nearest rooms looked like surgery bays with large double doors. Past them were the recovery rooms and further on the waiting rooms for people who needed emergency care. At the very end beside the reception desk stood two Holy Calligraphers—a dark-skinned man and older woman—armed with brushes and blocking the entrance.

Cat dove back behind the wall, heart pounding through her side and out of her chest. The doctor trusted her with her research, was that enough to not turn her in? What if she revealed she was lying about her name? If the Calligraphers tracked her, turning her in wasn't the issue. Did this mean her friends were already captured? The little strength she had drained through her soles. Was there a back door? A roof exit?

A hand grabbed her by the shoulder.

"Ahh!" Cat threw a punch.

Nurse Damini leaped out of range. "Relax! It's me!"

"Dustin?" Cat wheezed. "The Brushcasters are here!"

"I know."

"I can't let them find me!"

"Follow me." Dustin beckoned her further down the ramp, past the first floor exit, to a basement service area. The room was hot and dripping with condensation. A field of cylindrical power retainers like those Cat saw in the windmill in Wind Town clanked and hummed in stacks across the middle of the room. Cables ran from the bank to a panel of electrical switchboards built into the outer wall to a massive generator covered with meters and lights. A constant high-pitched whine buzzed on the edge of audible sound.

Dustin stopped Cat before a deep-set, reinforced metal door, his face grave. "You trusted me with the secret about your friend earlier. Now, I'm going to trust you with a secret. Promise not to tell anyone about this, okay?"

"Okay."

"Good, put these on." He thrust a pair of thick rubber gloves into her hands. "The boots, too. They go over the ones you're wearing."

"What are they for?"

"Protection. Rubber doesn't conduct electricity." Dustin pulled on his own set of gloves and boots and punched a six-digit code in the nearby number pad to unlock the security door. The door swung outward, the inside covered in thick rubber padding and tape. On the other side was a dark, cave-like chamber dug out of the raw earth. The low ceiling was hung with a single line of electric light bulbs. The walls were lined with wooden partitions placed every few feet like a stable.

Charged air raised the skin on the back of Cat's neck. She could feel eyes on her every direction. "Is this what I think it is?"

A low moan answered from deeper into the chamber, followed by the winding up of a high-pitched human scream. Dustin's head snapped up. "Stay here!" He took off full-sprint toward the sound.

Cat clutched her side as another chill shook through her. The door behind them had closed. A similar number pad was built into the bare cement wall. The red light above it probably meant it was locked with the same combination lock. Dark shapes moved in the shadows of the dirt-floor stalls. Moans rose from different corners, punctuated by sparks illuminating a leg, a hand, a shoulder. The overhead bulbs flickered with fluctuating wattage, like when the generators malfunctioned back home, although these felt more in danger of breaking than going out. One of them swelled with light, emitting a louder and more highly pitched buzz. The swell illuminated a pair of human legs lying in a stall a little further ahead. The barefoot girl couldn't have been older than ten. She lay prone, dressed in a vinyl jumpsuit with cut-off legs and sleeves, with raised scars branching like veins across her pink skin. Her short-cut blonde hair stood on end from her head, which was propped on a block of something like stone or maybe rubber. Two blinded white eyes stared from within the shadow of the wall.

Cat gasped. Her eyes adjusted, revealing two more people with the girl, and three more in the stall across from hers. All lying flat, awake or asleep, throwing sparks and breathing heavily between low groans. The same scream split the air.

At the very back of the room, Dustin crouched over a girl in the throes of a full-body seizure. Her hands were curled into claws near her chest. Froth gathered at the corner of her mouth as a convulsion forced another scream from her tightened chest. Dustin had one gloved hand under her head as a cushion; the other held a pocket watch. The scream ended and the girl's limbs uncoiled like a deflating balloon.

Dustin noticed Cat over his shoulder. He pulled his hands from the girl's bush of dark hair with a sigh. "It's passed for now."

"Does that happen often?"

"Yeah." He clenched his jaw. "I thought I told you to wait by the door."

"I waited for a minute. If you'd told me what was happening, I could have helped."

"Nothing to be done about this, I'm afraid," he sighed. "Restraining limbs could make her hurt herself. Just cushion her head and wait."

The girl's eyes fluttered. "D-D-Dustin?"

"It's okay, Nell, I'm right here."

"Did-did-did-did you give me med—? Give mmmed—?"

"No, no medicine. I came in a hurry. I wasn't able to time that one accurately, but it was a minute since I got here. Do you feel okay? You're stuttering more."

"Wwwworse." A wave of sparks snapped along the girl's hair from root to tip as she sat up. She saw Cat and an arc of white flashed in a bridge from her eye to her mouth. "Whoooooo's that?"

"This is Ildri. She's a friend."

Cat's stomach turned. She really wished she'd used another name. "Hi. You're a Lightning Curse, I assume?"

"Yyyyyyyyyeah."

"Ildri, this is Nell." Dustin put one gloved hand on Nell's back. "She's my little sister."

"Sister?" Cat confirmed it in their eye shape and the color of the skin between Nell's scars. "I see..."

"I was a teenager when Dr. Tyrus diagnosed her as a Curse. I used that connection to apprentice under her out of nursing school. I'm not saying it's the same thing with you and the friend you lost, but it's similar, isn't it? At least a little? I'm risking a lot to make Nell better."

Cat's heart swelled at thoughts of Peter, Lynn, Aiden, and meek little Zephyr hiding in the mountain caves. She hoped they weren't too worried, or running out of supplies, or caught by Calligraphers. "I definitely understand."

"Good. You'll be safe down here, only the doctor and I know the code. Just sit tight until the Brushcasters are gone. And if the doctor comes in, for the love of Our God don't let her see you."

"Why not? She seems to trust me."

"Trust *me* on this one. No one's supposed to be in here except the church staff and doctor during comptroller duties. If they find out I let you in I'll get fired or worse." Dustin turned his attention to Nell. "Stay here and recover your strength. I'll be back later when it's time for more medicine."

He nodded his goodbye to Cat and paused to punch the combination lock before dashing back through the hospital door. Nell balled up on the ground, her eyes clear but watery. The tears threw sparks as they reached her skin. Cat lowered to the ground next to her, holding her bandaged side. "So... you and Dustin are siblings, huh?"

Nell nodded against the dirt.

"It's good he's here to take care of you. I'm excited to learn more about the medicines."

Her body shook as she grunted.

Cat gnawed her lip. This wasn't like talking with Peter or the others, Nell was a stranger and it was rude to be so personal with someone you hardly knew. "Sorry. I can be quiet if you want."

The Lightning Curse sighed. "It'sssssssokay."

"I'm just curious. The doctor asked me to help her develop her medicines. I need to learn about how it works."

"It... heeeeeelps others better. Don't knooooooooow why... doesn't work... so well... for me."

"You feeling better though?" Cat asked. "You're speaking easier."

"Sp-p-peaking is hard always." Nell rolled onto her back, her arms still twitching but not as badly as before. "Doctor says it's brai— it's brai-ain damage."

"That's awful."

"At least I can sssssssssssee," Nell said. "And walk."

The scars branching across Nell's face spidered from her eyes to her mouth, and arced down her neck along the veins and arteries much like Aiden's sores. Was the lightning carried in the blood like his fire was? Or did it simply ride the blood like a river? Water *was* a conductor after all. "So is this Lightning Town, or are you a small number for the doctor to treat?"

"Town."

"But there's so few of you."

Nell whimpered a little.

Cat cringed and changed topic. "Is it completely underground? Like on all sides?"

"Uh...huh."

"No wonder I couldn't see it from the windows. I knew Tyrus was in charge, but it didn't occur to me it was actually on-site. Or *under*-site, I guess. In retrospect it makes sense."

"Dr. Tyrrrrrrrus moved here when she became com... became com... was elected. Trying to fixxxxxx us."

"How does the medicine work, actually? Does it reverse the damage or prevent it? Or, um, maybe it's a difficult thing to explain. Would it be easier if I asked 'yes' or 'no' questions?"

"He- he- here," Nell shoved herself shakily to her knees. "Shhhhow you."

Nell's walk was gangling and uncoordinated. Muscles twitched under her bare skin as she struggled to move. Sparks of electricity popped from her mess of hair at each flat-footed step. "Taren." Nell used one of the wooden walls for support. "Awake?"

"Ughhh." Taren rolled on his woven mat. "Whaaa?"

"Ildri." Nell pointed. "F-f-friend."

"Heeealthy?"

"Yes."

His scars stretched as he rubbed his eye. White strings of electricity snapped from the tips of his fingers to his prominent nose. "Why is she here?"

"Asking... the d-doctor's meds work?"

"What?" Taren asked. "Yeah."

"Are you sure?" Cat surveyed his sleeping companions. "You don't seem particularly well."

"Used to have seizures every day. Now barely have any." Taren flinched with a muscle spasm and lay back. "But makes me sleepy."

"Is that a side effect?" Cat asked either of them.

Nell shrugged, beckoning her toward an opposite stall. "Audra."

Audra was fast asleep. Electricity from the rustling raced along the fibers of her mat to a wire that snaked away to vanish under the other sleeping Curses.

Cat gestured to the cords. "What's that about?"

"Beds?" Nell asked. "Have wi-ires."

"For what?"

"Power." She pointed to the bulbs along the ceiling. "Lights."

"Just the lights?" Cat gnawed her lip. Memories of Wind Town nagged her cynical mind. She passed a lot of generators on the way through the basement, and there was an impressive amount of advanced technology in the hospital above. "Do the mats hurt you?"

"N-no. Takes the chaaarrrge," Nell said. "Helps."

They met six other Lightning Curses: one without the power of speech, one without a sense of hearing, and others who'd lost the use or feeling in different limbs. Those who could talk insisted the medicine was helping, but few were up and moving and there were far less of them than Cat would have expected in a Curse Town. Young children dragged their feet from stall to stall, muscles sluggish. Hardly anyone was old. The smell in the basement was overpowering. Cat realized there were no apparent food or bathroom facilities anywhere in the cave. "Do you guys ever leave here?"

"N-no," Nell said.

"What about food and water?"

"Packages."

"The doctor brings them?"

"And Dusssssstin—" Nell stopped mid-answer, face blanked as if a switch was flipped in her brain. She grabbed to support herself on Cat's shoulder. Cat ducked away and supplied her gloved hand instead. She could feel Nell's hand muscles involuntarily contracting. Nell regained her balance and released Cat's hand. "S-sorry. Wh-what did you say?"

Cat bit her lip. "Was that another seizure?"

"Wasssss it?"

"Are you okay?"

Nell blinked, still bleary. "It happens."

"Who's that?" another voice called from the dark. "Who's that voice? Who's that?"

"Hanish," Nell whispered. "Blind."

"Speak up!" Hanish demanded. He was propped against the partition between stalls. His eyes were bleach white, surrounded by scars like broken glass. "Identify yourself!"

"I'm Ildri." Cat waved although he couldn't see her. "Hi."

The right side of his face sagged as he spoke. "A new Curse?"

"Uh, no," Cat replied. "Just visiting."

"Visiting." Hamish repeated with the same inflection. Cat wondered if it was for comprehension. "Why?"

"Brushca-ca-casters," Nell said. "Doctor trusts her."

"Doctor trusts her." Hamish calmed down. "Okay, then."

Cat could feel a weight in his words, as if the fear and alarm was all the energy he had. Nell whispered to her, "Haaaanish old. Ooonly one here longer than me. Everyone else... gone."

"How long have you been here?"

"N-n-not sure." Nell's face twitched. "Ei-eight years."

"That's a long time."

"More tiiiiiime in thannnn out," she said. "Seizure as bbbbaby. Dr. Tyrus treated. Helped. But then found I was a Curse. Then chute."

"Chute?"

Nell's arm jerked as she gestured. "Here."

They walked to the back of the chamber beyond the stalls of Curses. A boy half Nell's age wandered, distracted, over his sleeping friends and bumped into one of the partitions. The far back wall was poured cement, just like the one with the hospital door built in it. Half a metal tube hung out of the wall, above a pile of scrap cloth and pillows. A Lightning Curse lay on it, mouth agape and eyes unfocused. Nell tapped his leg with her foot.

"Whoa? What?" The young man lurched to his feet with twitching arms. "Chute?"

"Not yet."

"Ohhhh." He limped away.

Nell stood in the spot that he'd left. "See?"

Cat gnawed her lip. "I hope that's not used how I think it's used."

"D-d-door at the top." Nell said. "Parents open. Kids slide."

"They walk up and drop their kids like bags of garbage?"

Light arced through Nell's hair. "We are n-n-not garbage!"

"You're right, you're not." Cat's anger flared at the thought of the poor Lightning Curses, scared of the twitches and seizures they couldn't control, being dropped into the dark, stinking underground to never see daylight again. She craned her neck for a better look up the slide. The door at the top was obscured by the slanted roof. "Can you climb back up?"

"Why?"

"Because you're trapped here."

"Meds here," Nell said. "And food."

A clatter sounded from the opposite end. Voices, but thankfully not screams or moaning. Cat recognized the doctor's voice. Dustin's rose, almost shouting, over her casual tones. "Are the Holy Calligraphers sure they want to visit such a sinful place?"

Cat's blood went cold. "Brushcasters?"

Nell's eyes sparked. "In c-c-c-cushions!"

Cat dove into the pile of pillows and blankets, breathing a nose-full of sweat and urine from the cloth. She gagged, coughing as Nell piled more on top of her.

A foreign voice spoke. "What was that sound?"

"The Curses. They have muscle spasms," Dustin said quickly.

"Nurse, let me handle this," Dr. Tyrus snapped.

"Yes, ma'am."

The doctor continued, more cordially as the group advanced into the room. "I assure you, your honors, an inspection is unnecessary, the mayor and I have our duties well in hand..."

"Was that in doubt?" an older woman asked.

"No! It's just that we have never had the Order investigate our location in person before. Usually the mayor's reports suffice—"

"Regardless," the Calligrapher cut in. "It is our duty as religious and moral authority to make sure our laws are being well carried out."

"Oh of course. I just wanted to reassure you," Dr. Tyrus said.

"I am reassured. Now continue."

"Y-yes." The doctor cleared her throat. "You can see that Lightning Town is completely protected by earthen insulation. It keeps the place cool and comfortable for them, while protecting the minds and bodies of those walking the streets above."

"Explain to me these mesh blankets they sleep on. They appear electronic, not organic."

"Yes, they are collectors."

"What do they collect?"

"Lightning Curses are always putting off electricity. We use the pads to harness it and fuel the generators in the next room."

"So this electricity goes to the entire hospital?"

"Yes." She switched to a more positive, salesman-like attitude. "The utility discount allows me to funnel profits toward my research."

"Research for your patients," the Calligrapher said. Papers rustled. "My reports say you specialize in seizures and brain disorders."

"Yes, it is a passion of mine."

"I assume this passion is also fueled by the Lightning Curses."

"Many of the Lightning Curses have issues that can resemble non-Curse illnesses: burns, blindness, and others in addition to seizures. In that way they've been a tremendous resource."

"In what way do you mean."

"Well, for research," she dodged. "I can observe the symptoms, test medicines, other things."

The female monk sounded wary. "So it's not for the benefit of the Curses."

"No, of course not."

"And are there records of these tests," the monk pressed.

"Yes, we keep internal records. My chief nurse Damini, here, is very diligent."

"Nurse Damini," the monk addressed. "Perhaps I should be asking you these questions."

"I, uh..." Dustin stammered. "Dr. Tyrus is in charge."

"Perhaps you would like to observe me administering the medicine directly?" Dr. Tyrus said in a rush. "That way you can witness the process I take first-hand?"

The monk paused. "You are prepared to do this now?"

"Yes, it is about dosing time. We administer it with the morning and evening meals."

"Doctor," Dustin interrupted. "It's a bit early still. Perhaps a verbal demonstration—"

The monk grunted. Dr. Tyrus cleared her throat. "Go draw the medicines, please."

"But doctor—"

"Damini. The medicines."

"Yes, ma'am."

The door opened and closed. The monks rustled more papers. The woman spoke. "My companion will be taking diligent observations of the proceedings."

The doctor stammered. "Yes, of course."

"Our report will find its way to the Holy Elder." The monk dropped her pitch on the word 'elder.' Cat swallowed a knot. She shuffled deeper into the cover of her blankets. Nell gestured for her to stay put and crawled to the partition where she pretended to sleep.

"Here, ma'am," Dustin said. "Shall I begin at the back?"

"How about you attend to the monks, Damini, I will give the medication."

"But we always do it in halves." Dustin's suppressed a note of panic. "I'm familiar with certain patients."

"They're subjects not patients," the doctor stated. "You are a good nurse. I trust your charting. Stay with our guests."

Cat carved a peep hole out of the blankets. The Calligraphers were still hidden behind the stalls.

"This one is... subject 14," Dr. Tyrus said. "When he arrived, the electrical rampancy in the brain caused full-body spasms and you can see how calm he is now." There was shuffling and the clink of glass. "This one developed a stammer. Speak, number 12."

"Speak number 12?" Hanish repeated.

"Tell us how you feel."

"Tell us... how you feel..." he mumbled. "Tired."

"See? A success!" The group stepped into view. Dr. Tyrus wore a leather case across her white uniform with a row of capped syringes loaded in the side. The two Calligraphers Cat saw upstairs followed a few paces behind. The older woman wore the white stole of a senior monk. Her associate was in his twenties, painting notes on a stack of clipped paper with a tiny calligraphy brush. Dustin stuck to them, eyes darting wildly. He started tapping a hand against his leg as the doctor knelt next to Nell. "This is one of my oldest cases. I treated her as a child and have kept the same treatment through her incarceration to see what would happen."

Dustin cleared his throat. "Um, Doctor? Perhaps I should..."

"Damini, please." She drew liquid from a vial and injected it into the meat of Nell's arm. The Curse flinched but kept quiet. The doctor placed the medicine back in her case and stood. "And there you have it, your honors. You see how I've been able to use these creatures for the benefit of humanity."

"Hmm." The senior crossed her arms. "Are any part of these Curses used on the patients of the hospital?"

"No, your honor."

"Is there any cross-contamination between the hospital and the Curse Town?"

"Oh no. I mean, not except the power."

The note-taking monk flurried a long response on his pad.

The senior continued. "And does the tax money provided by our Order's direction go to this power system or to these experiments?"

"Well, we only have the one generator," the doctor said. "And the medicines are for the patients."

"You mean human patients," the female monk prompted. "The otherwise healthy patients."

"Yes, that is what I said."

"I'll be more clear." She gestured for her companion to stop writing and stepped toward the doctor. "The monastery cannot be seen supporting anything that could be perceived as trying to heal these monsters. Curses are not able to be healed. They do not have *illnesses*. They are the sickness themselves. A supernatural plague. Sin incarnate."

Dr. Tyrus flinched. "Yes, of course."

"We are entertaining this demonstration for the sake of clarification. My associate and I came to your city to pursue a False Prophet—someone who has sacrificed their soul to serve sin. The one we are following is doing this by assisting Curses in all their forms. These creatures in affront to Our God and you, doctor, are currently one magic spell short of fitting that description as well. I am giving you the chance to clear your name. Is any of this to benefit these Curses?"

"I am nothing like the False Prophet," Dr. Tyrus exclaimed. "These creatures are lab rats. I don't care how they are affected, except for the benefit of the healthy people upstairs. The generator system falls well in line with the monastery's Edict of Charity, and only the funds for the food and water for these is currently derived from the population's taxable support fund."

"Of which you are comptroller."

"That is correct."

"Master." The male monk held a book in his hands. "There is no precedent in the law of the Order for medical funding. The commandment was written before science like this was abundant. I'm not sure if this practice is holy or not."

"Then such a decision requires research and prayer," the senior monk said. "Thank you for this demonstration, Dr. Tyrus. I will confirm your report in the town hall records. Come, Quill, let's leave this unholy place."

Dustin and the doctor escorted them back to the hospital door. Cat waited for it to open and shut before climbing from cover. "That was way too close."

Nell didn't move from her place on the ground. Cat frowned. "Nell?"

The Lightning Curse didn't respond.

Cat gripped her by the shoulder. "You okay?"

"Nell!" Dustin burst back into the chamber, running full-speed to fall to his knees beside the Curse. "Nell, speak to me! Please."

Nell blinked for the first time in seconds. "What... happened?"

"The doctor gave you medicine," Dustin said.

"But the... doctor always gives me medicine." She gasped. "I... I can breathe easier."

"Shh, stay calm. How do you feel?"

"I feel... better!" Nell shifted in her seat. "Why am I so weak? Did I have another seizure?" Her eyes widened. "Talking is so much easier, now!"

"Nothing's changed. Please stay calm."

"But it feels so different. Did she give me a different kind of medicine?" Nell frowned. "You usually give me the medicine. It's never worked like this before."

"I thought it was all the same medicine," Cat said. "Was what the doctor saying to the Brushcasters the truth? Is she experimenting on these people like lab rats?"

"No, it's all the same medicine. That was a lie," Dustin answered. "She couldn't tell the Brushcasters she's trying to cure them."

"How can you be sure?"

"Because I draw all the medicines from the same bottle."

"Dustin, look at me!" Nell turned her hands in front of her face. "I'm not shaking. Nothing's twitching. I bet I can even stand up—"

"Don't get too excited," he pressed. "Strong emotions generate more electricity."

"But I feel so much better!" Nell pulled her knees up, but Dustin forced them back down.

"Nell, I'm serious." His voice was edged with fear. "Rest."

"What's wrong?" Cat asked. "The medicine's reversed her speech problems, her coordination... If this is what the doctor's medicine does for Lightning Curses, imagine what it could do for the rest! It will save hundreds of lives!"

"It's not—!" Dustin caught his tongue. "It's a treatment."

Cat's heart skipped. "What do you mean?"

"I mean it's not what you think it is—" He stopped himself again. "I have to go."

Nell's eyes sparked at the corners. "Go where?"

"I'm sorry, sis."

"Hey, wait!" Cat held her side and staggered up as Dustin marched across the chamber. She caught his sleeve halfway to the door. "You can't leave until you explain more. The doctor asked me to help her cure Curses. Is this treatment not a cure?"

Dustin made sure Nell wasn't following, then stepped close and spoke in a hoarse whisper. "Not yet it isn't."

"Not yet?"

"The doctor talked it up to you. These experiments you plan to help with are a patch on this problem. She's not treating a magical cause, she's treating the specific symptoms of them. The drug she has now won't affect the Water Curses. She's going to try dehydrating chemicals and pneumonia medicine. She will not cure the source." Cat's heart seized. "So Pete... I mean, these people. They're still going to die? They won't make it past eighteen?"

"It's even worse than that," he whispered. "The drug she's using on the Lightning Curses is a clinical prescription that limits electrical activity in the body. Everyone's body has electricity in it, just like every body has water and heat and bone. Lightning Curses have significantly more electricity than healthy people. The drug in small doses would have helped Nell if she were a normal person with a seizure disorder, but she's a Curse, so the doctor has been giving her and the other Curses bigger and bigger doses of these kinds of drugs. She's not a bad person. She's trying her best, but the drug is really strong and has other side effects besides suppressing electricity. The medicine helps with their minds but at the cost of their muscles, their livers, and hearts... leading to failures."

"Deaths?"

His expression changed to one of exhaustion and sadness. "They only tend to live a couple of years."

"They what?" Nell had limped closer as the two of them talked. Electricity sparked from her eyes. The air crackled. "The medicine kills us? But... I've taken it for ten years."

"I... you haven't." It was Dustin's turn to stammer. Tears welled in his deep-set, hooded eyes. "You took it as a baby, and while I was at school, but I knew what was happening. I couldn't lose you like that, Nell. Not so fast. When I took over the medicines I gave you shots of saline. Your symptoms came back, but you didn't die. You still aren't dead. I'm protecting you."

"Protecting me?' Sparks snapped in her hair. "By lying to me?"

"It was for your own good."

"You wouldn't give it to me because it would kill me, but you gave it to everyone else?" she cried. "Did you ask *them* if it was okay?"

He gulped. "Nell..."

"This one dose made me feel normal again!" A flash lit the back of her throat. "Do you know how much it hurts being a Curse? Muscles always firing, blasting nerves in your skin, not being able to talk or move right, always seizing or blanking out? Do you know how scared I've been?"

He gulped. "I'm sorry."

"I trusted you!" Lightning arced from her eyes, drawing new scars on her cheeks like a flurry of tiny scalpels. "You lied to me!"

"To save you!"

"No!" The sparks increased. "Selfish!"

Her face blanked, anger turning to heartbreak with a literal crack of lightning. The skin blistered down her neck and along both of her arms. White light danced in her eyes as they slipped suddenly out of focus.

"Nell!" He gripped her shoulders with gloved hands and guided her as she sank down the wooden partition. Snaps of electricity lanced from her fingertips as her upper body began to shake and twitch. Cat grabbed her shoulders, but Dustin batted her away. "Don't touch her." He handed her his watch. "Keep the time."

"Okay." Cat watched the second hand as the seizure progressed. Five seconds. Ten seconds. The quaking came to a stop. Nell's eyes shut and Cat inhaled for the first time. "Fifteen!" She looked to the nurse but he was missing. Cat turned on her heel. "Dustin?"

A familiar beep sounded from the combination lock on the wall, followed by a clank as the hospital door bolted shut.

"She is using donations to treat them with medicines." Vivian paced the desk in front of Ebensmith's mayor. "I insist you arrest this woman, and submit her to the church for trial. Then remove these Curses from the hospital. Protect your people from the damage caused by exposure to their sin."

"Your honor, there is no need for such a dramatic response."

"I believe there is." She tapped the stack of freshly printed 'wanted' posters between them on the tabletop. "We were sent here to protect your town against the possible attack of a False Prophet only to find you live with the Curses in your midst, keeping them alive to power your hospital and using their bodies to help treat your most vulnerable."

"With all due respect, using Curses as resources is not the same as caring for them."

"They are sin incarnate," Vivian insisted. "Located directly under your hospital. Children are born there! People come at their weakest, fighting for their lives. How could you allow this?"

"Because this is the modern state of God's Valley, Ms. Arch." The mayor straightened his waistcoat and came around the desk. "I know your monastery is removed from the comings and goings of us lowly average people, but let me remind you that we are suffering what many call a five-century drought. It has not rained in over a year and our resources, industry, and population are suffering. We adapted to our surroundings, you can't condemn us for that."

"On the contrary—"

"The one thing we do have in abundance is power," the mayor continued. "Lightning Curses arrive here more and more each year. We spend what little money we earn to feed and clothe them according to *your* rules. What's wrong with us taking our investment's worth?"

Vivian stalled mid-step. "Your what?"

"Do you know how much energy Lightning Town creates for Ebensmith? It makes life out here possible. Every city in the valley has made compromises over the years. Protect us from False Prophets if you must. Religion and Prophets and that nonsense are your job, but my job is keeping this place running and your judgment not welcome."

"Our judgment?" Vivian couldn't hide the exasperation in her voice. "Our *guidance* is in service of reconciliation with Our God. Healing Curses, relying on them, using them for resources—this is the opposite of rejecting them. You are not only complacent to sin, you have structured your lives around it. You an insult to Our God!"

"Your honor, please," the Mayor said. "No need to overreact. We're merely trying to survive."

"Is surviving your only priority?" Vivian asked. "What about betterment? What about righteousness?"

"What are you suggesting we do? Close the hospital? Shut down our grid? How many lives do you think will be lost as a result?"

"But the moral cost—"

"Morality is not letting the people in my care suffer needlessly."

"Morality is choosing what's right!" Vivian nearly shouted. "Yes, the death of innocents is not a moral outcome to any choice, but that does not justify crime against Our God and nature, especially not one of this magnitude! I had my suspicions, but I never dreamed such disregard and corruption was possible. And at such a scale."

"It is the way things are."

"But not the way things have to be."

"I don't mean to disappoint you, your honor," the mayor said. "Holiness is ideal, but I'm afraid such aspirations, however noble, are simply beyond our reach."

"Then we are well and truly doomed." Vivian drew a measured breath and felt the weight of despair as she gathered the wanted fliers into her arms. "I understand why this has happened. I can imagine the steps taken to this point, but I cannot condone such willful opposition to Our God when men and women tear their own families apart to facilitate his return. I go now to contact the Holy Elder. Your city will face judgment. I recommend you take the intervening time to consider your position and begin change, because your size, your importance, and your connection to Castleton and its leadership will not save you from this. You will not be pardoned, and your city will not be spared."

She gestured to the corner where Quill was waiting at attention, and exited to the hall without being dismissed.

"Gather our things. We're leaving."

Quill shook his head. "Will he listen to the warning?"

"He will if he enjoys his power." Vivian's hand tightened around the papers. "What a world this has become."

The door to Lightning Town had no visible hinge or handle. It stood flush to the cement wall, with no gap for fingers or winches. The number pad for the combination lock was mounted in a rubber frame with rubber buttons and no visible wires. Cat beat it for a full minute with the heel of one of her protective boots before her meager post-surgery energy was spent and she was forced to give up. With no other doors or windows, the only other entrance was the horrible child-chute, which was too high for Cat to reach by herself. The only plan left was to wait for dinnertime and jump whoever opened the door. Cat paced, anxiously threading shapes in her loop of string.

Nell watched with her back against the cement wall. She'd recovered from her most recent seizure faster with the medicine involved, but morale was critically low. She slouched, breathing hoarsely and shuddering sporadically. "So what are you g-g-going to do when Dustin comes back?"

"Get out of here."

"And then?"

"Escape, I guess." Cat twisted a cup and saucer.

"To talk to Dr. Tyrus?"

"I'm afraid that chance is pretty moot at this point."

"You were really going to help her."

"Yes."

"But not anymore."

Cat sighed and slid down the cement wall beside her. "The medical cure isn't real."

"The medicine does help, though," Nell ventured. "I mean, I'm still a Curse, but I feel better."

Cat pondered a moment and shifted in her seat. "If Dustin had explained about the medicine long ago when you first came here, would you have said 'yes' to feel better even if you would die or would you decide to feel worse so you could live?"

"With as good as I feel now, I'd say yes to medicine!"

"But you've been here for years. If you'd said 'yes' back then, you wouldn't be here now."

"That... that's true..." Nell's hair sparked. "I mean, I didn't feel as bad back then, maybe I'd say no for a while. But it hurts all the time. How can I not want to stop it?"

"It's a tough choice to make."

"If he asked the other Curses if they want to try it they might have said yes, too," Nell said. "Dustin and the doctor didn't ask, that's the problem. If you ask people to help you treat the Curses maybe they'll say 'yes' even if they die sooner. The point is you ask."

Cat's stomach turned. She *had* been asking. All the way around God's Valley she'd asked people to die to make the world a better place. If Peter, Aiden, or Lynn were approached to test medicine they would probably agree, especially if the tests meant other Curses would benefit. But none of them were Lightning Curses, so the medicine Nell took would not help, and by the time it would take to develop new medicine... everyone would already be dead.

Cat let her string go loose. Disappointment and realization sank like a hook deep into her chest. "There's something I want to confess to you, Nell."

"Confess?"

"My name's not Ildri. That was the name of a friend—a Fire Curse—who was killed. My real name is Catrina Aston."

"Catrina?"

"Cat's fine."

"But..." A tremor started in Nell's right hand. "Why did you lie about that?"

"Because I'm a Prophet." Cat was amazed at how matter-of-fact she sounded. "Someone God chose long ago to stop people from being born Curses. Lots of people tried before me, but the Brushcasters kept getting in the way. Ending the Curses requires taking away magic, and the Brushcasters are scared of a world where they don't have magic."

A current jittered in the dark of Nell's pupils. "You're serious?"

"I'm sorry I lied about it," Cat said. "But understand, ending the Curses is not an easy thing. It requires a sacrifice. Five Curses have to die for it. Like Ildri. I have four of them with me right now, hiding in the mountains. They are all friends of mine and I love them for how brave and selfless they are, so when I got here and Dr. Tyrus told me about a medicine that could cure them without the cost, I thought I'd saved them. No more running from Brushcasters. No more dead friends." She released a sigh. "Changing my identity wasn't so much a lie as a hope."

"I- I think I understand," Nell said. "You really have four Curse friends hiding in the mountains?"

"Yeah; Peter, Aiden, Lynn, and Zephyr. I left them in a mine shaft if you can believe it. They thought it was too dangerous to come in with me, and I guess this proves they're right. They're a lot smarter than I am, especially Peter. He's my dearest friend in the world. I would have done anything to save him."

"Wow," Nell pressed her lips. "I guess... Dustin felt the same about me, huh?"

"He still does, I'm sure," Cat said. "He made a bad choice, but he didn't want to hurt you and ended up hurting you either way." The ache in her chest spread outward. "I can relate to that."

"You're so sad."

"Yeah, I am."

Nell's hair sparked. "And your mission... it's real too?"

"It's supported by scripture and opposed by the Calligraphers, that's proof enough. I've had to explain it many times and it never sounds any less 'out there', but God needs to come back and fix this. My friends were willing to die to make it happen. The least I can do is be the Prophet they need."

"And so all you need is a Lightning Curse, You need me."

There was no choice left but to accept that Nell was right. The mission continued, and she needed one of these Curses to help. Tears burned in the corners of Cat's closed eyes. "Taking your medicine will help you feel better and kill you faster. Coming with me is going to kill you in days. I can't ask you to give up this new life you have."

"I don't want to die, but I didn't want to be a Cuuurse either, did I? And I got mad at Dustin for not asking my opinion but what I wanted was for him to tell me the truth." Nell stared at her hands. "I can tell the truth, too. I don't want to go back to the way I was. If I never get another dose of this medicine I'll be sssssick like these others. You asked me before if I'd die to not feel bad... and even if it's dying tomorrow, the answer is still yes."

A slurry of emotion from relief to pure sorrow dragged Cat towards a breakdown. She took a deep breath. "Thank you, Nell."

Something rumbled through the cement wall behind them. Cat leaped up, string at the ready, as the lights flickered overhead. People shouted in the distance. Nell sat forward. "The street?"

"Ahh!" one of the other Curses cried out. "Aahh! Ahh!"

Another Curse further in began shouting as well, joined by more and more. The flickering lights swelled with more light. The high-pitched ringing increased in volume as the Curses did, filling the space. Nell rushed into their midst. "Taren? Audra!" Nell's arm and face twitched. She tilted off balance, covering her ears. "Ahh!"

"Nell, what is it?"

"Buzzing..." She cringed. "Ah!"

Cat reached toward her, but electricity arced off Nell's shoulder to Cat's bare, unprotected hand. The snap was sharp and concussive like a whip smack, sending tingles up her arm and into her chest faster than Cat could withdraw her hand. She stumbled back, suddenly dizzy. The tingles gave way to burning as she fell to one knee.

A Curse in the stall to the left started convulsing. One to the right arched his back with arms extended straight up. The lights on the mats beneath them blazed and popped from their housings. Ripples of excess power throbbed up the attached cords into the earthen walls. Light from the overhead bulbs swelled to blinding. Several shook, their wires sizzling. The light and noise increased to painful levels. Curses frothed and twitched. Nell fell to her knees as the overhead lights exploded in a shower of sparks and hot glass. The buzzing and screaming ceased as the room plunged to darkness.

For a moment all Cat could hear above her damaged ears was the pull of her own breath. Orange coils of filament cooled in the broken bulbs. Static electricity flashed from the Curses around her in bursts. Firelight glowed in one of the stalls ahead and swelled to touch Nell's motionless body. The orange flickers sparkled like crystal on her blanket of broken glass.

"Nell..." Cat's arm had gone from burned to numb. Nell was alive and sleeping fitfully, likely victim to another seizure in the panic of the moment. Cat let her rest and continued deeper to investigate the flames. One of the Curses lay on a burning mat. One of the younger Curses had a pillow from the cushion pit. It burned with the girl still on it, her eyes wide and lifeless. Cat put a hand over her mouth, aghast and saddened. She stepped over the body and kicked the pillow from beneath it. The Curse lying beside the girl was dead as well, as were the ones in the stall next door. Lifeless bodies sparked and twitched as the electricity inside consumed them. Cat's heel crunched glass as she hurried back to Nell, only to be stopped by a blast of light and the sudden intrusion of sound.

"Stop there!" A squad of policeman in head-to-toe rubber suits flooded through the hospital door. "Hands up!"

She obeyed. "I can explain—!"

"Look, sir," one of the other officers held out a sheet of paper. "It's the False Prophet."

The officer snorted. "Okay, Catrina, on your knees."

Cat gulped and looked to Nell. The girl twitched, but didn't wake. Cat lowered to one knee. "You monsters killed them. Every one of them. How? Why?"

"Battery bomb. Mayor's orders." The policeman came to tie her hands, but Cat was already holding string. She stretched it blindly, weaving on instinct. He looked down at the white flash. "What is—"

A jet of fire bathed his boots. The policeman squawked and leaped away. The rest drew swords, but Cat was moving before a one of them could swipe. She brought the string to her front and staged it quickly, blowing more fire as she skirted them. A blast at the doorway cleared the passage and Cat rocketed through the basement.

The generator room smoldered beneath a rotating red light. Sirens blared from every generator left crumpled and useless in their housings. The remnants of the detonator lay in pieces on the floor. The ramp was lit only by waning daylight as she returned to ground level. The first floor was deserted, the halls dark without the generators save another rotating light. Four officers ran towards her from reception with even more running up the ramp behind.

"It's the False Prophet!" shouted the policemen from below. "Dead or alive! Dead or alive!"

Cat had no choice but to take the ramp, dumping wheeled chairs and hospital beds on the slant as she went. The second floor had no guards or patients. Cat ran past her old convalescence room, only to meet a blank wall at the end of the hall.

Footsteps pounded the polished floor behind her. Every bedroom was a windowless cell. She put her back to the wall and braced herself with string held armed and ready. She could take down two or three with more fire. Water could slick the floor. Perhaps earth in the eyes would blind the most people if she aimed the string high. A faint click sounded over her right ear. A panel slid out behind her. Two hands grabbed her shoulders and pulled her backward from the hall.

Dustin slid the secret panel closed before the policeman saw them. "You okay?"

"Somehow." Cat staggered. They were in a hidden stairwell lit by a handheld lantern on the floor. "What is this—"

"The doctor was afraid this day would come. It's a secret exit from her office."

"Did she escape?"

"No, she's been arrested. They cuffed her mid-surgery and evacuated the whole hospital. I've been hiding in these crawlspaces. How'd you get here? Where's Nell?"

"I left her," Cat said.

His eyes flashed. "You what?"

"I had to! They blew the place to bits. All the Curses died. Nell was spared because she wasn't on a mat—"

"Current reversal." Dustin cursed. "Shock induced seizures. I knew it was a risk. But Nell's okay? She's alive still?"

"As long as she stays sleeping and the police don't look close."

Dustin grit his teeth. "I should have gotten her out of here a long time ago. If I was willing to risk this, I should have been willing to risk that..."

"Risk is a lot easier in retrospect," Cat said. "Don't think about what you should have done, let's think about what we're doing now, which is standing around in a secret stairwell talking instead of anything useful."

"Right. We have to save Nell. Are there police on the first floor?"

"At this point they're probably everywhere. I'm the False Prophet they're looking for."

"The what?"

"A criminal. Dangerous." Cat rolled her eyes. "I cast illegal magic and they want to kill me."

"Whoa."

"I'll tell you more about it if we survive."

He lifted the small lamp and the two hurried down the staircase through the internal structure of the hospital. Cat rounded several landings, doing her best not to trip on her rubber boots as exhaustion crept back in. She was still wounded and the adrenaline was fading.

Dustin stopped at another sliding door. "Since we can't get to Lightning Town the normal way, we're going to have to go the more traditional route. Keep your head down. Follow close."

He pulled a thin blanket from the medical bag he carried and draped it over the top of her head before ushering her to the street. The air outside smelled fresh and clean compared to the burnt hair and ozone stink in the hospital building. Dustin took her hand and put his other arm around her back. She still had a bit of a limp from her various burns, scrapes, and surgeries, coupled with the tremble of adrenaline; they must have looked like an authentic pair of evacuees.

Cat heard the crowd before they reached it. She peeked out from beneath the sheet to see the hospital staff cowering, protecting their patients from whatever they thought was inside the empty hospital building behind a wall of armored guards. The hospital was even more massive than it had seemed on the inside. Evenly spaced windows climbed the building in slanted lines, highlighted by intricate archways and carvings. The front was supported by stone columns.

Dr. Tyrus was in a police cart under guard with hands tied behind her back.

"Release me! This is ridiculous, I'm comptroller! I was only doing my job!"

"You see that?" Dustin asked.

"Yeah, the doctor. She was arrested for helping the Curses?"

"Yes, but I'm not talking about her—the building behind."

Standing opposite the hospital was the thirty-foot Lightning Goddess statue bricked into a low building so that only her top half was visible. She stood with a lightning bolt in both hands like a flag pole, staring southwest toward Castleton as if she were emerging triumphant from the additional structure.

Dustin pulled the sheet off Cat's head when they were safely across the street. Even in a crisis, Ebensmith was bustling with people. Rubberneckers crowded the sidewalks as horses and carriages hurried past. The nurse moved Cat along the crowd until they were out of sight, then sneaked across the street again to the brick building beneath the Goddess where the child-chute to Lightning Town waited beneath an official metal sign.

"Ebensmith welcomes travelers from the five corners of God's Valley and thanks them for their sacrifice. Deposit Curse Here."

"Disgusting." Cat snorted.

"It's the only other way." Dustin knotted the end of the sheet. "If we use this as a rope one of us can slip in, and once we get Nell we can climb it back out. I hope it's long enough."

"Give it here." Cat tore the edge of the sheet with her teeth and ripped a clean line down the grain.

Dustin watched her tie the two halves together. "Is there a reason you knew how to do that?"

"I was a troublesome kid." She tied a square knot at the end and handed it to him. "I'll be back."

"I really think I—"

"You're a nurse in this city. People know you. Trust your face. I'm a wanted criminal with magic powers the cops want alive or dead. Also, Nell's still mad at you. I'm going."

He gulped and nodded. "Hurry back."

The child-chute was a two-foot square metal slab hinged at the bottom with a spring to keep it closed up at the top. Cat made sure her string was in hand, put the tail end of the sheet in her mouth and slipped into the opening. It was a short ride, maybe five feet total, and dumped her in the urine-scented padding with as much ceremony as she'd assumed from inside. She landed hard on her wounded side with a flash of pain. It was more annoying than crippling. No doubt it busted stitches but there wasn't much to do about it now. The sirens blared from the generator room, muted by the wood and dirt. Red light flashed on the floor like a bloody slash, highlighting Nell, sitting on her ankles at the mouth of one of the stalls. "Nell!"

"Wwhhhaaa?" She turned her head, static sparking in her hair.

"Nell, it's me." Cat knelt beside her. "You okay?"

She turned back to the stall. Hamish lay dead against the partition. Nell poked his body with a questioning sound.

Cat's heart broke. "Oh, Nell."

The girl looked at her, confused. Cat retrieved her protective gloves from the corner near the door where she'd left them and grabbed the Lightning Curse under her armpits. She walked unevenly. Twitching muscles curled her feet as she planted them, leaving Cat to keep her steady. They limped back to the chute.

"Nell, can you climb?"

"Cliiiiiimb?"

"Yeah, climb the rope?"

Nell blinked slowly. Cat wound the knotted blanket around her wrists and pinched the loose end in her two hands. "Don't let go."

"Don't..." Nell repeated.

Cat boosted from below as Dustin tugged from above. Cat's muscles strained. Her side ached and her shocked arm was back to burning. She breathed a sigh of relief as Nell slipped up the slide. Voices sounded in the generator room. A policeman appeared in the door.

"Does chief think she really came back down here?"

"Not like she left. We got the building surrounded."

"But she's got evil magic right?"

"She can't go invisible."

"You don't know that."

The sheet tumbled back down the chute. "Cat!"

"Shhh!" Cat hissed.

"Did you hear that?" one officer asked. They already sounded closer. She ripped the gloves back off and stuffed them in her shoulder bag before weaving a spell. The cops rounded the corner, swords drawn. Cat dropped the trigger string and blasted them with a whipping arc of white lightning.

The flash jumped straight to the swords like twin lightning rods, steering the electricity up their arms. The policemen recoiled, muscle contracting. Holding the string taught doubled the pain in her stitches. She felt a flood of warmth spread below her vest and pulled her hand from the string figure to grab hold of the rope. Her attackers started to recover but she was too weak and wounded to climb. The string went taut in her hands and with a jolt she lifted, vanishing up the chute with strength from above.

Dustin grabbed her arms at the top and spilled her out onto the pavement. The gathered crowd stared and shouted. Nell dropped her end of the rope and knelt beside her. "Cat?"

"Nell? You're okay?"

"Dus gave me a dose. What was that?"

"Police." Cat held her side and winced. "Oooh I think that one finally ruined me."

"Can't rest now." Dustin said. "Get up."

"What's wrong?"

"Got an audience. People don't normally come *up* the chute." Dustin dragged Cat to her feet. Police were closing in on the commotion, but there was little time to care. Cat was dragged out into the square where the evacuees gathered. The wagon with Dr. Tyrus was parked mere feet away, surrounded by standing guards with drawn swords. Cat tried to comb the knots of the lightning spell out of her string, but was shaking from exhaustion or nerves or both. Every eye in the square fixed upon them. Dustin pointed over their heads and shouted. "Hey! Look over there!"

The people obeyed like a thousand sheep. One of Dr. Tyrus's

guards flashed his blade toward them and Nell smacked the broad side with the palm of her hand. Her touch charged the metal, which sprang from the policeman's hand. Dustin flattened the officer with one punch and flung Cat through the opening to the back of the wagon where Dr. Tyrus sat, mouth agape. "Damini? What are you– ?"

"Sit up straight, ddddoctor," Nell said. Officers held the wagon in place, but jumped back when the Lightning Curse grabbed hold of the metal wagon rail. Nell flinched as well. She balled up on the floor as Dustin threw the wagon driver and sped through the busy streets.

The police yelled. The townsfolk screamed. Cat's heart pounded as the wagon careened through the crowded streets. A collision banged her wounded side into the framework. Another rattled her head against the hard floor. The chaos grew muffled. And dull. And dark.

"She said they were in the mountains, right?"

"That's what she said."

"Dark will help but not for long. They're still behind us."

Cat pried her eyes open. Stars stretched above her in a glittering canopy. For a second she thought she was back with her friends, riding in the wagon with Peter driving, but they were going much too fast for that. The dry smell of dust and desert air filled her aching chest.

"Don't move yet," Dr. Tyrus warned. She was stitching Cat's wound closed again. That explained the sting.

"Did... we make it?" Cat mumbled.

"I think so." Dustin looked over his shoulder. "I can barely see them anymore."

"There are still two. One dropped oooout," Nell stuttered. She sat in a ball, wearing Cat's rubber boots and gloves for everyone's protection. "It's been hoooours."

Cat waited for Dr. Tyrus to tie her bandage before sitting up. She raised her eyebrows to Nell. "Are you okay?"

"Yyyyyeah." Nell gulped. "It's kinda all setting in. I-I'm out. I'm okay, but everyone else..."

"I'm sorry, Nell."

"It wasn't much of a life for them but... you know. It... was a life. It was worth something," she muttered. "And they were my friends."

The horse slowed to a walk and wove the wagon upward along

the old mining roads. They stopped when they reached the tree line. Their pursuers were still behind them, the dust from their hoof beats visible in the moonlight. Dustin parked and came around to the back. "Here's as far as we can go. I'll take the wagon and draw the police away. Think you can you walk back to your people?"

"Yes." Cat planted her boots back on the desert road she remembered. "Nell, you still coming?"

Dustin flashed a look to her, alarmed. "What?"

"I-I'm going with her," Nell said. "She's gonnnna stop the Curses. Needs my help."

"You?" Dustin challenged. "No, you're coming with me. We're getting out of here."

"Nnnno." Nell shook her head sadly. "Ssssssorry Dus."

"But—" He glanced from her to the pursuers. "But I—"

"Thank you for hheeelping me," Nell said. "I know you meant well. But I have to go."

"Wait." Dustin dismounted, handing her his shoulder bag. Inside were a dozen vials of clear liquid.

Nell looked up. "Is this...?"

"Enough medicine to keep you feeling better for a little while. I rescued the bag from Dr. Tyrus's office when I knew we'd have to run. I won't tell you whether or not to take them. It should have been your choice the whole way. Just please, think about the consequences if you do. It's not a magical fix."

Nell took the bag and held it to her heart. "Thank you, Dustin."

"Pay attention, doctor." Cat looked straight at the penitent-looking woman in the wagon. "I don't think you're a bad person. You've worked hard to help Curses when no one else would, but they are people. Nell here has a mind and the power to choose for herself. Don't take that from them, even as you work to improve their situation."

The doctor forced the smallest hint of a smile. "I could still use an assistant. My name is ruined at this point. I'll have to start over again. But I will start over. I was on the cusp of a breakthrough. I really think these people can be treated."

"I'm glad to hear you say so." Cat reached in her shoulder bag and pulled out the map and stack of money tucked safely inside. "Here. I believe this is yours."

Dr. Tyrus took the stack, astonished. "You're giving it back?"

"You need it more than I do." Cat shrugged. "Look, I don't care about the Brushcasters or the laws they put in place, the Curses need taking care of. I'm glad someone's been trying. Do good, but be honest. And work with them. They're people, just like you are. Dustin can show you the way."

His eyes welled. "The cops are still coming. We have to go."

Nell took his hand with her gloved one. "Goodbye Dustin."

"Bye sis." He gulped with a look to Cat. "Take care."

"We will."

He swung back into the saddle and charged out into the plains. Cat and Nell headed up the mountain path on foot, through the shadows of the dark trees. Nell panted, her hair flashing like a great, bushy firework as she climbed. Cat couldn't move quickly, either. She searched the road and shadows for movement until they reached the wall of mine shafts. The place was quiet as a grave with no sign of life, but no sign of a struggle either. No Calligraphers leaped from the shadows to put her under arrest. Cat called out; her voice was weaker than she expected it to be. "Hello? Guys?"

No reply. Cat cleared her throat and tried again.

"Peter!"

"Cat?"

Her heart skipped at his voice. Movement echoed in the nearest cave as her friends emerged. Aiden appeared first, his sores glowing in the dark. He lit the way for Peter, who picked along with unsure footing. Cat met him in moonlight and wrapped both arms around his knobby chest. Folding around her friend felt so good, she hardly noticed how his heavy arm pressed against her damaged side.

"Finally. Wow, waiting was torture." Peter's voice echoed through him like an empty barrel. "You're shaking. What happened?"

"Nothing important." She pulled back reluctantly. "Guys, this is Nell. Our last volunteer."

Lynn went pale and backed away, but Zephyr rushed toward them. "Lightning?"

"H...i," Nell forced out. "Nice to m-m-meet you."

Lynn's brow knit. "Is she okay?"

"T-talking is... hard," Nell said. "Ssssorry."

"Nell, these are Peter, and Aiden, and Lynn, and Zephyr."

Aiden crossed his arms. "You sure she knows what we're up to out here? I mean the stakes."

"Y-es, I know," Nell said. "I am the last Lightnnnning Curse in the valley."

"The last one?" Peter's voice hitched in concern.

Nell took a deep breath. The sparks flashed brighter and faster in the dark. "I'm afraid so."

"You must be so lonely." Lynn ventured as close as she dared. "Don't worry, we're your friends now. We're in this together."

Nell breathed deeply. "Thank you. That means a lot."

"There's policemen chasing us out of Ebensmith," Cat reported. "We can't take the road down yet, and probably shouldn't stay here. Let's pack the wagon and find a new hiding spot."

"We did some exploring while we were up here," Aiden said. "Zephyr found a weird clearing in the woods. Said something about a Goddess? Anyway, there's a cabin there that might fit us all inside."

"Sounds good. Let's get going." Cat ushered everyone into the wagon. Lynn took the reins, her excess water a dangerous conductor now that Nell was riding with them. They wrapped the Lightning Curse in a wool blanket and sat her at the edge. Cat kept an arm around her and the group trundled back onto the forest paths.

Vivian finished her note to the Elder as soon as she and Quill returned to the monastery. She'd learned a lot about the Valley on her brief visit below—about corruption and power struggles and bending the rules. The mayor of Ebensmith had listened to her warning, but how many more like him were there? It frightened her to think. Quill was waiting for her in the clay yard, idly sweeping the smooth surface. Vivian pocketed the letter and spoke. "I thought you would be resting."

"I waited for you."

"That was not necessary. I'm sending a letter to the Elder, nothing more."

"I know, but this mission was hard on you." Quill leaned on the broomstick, his brush on his back. "I thought perhaps you'd like some emotional support."

She pressed her lips and conceded. "What are your thoughts on this adventure, your honor? Does it affirm your faith in our cause? Or skew your perception of humanity?"

"Are you asking my opinion or have you drawn a conclusion?"

"I wish I could," Vivian admitted. "Things are so much clearer up here. Much plainer. I understand the writings of the Prophets, at least as much as a mortal mind is allowed to understand it. I cannot comprehend people, especially those in power. To me there is only one power—that is the law and word of Our God. The mayor of the city didn't credit that. He said 'holiness is good but this is the modern age.' I can't help thinking my life's work has been passed by."

"Sin's more than just the Curses. It's lies, pride, greed... everything," Quill said. "We can't force people to listen, but we have dedicated our lives to leading and educating on Our God's behalf. As far as I can tell, this mission proves our own calling is still relevant. There's a long way to go before humanity is perfect enough for the return of Our God, so we have to keep trying."

"Is it in vain, though?" Vivian asked. "Is such a goal even able to be reached?"

"It won't be if we don't try." Quill smiled at his old master. "If it helps, you can think of it as job security."

Vivian chuckled. "Step aside. I have a courier to paint."

He poured a palette of paint. She loaded her worn brush, fitting her fingers to the groves she'd worn in it. This was the third golem she'd painted in almost as many days, a spike in creation after years of quietly working by candlelight. Her soul had been stagnant, and now it was time to put herself and her faith into action.

This prayer will carry his message//And so my word will travel distance//Our God said seek your leaders//Swift is the stride of nature's passing//...

She paused. It was always poetry, but Vivian's heart told her this one was supposed to be a prayer.

Find truth in all things, our God commands. For truth is the candle that lights paths of the mind. Lies are oaths kept by those who are afraid. Release your burdens and rely on truth for it remains no matter how darkly the world closes around it.

"Malachi," Vivian quoted. She wet her brush again and painted the lightning symbol at the center. Her golem rolled to life, spitting and sparking with pure energy as it took on feline shape. The creature opened its white eyes, the points gleaming even as its body was alight with whiteness. The creature coiled back on its haunches and leaped like a comet from the painting field, into the starlit night.

"A lightning golem, huh?" Quill asked. "A little visible."

Vivian nodded. "It seemed appropriate."

"The spell was a bit long for you, too. I thought you were known for artistic brevity."

"I was feeling wistful."

"Master," Quill said kindly. "You seem burdened by some kind of responsibility for the things you saw on our mission. Conviction's important but guilt's not the response to it. Be proactive. You always taught me when I was younger that our pasts are like our paper. It can be flawed or torn or mended, but writing can be done on any surface, and our stories are composed with thought and intention and honesty above all. Don't fret about what you've seen down there. You're a scholar. Learn from it. Write about it. Use it to compose a better story. It's all we can do."

Vivian's heart stirred. She smiled. "The student becomes a master himself."

"Heh, not I'm not a senior yet."

Vivian put her hand on his shoulder. "Then my first writing will be your recommendation."

The two went inside. Lights flicked out in the windows all around them. The lightning golem pounced over rooftop and hillside. It skirted the old mines, stepping with nimble feet over the crusted canopy. Bolts of lightning struck down on moist patches of mist and stone. In its mouth was Vivian's letter, explaining the events that had occurred, carried by lightning through the distance of unknown space and time.

Readers familiar with the modern writing rules of the 2010s will likely need no introduction to the argument over prologues. Prologues have existed in books, especially science fiction and fantasy books, since the novel began. Often they are included to explain rules of lore, tell backstory, and describe landscapes to readers unfamiliar with the new lands. These things are well intended, perhaps, but pedestrian without character or plot to surround them and give them context. For this reason, a percentage of modern readers skip the prologue in order to get started on the story itself. And its for that reason that the phrase "Gas the Prologue" is repeated in workshops and lectures across the globe.

Prologues can be done well when used to set the tone, establish important backstory for main characters, or impart information impossible to include elsewhere in the story. But for all the prologues that work well, there are just as many that distract or deceive the reader into thinking the book is about someone or something unrelated to the rest of the story. Often modern books take what would have made a good prologue and turn them into chapter 1. Others are easily integrated into the body of the novel like breadcrumbs to be discovered by the characters in the course of the adventure. This is the best way to impart backstory to a reader, because it turns the lore, landscape, and backstory into part of the experience instead of spoon-feeding it without context like homework that's required first.

This prologue was removed from Threadcaster after the first draft back in 2008, but was revisited in 2018 and updated to meet present canon as a promotional tool. Almost all the information presented in this prologue made it into the book as Cat learned more about her world and herself on her adventure. Consider what follows a bit of possible canon, a scene that very well could have occurred in Joshua's story, even if it wasn't included in the text of Cat's.

Prologue

An old man and young boy sat cross-legged on the hardwood floor. Outside the wide glass windows, evergreens rested peacefully in the dark. The boy twitched his feet against the boards, staring intently up at his companion as the old man smoothed his long white beard and listened to the natural sounds of the summer night. When he finally spoke, his aged voice was firm and even. "My son, do you remember what I told you about this house?"

"Yes sir," the boy answered. "You told me it has been in our family for centuries, and that we stay here so no one else can find us."

"Very good," the teacher said. "Do you remember why we stay hidden?"

"Because of your tattoos." The boy said, pointing to the markings on the elder's hands.

The old man tucked his wrinkled skin into the voluminous sleeves of his cloak, hiding the circles inked onto the palms of his hands.

The boy slouched as they vanished. "Will I get tattoos like that soon? Dad says I will."

"You're seven years-old, my boy," the man said, amused. "Don't rush yourself, you'll learn casting soon enough."

"But," the boy sighed, "only little kids don't have tattoos. James calls me a baby because I don't have mine yet."

"Your brother is jealous." The elder said, rising from the floor with a bit of a laugh. "Don't pay any attention."

The boy hung his head.

"Do you know why our family marks themselves?"

The boy hadn't thought about why. He twiddled one seven year-old finger in his mop of dark hair. The elder drew a couple even breaths and left the front window. He hesitated before locking the library door.

"I think it is time I tell you a story our family recorded generations and generations ago. It explains why we hide, and it explains why James needs to leave you alone."

The elder took a seat behind the oaken desk in the center of the room. The boy pivoted in his seat and stared up as the grandfather opened a large leather-bound book.

"Back at the start of time God made people, and the people were thankful but didn't know how to repay him. So they prayed and asked God to speak to them and tell them what to do." He turned the first page. "And what do you think God did?"

"He answered their prayers of course!"

"What do you mean 'of course'?"

"He always answers the people's prayers in your stories," the boy answered. "I'm almost eight, Grampa, I can see patterns."

"I hope you'll grow out of that sass someday, child," the elder said. "But yes. God sent a messenger. This messenger was covered in the names of the four elements in the language of God, himself."

"Fire, Water, Earth..." The boy counted on his fingers. "... the loopy one."

"That would be Wind," the elder corrected. "And you want to cast spells, honestly."

The boy frowned. "I knew the shapes! Most kids don't learn those until magic class!"

"Calm down, son. You need to learn patience."

"But I don't want to be patient!" The boy whined. "I feel like I've been really patient already. I know I can do it if Dad would just let me."

"Hush and pay attention." The old man shook his head and turned another page. "The loopy one, hah!" The story continued. "Because he was covered in runes, the people called him the Runian. And he was the first of our people."

"So the Runians started with one man?"

"Yes, and continued through his descendants after he died."

The boy cocked his head to the side. "He died?"

"He was a mortal man."

"But... but he was God's messenger..." The seven year-old pursed his brow, lip clamped between his teeth.

His teacher smiled and softened his voice. "What a sensitive kid you are. I'm afraid you'll grow out of that too, and it'll be a shame. Don't worry, the very moment the old prophet died, a new Prophet was born with the symbols of the elements on her body just like her great-grandfather. This woman heard God, wrote letters, lived long, and died. And another child, a nephew, was born with the symbols. And so the line of Prophets continued."

"But we don't have a Prophet now," the child said.

The old man put the brush back in the ink and hesitated for a moment of indecision before bracing himself. "That's not entirely true..."

"Huh?"

He pondered his grandchild's innocent eyes. They were deep and dark with twinkles like starlight that drew the mind toward them. There was time and wisdom in the soul there, far surpassing a seven year-old's. The elder let himself fall into them, steeping like tea leaves in the bottomless well until someone jiggled the door handle, and rattled him out of the warm haze.

"Grandpa!" Another boy shouted through the lock. "I know you guys are in there!"

The elder ignored him, speaking faster. "We have not had a Prophet in many generations. This is why we mark ourselves with the elemental symbols. It lets us use magic like the Prophets used to until God to sends us a new one."

The boy glanced between the old man and the locked door. "That's James."

"Pay attention to me," his grandfather said. "What I say is more important – "

"I'm telling Dad!" The boy on the other side of the door shouted. Bare feet padded like punches up the hall.

The old man's heart raced. He leaned forward, staring deeply into his grandson's eyes. Deep. Intelligent. All-knowing. The boy backed away. "Grandpa?"

"Five-hundred years we've been waiting for a Prophet," he pressed, "but not anymore. Someone *has* been born with the symbols – "

"Jethro!" It was a man's voice this time, shouting. The door clattered like thunder against the lock. The boy on the floor didn't blink, his pupils constricted the universe beyond to pin pricks.

"Speak truth." The elder demanded in harried tones. "Does God speak or whisper? Does he come to you in dreams?"

"I – I don't – "

A key jangled in the lock. The grandfather yelled in desperation. "Speak, boy! Tell me the future!"

The door sprang open and Isaiah charged in dove for the boy on the floor. The old man rushed to intercept, but was thrown aside by the man's shoulder as he scooped his son off the floor.

The elder felt a crack in his ribs as he was laid across the desk. "Wait!"

"Don't speak!" Isaiah snapped.

The seven year-old clung to his father, sparkling eyes quaking in terror. The old man faltered. Such eyes should never be frightened. Guilt and an overwhelming sense of responsibility levered him from the desktop. "He needed to know, Isaiah. He needed to!"

"Not now."

"Look at him, part of him knew already!"

"Stop." Isaiah glared daggers into the elder and tucked the boy's head against his shoulder.

Was Isaiah hiding those eyes on purpose? The old man stood as tall as his swelling ribs would let him. "His mother would have told him."

"Shuna's not here to have a say." Isaiah dropped his voice low. "Whatever claim we men think we had on her as wife, daughter, scholar – he is still her son. She would take care of him. What you are doing is not kindness, you will change his entire life."

"The entire world."

"That too." Isaiah ran a thumb through the boy's hair. "He does not need that burden right now."

"He is a Prophet."

Isaiah's grip tightened. Joshua's did as well. Fearful whimpers punctured the silence like pinpricks. Like the lights in his celestial eyes, now undoubtedly fearful, and sad. The old man imagined the stars flickering in a cloud of tears as clearly as if he could see them.

"Selfish, stupid man. Could you not be patient for even two years more?" Isaiah's voice growled through clenched teeth. "In the name of our absent God. On the soul of the Prophet Malachai. You will not speak to my boys again."

Isaiah rushed the weeping boy from the library as the old man staggered into the chair by the desk. Joshua had heard the definitive truth. That was what mattered. The fear he caused was necessary. It was for the greater good. Still, breath hurt as he drew it, heart broken like his ribs.

James lingered in the doorway, bewildered and frightened by the intensity of raised voices. He looked so much like Joshua – so much like Shuna – yet when the old man met his youthful brown eyes they were normal. Shallow. Insignificant. The grandfather turned his back and waited for James's bare feet to pad away up before collapsing against the desktop in sobs.

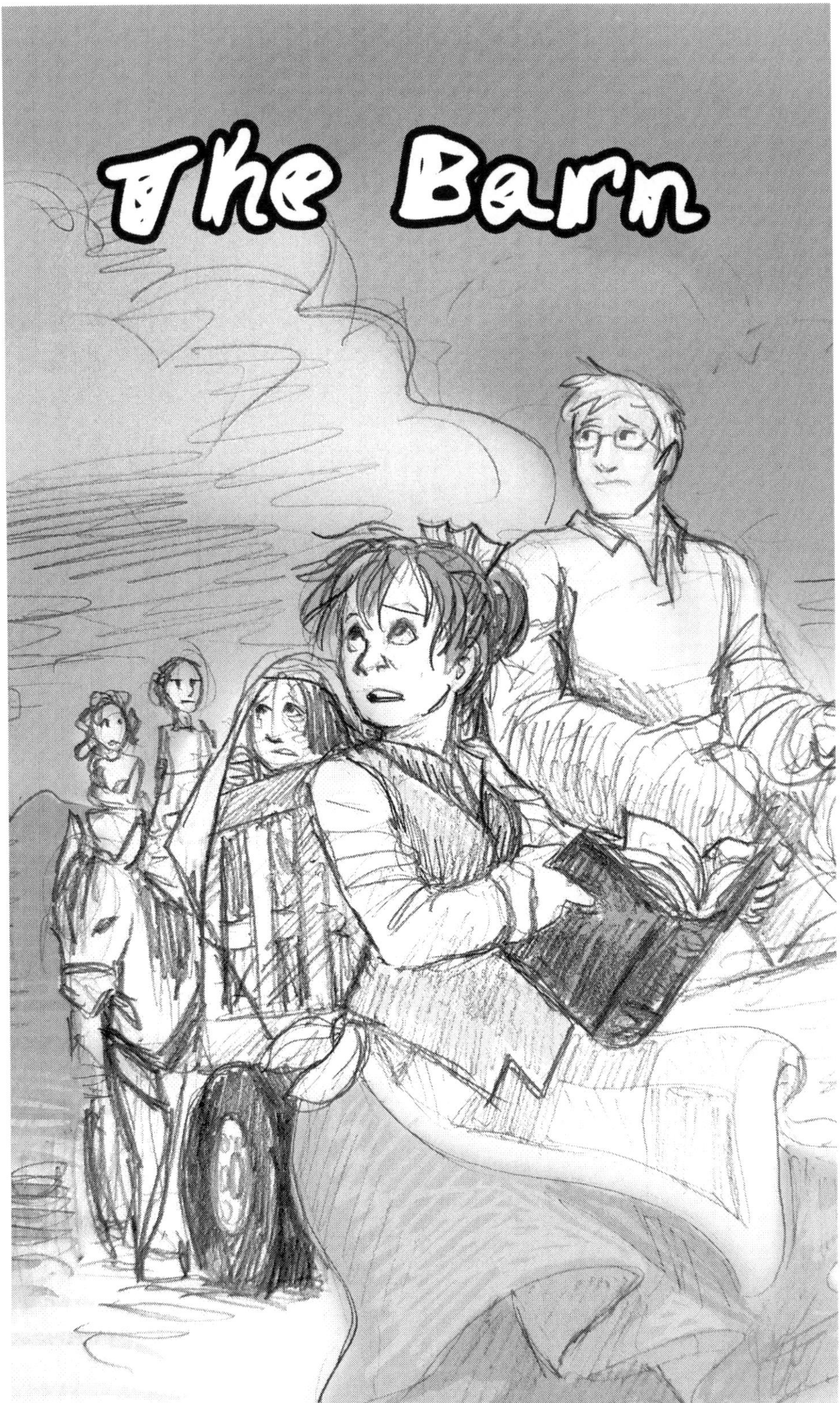
The Barn

This section is from the earliest draft of Threadcaster, way back in 2007. This first draft was written as part of National Novel Writing Month, which is a yearly challenge undertaken by authors around the globe. I did not complete the challenge that year but I did begin writing and that rushed draft revealed a lot of components that did not belong in the final version.

A couple important changes; originally Ildri's mother and younger sister joined Cat and company on their adventure. The characters names are Safara and Kindle, who later were reborn as Sharon and Kindle in Fire Curse. Calligrapher politics were more complicated. They were also fighting monks who used magic by different rules. Paige's original name was Karuka (Paige is a more on-the-nose pun). There was room for improvement on her relationship with Trace and how they used magic in the field.

Below is a slice of the past, a version of Threadcaster before all those changes happened. It is a testament to the long, evolutionary process of writing. Don't be afraid to throw yourself into imperfect first drafts. First drafts are SUPPOSED to be imperfect. You have to get your initial ideas out to make room for newer, better ideas, and having it written down allows you to edit and reevaluate what you have. So write without fear! To quote scifi novelist Michael Crichton, "Books are not written... they are rewritten." Threadcaster certainly was!

The cat's name was going to be Smokey.

The Barn

Safara surveyed the sky and urged the mule forward until she could look across into the driver's seat of her companion cart. "I don't think we're going to make it before dark."

"We'll make it. We have to," Cat said. "It's overcast tonight."

"That's a sign we're getting further south," Ildri said. "It's wetter down here."

"Is it going to rain on us?"

"Not up here, its out of season," Safara answered. "Maybe tomorrow though."

"We'll have to get out the tarps," Cat noted.

"Where are these tarps?" Ildri asked. "I want them handy."

"They're under the seat.... on the left I think."

Ildri began digging through boxes. Safara pulled her arm from under a sleeping Kindle and elbowed Aiden in the head. He jumped, throwing his hand to his crown. "What was that for?"

"Get out the cover, it could rain."

"You didn't have to give me a concussion."

"Just do it."

Ildri pulled out the tarp and suddenly flinched. She looked close at her hand, one red pinprick growing a welt on her skin. "Uh oh."

Aiden looked up from the second wagon. "What?"

"I think I felt a raindrop."

"Uh oh," Cat agreed.

Peter turned in his seat. "It couldn't have been spit or something?"

"I felt it too," Safara offered.

Aiden suddenly jumped. "Ow!"

"Dangit!" Ildri hissed, doubling her efforts on the tarp. "It's raining! Hurry!"

"Kindle, wake up!" Safara said, kicking her in the leg. Kindle jerked awake and her mother barked commands at her. "Get back there and help Aiden with the cover. It's going to rain."

"Rain? Really?" Kindle looked up at the clouds. "When'd it get so dark?"

"Kindle!" Aiden called. "My life's in danger here?"

"Oh, right." She hopped the rail and grabbed the edge of the plastic canvas cover.

Cat did the same in her wagon, tying the corners of their crinkled green tarp to the metal walls. Ildri disappeared from sight just as the rain began to pick up. Cat secured the last corner and climbed back into the driver's seat, glancing backward. "Do you have confidence in our tarp?"

"No," Peter said, his voice shaking. "It wasn't meant to be a life preserver, we didn't leave Mason Forge thinking we were going to be traveling with Fire Curses."

Cat zipped her vest to the top and folded her hands under her arms as the rain began to pick up. "What are we going to do?"

"It'll only get worse with the clouds so low." He blinked through spotty glasses. "We'll keep going until we find somewhere dry."

The drizzle gained strength, turning into a full-out downpour. Cat was drenched clean through with excess water running down her face. She hunkered down and bounced her knees, her teeth chattering in her head. Strawberry was barely visible in the dark and the wet. After thirty chilling minutes, Peter nudged Cat with his elbow and pointed with his shoulder through the dark. "Is that a light?"

"What?" Her head jerked up. Sure enough, there was a tiny fleck of yellow shining through the storm. "How far away?"

"I don't know. My depth perception's off. But not too far if we can see it through this rain."

"Thank goodness." She watched it come slowly closer over the span of another cold, miserable half an hour until the shape of the front gate was visible along the side of the road. The wagons neared the entrance of a ranch with a creaking barn and a farmhouse with lighted windows. Cat bounded down into the mud and took off at a run. She splashed through the mud puddles in a sprint toward the house. The gravel path slid under her boots, but she muscled on, as desperate to get herself and her friends out of the rain. Cat jumped the three steps to the porch and pounded on the door, her fist throwing water at impact. "Hello!?" She banged against the door, pounding with both hands. "Somebody ANSWER!"

The wagons stopped behind her, Kindle unwinding from Safara and climbing down to join Cat on the porch. Kindle hugged her arms and shook raindrops from her hair. "There has to be somebody home. The light's on."

Cat heard the door unlatch and jumped back. An old woman pulled open the door, the chain lock catching and restricting the door. The woman peered out with one glassy eye. "Who's that pounding on my door at night?"

"Please ma'am," Cat said, actually bowing to the woman. "It is an emergency. We need to use your barn."

"Barn? What do you mean barn?"

"Yes, your barn." Cat pointed over her shoulder to the wooden structure standing obviously across the yard. "That barn."

"What do you want a barn for?"

"For shelter," she said. "It's raining pretty bad out here,"

"Humph," the woman said. "The barn is full."

"Full of what?" Kindle cried.

The lady became suddenly suspicious. "Who is that!?"

"This is Kindle," Cat said quickly. "Why is the barn full?"

"Can't stay in the barn," the woman said. "Stay in the house."

"Oh... The house is good," Cat said. "But we do have animals – "

"You can't stay in the barn."

"I know. You said that," Cat told her, starting to draw conclusions about their new hostess. "You know, we've got the horse and the mule. And we've got to get our friends out of the wagons."

"Who is in the wagons?" The woman asked.

"My sister and her boyfriend," Kindle said. "They're Fire Curses."

"No Curses in my house." The woman snapped.

"But that's not fair," Cat protested. "They need shelter the most!"

"No Curses. None in my house."

"Can they stay in the barn?" Kindle offered.

"Only wagons in the barn."

"So the wagons can stay in the barn?" Cat asked.

"Wagons in the barn. People in the house. No Curses," the woman snapped.

"Then what about my sister!?" Kindle protested.

"Send them along," the woman said, closing the door, her voice trailing into the house. "Send them along!"

"But..." Cat looked to her companion, "..wait."

"You're not agreeing to this are you!?!" Kindle cried.

"No, no." Cat looked over at the wagons, imagining the shivering Fire Curses inside. "But this is desperate."

Kindle growled. Cat strengthened her composure and knocked again on the door.

It jerked open, the old woman was waiting on the other side. "Yes? Who's there?"

"We sent the Curses away. Can we stay in the house now?"

"Yes," the woman said. "Put your things in the barn. How many of you are there?"

"Three."

"Three yes," the woman said. "Put your things in the barn." The door closed, unlocked and opened again wider. "Come back in when you're ready."

"Thank you." Cat's shoulders sank and she headed back out into the rain to where Peter and Safara were waiting in their respective driver's seats.

"So?" Peter asked.

"What'd they say?" Safara finished.

"She's letting us stay, but only the non-cursed people get to stay in the house."

Safara shouted. "WHAT!?"

"I know, I hate it too," Cat said. "I wouldn't have agreed if this wasn't life or death. Let's get Idlri and Aiden in the barn and we'll talk more."

Cat and Kindle rushed to open the doors and the others parked the carts inside. Contrary to what the old woman had said, the barn was quite empty excusing a couple overfed horses and bountiful piles of hay. The girls shut the doors and ran to the backs of the wagons to free their friends. Kindle unlatched the protective casing over Aiden who bounded to his feet and out of storage in a huff.

"That took FOREVER!" He dashed straight to the second wagon. The wagon was too wet for him to touch so it was up to Safara and Kindle to peel back the tarp. Ildri poked her head up out of the dripping wagon.

Safara held up her wet hands, fighting hard not to touch her daughter. "Baby are you alright?"

"I'm okay, Mom. A little shaken up." She stood up her bare feet nearing the damp edge. "How am I getting down?"

"I've got you." Aiden held up his hands. "Don't worry, I'm the driest thing here."

"My hero!" She jumped from the cart and into his waiting grip. Aiden placed her safely back on the ground.

Safara stepped forward to pull out a suitcase. "Cat, get dry clothes. We've got to go to that house so the woman doesn't become suspicious."

"Right." Cat climbed up into the back of her wagon and pulled out a knapsack, stuffing in a change of clothes from her travel case. She handed Peter a dry shirt and pants, feeling suddenly guilty. "Hey."

He looked up to her.

"I'm sorry to make you stay out here. I feel rotten."

"Its okay, Cat. I'm not mad at you."

"You should be I'm just as bad as that old woman, or the idiot at Creven's gate. I should never have let her muscle you out here." She climbed down from the wagon. "It was only because of Aiden and Ildri. If they hadn't been in danger I would have fought harder, but I buckled. Was that the right thing to do?"

"It was the right thing," Peter assured her. "I'm proud of you. You kept your head. Two days ago you would have torn into her like an animal. You did a good job."

She shrugged. "If you say so."

"I'm always right," he replied. "And since that is my final word, I'll feel free to change the subject and ask you a favor."

She perked up a little. "Yes?"

"Could you loosen up these bandages?" he asked. "When you leave, I'll be the only non-Fire Curse here, and everything on me is soaking wet."

"Of course!" she dropped her bag and attacked the metal clasps. "Hold still."

Safara and Kindle took care of the animals and began to hang things out to dry. Aiden and Ildri climbed up on a mound of hay to watch and wait, giving their new living quarters a thorough inspection.

"This isn't so bad," Ildri observed, fluffing some hay. "Better than a dirt floor."

"If you say so." Aiden's eyes drifted along the line of stalls. Cat and Peter were hanging elastic bandages out to dry. The Fire Curse shouted across the space to him. "Hey, are you going to be nasty looking without those?"

"No nastier than you." He gave Aiden a smile. "Wait until you see me without a shirt."

Aiden returned a suspicious look. "I'll look away."

"Stop you guys," Cat protested. "You're making me feel worse."

"Hurry up!" Safara called. Cat picked up her bag and went to the door where Kindle and Safara were waiting to give their parting words. The older woman wrenched open the door. "Don't come out and if anyone comes, hide."

"I told the old woman I'd sent you all ahead," Cat said. "So you'll have to stay out of sight if she comes to check on her horses or something."

"We'll be back to get you tomorrow when the weather clears up," Safara said. "But even then the ground will probably be wet, so be careful."

"Yes, Mom." Ildri nodded.

"Remember," Kindle called. "I may be staying in the house but I don't like it! I'm totally miserable and I'm thinking about you the whole time."

Ildri laughed. "It's alright, K, don't feel bad."

Safara nodded. "Goodnight."

The mother and daughter slipped out into the rain, but Cat tarried at the door, her stomach knotting. She looked back at her friends. "Sorry again."

She shouldered her knapsack and trudged back across the yard to the house where Safara and Kindle were waiting for the old woman to answer their knock. The door pulled open to reveal the bent, wrinkled shape of the old woman. In one hand was a long cane, the other held a striped cat held like a loaf of bread. "Is that you, girl?"

"It's me," Cat answered. "And Kindle and her mother Safara."

"That's all?"

"That's all, I promise."

"Okay." The woman traced the ground with her cane and turned back into the room. "Come in then."

The travelers stepped inside the stove-warmed room. The place was dark but tidy. Cats were sitting randomly around the fireplace. The old woman spoke without looking at them as she tottered around the kitchen table and back to a faded chair in front of the fire. "Rooms through there. Two. Choose as you like. I sleep here in my chair." She eased herself down. "Mind the cats."

"Thanks," Cat said, flatly. She trudged over the creaking wooden floor toward the only hallway, leaving wet boot prints on the planks behind her.

Kindle followed her mother into their room. "What's weird about that woman, Mom?"

"She's blind, honey."

Cat chose a dusty room and shut herself inside. The place hadn't been disturbed in a decade, layers of dust on the furniture and bedclothes thick enough to see in the dim light. Cat found a matchbook by a candle and gave the chamber some light. She could see the rain through the window above the headboard. The curtains were faded to white. So was the foot of the quilt where the passing sun had traced a fan-shaped path in the mismatched colors. Cat wrinkled her nose at the thick dust on the bed and threw the quilt to the floor, scaring a out a cat and sending a thick cloud up into the air. Cat ran to the door and released the animal into the hall and gulping fresh air.

When the dust had settled again, she went about changing into dry pajamas and hanging her wet things out to dry. She wiped off the foot of the bed with the underside of the quilt and draped her soggy vestments over the wood. They soaked up the leftover dust, leaving muddy prints on her yellow shirt. She rolled her eyes and tore the comb out of her hair. "Wet clothes. Wet hair. Wet friends...." She tossed her matted brown mane over her head and scrubbed it dry. "My luck. My fault it had to rain."

Heaving a heavy sigh, she collapsed face down in the sheets. "Why me?"

It poured all night. Trace and Karuka were huddled together inside an igloo of earth, a small fire glowing in a pentagram at their feet. The girl hugged her knees tightly, her head propped against the wall of their cover. She could hear the steady pounding through the carapace and let her eyes droop. She was nearly asleep when she suddenly noticed movement by her head. A worm was wriggling its way out of the wall, its juicy little tail twitching back and forth. She screamed, threw herself across the small space, hit Trace and jumped again on reflex, squishing herself against the back wall. "Geez!"

Trace frowned at her. "What's wrong now?"

"This place is awful!"

"Learn to like it." He turned back over and got comfortable on his arm. "We'll be here all night."

Her eyes sprung wide. "You're joking!"

"No. Now go to sleep."

"I'm not sleeping in this!"

"Uggh." He groaned and curled up against his wall. "Fine. Keep watch then."

"Keep watch?"

"Yeah. Quietly."

Karuka pouted and crossed her arms. The tiny fire flickered, its heat dispersing weakly through the small room. Her toes were warm in its flickering light, but her nose and the back of her neck were cold. She missed the comfort of the Dojo.

This time of year, Karuka would escape her dormitory and sleep on the porch listening to the sound of cicadas and tree frogs. The

164

trees would help her sleep easy every night, but instead of being warm and comfortable snuggled in her bed roll on her porch, she was here, cramped, wet, miserable and in the middle of nowhere. She watched the downpour through the doorway and grumbled under her breath. "Why rain? It's a desert."

"Every desert has storms once in a while," Trace mumbled.

"It's out of season," Karuka said, sad but angry. "And its not even a thunderstorm. Just monotonous, long-winded, rain."

She paused and let the overwhelming drum roll of drops on the roof pollute her ears. Trace looked up to the ceiling then back over his shoulder. "Stop." He spoke slowly. "I can't sleep when you're talking."

She growled to herself and waited, the noise in her ears itching its way down her spine. She felt like a subject of water torture. She spoke at a whisper. "Couldn't you stop the rain?" She didn't look at her master. "Can't you make it stop?"

"Hm?" Trace muttered, his eyes closed. "I'm sorry, I can't do something that big. The Calligraphers don't work on that kind of level. The Chief Elder can redirect a river with the help of the monks. I can build us a house out of rocks. But no one can influence the whole sky with just some paint and a magic spell." He found a more comfortable position. "The planet still has some control over itself."

She balled up tighter and frowned out at the prevailing wetness. "I hate rain."

He moved his shoulder to see her face. She looked exhausted and miserable, her eyes staring solemnly toward the curtain of water. He flopped over onto his back, looping an arm around her.

She was surprised, but consented to lean on his shoulder. His body warmed her where the fire couldn't reach. It felt so good that she forgot for a moment where she was. He laid his head back on the wall and closed his eyes. Karuka closed her eyes and balled her hand next to her face, feeling sleep pass over her. "This is just because it's cold."

"Hmph." He pulled his other arm up around her back and rested his jaw on her head. Her breathing slowed to a steady rise and fall against his chest. "Whatever."

The next morning was just as dreary and drizzly as the night before. Cat stared straight out the window and groaned. "Why me?"

Thoroughly disheartened, she rolled out of bed and pulled on the pink paisley shirt and khaki dress she'd brought with her from the wagon. Yesterday's clothes were still wet, the humidity too thick for proper drying even after eight hours of sleep. She balled them up in the bottom of her backpack, pinned up her hair, and laced up her soggy boots before stepping out into the hallway as quietly as possible. The old woman was asleep in her chair surrounded by her many dosing animals. Cat tiptoed cross the creaky floor to the exit.

Puddles of water stood in the wagon ruts from the previous night, tracing four canals to the barn. Cat trudged past last night's footprints and pulled the wooden door aside, expecting the Curses inside to be asleep on the hay. Instead she saw no one.

"Peter?"

The bandages were gone from the clothesline, and Strawberry stood in the corner stall munching hay. Cat slid the door shut behind her and called again a little louder. "Peter?"

"Cat?"

His head peeked out from around the haystack. She sighed a little as he left the shadow where he'd been binding his ankles for the day. She dashed up to meet him. "There you are!"

"What? You think we split in the middle of the night?"

"That or the old woman found you and threw you out in the rain." She took the roll of elastic from him and started wrapping his wrists. "Where are Ildri and Aiden?"

"They're still asleep back there," he said. "We stayed up pretty late last night."

"You guys had a party and didn't invite me?"

"Healthy people weren't allowed. It was a barn party."

"Did you guys bond and stuff?"

"Humph." He snorted.

She smirked at him. "What? Were you talking about me?"

"No, but we did find something you should see."

Ildri appeared around the haystack, sprigs poking out of her black hair. "Who's there, Peter?"

He gestured toward his nurse. "It's Cat."

"Oh right. Up at Dawn Girl." Ildri yawned and scratched some straw off the back of her head. "How's the weather?"

"Raining," Cat answered. "I'm afraid you're going to have to hide out here a little longer."

"Oh well." She tugged Peter's red shirtsleeve. "Did you tell her about the thing?"

"I was getting to it."

Ildri grabbed Cat's arm. "You've got to see the thing!"

"Thing?"

"Maybe you'll know what it is," Peter said. "It looks like something elemental, but I've never seen it before."

Ildri led them around the hay, shaking Aiden's shoulder as she passed. "Wake up, we're gonna show Cat the thing."

"You really need me for that?" he asked. He shoved up and fell in behind Peter. "And stop calling it a 'Thing', there's gotta be a more descriptive term than that."

"A cool thing?" Ildri shrugged.

"How about a shrine?" Peter offered.

Ildri pulled aside a curtain to reveal a wooden pedestal surrounded by burning candles and shelves full of white powder. In the middle, an intricate system of shapes was drawn with thin lines of what looked like sand. At the center was a pentagram. At the center of that was the water symbol.

Cat crouched for a closer look. "Wow!"

"See?" Ildri said. "I told you it was cool."

Peter leaned in. "Do you know what it is?"

"It's salt," Cat said, sticking her finger in one of the lines.

"Well duh," Aiden said. "But what do the patterns mean?"

"I don't know," Cat said. She hovered her finger over the lines, tracing the various shapes in the air. "I feel like it's familiar but I've never seen the Brushcasters use any of these triangle type patterns before. All they ever use are circles and stars."

"So this isn't a Brushcaster thing," Peter supposed. "But what does it do?"

"It's got something to do with water," Cat said, pointing to the rune. "Maybe an irrigation system for her crops. Or maybe..." She got an idea. "Let's experiment with something. Ildri, go stand by the door and tell me if anything happens."

"Okay." Ildri moved out of sight. "Ready!"

"Here goes!" Cat used the index finger of her right hand to slowly and carefully sever one of the arching lines of salt.

"The rain's stopped!" Ildri called. "Like turning off a faucet."

"Tell me if it starts again," Cat scooted the salt back into place.

"Drizzling!"

"I knew it!" Cat bounded out from behind the hay. "That spell causes the rain!"

Aiden grunted. "The salt controls the weather?"

"That's amazing," Peter said. "That old woman's been controlling the sky from a corner of her barn! The Brushcasters can't do that."

"This must be ancient spell casting," Cat pondered. "No one nowadays can use the elements like that."

"Cat!" Ildri shouted. Her heat-tanned face was white as chalk as she stumbled away from the door. The others rushed forward and followed Ildri's finger toward the house.

Every window and door was thrown open, the curtains streaming outward like wings. The window nearest the family room took on a bright red glow, a bonfire welling up inside. They heard a young girl scream.

"Kindle!" Ildri cried.

The fire extinguished in a cloud of smoke that twisted out the front door and traced its way along the ground, snaking toward the barn. The four of them backed away from the door, confused and terrified as a blast of air shred the smoke like paper and revealed the old woman, her milky eyes staring wildly and salt trailing through the gaps between her bony fingers. "WHO IS THERE!?!" She waved her stick about in front of her. "WHO IS HERE!?"

Cat choked out a response. "Just me!"

The woman's wrinkled nose sniffed the air. "Fire Curses!" She whipped around, salt flying. "THERE ARE FIRE CURSES HERE!"

"No!" Cat cried.

"THE WOUNDS!" the woman cried. "The wounds! The dirt! The ash! CURSES IN MY HOUSE! CURSES IN MY HOUSE!" She whipped her cane through the air. "GET OUT! Get out or I'll make you a ball of flame!"

She flung her fistful of salt out in front of her. It hit Aiden in the face, burning his eyes and open sores. "Ahhh!"

Ildri reacted. "Aiden!"

"Run you guys!" Cat shoved them behind the wagon. "Get everything together! Let's go!"

Peter dashed for the stalls to free the animals. Ildri grabbed Aiden's shoulders and steered him to a wagon. Cat laced up her string and prepared to face the witch head on.

"Stay back!" she commanded. "I'll fight you!"

"Filthy!" The old woman shouted, her head clouded by fury. "Filthy creatures! Holy rain!" She grabbed another fistful of salt from the gunnysack over her shoulder and flung it about in front of her. "Drown them all!"

"Don't you dare!" Cat twisted the thread into two waves. "Water of the Earth OBEY ME!"

She hit the woman with liquid like aiming a fire hose. The old hag wailed and covered her face, the salt on the ground and in her hands turning to soggy mush. Cat stopped the flow before her strength gave out, resetting the string into her starting position. "Try it again, lady! I dare you!"

The old woman struck out with her stick, swiping the air. She reached into her bag again flung a dry spray of it in the air. Cat covered her eyes just in time.

The woman used this moment to draw up another rune. "Holy Thunder!" The barn doors clattered open. "Strike them down!" A bolt of lightning streaked in over her head. It struck the ground by the wagons. The animals reared. Ildri grabbed her mule's reigns and pulled him down, covering his eyes with her arms. No one was there to take control of Strawberry. The horse threw its long yellow mane and tore out of barn with the wagon barely strapped on. The old woman was thrown across the yard with a howl, as one barn door splintered on impact with the cart.

Cat was knocked off balance by the rush of the cart and landed face down in the dirt. She looked up in time to see Strawberry hang a right onto the road, tearing a path for Chalsiville all on her own. Cat shoved herself up and ran for the remaining wagon, summoning her friends to her. "We gotta catch her! Come on!"

"But Mom and Kindle-" Ildri stopped.

"We'll grab 'em on the way!" Cat said. "Peter!"

He heaved up into the back of the Fiammetta's wagon. Aiden, recovered from the attack, sprinted back to the salt shrine and tore the curtain from the wall. With all his strength he slammed the curtain into the rune, spreading salt and dust in all directions. He took a second swing at the shelves, glass jars toppling and shattering across the wooden plank, then continued to beat the salt and broken glass with his weapon until nothing was left intact. He threw the curtain into the middle and ran to catch the wagon. Ildri lashed the reigns across the mule's back, driving it at speed out of the barn and out into the damp yard.

Cat got ready to jump. "I'll get your family!"

"Look there they are!" Peter called.

Kindle and Safara were climbing out their bedroom window, the girl with a cat under her arm. Cat stood in the back of the wagon and waved urgently. "Come on! Come on!"

Safara shoved her daughter ahead. "Kindle! Run!"

They met the wagon at the gate. The mule made a sharp right and followed Strawberry's tracks. Cat watched the old woman use her cane to gain her feet as the wagon's speed swept them away.

Safara let out a deep sigh and looked accusingly toward the others in the wagon. "What in Heaven's name was THAT!?"

"That was the demonic possession of a homicidal maniac," Aiden snapped. "And we're lucky to have escaped with our lives!"

"We ran when the house filled with smoke," Safara said. "A wind displaced every bit of dust in the place. We couldn't breathe or see. We were lucky to make it out the window."

"We left our suitcase and all our clothes," Kindle said, but brightened and held up her arms. "But I saved this cat!"

"I'm proud of you, K," Ildri said, over her shoulder. "Even in the bleakest situations, you find something to keep you entertained."

In the mountains outside Mason Forge lay the sprawling Elemental Calligraphy Dojo. It was the pearl of the region, and the only school in the world that taught element manipulation. The buildings were constructed pagoda-style of heavy tree-trunk columns, bright white siding and red wooden shingles. The sliding doors were all open to let in the summer breeze and connect the calligraphy students with the sounds of nature.

In the main building, stood importantly above the rest of the campus. The Chief Elder paced the floor. Around him the five Elder Monks sat cross-legged, their paintbrushes propped against their shoulders. They'd been sitting at council for two days now, ever since they'd received word of the Governor's request. Trace's offhand report had greatly troubled the Chief Elder who'd set the senior brushcasters on alert and summoned his five advisors to help him handle the situation. Each Monk stood for an element and dressed accordingly. They sat about the Elder in a circle, equidistant apart. In this way they mimicked the corners of a star.

"Catrina Aston," the Chief Elder muttered under his breath as he moved along the polished wood floor. "A simple girl with extraordinary power. I wonder how much she knows."

"Hayes said she wanted to give priority to the Curses," the Wind Monk said. His black brush contrasted greatly with his white robe. "Creven claims she wants to put him out of business."

"I've met this girl," the Fire Monk said. "Ten years ago when I was only a calligrapher. She had great talent but refused to join us."

"I met this girl too," the Water Monk said. "She is friends with that Earth Curse as I recall."

"She's just following a childish fancy." The Earth Monk said, adjusting the sleeve of his green robe. "When she tires she'll return to her home in Mason Forge and everything will go back to normal."

"I'm not convinced," the Elder announced, twisting his beard in his hand.

"Master, forgive me," the Lightning Monk ventured. "But your council agrees that one voice among millions is barely a threat. It pains us to see you so worried about this report."

"It is not our reputation that makes me dwell on this," the Elder said. "Even if the people of the valley listen to her and do as she says, it matters very little to me. I know that the second a well runs dry or windmill stops turning, they will come to our doorstep for help. And as for Creven's business.... I couldn't care less."

"Then why have you kept us in council for so long?" the Water Monk pleaded. "Let this girl pass from your mind."

"I will not rest until I know her motivation," the Elder told him.

"She is more than just a girl with talent."

"Master!" a young man rushed up from the path, his Senior Apprentice-issue paintbrush slung across his back. "Master! A letter to the Aston house!"

The Chief Elder halted in his tracks and rushed to receive the envelope from the bowing messenger. "It was intercepted? The Aston family didn't read it?"

"Yes, sir. I mean No, Sir, they did not."

The Elder nodded. "Good, back to your post." The young Brushcaster bowed deeply and scurried away. The Elder tore into the envelope and read. "Hm...."

"What is it, Master?" one of the seated monks asked.

"This confirms my worst fear," the Elder answered. "She aims to change fate of the world." He glanced over the letter again. "She says she has a map and instructions on how to end the curses."

The Wind Monk leaned forward. "Does this mean what I think it does?"

"I believe so," the Elder said. "She knows."

"What shall we do?" the Fire Monk asked. "Do we stop her?"

"We must!" the Wind Monk pressed. "At all costs."

"Let's not forget our man in the field." The Lightning Monk said. "Hayes is already pursuing. We could send a message to him and give him new orders."

"Hays is ill equipped for this task." The Elder said. "He is weak. He doesn't know his true purpose. No, we need another."

"Who, Master?" the Earth Monk asked.

"I know of the perfect candidate," the Elder said, stonily. "A man both devoted and feared. Send our instructions to Torloff. Tell him to track down his old apprentice."

"Fire Curses. Fire Curses. Fire Curses. Everything smells like Fire Curses!" The old blind woman pawed at the scattered remains of her salt shrine, her wrinkled skin cut and burning from the broken glass. She worked slowly, sweeping mounds of sparkling white crystals and fractured bottles into gracefully perfect rings on the dirty wooden plank. She barely noticed the sting and she muttered incessantly to herself. "The smell of dirty bodies and oozing wounds. The smell of decay. The smell of death. It fills everything. It has ruined my barn."

"Salt caster Groa."

The woman snapped her head up at the foreign voice, pointing her ears to all corners of the barn. "Who is there!?" She stuck her hand in her gunnysack. "Speak again!"

The young man in the rafters smiled to himself. "Up here."

The blind woman tensed her arms. "How do you know me? What are you doing here?"

"I came to see you," he replied. "You weren't easy to find."

"What do you want?" she demanded. "Who sent you!?"

"Your great great great great grandfather."

The woman narrowed her clouded eyes. "What is your name?"

"Bastian."

She pondered the name, her brow furrowing deep over her wrinkled eyes.

Bastian took pity on her and answered her internal question. "You don't know me."

"Then why have you trespassed!?"

Bastian sat on the lip of the hayloft, his legs hanging down over her head. He leaned forward to get a clear view of the canvas where she was working. "I have a quad-great grandfather too. More like an uncle give or take a couple greats. You see, he died without an heir."

The story struck a dreaded chord in the old woman. She turned sickly white and tightened her grip on the salt in her bag, her voice hashing to a whisper. "Malachi."

Bastian nodded slowly, his eyebrows leveling over his piercing black eyes. "I was lucky to find you, considering you've got daughters in your ancestry. Some of your peers were very easy to find."

She steeled herself to him, withdrawing her hand from her bag and straightening as well as she could to her full height. "If you have come for revenge then take it. If I am all that's left in your game then strike me down. I could ask for nothing more."

"Apparently your guilt is as inheritable as your salt casting," Bastian said. He reached into a travel bag laying beside him and pulled out a leather notebook and pen. "No, I'm not going to kill you, calm down. I'm an observer." He flipped to a blank page. "I would have you complete that base you are building. It's the first of its kind I have ever seen." He sketched the concentric circles, his pen hovering over the spot she'd left unfinished. "Go back to work. Build your rain spell, your family has notoriously favored water."

"I'll do no such thing." She hissed.

"It was what you were going to do anyway."

"Not the point."

He lowered his voice and spoke in serious tones. The woman shrank under the weight of his aura, his pen resting solidly against the page. "Draw the rune." He growled a little in his chest. "Now."

She blanched, grabbed her salt and went straight to work. The symbol took shape with precision only possible through decades of practice. Bastian's pen followed her shapes as they formed on the ground directly below him until the arching pattern was complete. The old woman scowled to herself and reached into her satchel again. Bastian read her movements and un-clipped the shoulders of his shirt, the back fell away to reveal a swooping symbol between his shoulder blades. "Thank you, you can stop now."

"It is incomplete without the element," the woman said. "Shall it rain? Or gale? Or quake? Or storm?" She tossed salt from the hollow of her hand. "Burn the land in a column of fire?"

Bastian stretched the palm of his hand, aiming straight downward and whispering his incantation. "Holy Wind..." The pentagram on the back of his hand glowed white. "Remove all trace of this power from the world."

A column of wind welled and exploded from his palm, sweeping down and cutting between the artist and her canvas. Salt scattered in a million directions. The woman fell backward, her satchel spilling across the dirt floor. Bastian closed his eyes and concentrated. The wind blew around the space, gathering the spilled salt and broken glass up in a cyclone. Bastian funneled his hand, the tornado constricting to a column. He sent the wind spiraling out through the barn, gathering dirt and hay as it went. The column hit the doors and Bastian released his control on it, showering the courtyard in debris.

The salt caster wrenched herself from the dirt, her wrinkled face pulled in an expression of complete confusion and fear. Bastian grinned and levered off the loft, using a gush of air to slow his landing. He clomped down on the wooden stage and pulled up the flap on the back of his shirt, snapping it closed at his shoulders. He spoke to the prostrate form lying before him, his arms crossed across his chest.

"Hurry up and avenge your greatest uncle," the old woman said. "It's what you came for."

"It's really not," he said. "I came for your rune. Whether you live or die afterward is really not my problem." She bowed her head. Bastian stepped down from the platform, unstrapping the flap on his left forearm. "Holy Ground." He watched the matching pentagram on his left hand light up.

The old woman let out a startled scream as a spike of rock forced its way upward through the wooden planks, sending splinters flying. The woman reached forward, her fingers touching the six-foot spire in amazement, her spell casting shrine destroyed.

Bastian smirked and left the barn without a word.

the Hotel

Exposition is a dangerous monster. On one hand it's the writer's best friend. Being able to put ideas on paper is how we organize thoughts and express ourselves. By writing Lady Creven's explanation of the scripture, the prophets, the Curses, the purpose of magic, etc, I was able to form a clear understanding of the rules of my universe. Unfortunately it created quite the slog for the reader, and reduced my principle characters to glorified "yes men" prompting the lady for more backstory every time her paragraphs needed to break. So I moved the conversation from where it originally took place - a Catleton hotel - to the library below Lord Creven's manor, allowing me to tell the story of the past using all five senses in addition to verbally explaining the most relevant bits of information. The rest of the backstory was scattered throughout the novel like easter eggs for Cat to find on her journey. It was important for me to have written it, but just because a thing is written doesn't mean it's perfectly done.

I won't pretend the final version of the marching orders scene is the best way I could have possibly started Cat's journey, as it is still one of the talkiest portions of the book. Nor will I subject you to a recreation of that long exchange here, but I did want to include the framing elements of the old commission scene taking place with Lord (then Earl) Creven and Lady (then Countess) Orella and the hotel. This is the first draft after the zero draft used in The Barn, allowing you to see the evolution of the language, character, and world.

The Letter

Creven dusted his hands, his three servants bowing and heading back to their previous tasks. He returned to his dinner, immensely proud of himself. "Good riddance to that." The Governor picked up his fork and looked to his wife. The woman hadn't moved from her place, her head bowed nearly to her chest with graying black hair falling in strings from her elaborate up-do. He scoffed. "What's with that posture? This was a close call, you should be proud of me."

"What for?"

Creven stalled in mid bite. His wife's voice was hoarse from neglect and saturated in resentment. He lowered the fork slowly to the plate. "What was that?"

"What is there to be proud of?" Lady Creven asked, looking sidelong at him. "What is any of this wealth worth? You stopped caring about the welfare of the world a long time ago. Is all this suffering an adequate price for your own success?"

"This house and this town have been handed down my family for generations," Creven said. "Don't speak like this is my fault. I'm merely maintaining a tradition." He stuck a chunk of turkey in his mouth and shook the empty fork at her. "Besides, the planet has plenty of mileage in it, we'll die before it does, then it will be someone else's problem."

"How can you live with yourself!?" Lady Creven cried, finally coming to life and grabbing the arms of her chair. "I can barely function and you stuff yourself. My conscience gnaws at me day and night. How can you draw up contract after contract with farmer after oblivious farmer systematically claiming the whole valley for yourself? I can't sleep anymore! I can't eat! And you - you lure people into a false sense of security. You're dishing out heat and power like favors, trafficking the elements freely like you actually owned them."

He grinned smartly to himself. "I do own them."

"You do not!" She rose, gathering the black train of her dress in her hand. "You think you do but you don't! It's the blood of the very planet itself! You can't own something like that, you're not a god!"

"I'm ashamed," he said. "I can't believe you've bought into this God-blood superstition. The elements are just part of nature. There's nothing divine about them."

"That's what you think." She threw the hem to the ground and headed for the door. "Just wait, Our God will see you lose everything. Our God will take back what he's owed, and it'll be more than curses then, oh yes, you'll see wrath, and I won't be on the receiving end!"

"You wont leave me," he said, cockily. She stopped in the doorway, her stomach twisting with his words. Her husband smiled, insufferably smug. "You can't. You can't face the world out there. Even if you run from this house I know you will return." He lowered his voice. "Luxury is a fierce master."

She closed her tired eyes tightly in shame, one pale hand clenching the edge of her embroidered silk dress. She looked over her shoulder into the room, her voice again raspy and sad. "Perhaps. But it doesn't mean I have to take your fall with you." She exited to the hall. "Escape isn't the only way to resist."

He shot a defiant laugh after her and took the rest of his wine in one gulp. The hallway door closed with a clack and he sank into a slouch. "Devil woman." He reached for the rest of the bottle. "What does she have in mind? I'll bet it's got something to do with that loudmouth girl." He splashed the alcohol into his goblet, staining a trail of red across the tablecloth. Swirling the spirits, he pondered the situation. "That girl is going to try and change things? That won't last long. But if Orella gives her a tip…" He placed the wine glass back on the table. "Then… we might have a problem. I've got to deal with this."

Another servant came in from the kitchen with the dessert tray. He stopped and lifted the lid off a dish. "Rhubarb pie, sir?"

"Send a letter to that magic calligraphy school in the mountains," he commanded, waving the pie away. "Tell them to send a volunteer. I have a job for them."

The travelers recovered Peter's atlas from the wagon for a small access fee and tried to find a place to discuss their options. They both knew it was useless to try sitting in any of the restaurants and cafes they passed, it was more than evident from Cat's experience in the mansion that Curses were little more than tolerated. They walked until they found a fountain with a bench built into the outer wall. It was close to the traffic, but no one could throw them out. At that point, Peter was just glad to have a place to sit down.

"So," he said, flipping the book open to a map of the Valley, "we're dead center and it's one hundred miles to anywhere in the basin. Where do you want to go?"

Cat looked at the map in deep concentration. "You suggested a small town, where do you think is best?"

"Most the small towns are in the mountains," he answered. "Everyone else has moved here because the land is so bad. There are three or four little places on the other side of Dire Lonato if we want to head that way."

Cat leaned down over the map. "It looks pretty barren, do you think there are trees?"

"Probably near-dead ones like home," Peter answered. "The road that direction is all desert."

"Yuck," Cat said, wrinkling her nose.

He grinned at her. "Well, now's your chance, if you like trees so much we can go to Veneer. Its a big town, but its in the middle of the largest and oldest forest in the Valley."

"Wow really?" Cat marveled. "A forest? I'd love to see that."

"It's kept alive because of Water Town," he said, indicating the region. "The Water Curses live right in the middle."

"That's pretty impressive," Cat said. "I bet we can find a place out there somewhere? Are there any small towns?"

"Not on the map," Peter answered. "And it would take a couple days to get there."

"Days?" Cat's interest was instantly thwarted. "So we won't make it there today?"

"We won't make it anywhere today," Peter answered. "Dire Lonato we might make by morning if we pull another all-nighter, but I'd rather camp anyway."

"Camp?" Cat asked, uneasy. "Do we really have to?"

"Well yeah," Peter answered. "Why do you sound displeased?"

Cat fidgeted. "I'm not big on camping. Isn't there an inn on the way or a hotel or something?"

"Hold on," Peter derailed. "Are you scared? Are you scared of camping? Why haven't I heard about this sooner?"

"This isn't in the backyard or under the kitchen table, Peter," Cat insisted. "This is camping by the side of the road out in the open. There could be bandits or something."

"Bandits? Really?" Peter asked.

"Yeah, bandits!" Cat insisted. "It's a legitimate concern!"

He shook his head. "We can protect ourselves from bandits. People travel the road over-night all the time, it's perfectly safe."

She fiddled with her scarf. "Can we protect ourselves against having to use a latrine, because I'm not big on that either."

"That, you'll have to get over," Peter answered.

Cat sighed. "I'll just focus on the trees, its worth it for the trees."

"There you go." He directed her back to the map. "We should probably start right away. We will take Fourth Street out of Castleton and cross the Outer Road at this intersection here."

"Ahem, Miss Aston?"

The two of them looked up from the book to find a female stranger in a wide veiled hat and corseted red dress standing with hands folded a few paces away. She was thin to the point of emaciation and looked so out of place amid the dusty travelers that for a moment they thought she was a mirage. Cat recognized the gravel in her voice and the wealth that she wore as branching black embroidery on every inch of her gown. Cat folded the atlas onto Peter's lap and stood quickly, unsure how to react. "Lady Creven?"

The woman held up a hand to silence her and pulled an

envelope from her handbag. "We cannot speak here. I have bought you a room at the Freemont Hotel. Show the seal on this envelope and they will let you in. Break it when the doors are locked."

She gave the paper to Cat who held it in both hands. "Okay?"

"More is written inside," the woman said. She turned to Peter with a look of awe. "This must be the Earth." She reached slowly out to him, hand shaking slightly. "To think – a mortal man surviving while his blood turns to dust, you truly are an amazing thing." He drew away from her hand, she snatched it backward and rested it on the clutch of her bag. "Do as I ask and we'll meet again." She gazed longer on Peter, then walked away like a wraith in fog.

Cat looked to Peter. "That was the Earl's wife."

"The Earl's wife?" he repeated, looking paler than usual. "Why did she come looking for us?"

"I don't know," she said. "What do you think we should do?"

"As she says I suppose," he replied.

Cat looked to the envelope. "Do you think its safe?"

"It's an unusual situation," he said. "But a hotel isn't camping."

"That it's not." She pulled him to his feet. "And its free."

"Free is good."

"I don't know," Cat said warily.

"Don't worry about it," Peter consoled. "If anyone comes by I'll scare them off."

Cat pulled Peter to his feet and they headed off into the city again. According to the map of Castleton Peter had in his atlas, the Freemont Hotel was on the north side of town separate from any of the major streets or entrances and as they picked their way closer, it was obviously one of the wealthier places to stay. The building had an elaborate wooden facade with a veranda, garden, and private stables for its well-to-do clientele. The lobby was done up in grand fashion with inlaid wood and velvet chairs full of patrons who looked up in repulsion when they entered. Thankfully it appeared the receptionist was expecting them.

"Miss Aston?" The uniformed rushed quickly to the door.

"Yeah, hi." Cat presented the sealed envelope. "We got this?"

"Yes of course." The woman nodded, quickly. "The lady called ahead. Please this way."

Without another word, the two travelers were rushed down the hall and ushered into a cushy suite with an armchair by the fireplace and private bath. The woman bowed quickly, avoiding eye contact with them both. "Your things are on their way up and your horse is already in our stables, miss, free of charge."

Cat was overwhelmed. "Uh, thanks."

"Of course, miss," the receptionist said. "I'll return now, thank you very much." She bowed in haste and dashed away leaving the two travelers standing dizzy in the middle of the room like they'd been caught in a whirlwind and left spinning where they stood.

Cat noticed the letter in her hand and recovered her bearings. "Well, shall we?"

Peter stared at the elegant décor and nodded. "Lock the door."

"Right." Cat took the key from a nearby side-table and secured the door before dashing to the double bed and hopping up onto it as Peter sunk the mattress beside her. She tore open the envelope, the plaster seal splitting cleanly when she broke the wax. Inside was a single paper folded in half. Cat flipped it open:

'Stay here for the night. I will visit this room tomorrow with more instructions. -Countess Orella Creven'

Cat gaped at the handful of words. "What, that's all?"

"This is getting kind of spooky," Peter said. "I feel we're on a scavenger hunt, how much you wanna bet she shows up tomorrow with another envelope telling us to meet her somewhere else?"

"I hope it's in our new cottage with free running water," Cat said, rising and pacing. "Or maybe this is our one night of luxury before she turns us in."

The lock turned again. Cat sprang to her feet as a tiny maid entered with a covered pushcart. "Evening Miss, I was told to bring some amenities to make your stay with us more comfortable." She noticed Peter and squeaked. She turned on her heel and hurried out of the room. "G'night Miss."

Cat waved to the door as it locked behind her. "Good night, small frightened lady."

"See?" Peter dragged himself over. "The mere sight of me sends people running."

"At least she left food." Cat pulled the cover off the tray to reveal bowls of fruit and stacks of sandwiches with a pile of fancy tarts on the side. "Wow."

Peter nodded. "This is the best kidnapping ever."

Cat woke the next morning with the sun. The sky out the window held a pink and gold dawn with birds chirping in the flower garden just outside. Peter was still sleeping in the armchair nearby, his glasses on a side table and his un-bandaged arms hanging down to either side. Cat flipped her shoulder-length hair out of her face and tiptoed to the bathroom to change clothes.

The hotel washroom was twice as big as hers had been back home. She pulled on the same dusty blue skirt and vest from the day before, taking a moment to wind her trusty string over the billowy yellow sleeve that covered her left wrist. She took her antique comb off the sink and watched the mirror as she ripped knots out of her hair before securing it all up in a sloppy bun.

The faucet ran spring water, frigid cold. It shocked her awake as she washed her face with it. It was also deliciously pure and clean. She realized quickly this was probably the legendary free water running out of Creven's mansion, so when she was done washing and drinking, she left the faucet on full blast and turned turned the bathtub on to drain out of spite.

Peter was yawning awake when she re-entered the main room to put on her boots. "What time is it?"

"Sunup," she answered. "Sleep well?"

"About normal." He stretched. "Oh my aching self."

"Is it at least better than yesterday?" she asked, pulling on socks and buttoning her traveling boots up the sides.

"Yeah, it beats sleeping in that wagon," he admitted. "Although it would be nice to have been home."

"Yeah," she agreed, a little sadly.

He balanced his glasses on his thick wrist and slid them on with practiced ease. "Do I hear water running?"

"Oh, yes." Cat retreated in to turn off her revenge. "My mistake. You want some breakfast?"

"In a minute, I gotta do this." He grabbed a roll of elastic bandages off the table and bent forward to loop it around his foot.

He had a method that worked around his the physical limitations, but wrapping up his legs got harder every day. Cat walked over and sat on the ottoman. "I'll do that, it'll go faster."

"Okay." He tossed her the roll he was using and grabbed another to start on his arms. Cat wrapped him up good and tight, putting extra layers at the ankles, and secured the elastic wrap at his knee before moving to the other foot. There was a knock at the door so she handed him the rest of the roll to finish by himself and answered it. "Hello?"

It was the same maid as the night before. "G'morning, Miss. Did I disturb you?"

"No, what is it?" Cat asked, hoping it was waffles.

"You have a guest waiting for you in the lobby," she said.

Cat looked back over to Peter who'd stalled halfway up his right arm. She turned back and nodded to the woman. "Thanks."

"Very good, Miss."

Cat closed the door. "She's early. I gotta brush my teeth."

"Lucky you're an early riser," Peter said, levering out of the chair. "I never expected her to come at dawn."

"Yeah no kidding." Cat rushed back out and tied the checkered sash around her waist. "Are you ready?"

"Ish?"

She looked up to give him an inspection. "Here." Cat climbed up on the bed and smoothed down his blond hair in back. "Good enough."

Lady Creven was waiting for them in the lobby wearing an extravagant lace dress and veil. She nodded as they approached. "Good morning Catrina."

Cat gave an awkward curtsy. "Lady Creven."

"Orella, please," the lady bade. "Should I address you as 'Your Honor', Miss Aston? You're the first Prophet in five-hundred years."

"Please don't." Cat said. "I'm stressed out enough."

"And you, sir?" the lady addressed Peter with a cordial tilt of her head. "How was your rest?"

"Just fine," he said. "Best I've had in a while, actually."

Orella paused a somber moment. "That's good to hear."

The receptionist was standing guard at the front door. He unlatched it quickly to permit a young man. Cat recognized him as the brown-haired attendant from the Lord's Manor. He bowed awkwardly. "All's ready, Ma'am."

"Thank you, Matthew," Orella said. She took a nervous breath and returned to her guests. "I've handled your affairs, my assistant will see you safely out of town. I regret I cannot see you myself..." She checked the time and pulled another envelope from her handbag. "Here are your instructions. Do not use my name or make any attempt to contact me here. There are many very important and very powerful people who don't want God to come back... ride fast to stay ahead of their suspicion and tell no one who and what you really are."

Cat took the envelope, wholly overwhelmed. "But what if we need your help?"

Lady Creven patted her hand. "Try your best not to." She donned a wide brimmed hat at turned to the nervous receptionist. "Call me a cab please, hopefully my husband won't question my absence." She touched both Cat and Peter on their shoulders with a blush on her high cheekbones. "Good luck. Peace and great love to you both." She gathered a bag and slipped out through the front door without a word.

Matthew led the two of them toward the back of the hotel and out to a private stable she hadn't seen from the street. There Strawberry waited with their stuff packed and ready to go. She stepped forward and pressed her nose to the center of Peter's chest. "Hey girl." He rubbed his hand on her neck. "You're a surprise."

"The attendant said you incurred a fine." Matthew said. "That'll be ten dollars."

Cat frowned. "The lady said she took care of that."

"She meant the hotel tab," he answered. "This place is hers. The fine is her husband's."

Cat pulled their money from her pocket and squared up their bill. Matthew pocketed it greedily and ushered them in. "In back please, Your Honor. Leave the rest to me."

She gave Peter a shrug and the two took their seats. The young man at the reins stood with a salute.

"None of that!" Orella bade. "Take us to the West Gate."

"Yes ma'am," the attendant said. "Er.... I mean sir."

Lady Creven invited Cat and Peter with her into the back as

Matthew pulled them all off down the hill. The quaint houses and shiny copper irrigation pipes made the adventure feel more like a country stroll as the Lady sat convincingly like a posh Castleton aristocrat with both hands on her walking stick and back extremely stiff. The wagon pulled left and into the warehouse district where farmers and field hands were hard at work delivering produce to storage sheds. Other workers sorted the goods into larger wagons bound for sale in the other towns of the Valley.

The pack neared the west gate checkpoint and drew to a stop. Matthew helped Cat and Lady Creven down but let Pete move himself with a touch of nervous tension in his eye.

"I'm afraid this is where we part." Lady Creven pressed one of her crisp white envelopes into Cat's hand. "I wish I could spare more. Do not open it until you are safely out of the city... I can't risk further implication." She took both Cat's hands in hers. "There are some in this valley who don't want God back. They'll do anything to stop you – don't give them that chance. Go fast and quiet then return back here. I will leave Matthew at the Freemont Hotel. Bring the four Curses there as soon as you can."

"Don't worry." Cat nodded.

Lady Creven drew a deep breath and touched both of them on the shoulder. "Good luck."

She and Matthew took off in separate directions, mingling seamlessly into the crowd. Cat glanced down at the note then up at Peter with a wincing smile. "Well... I guess that would be that."

The two climbed in the front seat and took off for the wall. The same man was tending his post at the gate. He took note of their wagon number and ushered them through. "Hope you enjoyed your stay."

Cat saluted him sarcastically and pulled out of town.

Night fell on Castleton as well, its tenants leaving the streets as the sun did and leaving the city quiet as if it, itself had gone to sleep. At the top of the hill, the lord and lady of Castleton were in their drawing room taking wine before bed. The countess sat straight and poised, reading a book of poems silently as her husband swilled alcohol in the seat behind his over-sized desk.

The earl eyed his wife suspiciously. "The guard at the third gate tells me that Aston girl left town this morning."

His wife did not move.

"I suspect." He paused for a dose of spirits. "You, had something to do with it."

"Why would you suspect that?" she asked, shortly. Her eyes did not leave the page.

The earl studied her. "And I hear you visited the library."

She turned a leaf and returned a sharp retort. "Is that a crime?"

"No." He said. He swirled the red liquid in his glass, gulped all that was there and stood, voice raised in sudden anger. "You told her, didn't you!?"

Orella flinched at his outburst, but hardened herself against it and pretended to read on. "I have no idea what you're talking about."

"You did!" he raved. "You told her everything!"

"Dear, you're shouting."

"Damn right, I'm shouting!" he cried. "Do you realize what you've done!?"

"Yes!" She cast the book aside. "Yes and I'm glad of it!"

"When did you get so bold!?" he said, charging around the desk. "If she succeeds in your little religious crusade she'll destroy everything! She'll break the very foundation of mankind! It'll be a dark age of pestilence and poverty and death!"

She rose, standing taller than he by a head. "With Our God among us we need fear nothing!"

"Our God!?" He laughed. "Ha! Our God is dead! We killed him ourselves five-hundred years ago!" He threw back his head to look her in the eye. "What you've done here won't bring him back, all you're going to do is ruin us. Yes that's right, us. You'll be in the poorhouse too, Orella. We'll be penniless, and Your God knows you didn't marry me for my looks. You've doomed yourself."

"I deserve it!" she announced, voice strung with righteous conviction. "I deserve punishment for staying quiet all these years, but I've corrected that now. Perhaps Our God will pardon me for that. You though, Orson, deserve everything you'll receive, your sins were the soil feeding mine."

"You have no idea what you're dealing with, woman." The earl growled. "I will see this Aston girl stopped at all costs. You see, I know a certain order of mountain calligraphers who will agree with me heart and soul."

Lady Creven was taken aback. "The Holy Calligraphers are servants of Our God!"

"Sure they are," he said, pulling pen and paper from a desk drawer. "We'll just see about that. When they learn what you've started they'll come at this in full force and that'll be the end of it. What's one girl against all the powers of nature?"

The countess was shaking, her hands clutched into white fists. "If it is Our God's will, it cannot be stopped!"

"Our God has no say in the matter." He scribbled furiously across the paper.

Overwhelmed, his wife could stand it no longer. She gathered her embroidered dress and dashed from the room. "I'll be in my chambers praying for your wicked soul."

"Yeah you do that." He spoke over the slam of the door. He flourished his signature on the letter, tucked it in an envelope and sealed it with his official crest, then he rang for his manservant.

The man appeared in his uniform blue waistcoat and wig and bowed to his master before taking the envelope.

"Make sure that reaches the mountain monastery before sunup," the earl said. "It's extremely important."

The man bowed again. "Yes, sir." He turned to leave but the Earl stopped him short with one more request.

"Oh, and my wife is in her chambers." He poured more wine. "Lock her in."

The servant gave a third bow. "Yes sir."

One of the wisest lessons for authors to learn is to "Kill your Darlings." A "Darling" in this context an be anything from a stretch of dialog to whole characters and places occupying the pages of a story solely for emotional reasons. There is nothing wrong with loving the things that you make, but nothing in a story is immune from pulling its weight. Often Darlings stick around much longer then they're needed, complicating the story causing problems with the pacing or plot. I had a lot of elements in Threadcaster that stuck around far later into the game than they should have simply because they had always been there, and I couldn't imagine the book without them.

I've already mentioned in this anthology the characters Sharon and Kindle. They were in the original outline back in 2006 and persisted through name changes, age shifts, and revision after revision until 2011 when they were finally written out. The bits of the story they occupied dragged. Their presence displaced the main characters or created a repetition with other characters later on in the book yet it didn't occur to me that perhaps they, themselves, were the problem. When I got rid of them, everything fell into place.

Sometimes it's hard to get rid of something you worked so hard on for so long, but when you refuse to kill your darlings you'll never know how much better a work can be when you are brave enough to let go.

The following is a selection of scenes featuring Sharon and Kindle in several incarnations of their characters. The first scene is the introduction of these two characters. It is also the scene that stayed in the book the longest in one form or another. Compare it and its two companion pieces to the version existing in Threadcaster and I hope you'll agree that my decisions were the right ones.

Ferry to Bren

A forest of grabbing hands seized Cat from all sides and carted her off. The surrounding rooftops were empty with no sign of dark strangers or anyone coming to help her.

They dragged her past the sign for the Fiammetta's inn. Cat spotted faces in the front window just before the door burst open and a middle aged woman in a headscarf and curls rushed down the steps. Cat was grabbed by the arm and wrestled away from her captors. The spell caster fell to her knees on a musty, foot-worn antique carpet. The polished floor was dusty and covered with visible burn marks. The hooded woman locked the door and pulled Cat up by the arm. "Alright, Girl, what's with the magic?"

"What?" Cat's mind flashed back to the man on the roof, unsure she'd been dreaming. "I didn't-"

"I saw you!" The woman shook her. "And that Curse you were with - explain yourself!"

A brick crashed through the living room window to their left. The woman swore again and charged deeper into the house. The halls were lined with yellowing wallpaper and faded paintings. Cat caught glimpse of a loom and thread through an open door.

"Cat!" Edana met them on the steps.

The tall woman with a loose white scarf locked the door

"Wait!" Edana shouted. "What about Mommy!?"

"Stay back, little one - she's saving you both."

Edana dashed to the front room and plastered her face to the window. Cat followed leaving the strange woman with her hand on the doorknob. The crowd was taking Isolde prisoner. The men started pounding on the door. "Open up, Sharon!"

"Get off my property, Richard!" the woman in white barked.

"She's a heretic and a criminal!" the man yelled. "We're taking her to the Calligraphers!"

"Your shop's still on fire!" Sharon yelled. "Take care of yourself! Leave the magic user to me!"

"This isn't one of your Curses, that girl is dangerous!" he shouted back.

"That's for me to judge!"

Edana pressed her wounded hands against the glass and began to cry. Cat bent and took the young Curse in her arms. Edana face burned where the tears rolled, she buried her face in Cat's yellow sleeve. Her skin was dry as paper and feverishly warm. Cat held her lightly and glared at the woman hunting the hallway. "We could have done something."

"She's buying us time." Sharon stormed over and placed a hand on Edana's back. "We have to go now, little one."

"Go?" Edana asked.

Cat frowned. "Where are we going?"

"Out of town." Sharon took Edana's hand and peeled her from Cat's side. "I'm taking this girl to Fire Town while it's safe. There's no telling what the Brushcasters will do when they get here. You're lucky to have sympathetic friends - when Kindle gets back with your rock monster we're leaving."

Cat's stomach clenched with horror and guilt. She sprang to her feet. "You've seen Peter? Is he okay!?"

"Mom!"

A screen door clattered within the house. Sharon dropped Edana's hand and rushed from the room. Cat followed to the kitchen where a young girl in a pink hood was struggling to yank Peter up the stairs. He struggled for steadiness against her yanking but all his limbs were as she left them. Cat felt weak with relief. "Pete!"

"Cat!?" He relaxed and let Kindle coax him into the house. Cat elbowed her aside and held tight to his chest. He blanketed her in his arms. "What happened? Are you okay?"

"Fine - I'm fine!" she answered. She stepped from his embrace for a better look. "Are you hurt?"

"Nothing serious," he replied.

"You're welcome by the way." Sharon's fifteen year-old daughter smiled and pulled her pink scarf down to fluff her mane of brown curls. "That was intense! Edana saw you guys through the window and -"

"Thank you so much!" Cat cut her short with a fevered handshake. "You saved his life! I don't know what I'd do..."

"H-hey!" The teen smiled. "My pleasure - really!" She used both hands to stop the shaking. "I'm Kindle by the way. Your friend is just awesome! Where'd you find him!?"

"No time, Kindle," Sharon said. "Get the wagon, we're leaving."

"What? Now?" Kindle asked. Another brick shattered the dining room window beside them. Kindle elbowed. "Never mind. Not safe. Climb in the wagon, we're escaping!"

"From what and to where?" Peter asked. "Did the golem get killed? Tell me what's happening!"

Cat patted his shoulder. "I'll explain to you later. Right now we're outrunning a mob."

"We're doing what!?" he cried.

A musty mule cart was waiting in a garage at the back of the house. Sharon put Edana in the back of the wagon and Kinde ran to a pair of massive wooden doors. She hooked her shoulder under the latch and used her legs to lift it. Cat pulled Peter up with her into the back and sat beside him, Edana trembling under one arm.

The sound of the mob filtered in through the walls. Kindle dragged the heavy door open revealing miles of rough desert and the mountains beyond. "Drive!"

Sharon lashed the mule hard and sailed out into the desert. Kindle jumped aboard as it past, joining Cat in the cluster of Curses. The mob stopped at the wall in frustrated defeat.

in the first draft, Sharon and Kindle followed Ildri out of Fire Town and stayed with the party throughout. When I realized they were taking valuable character development time from my heroes, I decided to delay them so Cat, Peter, Ildri, and Aiden could have a bonding moment without them interfering. This is how Sharon and Kindle's inclusion looked in the second major revision.

Chase Across the Desert

Cat, Peter, and Fire Curses Aiden and Ildri were traveling away from Dire Lonato. Ildri tried to hold it together, feeling sad but being strong when a rattling noise drew everyone's attention. It got louder and louder as a plume of pale smoke rose into view behind them.

Sharon Fiammetta's old mule cart bounced and clattered as if it would break. Ildri latched on to Aiden's shoulder in near terror as they approached. "What is she doing!?"

"Chasing you," Aiden said with a roll of his eyes.

Peter braked to a stop and waited for the hellish clamor to catch them. The old mule was soaked and foaming at the mouth. Sharon dropped the rein and leaped onto the dusty road. "Ildri! Ildri! Thank goodness!"

"Mom!" Ildri drew back but was snatched down from the wagon and into a pinching embrace. "Why are you here?"

Sharon held her at arm's length, eyes wide and red, face lined and sallow like she'd aged ten more years. "Are you hurt?"

"No." Ildri shrugged away from her mother's petting. "I'm fine."

"Thank goodness we made it in time!" Sharon stroked her scarred face with one shaking hand.

"Ildri!" Kindle braked the poor mule from the back of the wagon and joined her mother on the ground, "I'm so glad to see you!"

"Oh no, her too?" Aiden groaned.

"Kindle." Cat climbed down to meet the cart. "What are you doing here?"

"We came for Ildri," the thirteen year-old replied. She rushed from the cart to her sister's side. "Are you sure you're okay?"

"I'm fine," Ildri insisted. She pulled Kindle into an embrace. "I'm glad to see you."

"We brought more gauze," Kindle replied. "And new clothes and scarves. Mom's wagon was still full."

Ildri gaped. "You followed from Fire Town?"

"What about Fire Town!?" Aiden cried. "You rode off with their supplies!"

"Don't worry, Cat left them a miracle, remember?" Kindle turned to the young spell caster with hands folded in prayer. "Don't send us away, Cat! You're the most amazing person I've ever met - I want to help you recruit Curses!"

"Kindle!" Sharon said aghast.

"I feel like I've waited my life for this!" Kindle insisted. "All this time looking after Ildri and doing research – it's like we were meant to be a team! Please, Cat, I'm begging you!"

Cat stared uncomfortably into the thirteen year-old's pleading brown eyes. Ildri nervously bit at the dead skin on her lip. "They are my family, Cat." The spell caster looked over with one chestnut brow arched. "We need all the help we can get, right?"

Aiden stood in back. "Hold on!"

"She has a point," Peter said hesitantly. "Considering our next member is a Water Curse, we could use another wagon..."

Kindle gasped. "Really!?"

"Not so fast," Cat warned her. She flitted an eye to Sharon. "This isn't a vacation. You know what's at stake if you two come along..."

"I'm here to protect my child," Sharon said. "No matter what."

Ildri paused a moment in pity. "That's good enough for now."

"Il, honestly," Aiden joined her. "They'll just slow us down."

She put her hand on his shoulder. "Is that such a bad thing?"

Cat heaved a sigh and sent Peter a longing look. "Okay, let's go."

Cat and the Fire Curses loaded back up. Sharon and Kindle did the same and the two wagons pulled back onto the road. Plains of dry grass stretched like a woolen blanket toward the mountains dotted with the occasional abandoned farm house or broken bits of an old fence. It was late into the evening by the time they reached the campsite at the intersection of the Outer Bend and the southern road. Peter stopped near a copse of dead trees. "We're here."

Sharon braked and turned with a fierce look. "What do you think you're doing?"

"Camping," Peter replied shortly.

"No you're not!" Sharon stood in her wagon with a decisive scowl. "It's not safe out here."

"It's dark, it's fine," Cat answered. "Everyone's exhausted, we'll sleep a bit and be off in the morning."

"No," Sharon said, acidly. "We use the cover and get to the southern forest."

"The forest is another five hours away!" Cat protested.

"So we leave now!"

"No!" Cat rocked the wagon as she stood. "I'm in charge, here. If I say we rest, we rest!"

"You're naive and selfish." Sharon cut her short with a snarl.

Cat's face flushed. "Why you - !"

"These Curses are dying for you; you owe them every living breath," Sharon spat. "They can sleep in the wagon. You can rest when they're dead."

Cat's blood ran cold. She sank back to her seat as Sharon lashed her panting mule and moved off down the southern road. Cat kept a bleary eye on the trailing end of her wagon and followed subserviently through the dark.

Cat awoke beneath a canopy of distant branches. The naked boughs clawed at the mid-morning sky, dappling the sunlight in patches across her face. The two wagons were parked between the silver-barked old-growth forest and the unevenly-stacked stone wall around Chalsie-Veneer. Cat vaguely remembered camping here. She dragged her head up from Peter's shoulder and met Ildri's red-rimmed eyes. "Morning."

"Morning." The Fire Curse whispered. She and Aiden were tucked beneath a woolen blanket at the foot of the wagon. She nodded to Peter propped against the front benches. "You two okay?"

"Yeah." Cat reluctantly pulled herself up off her human pillow. "It was a long night. What about you guys?"

"We had it easy," Ildri replied. "I'm sorry about Mom. She's got a strong will."

"No kidding." Cat yawned. "Is she around?"

"She went to check the town," Ildri replied.

"Ever diligent," Cat sighed. "I guess that's what it takes to take care of Curses."

Kindle appeared at the foot of their bed with with her dark hair up in a messy bun and her blue scarf tied as a sash around her waist. "Morning!"

Aiden jumped awake. The motion stirred Peter who dropped his arms from the benches on either side. Cat gave their unwelcome alarm an impatient look. "Kindle."

"What do you think of my outfit?" Kindle posed glamorously. "I'm calling it mountain chic - only the cool people wear it."

"Them and all of Mason Forge," Cat grumbled. "You look like my mom."

"I think it's a compliment," Ildri said with a wink. "You wanna be Cat when you grow up, Sis?"

Kindle blushed. "Can I get you guys breakfast?" She grinned at Ildri. "I made it clumpy like you like it."

"Sounds great, Kindle." Ildri climbed down and drew Aiden with her. "I could use a hot meal and a little time to stretch. I feel like we've been sitting for ages."

"No kidding." Peter propped himself on the bench with trembling effort.

Cat winced in sympathy. "How's your back?"

"Stiff." He replied. "Calcifying."

"Climb out, let me look at it." She coached. He scooted and lowered down with an audible grunt.

"I'll help!" Kindle clamped on to his arm with a tug.

Peter grimaced and shrugged her off. "I can do it." He straightened with a grimace and a troubling cascade of popping joints.

Cat walked around and pressed her palm to lump she discovered the previous morning. It had doubled in size, occupying a visible spot between his shoulder blades. "We should have camped last night. This is horrible."

"You're being dramatic," he said flatly.

"I'm being concerned." She rubbed the spot comfortingly, "You sure you don't want me to run a bandage around it?"

"No," He said quickly, "I can still feel my legs, it's fine."

"Wow! You're growing more stone?" Kindle pressed in for a better look. "Will a bandage slow it down?"

"They're for the ache." Cat answered. "Pressure helps."

"I never thought about aching." Kindle turned her attention to binding on his arm. "Does it ache all over or just at the joints?"

"Kindle," Peter said. "I warn you, I'm not a morning person."

"I just want to help." The thirteen year-old ran a finger under the bandage at his elbow. "Do you rebind them every morning or -" She accidentally dislodged the metal clasp on his arm. The elastic bandage sprang immediately out of place and coiled loosely around his wrist.

Peter groaned. "Kindle..."

"Sorry!" Kindle was mortified. "I can fix it! Let me -"

"Just stay back, he's not your toy." Cat reprimanded. "You okay?"

"Fine." He shook the elastic loose from his patchwork sleeve. "Hand me that..."

"I'll do it, hold still."

Kindle watched Cat gather the fallen bandage and flurry it up his arm with practiced speed. Cat started in the palm of his bandaged hand and stretched the elastic tight. Peter winced as she went, hurting in both body and pride. She ran out of bandage at his bicep and held a hand to Kindle. "Clasp?"

"Oh," The thirteen year old placed the piece of metal in her hand and bowed her head.

"It's okay, sis, he's not mad..." Ildri cooed up at Peter. "Right?"

"Mmmm..." He pressed his lips and waited for Cat to secure the bandage. "Sure."

"See?" Ildri patted her on the head. "It's okay..."

"I'll um... I'll go get that oatmeal." Kindle hurried away.

Aiden crossed his arms. "I told you they'd be trouble."

"She means well." Ildri said compassionately. She stepped close to Peter and lowered her voice. "She wants so much to help you, Peter, I can tell she really admires you."

"Nah," He dismissed. "She only likes me for my body."

"Here." Kindle reappeared with three bowls of oatmeal balanced along the length of her arm. "These are for you and..." She peered apologetically up at the Earth Curse.

"Girl!"

Sharon's shrieking voice preceded her. She stopped at the edge of the gathering and glanced around. "What are you doing?"

"Breakfast." Cat answered between bites. "Problem?"

"Yes!" She snapped. grabbed Cat by the arm. "Follow me!"

The two women hurried to the shelter of the trees and onto the gravel road. The Curses followed as far as the treeline, watching with interest as Cat and Sharon peeked around the wall and through the open town gate. Kindle whispered across the yard, "What do you see!?"

"Chalsie-Veneer. We are camped outside one of the largest cities in the Valley mere feet from the last body of standing water and a town full of people who leak." Sharon replied. "Yes, I have a problem."

"Cat can't help those things," Ildri appealed.

"It's okay, she's right." Cat swallowed and placed her bowl on the runner. "You good Pete?"

"I'm with you until the end..." Peter smiled, "Assuming I don't have to jump, run, crawl, climb or get in boats."

"Kindle?" Cat asked with a forgiving smile. "You can still come if you want to."

"You bet!" She cried. "We'll pick up a Water Curse so much faster with me along!"

"You most certainly are not!" Her mother snapped.

"Come on, Mom - Water Curses! This is amazing!"

"I forbid it!" Sharon cried, "I'm already losing one daughter to this adventure. I'm not risking two."

"Pfft! It's fine!" Kindle loaded in next to Peter, bouncing with bottled glee. "Come on, Cat! Drive!"

After the second revision attempt did not solve my problems, I broke out the ax. I eliminated Kindle first, giving what few narrative jobs she had to the other characters. I also decreased Sharon's involvement to the bare minimum -- going as far as knocking her unconscious with heat stroke to make her shut up. All this was to preserve the scene after Ildri's death, which you'll read in this section. This was the darling that was so hard to kill, but once I figured out that I could, I was able to write Sharon out completely. What a relief.

A Tragic End

The dead trees around Mason Forge were nothing compared to the towering splendor of the Southern Wood. The wagons were spent the night wedged together into one of the many empty camping spots along Chalsie-Veneer's outer wall. Cat knew the place was impressive, even in the dark, but as dawn light lanced down through the crowns of naked branches she was able to see the full extent of it's enormity. Thirty-foot trees with peeling gray bark scraped at the sky above their small campsite with hundreds more like them in every direction. Cat watched the wind stir the canopy from the back of her wagon with her head on Peter's shoulder. She could hear him breathing shallowly, stirring in his sleep. He smelled like turned soil; it reminded her of camping in the woods behind their house when all the trees felt giant and magic was still fantasy.

Her pillow snored a bit and pressed his to her forehead. She could feel the lumps growing just under the skin and clung tighter.

Sharon's mule snorted and nosed a bowl on the ground near its cart where Sharon Fiammetta was still sleeping soundly. Ildri moved around their campsite on tiptoe. Cat heard her empty the last of their canteen into the mule's bucket and pulled out of Peter's embrace. "Morning, Ildri."

"Morning." The Fire Curse said wearily. "Sleep well?"

"Well enough." Cat slid to the edge of the wagon and climbed out. "How's your mom?"

The Fire Curse glanced to the bed of her mother's wagon with a sigh. "It's heat stroke. I see it all the time in Fire Town; kids playing outside without their scarves, sixteen-year-olds taking a turn for the worse." She took a moment to adjust her lavender headpiece. "Of course I've never had to treat my own mother before."

"You're doing fine," Cat assured her. "Any way I can help?"

"You can buy us more water." Ildri held out the empty canteen. "This is Chalsie-Veneer so they should have plenty for sale. If you can find a vender this early – "

"Or I could just make some." Cat snapped of her string.

"Or you could make some." Ildri blushed and pressed her wrist to her forehead. "Sorry, I guess it's been a long night."

Cat noticed the fresh scars framing the Fire Curse's eyes. "You should take a break for a while. Leave the wet stuff to me."

Ildri sighed. "Thanks, Cat. I appreciate it."

She climbed in the back of the mule cart with her mother. Cat took a rag from among Sharon's things and used it to dab the last drops from the canteen on the sleeping woman's forehead and wrists. "This is how we deal with heat stroke at home. It's a fast way to break temperature down."

"Smart." Ildri noted. "What do you do at home?"

"Farm mostly. Some logging, but not for sale." Cat tucked the rag around the back of Sharon's neck. "We mostly fend for ourselves."

"I'm jealous." Ildri grinned. "Fire Town relied on Mom for everything. I have no idea what they'll do with her gone." Her brow knit into a stiff crease. "I can't believe she abandoned them to come after me. She left everything – she nearly died. What was she thinking?"

Cat softened her voice. "The same thing Aiden thought when he jumped in our wagon;" Cat glanced pointedly toward Peter, "if you love someone enough you will follow them anywhere."

Ildri bowed her head, "Is that why he volunteered?"

Cat shook her head 'no', "It's why I did." She smiled sadly and climbed out of the mule cart with the empty canteen. "Be right back."

She took the canteen with her back to Strawberry's wagon and shook Peter awake. "Morning, Sunshine."

"Blah," he peeled his eyes open. "Five more minutes?"

She smiled at him, "Sorry, you're blocking the storage."

Peter groaned and lifted himself painfully from the floor to the forward bench. "You're making breakfast?"

"No, I'm making more water." She pulled a rusted metal pail from storage, propped it against the railing and laced up her string.

"Whoa there!" Peter cried. "Back up a few paces."

She raised an eyebrow. "What's wrong? Don't you trust me?"

"No way. I've seen you in action," he answered. "Containment has never been your strong suit."

She smirked at him, "Relax, I'm a Prophet, I can handle this."

He scooted toward the far corner of the bed. "Okay, but don't say I didn't warn you."

Cat twisted the string into the smallest water symbol she could and aimed it at the bucket. Peter cringed as thin blast of water hit the bottom of the bucket and sprayed back into her face. "Ahh!"

"Ahh!" Aiden dropped an armful of firewood and leaped for cover behind Sharon's cart.

Cat balled the spell in her hand. "Sorry, Aiden."

"Stop doing that!" He shouted. "You trying to kill someone?"

Ildri patted his head, "It's okay, Aiden, she was trying to help."

"She can help by getting us out of here as fast as possible." Aiden reported. "I took a look through the town gate – there's something going on on there. Everyone's gathered at the courthouse."

Cat cocked her head in suspicion. "Did you see what it was?"

"No but I don't like it." Aiden said. "When healthy people congregate it's nothing but trouble."

"Sounds like an opportunity to me." Cat poured some water for the animals and left the bucket near Sharon's wagon. "Will you two be okay here by yourselves?"

"We'll be fine," Ildri placed a hand on Sharon's shoulder. "Don't take too long, though."

"We won't." Cat gave the Fire Curses an encouraging nod, took Peter's arm and struck off along the wall toward the city gate.

Ildri dabbed her mother's forehead with a wet cloth tied to the end of a long stick. "This is really smart, Aiden."

"I'm letting you burn yourself for her." He assembled his bundle of sticks into a bonfire.

Ildri smirked at him. "She is my mother, you know."

"She's insane." Aiden said shortly.

"She's protective." Ildri replied.

"Then she shouldn't have attacked you back in Fire Town." He angrily adjusted the gray cowl on his head. "Protective people don't chase them across the desert."

Ildri looked over, stiff brow leveled. "Like you?"

He glared back. "That was different."

"You left everything you had," she reminded him. "Heather, the kids, Tyson..."

His forehead wrinkled into a well-worn frown. "Stop it."

"Just admit that it's the same."

"Fine." He threw a stick at his fire pit and knocked the logs apart. "I'm crazy too, then."

As if cued by the conversation, Sharon dragged herself into consciousness. "Where am I?"

"Chalsie-Veneer." Ildri answered.

Sharon shoved up onto her elbows. "Ildri!"

The Fire Curse shrugged. "Hi."

"Thank goodness!" Sharon nearly tackled her into a hug. Ildri winced but held her back as Aiden rolled his eyes. The distraught mother grabbed her daughter's shoulders and held her at arm's length. "Are you hurt? Are you okay?"

"I'm fine, Mom." She answered a little stiffly. "What are you doing out here? You could have hurt yourself."

"I came to take you home." Sharon said. "Where's the Prophet?"

Ildri frowned. "She's in Water Town."

"Perfect." Sharon hopped out of her cart only to stagger and grab for the rail.

Ildri crawled up next to her. "Lay back down, Mom, you're sick."

"I'm fine." She shoved off and herded her mule away from its water bowl. "Get in the cart, Aiden, we're going."

"No." Aiden stormed over. "You can't barge in and order everyone around!"

"I'm protecting my daughter." Sharon said firmly.

The veins in his face pinked. "So am I!"

"Oh a lot of good you've done," Sharon sassed him. "Riding with her to her death? If you love her you should help me."

"You just love the idea of her!" Aiden challenged. "You don't care about her opinions or her convictions or any of that – just that she's your daughter and you've got some kind of contract on her!"

Sharon stomped over to stare into his face. "So letting her commit suicide is your idea of love?"

"Supporting her decision is my idea of love!"

"You both stop it!" Ildri climbed out of the wagon and shoved the two apart. "You're both going to overheat! Calm down!"

The conversation was interrupted by a bright flash of white light on the other side of the city wall. The three of them paused and watched as a mass of rippling power rose into view over the rooftops. Sharon grabbed each Fire Curse by the sleeve. "Get in the wagon. We've got to go. Now."

Cat entered Chalsie-Veneer through the east entrance and crept toward the square. The town was eerily quiet. Pieces of loose stone and splintered wood littered the road, growing thicker as she picked her way toward the square. The town hall was mangled beyond recognition with bodies draped in fabric spread before it in lines. Cat spotted the Calligraphers' horses up the road past the ruins and ducked into a damaged building. Trace was speaking. He sounded hoarse.

"I dredged the lake from one side to the other sir." He said. "My golem dragged up body after body but none were Catrina Aston. She simply wasn't there."

"It's impossible." The Elder said pompously. "I saw the accident."

"Accident?!" Sharon Fiammetta screeched. Cat sneaked through the shop to a side window. The whole town was gathered in the square like refugees tending the wounded and huddling for comfort. She spotted Peter and Aiden waiting with a pair of familiar wagons. Sharon was wild and tear-streaked with hair and clothes askew. She pressed into the Holy Elder's face with red rings around her eyes. "This was no accident! You did this with your magic!"

"They are miracles, dear woman." The Elder said coldly. "Miracles twisted by dark forces – "

"My daughter is dead!" Sharon roared. Cat's stomach clenched. "You killed her, you monster! Just like you tried to kill the Prophet! She'll get you! You wait and see!"

"That is treason," he replied, "but I can see you are grieving. I'll let you find peace in your own way. Our work here is done."

"But sir." Trace insisted. His well-oiled hair was frayed and dirty. "Miss Aston..."

"We'll launch countermeasures," he said briefly. "Believe me, Hayes, I have this under control. Assuming she lived there is only one place left for her to go. Get to your horse."

Trace shook his head in disbelief, "But...!"

The Elder slid the gold brush into the holster on his saddle and swung up. Paige stood holding the rein of the second. She passed Trace an unsettle look. He swallowed and smoothed the loose hairs back into place. "Excuse us everyone." He gave the gathered townsfolk a bow. "We will send aid from the monastery as soon as we can. Today has been bleak, but it was a victory for God's memory. Everything will work out for His intention, I promise."

He mounted the horse and let Paige climb on behind him before following the Elder past Cat's window and out of town.

Sharon ripped her fingers through her curls in rage and stormed back to her wagon where Aiden sat with his head hidden behind his cowl. Peter leaned on the rail beside him, a picture of melancholy. Sharon shoved him aside. "Come on, Aiden, we're leaving."

The Fire Curse barely stirred.

"Get up!" She yanked him out of Strawberry's wagon with both fists. "We're going! Now!"

"Wait!" Cat climbed out of the broken window and rushed across the yard.

Peter's head snapped around with a stagger. "Cat!"

He ran the best he could and met her in a forceful embrace. She clamped her arms tight around his barrel-like chest, relieved to find all the knobs she remembered in the places she left them. "You okay?"

"Hardly." He blanketed her in two heavy arms and planted a kiss on the top of her head. "Don't you dare do that to me again."

She closed her eyes and listened to the hollow sound of his heartbeat through stone. "I'm sorry."

Sharon charged in, hand raised for a slap but Peter hid her within the shield of his arms. Sharon lowered her hand and struck with words instead. "Murderer!"

Cat flinched.

"Ildri's dead!" Sharon's face reddened, her nostrils flaring. "You killed her! It's your fault!"

"Sharon," Aiden spat. His voice was bitter and gruff. "Stop looking for someone to blame."

"Well it wasn't my fault!" She raged. "I tried to stop it! It was this False Prophet and her awful mission that did it! If it wasn't for her we'd be home right now – !"

"Sharon!" Aiden looked up from the shadow of his cowl. Sharon took one look and staggered; a blanket of horrible, blistering scars lay in trails beneath each of his eyes.

The woman recovered with more concern. "Aiden, your face..."

He pulled he hood lower over his eyes. "It's nothing."

"I'm getting you home." She rushed to her mule. "I'm not losing another Fire Curse to this menace. Get in the wagon."

"No."

He took a deep breath. The veins glowed orange within his neck. "I'm not going. I'm taking Ildri's place and finishing her mission."

Sharon's jaw dropped in crippling outrage. "No!" She balled her fists. "No, I forbid it!"

"It's what she would have wanted." Aiden said. "Cat still needs a Fire Curse."

"You'd die for her?!" Sharon shouted. "After Ildri – "

"Ildri's dead!" Aiden stood, a mote of orange flame flashed in the caverns of his wounded face. "What else do I have to live for?"

"You're being stupid!"

"I don't care!" He shuddered. "Just go."

"Fine!" Sharon straightened her dress. "Go kill yourself. See if I care!" She climbed in her hastily repaired vehicle and gave the wounded mule a lash. The cart limped out of the city the way it came, leaving Cat, Peter and Aiden amid the ruin of the city. Cat took a shaky breath and glanced to the Fire Curse. His eyes were unfocused and downcast. She hugged tighter to Peter and let a moment of silence pass for Aiden, Ildri, and all that was lost.

There's a concept in role playing games called "Player Knowledge vs Character Knowledge." Player Knowledge is what the player, aka the author, knows based on all available information. Character Knowledge is what the character they are playing has seen and experienced. It's important for an author to know there is a monster in the dungeon, but the character won't find out until they see it for themselves.

Writers – especially those who enjoy plotting – face danger when they forget the the their characters are experiencing the story first hand without the omnipotence of having an outline in front of them. I ran into a bit of this while writing the second half of Threadcaster. For the first half of the book, there was a clear pattern that breaks at the black moment when the Calligraphers attack her in the mountains. I had all the towns and cities mapped out, so naturally if I was sending Cat to Earth Town, I expected her to visit neighboring Astonage as well.

But the stakes had changed on either side of the black moment. Cat was shaken from leaving Peter and Calligraphers were hunting her with ten times the effort as before. It became apparent from Cat's perspective that going into a heavily populated city as a wanted criminal was a bad choice for her to make. I realized I was being foolish. It made no sense for Cat to risk her life and the lives of her friends so I could show off the city I outlined. Her priorities were grown out of the events of the story and state of the world around her, and so character knowledge won and Astonage came out, but not before I wrote some of the intended portions.

Here are those scenes in incomplete form, taking place while the rest of the Curses were hidden in the desert outside Earth Town after entry was refused.

Astonage

Astonage's slate wall was low compared to Earth Town's. Cat could scale it easily and pass like a whisper into the city. The roads were made of mortared slate that made chipping sounds under her feet as she walked. She hugged the walls of the alleys, her heart pounding in her ears. Two men in black tunics stepped into the moonlight at the end of the alley, the shorter of the two carrying a stack of paper beneath one arm. They paused, selected a page from the stack, and plastered it to the wall of a bookshop within view of her hiding place. She heard the chink of the stone resisting nails and watched them wedge it between the slats of the store window instead. The two moved on.

The next strong gust shook the sheet loose and sent it swirling across the road. It got caught against a trashcan near the street, Cat sneaked over and found a wanted poster with her face on it. She expected as much. The likeness was spot-on, at least it was before she started wearing her hair down. Perhaps that would keep her safe. She untied her scarf on her waist and retied it like a hood over her head.

The town was built entirely out of of gray and white stone quarried from the mountains nearby. The roads, walls and roofs would have shone majestically during the day, but now sat painted in blue moonlight. Smokestacks from distant factories leaked white steam into the night sky. Cat ducked beneath a lit window and checked both ways before scurrying across the main thoroughfare to another dark alleyway. She could see the town square out of the corner of her eye, and zig-zagged her way though covered places toward it, passing Calligraphers and tearing down Wanted posters as she passed.

By the time Cat wove her way to the center town square the storm had faded and the night was clear with stars. The Calligraphers and their horses gathered beneath the Goddess of Earth forlornly offering a block of stone to the sky over their heads.

Cat peeked out from between a pair of closely-placed storefronts scanning the houses for what could be considered the richest one. The one at the far end had red and white stained glass windows, she knew it had to be the one. She backed out and crept her way around the ring of buildings, keeping both eyes and ears on the gathered Calligraphers she prayed would not notice her.

"You have some left?" one was asking another.

She missed the second's response on her way around a building.

The first spoke again. "I haven't seen her either. Everyone's obeying our curfew just like we asked."

"Do you really think she'd come here?" another asked. "The mayor seems to think he is her next target."

"She's visited the other major cities," the first answered.

"If she was smart she'd stay away," his fellow said haughtily. "My golems look like lions."

"It doesn't matter what your golems look like."

A different voice grumbled into their conversation, "Is he going off on that again?"

"You don't like it because yours look like bugs."

"Bugs frighten people," said the grumbler. "They at least still exist in this dead world."

"The world's not dying. It's a seasonal anomaly."

"The world is ending."

"It's fine," the stubborn one said.

The grumbler's voice hissed through his teeth. "The Holy Elder's dead. It's not fine."

"Shut up!" The first one snapped. "That's what the False Prophet wants you to believe. That's why she's a terrorist."

Cat paused and watched one of the group march off. He

vanished from view. She pressed herself to the wall of her alleyway and held her breath. There was no sign of him. She sidled to the edge and peered around the corner. There was no sign of the patrolling Calligrapher so she continued on.

After ducking in and out of a dozen more shadows, she finally found the house with the stained windows. It was two stories tall and built with white stone. The wall she hugged was bright in blue moonlight, she scuttled quickly toward the front door. The facade faced the square in plain view of the Calligraphers. After overhearing the bit about curfew she knew she couldn't knock. She rushed back to the rear to sneak around behind.

She took a step out into the street and spotted the bob of a dark shape out of the corner of her eye. The patrolman was coming this way. She saw him jerk and threw herself against the moonlit wall, "He saw me!" She covered her mouth and searched the bright alley for a place to hide. The opposite building had nothing to offer and no box or can was set in the street. Her only choice was the red and white paned window over her shoulder. It was set high in the wall and cracked a sliver. She aimed her string and flurried a quick wind rune and it swung inward the rest of the way.

She could hear the slight crunching footsteps coming quickly. With a bound she threw herself to the window ledge and sent herself tumbling inside. She landed in the kitchen sink, hitting a pile of dirty dishes before flailing to the floor. A voice called from within the house. She sprung to her feet and locked the window shut before the guard outside could see or hear anything.

The light of the kitchen flashed on. Cat shielded her eyes from the painful brightness. A man's voice barked at her, "Hands up!"

She opened her eyes and saw him standing at the doorway in a nightdress with a crowbar held over his head. He stared out from lopsided glasses, furious, "Don't move! I handle a scapel!"

"Mr. Preston?" Cat asked.

"Doctor," He weilded his bar higher, "What is it to you!?"

"Dr. Preston," Cat quickly fished out the letter and presented it, "My name's Cat. I'm a friend of your daughter. Rebecca sent this letter!"

The crowbar sank behind his head, "I don't believe you."

"It's her handwriting," Cat said, "Look. It's the truth!"

He couldn't resist his curiosity. He inched into the room and snatched the letter from her hand, "This is her handwriting." He dropped the crowbar in an instant. The metal instrument clanged on the stone floor, "How did you get this?"

"I met her in the mountains," Cat replied, "She said you could help me."

"Dear?" The voice of Dr. Preston's wife echoed through the house. The eerily familiar tone gave Cat pause. She heard the heavy sound of footsteps coming down the stairs, "Benedict, is it a burglar? What was it -" The woman entered the room, her round lined face framed by a tangle of graying brown hair. The two women exchanged glances, the same look of shock on each.

Cat frowned and gritted her teeth. How could she forget the mother who heartlessly abandoned her fire cursed daughter to strangers then stole food and vanished without even a goodbye, "You!"

Dolores, mother of the young Fire Curse Edana, stood with her face drawn in terror.

An hour later Cat was sitting at the Preston family table. Isolde Preston-Preston was pouring tea for all three of them while her husband poured over Rebecca's letter repeatedly. Cat's eye wandered about the kitchen to escape the awkwardness, catching on every remnant or sign the child she knew once lived there. There were no drawings or pictures pinned to the bulletin board or the icebox, no portraits on the walls, but in the unfrequented corners she could see remnants; a storybook on the dusty shelf near the cookbooks, an old box of sugary cereal in the corner of the pantry, an unopened package of white gauze at child-level.

Dr. Preston placed the letter firmly on the table and looked up with a tightly set jaw. "She didn't even give me a name! I keep searching for a name!"

Cat fidgeted in her seat, "A name for what?"

"Her husband!" The doctor exclaimed, "The blaggard she ran off with!" He leaned over the table, "You said you saw her right. You met him? What's his name? Where is he so I can cane him!"

"I can't say," Cat grimaced remembering James and their long walk through the woods. "He comes from a good family if that helps?"

"It most certainly does not!" Dr. Preston scoffed.

"Did you get to the part where she asked you to help me get into Earth Town?" Cat prompted. "Because I hate to be so pushy, but I really need to get to Earth Town."

"Why would a healthy person want to get to Earth Town?"

"Because of this." Cat offered him one of the wanted posters. The likeness was uncanny.

Dr. Preston drew back, knocking his chair aside as he stood. "You're a criminal?"

"I'm wanted by the Brushcasters because I'm trying to help the Curses," Cat said. "Dolores can tell you. We met each other on the road before when she was on her way to Fire Town – "

"Don't!" Dolores cut her short, lip trembling.

Dr. Preston regarded his wife. "That's a very fresh – very tender – wound you're touching, Miss Aston."

"I know. I know what she did," Cat said. "My friend Peter and I met your daughter on the road. We fed her and cared for her. Dolores was practically out of her mind with sadness and a lot of self-loathing, too. I know she didn't want to take Edana to Fire Town, but she was doing as she was instructed to do by people who said they knew best."

Cat took Dolores's hands. The woman started, staring down in shock as Cat gently held her fingers.

"I did the same thing in a way," Cat said. "I have been on a mission since you met me, trying to get God to come back and take away magic, and to do it I have to lose friends... some sooner than I thought I would." She breathed heavily. "Peter's gone, Dolores. You know how much he meant to me. He was taken from me by the Brushcasters, the same way their teachings took Edana from you. You're not alone."

Dolores sniffed. "You're... not the Goddess... are you?"

"No," Cat said. "I'm a Prophet. I've come to change the world."

"This is madness!" Dr. Preston cried. "You are a wanted criminal, and our daughter... Edana was sin incarnate, it's painful but it's a fact."

Dolores cringed. "Ben, please."

"These last two weeks have been torture."

Cat released her hands and stood. "I know you didn't want to hurt your daughter, Dolores. I did as you asked me. Edana's safe. She's in Fire Town where there's a safe roof over her head, and food for her to eat, and friends. She met a little boy named Kory when we arrived and by the time we left her, the two were best friends. She misses her parents, but she's being cared for. She'll be as happy as she can be. I'm confident."

"Thank you."

Dolores began weeping. "Thank you."

The doctor took his wife by the shoulders and spoke to Cat. "You really are who you say you are. You're really on a journey to ransom back Our God?"

"I am," Cat said. "Will you help me?"

"I've lost both my children to this unhappy world. You helped Rebecca, but even more importantly, you helped Edana. I think I can help you." He sighed. "Meet me outside Earth Town. I will get you inside."

Writing is complex and sometimes intimidating, but it's extremely plastic and freeing, too. A lot has been in these intros said about writing without hesitation and not being afraid to make mistakes, but this goes for structure and pacing as well. This scene was removed from the original novel not because it contradicted anything or clashed with the direction of the plot or themes. This perfectly good scene was removed because of the inpact it had on the reading experience.

The fire golem attack in Dire Lonato is Cat's first encounter with with Trace as a solo antagonist and the scene in which he and Paige observe the destruction of his casting circle is only the second time the point of view shifts from Cat's perspective. From this point on, the narrative begins to cut back and forth between Cat and company's "A Story" and Trace and Paige's "B Story" with several intersectiosn between them. This is where balance comes into play.

While Trace and Paige are very interesting and their change of allegiences worthy of investment by the reader, they are not the main characters of the book. To achieve pacing and balance, I limited "B Story" asides to one scene per chapter and located them either at the beginning or end of each. The goal was to keep the "B Story" relevant and present in the reader's mind, but not let it eclipse the "A Story" in terms of scope and attention. This scene took place within the same chapter as the much sweeter, meatier scene featuring Trace teaching Paige how to paint and the arrival of the Holy Elder to their traveling party, so I took the reveal of Trace's ambition from this scene and put it in that one, allowing this moment to come out easily in favor of the other.

The Fire Goddess

Dire Lonato was still reeling hours after the attack the golem. Trace did his best to repair the damage to both the town and the Order's reputation but none could deny the loss of property and the Fire Goddess was still irreparably damaged.

Trace paused by the broken arm with a weary sigh. The townsfolk had draped it with paper chains and flowers, mourning it as they would a fallen dignitary. The plume of flame sat perfectly in the palm of fire in the Goddess's amputated hand, it's base was covered in red jewels invisible from the ground until it fell; a mournfully poetic detail meant only for God. He studied it until Paige stepped up beside with her pail in hand. "Here's the paint, Master."

"Good." Trace placed the bucket on the ground and drew the well-used paintbrush from his back. It's bristles were stiff with old paint. They loosened back to silky smoothness as he bathed them in white. "Thank you."

The people closed in to see what he was doing. He turned to them with his trademark showman's smile. "Ladies and gentlemen, thank you for all your hard work. I know how tough the last twenty four hours have been for you and I want you to know how deeply it pains me to to know my creation was the cause of your hardship."

He dipped the brush again. "As a monk, the golem is much like a signature; its shape unique to each calligrapher and it's life is derived from the force of it's creator. This is why during the anointing of our Holy Elders they paint a stone golem for us in the halls of the monastery. This Living Golem is a portion of his strength so that in his followers can feel the Holy Elder's presence when he is away."

He gestured to the Goddess. "This sculpture is the same; it was created hundreds of years ago as a tribute to God to inspire hope in all of us and while I cannot restore this historic landmark, I can leave you a personal gift. Please accept this gift as a reminder that sin and suffering will not last, that the power of God still lives in the wisdom of his scripture, and that I vow henceforth to stop the heretic that caused your pain."

The people drew a calming breath and waited as Trace began to paint. He laid nearly ten verses in the ring; writing each with care. Paige recognized a couple but most were above her library clearance level. This was a true monk at work, performing a miracle for its own sake, not the approval of others. He finished the spell with the symbol for earth and his strong-armed golem took shape above the circle.

It grew to life from smooth gray stone, nearly as tall as the Goddess with deep passive white eyes. The next verse caught light and the golem started moving. It took the broken pieces of the Goddess's arm in its massive hands, balanced on its short, squat back legs and lifted the fragments into the air. It held them precisely in place where they'd been. It reached the last of its instructions and grew still staring as reverently skyward as the Goddess herself.

The locals marveled with hearty applause. Trace smiled and dismissed them back to their lives then turned and saw Paige admiring his work. "Not so useless, am I?"

"I didn't know you could paint like that." She said. "How can you recall such precise verses?"

"There's more to being a monk than just making miracles." He replied. "Close study of the scripture is part of our strength." He nodded up at his work, "Some day one of these will stand in the Hall of the Elders and I'll teach you the holiest secrets of the highest library."

She rolled her eyes, "Don't shoot for the stars just yet, Master."

"The locals say the False Prophet through the south gate." He slid the brush back into its holster. "If I do this well, my dream may still come true."

Noah – like Sharon, Kindle, and others – was given new life in a short story after being forced out of Threadcaster proper. He was what I call a "plot-business" character, meaning he was a prop for me to force the main characters to behave the way I wanted them to, even when their own logic or motivation made them resist me. It's a rare exception that a plot-business character is the best tool in the author's kit. Ideally every significant movement in an adventure is triggered by a choice made or consequence faced by the principle characters, making every step of the journey personal to both protagonist and reader. In the case of Noah, I could not get Cat down the stairs to Water Town but instead of attacking the trouble at its source and writing the scene in such a way that Cat could get past Ford on her own, I invented a whole cast of characters to try force her through external means.

At first it was Lynn and friend named Kendra who happened to be on the way home from shopping in Chalsie-Veneer that got her inside, then it was Lynn and a Water Curse named Wade running errands for Douglas who got her past Ford, then it was just Wade, then it was just Lynn, then it was Noah, then it was no one. No one was better, because no one meant that Cat was an active agent in her story and that everything that happened as a result of her choices – including Peter's capture and Ildri's death – weighed heavier because she didn't "coincidence" her way into the problems that resulted.

Noah survived all my critique partners, existing in the manuscript all the way to the final editing pass. It was on my final read-through that I realized he was extraneous – that Cat could do this herself and didn't need a crutch. In this way, Noah was the last major element cut from the finished book. Here are the final version of his scenes.

Noah

Thick, heavy, coughing sounded below.

Ford frowned and called down the stairwell. "Lynn was that you?" The coughing repeated closer. Ford cleared his throat. "Lynn? You all right?"

A teenage boy appeared on the landing below, his platinum blonde hair stuck to the loose, heavy flesh of his face.

Ford gargled. "Noah go home, you're a mess."

Noah spat over the stairwell. "This is my shift."

"Lynn took you off the roster, remember? You're retired. Douglas's orders." Ford studied his hooded eyes. "Are you feeling ok?"

"I'm fine." Noah noticed the two travelers. "Who's this?"

"I'm Cat, this is Peter," she said. "We're going to Water Town."

"Over my dead body." He took a sharp breath and fell, coughing, to his hands and knees. The hacking turned to retching as he heaved lungfuls of water onto the sagging planks.

"Noah!" Ford climbed down to meet him. "You okay?"

"Get rid – " A deluge of clear water gushed through his fingers. "Get rid of her."

"Noah, for real, when'd you start this cough?"

Noah swallowed and wiped his mouth with the back of his wrinkled hand. "It's not a big deal."

"It's in your lungs, its absolutely a big deal." Ford rose. "That's it, I'm carrying you down."

"No!" Noah grabbed his wrist. "Don't leave the post. That's how it happened before – when we weren't looking – "

"I know," Ford said. "Fine, sit tight. I'll call Lynn up to get you."

"You can't." Noah lowered his voice. "She's not there."

"Where'd she go?"

"I sent her away," he muttered. "I knew she wouldn't let me through so I told her Doug wanted to see her, so I..."

"Noah, this is stupid."

"You're right about my cough," he gargled. "I don't have time."

Cat stepped forward. "We'll carry him."

Ford swallowed. "You?"

"I came here to help," she said. "Pete and I will take Noah so you can keep your post. While we're there I'll talk to Douglas about my mission."

"No," Noah rasped. "We can't trust the healthies..."

"Then let's make a deal," Peter offered. "Cat goes down and you keep me as collateral."

Cat turned sharply. "He what?"

"That way Ford can keep his post and Noah gets downstairs."

"Collateral, huh?" Ford studied Cat's distress with a pout. "That could work."

"No deal," Cat said. She pulled Peter aside. "What are you doing? Are you nuts?"

"I'm getting you in."

"I won't let you put yourself in danger, you've done that enough of that already."

"Look at me," he said. "I can't climb those stairs. It'll be just like Castleton – "

"Because that worked well." Cat pressed close. "Pete, I need you. I can't do this myself. These people don't trust me; I'm healthy. You're the reason Ildri agreed to come, she heard your conviction and respected your sacrifice. You're my credibility."

"Cat, listen," he said. "God chose you, not me. Trust in yourself. That's why I'm convincing – not because I'm a Curse, but because I believe. I have faith in the scripture and I have faith in you. I think you can do anything."

"Well?" Ford asked. "What'd you guys decide?"

Cat bowed her head. "Okay, but I have a condition of my own." She turned. "If I find one crack in him when I get back..."

"Don't worry," Ford said. "You take care of my friend, I'll take care of yours."

Cat pulled Noah with her down the rickety staircase. The Water Curse fought her every step, coughing and wriggling as water sloshed through the soft tissues of his body.

Morning sunlight revealed Water Town cloaked in shadow. It was a sprawling labyrinth of pontoons, platforms, and barges lashed to the rotting legs of the pier. Interlocking catwalks wound between driftwood homes where Water Curses moved slowly, silhouetted by fog.

Noah twisted his slimy arms free of her grip. "Enough of this – " Water caught in his throat. He heaved it into his hand "... I... won't..." He slipped on the stair and tumbled to the landing.

Cat knelt at his side. "You okay?"

"I..." A stripe of inky blood mingled with the water at his hairline. Cat wadded her sleeve in her fist but Noah smacked her away with a spray of cold water. "Don't touch me!" He drew water in and out of his lungs. "I'm not helpless."

"I can see that." Cat forced the fabric to his face. "Listen, I know a lot about Curses. Stress affects your symptoms. And I understand why it might be hard to trust me, but I'm trying to help."

"We don't need your help."

"So I've heard."

"Douglas made the rules for a reason." Noah clung to her shoulder. "No one here remembers. They carted us off by the boat-full... every night... screaming. Snatched me out of my bed."

Cat shouldered his weight. "How did you escape?"

"Douglas." Noah coughed. "He came after us. Threw a man out a window." He rose and heaved another cough. "A ten-year old."

"He was strong enough to do that at ten?"

"He was crazy." Noah wiped his mouth. "He burned down the warehouse. He burned everything." Noah shuddered. "The healthies never expected us to fight back, especially not with fire. They're still scared... scared of him..."

"You're scared of him too, aren't you?"

"No." Noah paused for breath. "You healthies deserved it. You treated us like animals, and that's what we became."

"You're not animals."

"We're sin incarnate."

"You're people who are sick," Cat insisted. "God said so. I read the scripture, myself."

"You read scripture?" Noah gargled. "Like real scripture? From history?"

"Yes," Cat warmed a little. "God sent me to help you."

"God abandoned us. We're sin."

"I'm saying you're not," she insisted. "You're victims of the same sin that's killing the world. I'm here to help you and bring God back."

"You?"

"I'm a Prophet."

Noah swallowed. Tears swam in his reddened eyes. "Why did you take so long?"

"I don't know." Cat sobered. "I'm glad I'm here now."

The humidity at water level was overwhelming. Noxious fumes rose from the dark, filmy water. Cat led Noah to the first floating platform and let him lean against a wooden table, strewn with bits of slate and grease pencils.

He released her. "Thanks."

The clock above city hall dolled the time. Cat bit her lip and glanced to the top of the stairs where water dripped through the pier. "Can you make it home from here?"

"Yeah. It's not far. You're hurrying back to your friend?"

"I wish I could." Cat gulped. "I need to see Douglas."

Noah blinked water from his eyes. "He'll kill you, you know."

She paused. "I'll have to take the chance."

"Noah!" A teenage girl appeared through the huts. "Brooke said Douglas isn't seeing anyone. Are you sure he asked for me?" The girl spotted Cat and stopped. "Is that a healthy?"

"Lynn, hush," Noah coughed.

Lynn's eyes ran like rivers down her face. "But she's a healthy – "

"I know. Cat's a Prophet." Noah hesitated. "Douglas sent for her.

She's here to help us."

"But there are no Prophets. And Brooke said – "

"He asked for her specifically."

Lynn studied him. "Why did she tell you, not me?"

"Trust me on this."

Lynn considered Cat and shrugged. "Alright, I guess Douglas is the boss. Stay close, Cat, it's a bit of a maze."

Cat mouthed a silent 'thank you' to Noah and followed Lynn along the interlocking pathways.

Return to
Mason Forge

More than dictating events in order, a big part of storycraft is guiding your audience througoh an experience. This involves managing the emotional state of the reader by choosing scenes and character moments that set a specific tone and not including elements to sabotage it.

When tones vary widely within a single sequence, the audience becomes confused about how seriously they're supposed to take the situation. Readers will adopt the moods of the characters, but they will also make judgements about those characters. The scene that follows was in the original outline, but as I learned more about my characters and writing in general, I realized that the tone and the ideas presented in this scene conflicted with those put forward in the ones before and after. Peter has been mortally wounded. Cat's risked the mission and the lives of her friends to transport him halfway across the valley so that he can die at home. The tone is somber and serious until Joshua shows up and refocuses Cat's attention to the quest. After training the audience away from the drama with Peter it relieves the sadness, and watching Cat show interest in Joshua at this moment teaches the reader where her priorities lay. It did not feel right for Cat to forget Peter so quickly, so I moved the relevant bits to Joshua conversations before and after the return to Mason Forge and cast the rest aside. Here it is restored to its previous version.

Return to Mason Forge

The woods felt more like home than anything. It was the only place still perfectly preserved from her childhood, she recognized the spacing between the trees, places she and Peter used to set up their tents, even scrapes and scars from practicing magic. Cat took several deep breaths and pulled out her string and began weaving ladders to settle her nerves.

She heard a voice from directly above her. "Casting spells?"

Joshua sat on one of the branches. Cat shoved up from the trunk with a start. "How long have you been there?"

He nodded to the thread on her hand. "Are you casting spells?"

"What?" She looked down and pulled one hand out of the web. "No I was just playing."

"Hmph." He dropped down beside her and dusted a fine powder from his mop of dark hair. "I believe there's irony in that."

"What are you doing here?" She asked. "I thought you said you couldn't travel with us."

"Just because I'm not in your wagon doesn't mean I'm not with you," Joshua noted. "I've been watching the skies and the roads. The Calligraphers are flooding all corners of the Valley. They're on their way here, but don't worry, you still have some time. Still, you should leave first thing in the morning."

"So soon?" Cat bit her lip.

"There's a storm coming up," Joshua said. "It's the most reliable cover you can hope to expect. You can use it to get to Astonage."

"Okay, but..." She glanced over her shoulder at the lights of the house. "I promised Peter I'd be here to the end. If I leave tomorrow will I make it back in time?"

"I can't answer that."

"I know you can see the future," Cat said. "If you know the answer, just tell me. Why leave it to me to make the call on my own?"

His look softened. "Because I care about you, Catrina."

"You have a funny way of showing it." She grumbled. "You were there when the wagon turned over, why didn't you warn me the Brushcasters would attack? Why didn't you let all this happen?"

"Please don't be mad," he said. "Sometimes the journey has value in itself. There are hard turns for all of us – even for me. Everything that happens does do for a reason."

"Are you trying to tell me Peter dying is a good thing?" She demanded. "That the Curses and the drought and all this is considered good?"

"That's not it at all," Joshua consoled. "Value isn't intrinsically good. Life is hard, but sometimes the journey, itself, is what's valuable. Judging a life based on episodes isn't fair to anyone."

"I guess I just don't understand." Cat said, shortly. "If I had that knowledge I'd use it to warn people. There's no reason people should suffer if they can avoid it."

"That's what Malachi thought back in the day." Joshua noted. "He tried to warn the future but they still wouldn't listen. He was still killed by the person he trusted the most."

Her lip quivered again. She bit down to keep is still. "I feel just like him."

"He'd like you," Joshua noted. "You've got the same spirit."

"Joshua," Cat said more forcibly. "If we leave tomorrow, would you travel with us? Maybe only a part of the way?"

"I do travel with you."

"I mean for real." She insisted. "Not the creepy, stalker way."

He smiled. "I'm not stalking you." Something out of sight drew his attention. He glanced toward town and back with a hush in his voice. "You should get back."

"What?" She turned to see torchlight moving up Cross. The orange light stopped at the Montgomery's front door. Cat glanced up at Joshua but he was gone.

Cat charged out of the wood and met a crowd on the stoop. The whole population waited behind Mayor Lane. The aging man removed his had with a nod. "Can we talk to Sheila?"

"No." Cat said, darkly. "She's busy."

"I see." The mayor fidgeted guiltily. "We brought her some things – prepared meals, that sort of thing – to help her through this, and of course for you as long as you're here." He looked her sincerely in the eye, "You and your cursed friends can stay as long as you want. If the Brushcasters are right and their presence ruins our town, it doesn't matter. It's less than we deserve for driving you out in the first place."

Cat scanned the crowd, the same faces she'd seen there a week ago. She wanted to hold a grudge, blame them for everything and relieve her guilt, but she was wiser now and knew better. She closed her eyes and released a defeated sigh, "Thank you. I'm sure Peter would appreciate the thought."

Sunrise

When you write any project, especially a long project like a novel, never expect to do it in one draft. The importance of revision has been reiterated often in this anthology, but for this passage, I wanted to emphasize the need for saving iterations and keeping a graveyard. These are pretty self explanatory; an iteration is saving multiple copies of your work along the way. and a graveyard is saving parts of the draft you've decided to delete in a spare file. The graveyard is especially important for keeping little sparks of brilliance that tend to leap involuntarily out of a writer's hands in the middle of scenes or exchanges that don't survive the drafting process. I can't tell you how often I cut bits of dialog or description and dropped them in the graveyard only to salvage them out later. Other times the story changes and beloved scenes are removed.

I loved this scene. I worked a portion into the final draft. If readers compare the two, some of it is even word-for-word, but moving the Earth Town sleeping arrangement from outside in the wagon to inside in Will's house meant a lot wouldn't save. When I got to assembling this anthology, I knew I wanted to include it even if it was very short.

I thank you all for reading Threadcaster and exploring this anthology with me as I walked down memory lane. Hopefully seeing where I've been as an author will give my readers inspiration. Know if you love something, it is worth doing. Nothing of value is ever done quickly or easily. Making mistakes is not only okay, but encouraged. Correcting mistakes is a constant challenge and their results a reward. Never be afraid to think outside the box. Try new things. Fail occasionally, but keep those experiences as so many steps forward. You can't edit a blank page. You never stop getting better. Always remember to save your progress.

Peace and Great Love,
Jennifer

Sunrise

Cat spent most the night under the wagon coughing up brown mucous. Strawberry lay on the ground nearby, in the shelter of Earth Town's open gate. Breath wheezed through her congested chest, punctuated by snuffles and deep cough. Guilt chewed through Cat's empty stomach. The illness was her fault. She pushed the horse too hard. Strawberry was a living creature who deserved rest as much as the rest of them. Peter would never have hurt Strawberry, he loved her like a pet. Cat apologized to both of them in silence and heaved another cough. If she closed her eyes, the wheezing sounded like he was sleeping right beside her. The thought calmed her aching heart enough to let her fall asleep.

Morning broke with high wind and a hazy sky. Astonage sat dark and quiet, fifty miles to the south. Smoke rolled from the thick chimneys in ribbons. Cat studied it through the gap between the wagon wheels and heaved a gritty sigh.

Something moved in the wagon above her. "That's your ancestral home, huh?"

It was Aiden. She adjusted her arms beneath her scarf. "I wouldn't call it a home."

"It's named after you. You never wondered?"

"Did you wonder it when you met me?" Cat asked. "'Hey, her

239

name is Aston. I bet her grampa made that town?'"

"I suppose not." He slid from the back of the wagon and sat beside her on the ground. "Want some bread?"

"I'm not hungry."

"You should eat some anyway." He handed her a slice. "Ildri used to mope like this whenever someone died."

"How'd she cope?"

"We're Fire Curses," he shrugged. "We didn't really have a choice, we got up and moved on."

"I don't know if I can do that."

"I'm pretty sure you can," he said. "Although it's not fair for me to expect you to be as good at is as we are."

"I'm sorry you've had so much practice."

"Heh." Aiden swallowed and studied his bandaged hands. "I'm sorry about Peter."

"I'm sorry about Ildri."

He looked to the horizon. "They're both making us stronger."

Resources

A lot of lore and world-building went into the preparation of Threadcaster, but not all details made it into the final book. Here is a handy series bible for readers curious enough to delve deep into the cogs and gears of God's Valley.

The World of Threadcaster

Threadcaster takes place in a land different from our own where a singular God created life from the cradle of a valley surrounded by mountains on all sides.

All of nature, including humans, is controlled by God using the power of life itself. He instructed his people through Prophets who were marked with the symbols of fire, water, earth, and wind written in the unspeakable language of God, himself. These markings allowed the Prophet to endure the power of God's voice and harness nature in the form of miraculous signs and magic.

Five-hundred years prior to to the events of Cat's journey, a devastating sin separated God from his creation, causing nature and magic to fall into gradual corruption. Her journey to reunite God, nature, and the valley leads her to the four corners of her small world.

God's Valley

In ancient times, when Prophets walked the world, the place was simply called "the valley." After God left, the Holy Calligraphers declared it "God's Valley" as a way of reminding the population what they were missing and to whom they belonged. In truth, it is less of a valley and more of a crater surrounded by an unbroken ring of mountains. This ring is sectioned into ranges and labeled by the four cardinal directions; north, south, east, and west. Once lush and green, the valley slowly decayed into a desert over a steady five-hundred year ruination. The topography of the land shifted as forests died, farms failed, and towns were abandoned in favor of larger cities. At the center, the capital city of Castleton stands on the basin's only hill. Around it, a beltway known as the Outer Bend connects a collection of spoke roads like a wagon wheel. The major roads are also tied to the compass rose and match up to the four mountain ranges and the four directional gates of the capital city.

At the time of Cat's journey, no one has ever ventured beyond the rim of mountains that surround God's Valley. Those who have climbed to the highest peaks describe more mountains obscured by clouds, and those who've ventured even further find ragged cliffs and impassable terrain. Are there more lands outside of the valley where life is preserved? Perhaps one day, brave adventures will find out.

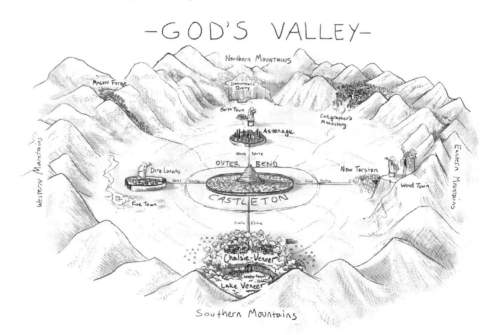

−GOD'S VALLEY−

Mason Forge

A farming town tucked deep in the Western Mountains, Mason Forge is known for self-sustainability. Protected from view of God's Valley by encroaching mountains and dense dead forest, the town is accessible by a single road that becomes the main thoroughfare once past the gate. The town consists of Main Street and Cross Street which intersect halfway up the slope at the town square whre the centers of government, religion, and education stand. Service and commerce take place near the gate at the base and recreation and residential areas are located further up. Farming terraces above the town grow grains and other staples, irrigated by water from a snow-fed river. The people of Mason Forge buy and barter, helping each other survive through the ongoing drought with extra crops or handmade goods going by cart to sell in the Castleton markets.

Castleton

The capital city of God's Valley, Castleton is the largest and most affluent city in the world. It is home to Lord Creven, patron of the city and deed-owner to hill and surrounding farmland. Those living in the city pay tribute to the lord in exchange for amenities like heating, cooling, running water, etc. The wealth precipitates down the hillside with Lord Creven's house at the top, surrounded by a layer of mansions that lose splendor the further toward sea level they descend. At a certain point the cone of the hill breaks into wedges of commerce including directional warehouse districts for crops harvested in the surrounding farmland, markets, storefronts, health services, recreation, education, religion, and law enforcement. Far beneath the city lies an ancient sea of magic. The white light of this well is the sum of God's pain and wrath left behind after he retreated from the people. This well was buried by God for safekeeping until he returned, but was tapped by Lord Creven's ancestors and used to control the city and its ignorant citizens. Castleton is one of the few patches of lush farmland left and an expensive refuge for all people unable to sustain themselves in the harsher environments.

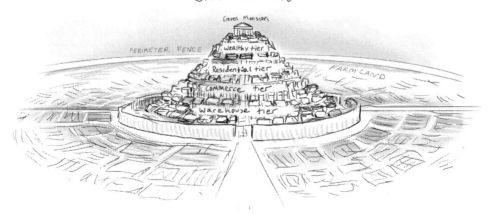

Dire Lonato

The ancestral home of Uzzah's son Lonato and location of the Fire Goddess statue, Dire Lonato is located in the western quadrant of God's Valley. Once in the heart of wine country, the city is now surrounded on all sides by desert with a brick retaining wall to protect against wind and dust storms. The buildings are mostly mud-brick and stucco with squat, square designs and colorful awnings. It's chief industry is weaving and textiles. The fibers were once supplied by herds of sheep, but after the death of surrounding pasture they were forced to import materials from Castleton by horse-drawn cart. The historic district of the city dates back to it's founding and features the impressive statue of the Fire Goddess, sculpted by the last Prophet's holy architect. Fire Town used to be located in this district until controversy prompted local lawmakers to move the slum beyond the walls. Afterward, Dire Lonato's historical society raised money to restore the district as a point of tourism and civic pride.

Chalsie-Veneer

The city belonging to Uzzah's son Chalsie is located at the southernmost point of God's Valley on the banks of the valley's last remaining lake. Lake Veneer feeds the Gatekeepers Forest which enables Chalsie-Veneer's still viable logging industry, although at the time of Threadcaster most the trees have died and few are growing anew. In its heyday, Chalsie-Veneer was a fishing village and the valley's premiere vacation destination, although the dropping lake level and general destitution of the valley's population has all but eliminated those industries. Instead, the city relies heavily on lumber and paper-making as well as the bottling and exporting of drinking water borne out of Water Town.

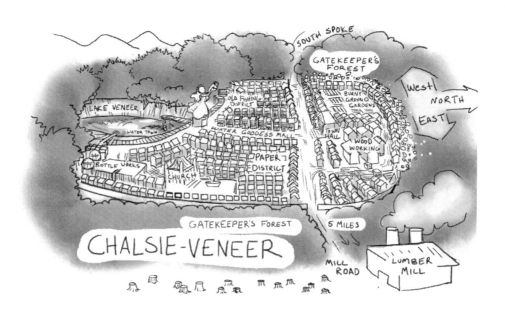

New Torston

As God's Valley deteriorated, the road to the mountain city of Torston degraded to a hazardous level, and so the citizens moved their homes down the bluffs to establish New Torston, a thriving city of art and innovation. It is home to one of the valley's few higher learning institutions and has invented everything from the steam engine to the first electric generator. They are also known for glass blowing, ceramics, and crafts like carving and jewelry making. The old town of Torston was given to the Wind Curses and is accessed via steam-powered elevator bolted into the hillside. This elevator was originally built to move the citizens of old Torston to New Torston along with all goods and building materials they could salvage from the abandoned city.

Astonage

Astonage is built of stone taken from the Stonemason's Quarry located in the mountain range directly north, which is where the marble for the Goddess statues originated. A factory city, Astonage is known for mass producing goods and building materials as well as stone bricks, slate, minerals, and architectural elements. It is the largest city after Castleton and the poorest of the municipalities. It is also known for its privately owned breweries and distillation of spirits, creating a wide gap between rich brewing families and poor blue-collar workers. Originally located closer to the Earth Goddess, Astonage has slowly crept south toward the Outer Bend, leaving the statue standing alone in the desert between the city and Earth Town.

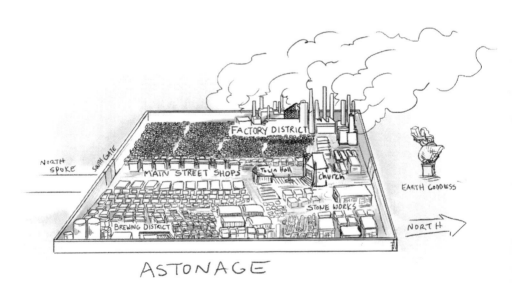

ASTONAGE

The Calligrapher's Monastery

The monastery is located in the gray area between the Northern Mountains and the Eastern Mountains. It is an ancient structure, built in the days of the Prophets as a retreat for the messenger and his family. The compound is comprised of religious spaces such as temples and libraries, living quarters complete with craftsmen to keep the place comfortable, and a large outdoor element for growing food and breeding horses. The place is partially carved into the mountainside, and is accessible by a mountain road guarded day and night by monks.

The monastery is full of history, and treated as sacred by its occupants who spend their days studying scripture and practicing magic. Pledges are accepted at all ages, even as foundlings. There are four ranks of Calligraphers; acolytes, monks, senior monks, and the elder monk of which there is only one. Acolytes seeking monkhood will enter an apprenticeship with a senior monk who is responsible for teaching the acolyte magic and proper conduct in the valley. The graduation of acolyte to monk is entirely up to the acolyte's master. The graduation of monk to senior monk is decided by a jury of seniors based on mastery of scripture and charitable accomplishment. The mission of the Holy Calligraphers is to provide guidance and moral teaching to the people of the valley in hopes of speeding God's return.

The Curse Towns

Part of the Calligraphers' mission to turn the valley into a god-favoring environment is the rejection and abandonment of the Curses, who they believe to be the embodiment of the sin that drove God off to begin with. Unfortunately for the Calligraphers, even the most pious people had a hard time abandoning children in the desert, so the monks also put religious law in place demanding a certain amount of food, water, clothing, and other supplies be donated to the Curses Towns to ease their suffering. The four towns grew up around the four elemental Goddess statues carved by the last of the holy architects, although some of the Curse Towns have have moved away from the statues due to time and necessity. The Curse Towns have very little interaction with the healthy population, and anyone considered "accepting" Curses is condemned by the church's purity laws. In this way the Curse Towns are both rejected by the people of the valley and wholly reliant on them at the same time.

Fire Town

The home of the Fire Curses is located in a dried up lake bed several miles outside Dire Lonato. The town is comprised of twelve dug-out houses with underground living space safe from rain, dust, and the heat of the sun. They survive off donations from Dire Lonato and haven't the ability to dig wells or farm on their own. A fire field encircles the town, raising smoke and raining soot. This field is both beacon for travelers and cemetery for the Curses whose smoking bodies are added to the field upon death.

Early on, Fire Town was located in the historic district of Dire Lonato, but after an unfortunate circumstance concerning a riot and some structural damage, the Fire Curses were moved to a new location in the desert. Supply wagons arrive once a month with food, water, clothing, and new Fire Curses abandoned by the Goddess.

Water Town

Water Town is a floating village on the surface of Lake Veneer. It is accessible by a staircase built into the pier intended originally for Chalsie-Veneer's fishing boats. Once a simple collection of barges, after their leader Douglas arrived and forced out the water traffickers, it grew rapidly into a complex network of pontoons, boats, and walkways. Water is collected from the Curses into drums and sold to the healthy residents of Chalsie-Veneer for money to buy building materials and supplies. The Water Curses bury their dead in the lake by tying their bodies to weights. Submerged, the corpses continue to transform until the entire body has dissolved.

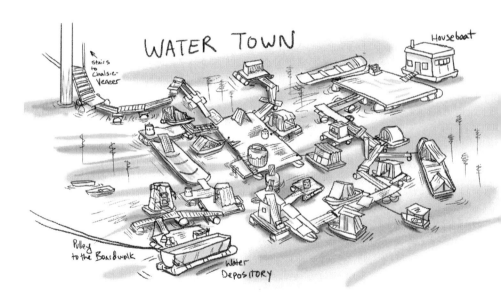

Wind Town

Wind Town is located in what was once the town of Torston, home to Uzzah's son of the same name. As such, Wind Town still holds the Wind Goddess around which the local Curses have crafted a religion. Aside from the statue, the dominant feature of Wind Town is the windmill that provides the Curses with electricity and dredges up water from the mountainside. The windmill has the capacity to grind flour but the Curses long ago lost that knowledge. The windmill is instead used as a ritual part of their religion and storage for their dead whose wind turns the propeller. The Curses live on mushrooms and potatoes grown in the moist soil around the mill and the regular supply of food and clothing sent up the elevator from New Torston below.

Earth Town

Earth Town is located a mile north of Astonage on the other side of the Earth Goddess. It is an extremely isolationist society that refuses help from outsiders and only begrudgingly accepts the donations of food and water. Built literally on the backs of its residents, the town is made of stone huts surrounded by walls of heaped up rocks around a central well. Young Curses live in houses built from parts of the expired previous residents and old Curses rendered immobile often wait in the spot their materials are intended to shore up, so that their stone may be easily moved when they die. The result is an unnerving collection of vaguely human shapes. The town is small, filthy, and crowded. The Curses inside are never seen by visitors. Children are left outside the main gate, which is made of wooden panels re-purposed long ago from the bed of an abandoned ox cart. Children left there can sit for hours or days but will not be let in as long as healthy people are present.

256

The Runian Mansion

The house where the ancestors of the Prophets live is located in the Northern Mountains high above the quarry. Originally a somewhat humble private meditation space for the Prophet, this house has been greatly enlarged and elaborately decorated in the five-hundred years since Malachi's passing. It is unknown to the residents of the valley including the Calligraphers, and does not appear on any map. It is hidden from sight by mountains and trees and can only be accessed with magic. In the culmination of a young Runian's magical training, they are allowed to leave the safety of the mansion and explore the valley in secret, looking for helpful inventions, additional supplies, or sometimes even spouses among the valley's residents. Those who agree to marry into the family forfeit their previous lives including any written contact with the people of the valley. They are not taught magic or tattooed with the symbols of the elements, and are therefore unable to leave the mansion on their own.

RUNIAN MANSION

Magic

Magic in the world of Threadcaster is a divine force the planet's god uses to control and direct nature. It is the blood of the world, connecting all its tissues, healing it, and growing it like a body with God at its head. It is life itself. Magic without direction is a non-sentient force that follows the natural patterns put down by God at creation, so when God left it unattended five-hundred years before the events of Threadcaster, it was fully equipped to run the world without trouble even with a certain amount of corrupt magic use.

All magic is generated by the symbols of the elements, which are the names written in a holy language only the god of Threadcaster's world can say aloud. Casters can activate the magic by simply drawing the shape, although such action has no longevity. By encircling the symbol, the spell can be given direction and a certain amount of persistence. Cat draws the elements with an unbroken loop of string, allowing her to project whatever spell she wants outward from her body in a jet for as long as she can hold the shape in place. The Runians use a similar system by marking their arms with the four symbols in a tattooing ceremony and placing the circle element on the palms of their hands. By pressing the circle tattoo over one of the element symbols, they activate the spell and project it outward through the opposite hand. Their clothing is stitched with special pockets to allow the hands to touch the symbols through their sleeves.

The Holy Calligraphers have refined magic even further through the creation and use of golems. Golems are an application of the caster's will impressed up on nature. Each golem is granted a unique shape by their painter determined by their handwriting and spiritual continence. The shapes are not of specific animals but can bear a resemblance to known species in a lot of cases. The Calligraphers control their creations through commands issued by God within the body of scripture. Commands can be direct or implied, but must be divine otherwise the golems created will stall, evaporate, or in worst cases, become wrathful.

A wrathful golem is the result of undirected magic and takes on the anger that God left behind when he vanished five-hundred years before the events of Threadcaster. A wrathful golem will attack any evidence of the sin that drove God away which includes Curses, active spells, and other golems. Golems are actionable spells that only exist as long as they have direction. Golems without direction die as soon as they are born, but death can be delayed by painting a coiled line about the element symbol at the center of the circle. There are verses of scripture that enable a golem to persist indefinitely, although they, along with the verses for spawning multiple golems and directing golems verbally, are included in the highest library and reserved for the Holy Elder, himself.

All elements used by mortals are created from raw magic and therefore seem to appear out of thin air. In other words, an earth spell does not manipulate the ground that already exists, but creates new stone instead. This rule applies to all people including the Runians with the exception of the Prophets who manipulated nature under God's direction, using the elements provided by the world without any loss to the life cycle.

Runians

The Runians are the extended family of the first Prophet.
Long ago, when life was new in the valley, the people asked their god
for a way to communicate with him directly. in response, God sent
the first Prophet, a man marked with the symbols of the elements
along his spine. From that point on there was always a Prophet among
the people, all stemming from the blood of the first Prophet by one
path or another. Those carrying his blood take on a similar complexion;
bronze skin, dark hair, and deep brown-black eyes; no matter what
coloration the parents may have. There are a vast array of naturally
occurring skin tones in the valley, but none with the same metallic
sheen as those containing holy blood.

Because the Prophet was covered in symbols, the people began
to call him the Runian, and because his children and grandchildren
were all born with the same coloring, the name extended to them.
After the death of Malachi, the Runians retreated to a hidden manor in
the mountains. Although no more Prophets were born, those with the
coloring were marked with tattoos when they came of age and taught to
use magic to keep their heritage alive until a new Prophet appeared.

Curses

The four elemental afflictions (known by the people as "the Curses") are a direct result of mankind taking control of magic it was unfit to wield. When God uses magic, it returns to the well of the world and maintains homeostasis. When humans use magic, it doesn't return to where it came from and is instead released from the natural cycle. But the world craves balance, and since magic is the power of life, the world uses life to return the magic to nature, creating the Curses. Because the world has no ego controlling it, it strikes the population randomly without regard for guilt or innocence, using the deaths of the people it afflicts to reclaim the elemental magic.

The victims are Curses from birth, although it takes years for the illness to present visibly. The average Curse is identified between five and ten years old. Curses advance steadily but can be accelerated by physical injury, heightened emotion, or anything leading to elevated heartbeat or bleeding. The transformation starts deep in the bone marrow before moving to the bloodstream where it slowly transmutes soft tissues into one of the four elements. The raw life found in magic tempers the effect for a short time, allowing Curses to continue living even as portions of their bodies transform, but the effect does not last for long. As a result of the transmutation, Curses are impotent, sterile, and magically immune to human illnesses due to the forces at work in their flesh. At the time of Cat's journey, no Curse on record had lived past eighteen years old.

Fire Curses

Fire Curses are people slowly turning to fire. Symptoms suffered by this Curse manifest most obviously in the skin, which is vulnerable to wetness. Contact with liquids or other sources of rapid cooling cause blisters, cuts, and skin-loss. This aquaphobia is often the determining symptom when diagnosing young Fire Curses. Other symptoms include a gradual raise in core temperature, burns (especially in areas of moisture such as the eyes, nose, mouth, and in shallow areas where the blood flows close to the skin), blisters, scars, and open wounds with wet discharge causing further burns. Advanced Curses will exhibit a faint glow through thin parts of the skin and deep in the eyes or mouth. Intense flares of heat can cause blindness, loss of digits, or sealing of orifices. These flares can kill an older Curse, although death is also caused by dehydration, brain damage from intense fever, and in some cases spontaneous human combustion.

Water Curses

Water Curses are changing to water from the inside out. The liquid inside lowers body temperature, making them vulnerable to cold. Other symptoms include swelling in the face and extremities (especially at the joints), engorgement of veins and arteries, excessive bruising, and a constant excretion of water from every orifice including the pores of the skin. The water created by Water Curses is as pure as spring water, turning them into valuable resources in the drought-parched world of God's Valley. Many Curses are taken against their will and used as living wells in farms and towns. This mistreatment has killed many through poor health, stress, and abuse. Other more natural causes of death are hypothermia, hemorrhaging, and pneumonia. This last one is the most common death among Water Curses as the water within them overwhelms their body's ability to clear the lungs.

Earth Curses

Earth Curses are slowly turning to stone. The heaviest of the elements, the earth has a hard time filtering to the blood and instead takes root in the bones where it grows outward, spreading to tissues. Earth Curses are especially vulnerable to physical trauma, as each new crack in their internal stone creates more surface area for additional growths. While bone protrusion is the most obvious symptom, others include paleness and poor circulation as the blood thickens with stone powder, increased weight and size, and loss of mobility. Larger pieces of stone can block nutrient flow to portions of the body causing tissue death (and rapid calcification) in the body and strokes in the brain. Growing stone crowds the organs until they also start calcifying or are pierced or crushed by the pressure. Curses in the advanced stages often die of crushed brains, hearts, or windpipes, although few Earth Curses reach such a stage. More often physical trauma from a blow or fall, or the simple inability to care for themselves claims their lives.

Wind Curses

Wind Curses are essentially evaporating into air. It's a withering condition, leaving sufferers gaunt and skeletal. Their bones are hollow, and as a result are weak and very light. They emit a constant breeze which gains strength as the Curses age. The ceaseless bluster of wind makes it difficult for Wind Curses to breathe and eventually eat and drink as well. The most devastating symptom however is to the mind. Unlike the other three afflictions, Wind Curses do not retain any of the materials they transform into, preventing the magical property that maintains normal function in the other Curse types. Damage to the brain can cause amnesia, loss of organ and muscle function, disorientation, hallucinations, and sometimes seizures. In this way, Wind Curses lose use of their minds long before they lose use of their bodies and as a result die in vegetative states before the physical degradation can claim them.

Lightning Curses

Lightning Curses are a concept featured only in this anthology as a bit of fun but are not canon to the world of Threadcaster. Lightning Curses generate their own electricity and can discharge that electricity to any conductive surface. These transferences cause fractal burns across the Curses's skin, waves of static through their hair, and sometimes magnetic fields to attract small metal objects. Large surges or discharges of this electricity can cause seizure, blindness, and nerve damage. Despite their magical ailment, Lightning Curses die from very human causes; organ failure, brain death, and loss of bodily functions due to the misbehavior of their electrical system.

Although Nell only joined Cat's journey in an alternate reality, if she had continued she would have worn rubber boots and gloves to protect her fellow travelers. Further adventures with the group are up to the reader's imagination, as are any other kinds of Curses there could possibly be. Once we're outside canon, almost anything goes.

The People of Threadcaster

Cat's journey to follow Malachi's last scripture takes her to many places and introduces her to many different kinds of people. From the powerful in wealth and magic to the socially outcast, from the most selfish and cruel to those willing to make the ultimate sacrifice.

These people represent the best and worst of the valley, but all had a part to play in its restoration. When writing the book I had faces in mind for all of them, but my interpretations are no more valid than the readers' imaginations and is not meant to supplant the characters in their heads. This list highlights only the most prominent characters from the novel and this short story compilation, and is only a fraction of the characters Cat encounters on her journey.

Catrina Aston

Aspiring Prophet
Age: 16
Eyes: Green
Hair: Brown
Height: 5'6"
Meek but powerful with an affinity for string games.

Catrina "Cat" Aston was born in Mason Forge, a place she never expected to leave. She started playing with string at an early age and learned to use magic not long after. Her father insisted she keep her magic secret, so the rebellious child sneaked as much of it into her life as she could without getting caught. She would do anything for her best friend Peter who she has lived next door to all her life. Any fear or self-consciousness is forgotten in his defense, which gets her in trouble and sometimes prompts her to save the world.

Peter Montgomery

Earth Curse
Age: 17
Eyes: Brown
Hair: Blonde
Height: 7'0"
Patient, intelligent, a little sad.
Cat's official pet rock.

Peter found out he was a Curse at six years old after a sprained ankle swelled and turned to stone. He was supposed to be sent to Earth Town, but his loved ones argued his case before the city council who allowed him to stay out of loyalty to Peter's family. At first only Cat would speak to him, but over time his kind, patient soul won his neighbors confidence. Peter's body is a burden but his heart longs for adventure, which he can only find in books and the maps in his atlas.

Joshua

Runian
Age: 18
Eyes: Black
Hair: Black
Height: 5'8"
Mysterious and powerful, in-tune with nature, would really like to tell you more but can't right now.

Joshua is the youngest son of Isaiah, current patriarch of the Runians. He lives with his family in a giant house in the mountains where they've hid from humanity for five-hundred years. A natural at magic, Joshua gained power and respect very quickly, and was able to join his older brother James on his pilgrimage a full three years before he would have been allowed to go. This pilgrimage was when Joshua first observed Cat as a child, awakening a fondness for her he's nurtured ever since.

Artemis Ulrich

Holy Elder Calligrapher
Age: 65
Eyes: Gray
Hair: Gray
Height: 6'0"
Golem: Lupine with a spade-shaped head and club tail.
Cold, meticulous.

The Holy Elder joined the Order of Holy Calligraphers as a young man seeking strength and wisdom. He was apprenticed to one of the top Calligraphers in the monastery and excelled through the ranks. His exceptional painting and recall earned him a promotion to senior monk at the age of twenty-five, although he didn't take his own apprentices for many years. He was hand-picked to become Elder by the previous leader and ordained to the position a week after her death.

Trace Hayes

Senior Monk of the Holy Calligraphers
Age: 27
Eyes: Blue
Hair: Black (Brown)
Height: 6'0
Golem: broad, heavy forelegs and
squat back legs.
Wants to be Holy Elder one day.

Trace joined the Holy Calligraphers at ten years-old where he
fell quickly in love with the study and recitation of scripture. A
perfectionist by nature, he took some time mastering golem painting
and control before being chosen as an apprentice by then senior monk,
Artemis Ulrich and graduated to full monk shortly before his previous
master was ordained elder. As a monk Trace gained a reputation for
duty and loyalty, and was promoted to senior very quickly.

Paige Waverly

Apprentice Monk of the Order of
Holy Calligraphers
Age: 16
Eyes: Hazel
Hair: Black (Red)
Golem: birdlike with a short neck
Impatient, strong-willed, prideful
but loyal if you earn it.

Paige was surrendered to the monastery as a baby and raised in their
dormatories by the monks. Not particularly invested in the magic or
the doctrine, Paige continued her training in order to gain prestige
and feel important. She has no patience for her master, who she feels is
willfully indoctrinated to a group whose relevance is more social than
scriptural, but begins to change her mind when she sees the strength
and power in the world around her.

Horace Creven

Self-proclaimed Lord of Castleton
Age: 61
Eyes: Blue
Hair: Gray
Height: 5'5"
The wealthiest man in God's
Valley, owns Castleton and
surrounding farmland

Horace descends from Uzzah's son Chalsie, which makes him the
heir to one of the oldest families in God's Valley. When the drought
reached critical levels, the Crevens used their generations of wealth
to buy all of Castleton one peace at a time, establishing a monopoly
on it's agriculture and industry. Creven's public persona is one of
philanthropist, but his work contracts are stacked heavily in his favor
and as farms fail and towns die his wealth constantly increases.

Orella Creven

Lady of Castleton, Creven's wife
Age: 50
Eyes: Gray
Hair: Brown
Height: 5'9"
Studious, perceptive. Excellent at
reading people.

Orella married Creven when she was a young woman, drawn to him by
his wealth and power. Living in his manor, she uncovered the secrets
of his family legacy and from that moment, her singular goal was
to discover the New Prophet and see Malachi's final prophecy come
true. She is the polar opposite to her husband; rigid and controlled
compared to his gluttony and irreverence. She is also intuitive, a trait
Creven uses in his political meetings to detect lies and manipulations.

Dolores Preston

Distraught Mother
Age: 39
Eyes: brown
Hair: Black/Graying
Height: 5'4
Pious, faithful, tormented.

Cat and Peter run into Dolores Preston on the road to Fire Town.
Before discovering her daughter was a Curse, Dolores was a normal
mother living in Astonage with her only child. Upon Edana's diagnosis,
Dolores had no choice but to cross the world on foot to follow the
Calligraphers' edict and deliver her to her new home. The contradiction
of her devotion to god's return and need to protect her daughter has left
her a little unstable.

Edana Preston

Fire Curse
Age: 8
Eyes: Glowing
Hair: dark/greasy
Old before her time, frightened.

Edana was diagnosed as a Fire Curse mere weeks before Cat and
Peter encounter her. As an emergent Curse, her symptoms are
comparatively minor, although the walk from Astonage has advenced
them dramatically. She's grown up a lot in a short amount of time,
and ignores her own pain to comfort her mother. Bottling up these
emotions might work short-term, but primes her for an emotional
attack that could kill her if its too strong.

Ildri

Fire Curse
Age: 14
Eyes: Glowing
Hair: Bald, Lavender Scarf
Height: 5'4"
Gentle, giving, cautious. Ildri wants to protect her fellow Curses above all.

Ildri came to Fire Town with her mother who decided to stay and live in Dire Lonato beside her. Although her mothers's efforts were thwarted, her loyalty and sacrifice left a lasting impression on the young Fire Curse. Ildri grew up to become the mother of Fire Town, looking after young children who arrive and doing all she can to keep her fellow Fire Curses as healthy and happy as possible. She strives every day to make others lives less miserable.

Aiden

Fire Curse
Age: 14
Eyes: Glowing
Hair: Bald, Gray Scarf
Height: 5'5"
Brooding, introspective. Fiercely loyal to both friends and grudges.

When Aiden was diagnosed, his parents hired a stranger to carry him to Fire Town, a betrayal he's never forgotten or forgiven. Suspicious of strangers, Aiden's found a new family in the Fire Curses, especially Ildri, and will not hesitate to die in their defense if necessary. He's attentive to moods and deeply perceptive, although his reserved nature often means he keeps insight to himself.

Sera

Fire Curse
Age: 12
Eyes: Glowing
Hair: Patchy, Yellow Scarf
Height: 5'2"
Aggressive, frightened. Likes children, but keeps all others at arm's length

Sera and Ildri have grown close since Sera arrived in Fire Town. Her Curse symptoms have made her jumpy and frightened that anything or anyone could harm her at any moment. Ildri taught her to channel this anxiety into caring for the new additions. Soothing the children's feelings and calming them down helps Sera to control her own emotional outbursts. Although she has gained a lot of confidence over the years, she is full of doubt and was naturally drawn to Tyson, whose strong personality is both her shield and spear.

Tyson

Fire Curse
Age: 15
Eyes: Glowing
Hair: Bald, Green Scarf
Height: 5'6"
Strong temper, belligerent. terrified of his own weakness

Tyson has a lot of pent up aggression and is looking for a fight. His frequent outbursts have progressed his Curse further than any of the other Fire Curses living in Fire Town when Cat visits. He has taken the Calligrapher edict of rejecting Curses as a personal insult and returns the same hatred to any healthy person who comes near his home.

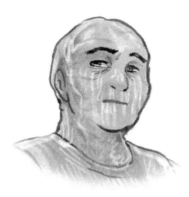

Douglas

Water Curse
Age: 17
Eyes: Pale
Hair: Bald
Height: 5'8"
An intimidating, powerful leader.

Douglas was always a strong and healthy kid, especially for a Curse. Forced by self-defense to kill at a young age, he is no stranger to doing what needs to be done. He refuses to forsake his humanity and leads Water Town in a way that demands the respect of the healthy residents of Chalsie-Veneer. The Curses in his care look up to him as both protector and example to emulate. Douglas has done all he can to exhibit the strength and potential Curses can reach if they remain confident.

Brooke

Water Curse
Age: 16
Eyes: Dark
Hair: Bald
Height: 5'5"
Protective, vicious.

Brooke was a child in Water Town when Douglas arrived, and watched in awe as he drove the raiders out of their town. She grew up beside him, at first trying to be like him and quickly falling in love. He was impressed with her as well and the two entered a vow of marriage when they reached their teens. She is physically and mentally strong, but dependent on Douglas to the point that she cannot see her own potential as a leader.

Lynn

Water Curse
Age: Unknown, early teens
Eyes: Dark
Hair: Dark Brown
Height: 5'4"
Naive, trusting, uncertain.

Lynn's abandonment by her parents was so traumatic it's blotted everything prior to her arrival in Water Town from her memory, including her own name. Brooke found her, named her, and with the assistence of the other Water Curses helped her regain a sense of herself and begin talking and opening up. Lynn chooses to see this trauma as a blessing. Because she doesn't remember the pain she doesn't have it as a burden. Although curiosity persists, she tries to be optimistic in all things and not dwell in the pain of the past.

Ford

Water Curse
Age: 11
Eyes: Pale
Hair: Brown
Jovial, confident. The guard at the end of the pier.

Ford's confidence comes from the ease that Douglas's leadership fosters in the people of Water Town. He arrived after Douglas's reign began and has known no other way of living. Fed by stories of the dark past and Douglas's heroism, Ford joined the guard as soon as he could. He is happy to be a part of the system that keeps his town safe, but doesn't fully believe in the danger he's been warned about until it arrives on his doorstep.

Wendy

Wind Curse
Age: 12
Eyes: Blue
Hair: Blonde
Height: 5'1"
Airy and spiritual. The priestess of
the Wind Curses

Wendy is recognized as the smartest of the Wind Curses because she retains a lot of her short-term memory. Wendy is self-important and haughty, blind to her insufficiencies thanks to her evaporating brains and cult-like belief in her goddess. Wendy believes that Wind Curses are holy, chosen among Curses, and superior to healthy people in both stature and appearance. Her distaste for other Curses is only surpassed by her pity for those who have the Goddess's blessing but not her likeness.

Gabe

Wind Curse
Age: 11
Eyes: Hazel
Hair: Brown
Height: 5'3"
Judgmental and suspicious.
Lore keeper of the Wind Curses,

Gabe is the second-smartest Curse in Wind Town. His superior long-term memory has put him in charge of passing on history. He tells the stories of the Goddess to younger Curses, hoping one will emerge as the new lore keeper after either he or Wendy ascend. His sense of superiority extends to his fellow Wind Curses, who he thinks are clueless and beneath him. Gabe really wants to be the priest in charge or everything. The only person he puts before himself is Michael.

Michael

Wind Curse
Age: 10
Eyes: Brown
Hair: Black
Height: 5'0
Bright and cheerful. Welcoming.
Attracted by sparkly lights.

Michael loves everyone despite the lessons taught by his religion. His positive energy has a strong affect on his fellow Curses who often take his ideas because of his charisma and enthusiasm. Michael's sense of time has degraded away, leaving him to live in the moment without cause or consequence. He is indifferent to Cat and ignores her presence, her negativity rolling like water off his back.

Zephyr

Wind Curse
Age: 14
Eyes: Hazel
Hair: Brown
Vapid and spacey with moments of lucidity

Zephyr has lived on scraps and scavanged resources for an untold amount of time. Her mind has degradedd to such a point that she's lost much of who she is except rare moments when a stimulus triggers deep memories of her previous life. All Cat knows for sure is that Zephyr is afraid of fire, loves babies, and constantly seeks companionship by clinging to those around her. This fear of loneliness is likely the result of her past solitary confinement.

Georgia

Earth Curse
Age: 16
Eyes: Blue
Hair: Brown
Height: 7'5"
Leader of the Earth Curses
Stern, unflinching, cold.

Georgia leads the Earth Curses with an iron will. Her no-nonsense rules about destiny and purpose keep all Curses in line. When her sense of order was challenged by Clayton in her youth, she played dirty to gain control of Earth Town. After his death, she took power back and maintained unwavering control over the Earth Curses. By the time Cat meets her, Georgia's legs and arms are useless. She'd be completely immobile if not for two assistants used as crutches.

Will

Earth Curse
Age: 14
Eyes: Brown
Hair: Brown
Height: 6'11"
Plucky, optimistic, flexible.

Will was born the son of a steel worker in Astonage where his natural clumsiness exposed him as a Curse at a young age. Despite his physical deficiencies, he strives to do his best in everything he attempts and finds a lot of reassurance in knowing who he is and what he's for. Death has always been a given for Will, so he's done his best not to worry about how or why. He sees the value placed in him through Cat's quest as far more important than his own fate.

280

James

Runian
Age: 21
Eyes: Black
Hair: Black
Height: 6'1"
Competitive, Loves his family and
its history more than anything.

James is three years older than his brother Joshua, but has lived in his shadow at the same time. Joshua's natural magic and leadership abilities propelled him through his lessons to match and surpass James in many ways including a future position as patriarch. While James is jealous of his younger brother's achievements, he's also fiercely proud of his accomplishments and wants him to have the best of everything. James hides his subtle resentment behind a loud and outgoing mask.

Marianne, Silas

Runian
Age: 20, 6 months
Eyes: Green, black
Hair: Red, black
Height: 5'6", 26 1/2"
Marianne is shy, but gracious. Silas
is a friendly baby.

Marianne was born in Astonage where she worked as a nurse. She encountered James while on his pilgrimage and left with him to live in the Runian mansion as his wife. Silas was born a year after their marriage. Like other children born to Runian couples, Silas has the Runian coloration and will grow up to be a magic user like his father.

Raymond, Mona Aston

Cat's Parents
Age: 55, 52
Eyes: Green, blue
Hair: Brown, brown
Raymond is paranoid and a conspiracy theorist. Mona is encouraging and bubbly.

When Cat started using magic as a baby, Raymond policed her closely to make sure she kept it secret. He would have forbidden her altogether but Mona hoped her skill would lead her toward a career as a monk and insisted she practice in private. Mona was born in Mason Forge and has lived there her whole life. Raymond was born in Castleton but left when his father's house was raided by Calligraphers looking for contraband. He fled to Mason Forge where he met Mona and settled down. The Astons love the solitude and security of small town life.

Sheila, Alan Montgomery

Peter's Mother and Younger Brother
Age: 53, 12
Eyes: Brown, brown
Hair: Light brown, light brown
Height: 5'3, 4'5"
Sheila's a busy, overeager server. Alan's curious and incorrigible.

Alan was an infant when Lionel Montgomery died and Peter was diagnosed as an Earth Curse. The Astons were already close with the Montgomerys and fought with the mayor of Mason Forge to let Peter stay. From then on, Sheila and the Astons worked together to raise the children to appreciate every moment they had together. Sheila and Alan cope with Peter's illness in different ways. Sheila does all she can to keep busy with crafts and cooking. Alan talks big and acts tough to hide his fear of death.

Isaiah

Runian, Patriarch
Age: 60
Eyes: Black
Hair: Black
Height: 5'9
Leader of the Runians. Knows more
than he's letting on.

Isaiah has led the Runians for over thirty years. He is well read and
wise, but quiet in front of his people. When he speaks to Cat he betrays
the festering resentment and pain he's inherited from Malachi's betrayal
five-hundred years prior. The story of the crime and it's affect on God
was passed down from generation to generation of Runians as they
wait for a new Prophet to come and put everything right. Isaiah shows
favoritism and perhaps a little fear toward his younger son Joshua and
intends to pass the mantle of leadership to him.

Henrietta Torston

Ex-Mayor of New Torston,
Age: 30
Eyes: Green
Hair: Rose gold
Height: 5'8"/4'11"
Cryptic, secretive, beautiful

The last of the Torston dynasty, Henrietta learned the secret of her
ancestry the day her father died. Inheriting her family library gave her
great power but also isolated her from the rest of God's Valley. Faced
with the temptation of magic and foresight, she internalized the sins of
the past and retreated to the moutnains to live out the rest of her days.

Vivian Arch

Senior Monk of the Holy Calligraphers
Age: 63
Eyes: Hazel
Hair: Gray
Height: 5'6"
Golem: sleek, four legs, long tail
Scriptural scholar.

Viivan is one of the Holy Elder's most trusted advisers and the top scholar of the lower libraries. She specializes in the interpretation of scripture used to paint golems and is known for her concise and elegant spells. Her deep study has sheltered her from the politics of God's Valley until the death of the Living Golem gives her reason to visit Lord Creven in Castleton and involve herself in Cat's journey.

Quill Gravadain

Monk of Holy Calligraphers
Age: 21
Eyes: Brown
Hair: Black
Golem: Serpent-like with a long rope-like body and four spindly legs.
Artistic, enthusiastic, broad-thinking

Quill was Vivian's apprentice as a teenager and maintains a close relationship with her as a graduated monk. He has an artistic flair, choosing to decorate his brush and books with colors. Laid back and personable, he gets along well with seniors but has yet to make an impression strong enough to earn promotion to their rank. In Lightning Curse he is shown to have drawn the portrait of Cat used in her wanted posters. In Threadcaster this remains true, although he draws it in Castleton from Lord Creven's description.

Imma

Water Curse
Age: 8
Eyes: Brown
Hair: Black
Height: 4'0"
Kind, sad, frightened

As a child, Imma was caught by the same farmer who captured Douglas while she was being transfered to Water Town. She was on a transport specifically intended to deliver Curses to their intended towns. These services traverse God's Valley a couple times a year, with private charters available to weathy parents. Imma's empathetic nature moved her to comfort Douglas while he was upset. She and the other prisoners of the well were rescued by him.

Noah

Water Curse
Age: 7
Eyes: Hazel
Hair: Blonde
Angry, vengeful. Ready to follow a worthy leader

Noah was one of the children trapped in the well with Imma and Douglas. He initially fought with Douglas, but became his friend after being bested by the other's strength. The two worked together to escape the farm and liberate Water Town from the oppression of the preying water merchants of Chalsie-Veneer.

Elizabeth

Wind Curse
Age: Middle Curse
Eyes: Brown
Hair: Red
Height: 4'5"
Vulnerable, generous, adoring.

Elizabeth is a giving soul who takes comfort in caring for the old Curses, especially her dear friend Gale. Captivated by Henrietta's beauty, Elizabeth became the Goddess's first worshiper and in doing so, founded the religion practiced in Cat's time. She is also the first victim of that religion, starting a practice that continued for fifty years.

Ayer

Wind Curse
Age: Middle Curse
Eyes: Brown
Hair: Brown
Height: 5'0"
Retains details and facts,
no imagination.

Ayer likes to tease Elizabeth about her lapsing memory, but actually thinks very fondly of her. He is the closest thing to a leader the Wind Curses have because of his level of retained lucidity and ability to think through puzzles. This trait is warped by Henrietta and used to convince the other Wind Curses to consider her a Goddess. Ayer acts as a big brother to the Wind Curses and only wants what's best for them.

286

Sharon Fiammetta

Ildri's Mother
Age: 33
Eyes: Blue
Hair: Brown
Height: 5'6"
Determined, stubborn. Won't be told she can't do something.

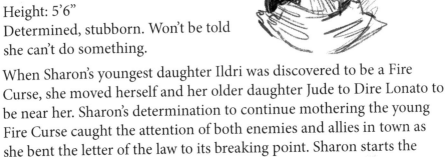

When Sharon's youngest daughter Ildri was discovered to be a Fire Curse, she moved herself and her older daughter Jude to Dire Lonato to be near her. Sharon's determination to continue mothering the young Fire Curse caught the attention of both enemies and allies in town as she bent the letter of the law to its breaking point. Sharon starts the volunteer group that eventually builds the new Fire Town and is also the reason Fire Curses began to wear scarves to protect their heads.

Kindle

Fire Curse
Age: 7
Eyes: Glowing
Hair: Dark brown
Rambunctious, extroverted, fearless

Kindle befriends Ildri the minute she arrives in Fire Town and wastes no time introducing her to her new companions and surroundings. The two get in trouble when they explore a burned building, causing Sharon to distrust her. In spite of her mother's wishes, Ildri comes to see Kindle as a sister and after Fire Town is moved to its new location the two live together happily.

Clayton

Earth Curse
Age: 12
Eyes: Brown
Hair: Brown
Height: 6"0"
Fair-minded, sacrificial.

Clayton bids against Georgia to become the new leader of Earth Town after the previous leader's death. His chief goal is to spread the responsibility of the Earth Curses evenly through the ages and abolish a system in which the young Curses become slaves to the old. This change causes division in the group and reveals both Clayton and Georgia's true natures. Clayton has a strong sense of family and firmly believes that the Helpers should feel safe and protected.

Mica

Earth Curse
Age: 5
Eyes: Brown
Hair: Dark Brown
Height: 3"0"
Angry, contrary, stubborn

Mica is a new arrival to Earth Town and Clayton's assigned Helper. They feel betrayed by the world for the way their life has turned out and spends most of their time pouting and refusing to obey instructions. When Clayton falls prey to Georgia's dirty politics, Mica is impressed by his strength and will to live.

Nell

Lightning Curse
Age: 13
Eyes: Brown
Hair: Black
Height: 5'4"
Sweet, trusting. Desperate to feel well again.

Nell was born in Ebensmith where she was treated by Dr. Tyrus before being diagnosed and deposited into Lightning Town. Because of her brother's manipulation, she received a placebo for many years, allowing her to maintain her energy and mobility while the other Lightning Curses lay idle. Nell has a companionable nature and a deep weariness concerning her Curse. Although *Lightning Curse* is not canon to the Threadcaster Universe, her influence early on helped shape the book that eventually took shape.

Dustin Damian

Nurse
Age: 19
Eyes: Brown
Hair: Black
Height: 5'8"
Perceptive, ambitious, cagey.

Dustin entered nursing school when his little sister Nell was diagnosed as a Lightning Curse in an effort to stay close to her and participate in her treatment. He is protective of his younger sister and although he trusts Dr. Tryus to find a treatment to help Curses, he is not willing to sacrifice Nell in the pursuit of it. Cat's compassion for Curses cuts through his suspicions even if trusting her is a dangerous choice.

Lightning Curse is not canon to the Threadcaster Universe.

Cat on a Fence (Oil Pastel, 2006)

The History of Threadcaster

    I've been writing and drawing my entire life, attracted to stories like A Wrinkle in Time, The Crystal Cave, and The Wizard of Oz that feature colorful characters, enchanting worlds, epic journeys, and true friendships. These stories conjured my imagination and set me on a path of creation and discovery from the moment I could hold a pen.

    I started writing Threadcaster in 2005 while studying animation at Webster University in St. Louis, Missour. The initial spark came in pictures; specifically the image of a girl crying rivers of tears from a completely expressionless face. Why was this girl crying when she wasn't sad? Perhaps she was cursed to fill up with water and it was finding its way out of her in any way it could. What would happen if people could fill up with other elements and how would that affect their bodies? The idea sparked a lore that percolated through fall of that year.

Cursed by Water (Graphite, 2007)

Another thing I enjoyed doing as a child was playing Cat's Cradle. I memorized a half dozen shapes and wove them out of any loop of string I could find. One day while playing around in my house I finished a Jacob's Ladder and aimed it down the hall like an anime character. It was spur of the moment, but I realized I'd never seen a magic system quite like that before. The two ideas collided and soon a story was born.

I am a plotter by nature, so pre-production started on the project through the rest of that year. I drew up characters and planned outlines and maps of the locations. I planned for five elements - fire, water, wind, earth, and lightning - and with it five Curses, five towns, and five cities. The key beats of Cat's story and Trace's story were planned along with a third path for the Joshua analog, Bastian. Other characters had different designs, names, and ages at the time.

Cast (Digital, 2008)

This brings us to November 2006 and an attempt at the National Novel Writer's Month challenge. This draft, the zero draft or pre-write, was only 26,000 words long but provided a stable foundation for me to build on. I scrapped that draft and began again, adjusting the lore to fix the problems I encountered and adding new inspiration as I went.

Hurry this Way (Graphite, 2007)

Fast forward to 2011. I've graduated school and have been working at a website doing graphics and animation for several years. It's been slow progress on Threadcaster. The first draft is about half done when I am invited to attend the Missouri Writer's Guild's 2011 writers conference. I knew nothing of the publishing industry and that weekend among my fellow writers introduced me to people and concepts that would change my life. I learned that this story I was writing was more than a blog entry, it could be a real book on a shelf at a store some day.

While at the conference I had the opportunity to pitch to agents and even recieved a partial request from my top choice. She gave me some instruction and sent me off. Six months later I submitted, and while I was not accepted, I successfully finished a first draft and was able to continue forward through the second, third, fourth, etc.

I can't tell you in the end how many drafts there were in total. The evolution was slow and meticulous. I ran it through beta readers and editors, changing what felt "off" and improving my craft with each new addition. I continued querying as well, sending letters and entering contests in attempt to make my dream come true.

Cast Photo (Digital, 2011)

While this was going on, the publishing industry was changing. Tools for self publishers and small presses became cheaper and more readily available, allowing more writers access to publishing. The traditional publishing world was restricting the types of books they wanted to accept. This was the time of the Harry Potter and Twilight movies. Fantasy stories for young adult audiences were big, and the industry's inboxes were flooded with queries like mine. I had a decision to make... wait for the smoke to clear and write something else to query in a couple years, or pursue alternate forms of publishing. It was a difficult choice to make. On one hand, the traditional route provides greater access to distibution, new contracts, and greater sales at the price of time and control, while the indipendent route provided higher profit per sale, complete creative control, and an opportunity to publish immediately. I let the question simmer, and in 2016 decided to pursue indipendent publishing. I hired a copy editor and took half a year to work exclusively on getting my book in shape for release.

Threadcaster's official birthday was March 11, 2017. It was a crazy ride, but I'm so proud of what I accomplished in the twelve years since that first brain wave. I have a whole universe worth of stories and characters to play with and the freedom with which to do it, including this bonus-disc of a book you are reading right now.

I hope this anthology proved entertaining and perhaps a little inspiring to my fellow writers out there. Threadcaster did not spring from the earth as a perfect creation, nor was it perfect at the time of release. Creating it taught me so much about storytelling, character development, design, narrative, and writing in general. I encourage everyone reading not to be afraid of making mistakes, never stop chasing your dreams, and try to think outside the box. You never know where the muse will lead you if you're willing to follow!

Thank you, everyone, for helping me make this dream of mine come true. Thank you for reading the books, participating in the contests, and following online. Thanks to my parents, my sister, my editors and beta readers for your time and advice. Thanks to the St. Louis Writer's Guild and the Write Pack for their wisdom and encouragement. Above all I thank God and his blessings for the skills and experiences that equipped me for this task. I love you all. Please join me on the next step in the Threadcaster journey!

Keep an eye out for Brushcaster, the sequel to Threadcaster, in 2020!

THREADCASTER

Thank you for reading!

www.threadcaster.com

Threadcaster

Chapter 1

Cat sat in her open bedroom window, weaving a pattern of string in the cage of her hands. Her mind wandered as her expert fingers completed figure after figure. A loop transfer made the Prayer Knot; a wrist turn created the Whirlpool Spiral; crossing her thumb under and dropping her pinky loops left the Cup and Saucer, which became the Spire Mountain if she grabbed it with her teeth. It wasn't a game, per se, more like a habit introduced by her frustrated mother, desperate to keep a fidgety six-year-old still at church. Ten years later, the trick still worked. Cat drew a breath and let the familiar movements quiet her anxious mind.

Below, Mason Forge spread like a blanket over the mountainside. Residents took their time walking Main Street to shop or visit neighbors happily resting from the week's work. A group of rowdy men gathered for afternoon drinks at the town's only bar. Their laughter carried over the staircase of rooftops, ushered by dry gusts of wind from the wooded mountain pass. Somewhere, concealed beyond the Western Mountains, lay God's Valley with its complicated mess of magic, religion, and politics. Mason Forge was peaceful, stagnant, and felt less claustrophobic when Cat had a string in her hand.

The thread pulled tight. She turned from the horizon to find the first stage of the Child's Cradle taught between her palms. Her hands knew the following steps – she and Peter used to play for hours in the forest behind his house – but without someone to transfer the string to, she was trapped in a cage of wasted potential.

Dust-scented wind swept flyaway hairs about her face and stirred the sapling below her window like a tiny green flag. Cat planted the fruit tree after Peter's sixteenth birthday party. His mother saved a whole year to order peaches from Castleton, and served cake to their families with tears in her eyes. Sixteen meant Peter was a state-sanctioned adult, and officially older than the medical books said he could get. No one expected him to last another year, yet he was still with them, even though the seed they planted in his honor was already three feet tall. Cat hoped looking after a living thing would lift her spirits. After months without water, the forest in the pass was leafless, and the river was dry. The peach tree was the only green thing standing on the whole drought-choked mountainside and still it made her sad. It meant Peter was getting older, and his condition was getting worse. The thought made her physically ill.

The sapling scratched the wall beneath her window like a begging dog. Cat swallowed the lump growing in her throat and managed a smile at the little thing. It wasn't Peter, but she still knew a string game they could play together.

Cat set her opening stage with a single loop around each palm and began the steps of the Whirlpool Spiral with casual ease. Halfway through she changed her pace, carefully twisting the threads into tiny knots and lacing her exchanges more delicately than in the previous shapes. The loops braided denser and tighter, zig-zagging a line through her web until one single step remained. Cat hooked the last string in her pinky and checked the yard for witnesses. Her mother and father were probably in the living room, Sheila was likely cooking, no one was in the yard to her right – it seemed safe enough. She aimed the web at her tree and snapped the final string into place.

The thread fell across the pattern with a flash of white light. A braided chain of knots and snags glowed in the center of her tight spiral and a blast of clear water exploded from the surface. Cat locked her elbows and forced the jet down toward the tree, scattering powdery topsoil, and churning the earth around the roots to soupy mud. The force of the spell dug the string into Cat's fingers as it tried as hard as it could to shake itself apart. She fought to keep it tight, when a shout exploded from the distant townsfolk. Cat jumped and the spell uncoiled like a serpent from her hand.

She dropped below the windowsill, the soggy thread balled in her fist. If they caught her she'd be grounded, not to mention the legal ramifications. With half a dozen lies at the ready, she poked her head back through the window to see three dozen shoppers gathered in the road a block down, staring – thankfully – not up into her yard, but eastward toward the mountain pass where a black carriage had emerged from the trees. The coach was huge compared to normal delivery carts, pulled by a team of eight dark horses and flanked by six riders dressed in black tunics with white collars. Each carried a staff made of polished wood with bristles of brown horsehair cuffed at the end like a six-foot tall paintbrush.

A brand new fear charged Cat's nerves like wild fire.

"Dad!"

She raced up the hallway to the sunlit front room. Raymond Aston sprang from his seat; the law book he was reading fell heavily to the ground. "What? What is it?"

"Brushcasters!"

"Brushcasters?"

Cat swept past him out the front door and up the ramp to her neighbor's house. The door was locked. "Peter! Alan!" Cat pounded it with both fists. "Sheila!"

To Cat's surprise, her own mother answered the door. Mona Aston frowned. "Cat, what's gotten into you?"

"Is Peter home?"

Mrs. Sheila Montgomery appeared, still holding her knitting. "The boys are out today. What's with all the panic?"

"Where did they go?"

"Brighton's, I think –"

Cat leaped from the porch. Mona charged out after her. "Stop right there, Catrina Aston! What in the world is going on?"

"Can't talk!" Cat shouted and dashed toward the street only to be caught by the arm as her father leaped from his house.

"Hold on."

"Let go!"

"I know you're worried. Just breathe." Raymond pulled her close and dropped his voice. "They may not know Peter's here. Use your head. Find a place to hide."

"A place to hide." She nodded. "Got it."

"And Cat." His grip tightened around her arm. "No magic."

"Dad, not now – "

"Promise me." His green eyes – the ones she'd inherited – burned with an intensity that cut straight through her mania and rooted her to the spot. "I'm worried about him, too, but I won't lose you to those false prophets. No magic under any circumstances. Do you understand?"

Lips dry, she nodded again. "Yes."

"Say you'll promise."

"I promise."

"I'm trusting you." He dropped her arm. "Run fast."

Cat gulped, riddled with panic, but thoughts of Peter brought her wits back into focus. She kicked dust as she tore away from the house, skirting porch steps and lawn ornaments until the road widened onto Cross Street. The town square was at the intersection of Main Street and Cross. Half the population congregated on the courthouse steps to greet their visitors. Cat scanned the masses, but couldn't see Peter over the heads. Below, a mass of celebrating townsfolk paraded with the carriage up Main Street. Cat elbowed through the assembly to reach the other end of Cross, where she wove at top speed through the crowd toward the river.

Brighton's Café sat across the street from town's power center with a clear view of the old waterwheel barely turning in the rain-starved current. A string of electric lights flickered above a patio dining area where a pack of weekend loiterers sipped coffee from bowl-sized cups. Peter sat at their usual table, his iced coffee garnished with a very long straw.

Although she saw him every day, his worsening appearance

was still shocking. He was blond with wire-framed glasses before slightly cloudy brown eyes. His illness left him deathly pale, with swelling from head to toe. Massive arms, heavy with ten years of steady transmutation, rested limply on the table where his gloved hands cupped his drink. The wrists and elbows were wrapped in more layers of elastic bandages than she was used to seeing, as were his knees and ankles above his heavy, trunk-like feet. Below his collared shirt, his broad shoulders and barrel chest were marred with craggy tumors where juts of cold stone grew from the marrow of every bone. Peter was a fragile giant, part man and part earth. His eyes brightened as Cat approached. "Hey, I thought you were sleeping in."

"We can't stay." She heaved one of his arms off the table. "We have to go."

"What's the rush?"

"Yeah, what's the deal, Cat?" Peter's twelve year-old brother Alan bounced in his seat. "The town's gone nuts! Is there a fight or something?"

"No." She paused long enough for another deep calming breath. "It's Brushcasters."

Peter's smile faded. "Brushcasters?"

"The Holy Calligraphers are here? So that's where my wait staff went!" A mustached man appeared, pen and notebook in hand. "You want the usual, Cat?"

"No, Mr. Brighton, Pete and I have to go."

"Relax, Catrina." Brighton laughed. "The Calligraphers are good people. They're God's messengers, you know."

"So they say." Cat gnawed her lip. "I'm not trying to be rude, Mr. Brighton. Do you think we can hide inside?"

"You know, I bet they're here to fix the river!" Mr. Brighton pointed to his flickering lights. "The power's been all wonky for months now! Bet Mayor Young called them."

"They can fix a *river*?" Alan beamed.

Cat slapped his arm. "This is not a good thing."

"Sure it is, it's the Calligraphers' job to bring miracles. Maybe they'll bless us, too. Our God knows we could use a blessing, right there, Pete?" Brighton elbowed Peter in the shoulder.

The blond's brow knit as he forced an uneasy smile. "Yeah, I mean, I'm a bit old to be banished at this point, right?"

"A'course ya' are! You aren't going anywhere, you're like our town mascot!"

"Yeah." Peter relaxed a bit and shrugged to Cat with one massive shoulder. "Tell them I'm your pet rock."

"This isn't a joke, Pete." Cat squatted beside him at the table. "I know it's scary to think about, but Dad's told us how dangerous they are."

"Your father's got too much passion," Mr. Brighton drawled. "It's been twenty years since I've seen a calligrapher here – if it'll help y'all relax, sit back and watch the show, the drinks are my treat."

"Mr. Brighton!" Cat glanced to the intersection where the first of the black horses pulled into view. They stopped at the crest headed for the river. Her hands shook on the tabletop.

Peter studied her a moment and slid his cup aside. "Thanks anyway, Mr. Brighton. Cat's right. We should go."

"Aw!" Alan slouched. "But free coffee!"

"I'll buy you as much coffee as you want later." Peter nudged his brother's knee. "Come on, help me up."

Peter shifted forward and waited for Alan to draw his chair aside before rising with a wince. He staggered, back and shoulders cracking, until he reached his full seven-foot height and peered down at Cat with a good-natured smile. "Okay, where to?"

She sighed and took his arm. "Thanks, Pete."

The population of Cross Street had already doubled. Farmers, dusty from the fields, arrived to the riverfront in droves. Brighton's porch was full of ogling diners who crowded the outside tables and blocked access to the door. The alleys on either side of Cross Street were full, with more revelers pushing in from the town square every second. The only clear spot was the riverbank where the Calligraphers were headed. It was a risk, but at least there she and Peter had an exit to the treeline. Cat steered her friend off the porch. "This way."

The sick man's stride was short and slow as he balanced his uneven bulk on fused ankles and feet. Alan took the lead, shifting townsfolk out of their path. They grumbled at first but apologized when they saw Peter, and parted without complaining.

By the time Cat reached the bank, the Calligraphers' carriage was closing quickly, with its parade of locals in tow. Those who escorted them from the gate herded the crowd ahead of them like a flock of bleating sheep. The farmers along the river were shoved backward toward its edge. An old field hand stumbled and knocked Peter from behind. He staggered. Cat released his arm and took his weight onto herself. She held tight, buried in the earthy smell of his cotton shirt, until his cumbersome legs found footing.

In their pause, excitable people had flooded in from all sides, surrounding them with heat and the smells of sweat, mud, and alcohol. The jutting tumors on Peter's ribcage pressed hard into her cheek. His heart pounded through layers of skin and stone.

"I'm good." Peter shifted back onto his heels and wrapped his heavy arm like a blanket around her back. "It's alright. I'm okay."

The waterwheel was barely six yards to their left. The treeline, now behind them, was too crowded to reach. Alan was missing, swallowed fully by the jostling gridlock. Their saving grace was the constant movement of the over-excited crowd and the trailing slope of the dry riverbank that disguised half a foot of Peter's unnatural height.

His voice echoed in his rib cage. "What do we do now?"

Cat tightened her grip. The Calligrapher's wagon and all of its brush-toting warriors came to a stop. She tried and failed another deep, calming breath. "Pray for a miracle?"

"Hah." Peter leaned heavier onto her shoulder. "Right."

Ask for Threadcaster at your
local library or book store.

And find more stories in the Threadcaster
universe and beyond - coming soon.

www.jenniferstolzer.com
@jenniferstolzer
facebook/tumblr/twitter